Cascade Falls

a novel

"[An] exploration of the struggles people go through trying to survive and do right, while still holding on to their dreams…about loss: lost dreams, lost love, lost money. But it's also a story of rising from the ashes…and redemption through honesty and forgiveness."

—*ForeWord Reviews*

"Seldom does the breach in a couple's bond spring from a simple, singular moment. The rift deepens subtly through trickles of concealed, vulnerable truths; wounding misinterpretations that erode trust and build defensiveness; the paradox of alienation alongside a drive to join; and faraway spaces of intimacy, ardor, and hope. In *Cascade Falls*, Bruce Ferber masterfully reproduces a relationship in its aching devolution."

—Holly Parker, PhD, lecturer in the Department of Psychology, Harvard University, and author of *If We're Together, Why Do I Feel So Alone*

"Bruce Ferber is that perfect combination of humorist and humanist. *Cascade Falls* is poignant, moving, and ridiculously funny."
—Dan Zevin, Thurber Award-winning author of *Dan Gets a Minivan*

"Bruce Ferber's gentle narrative style slyly masks a much more serious question, one the disillusioned suburbanites at the core of *Cascade Falls* might as well be asking on the part of us all: namely, what does the American Dream mean these days, and to whom does its storied set of tenets apply? Ferber reminds us that no matter how well off you think you are, there's always room to fall, and yet no matter how far you've fallen, there's also room in your remaining space and years to find your best self."

—David Kukoff, author of *Children of the Canyon*

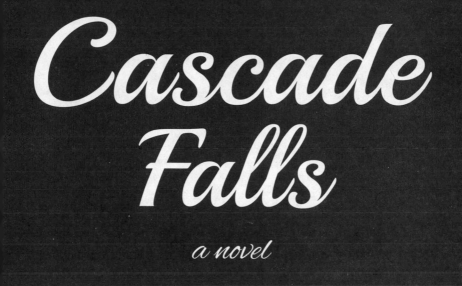

Cascade Falls

a novel

Bruce Ferber

A Vireo Book **V** Rare Bird Books
Los Angeles, Calif.

THIS IS A GENUINE VIREO BOOK

A Vireo Book | Rare Bird Books
453 South Spring Street, Suite 531
Los Angeles, CA 90013
rarebirdbooks.com

FIRST TRADE PAPERBACK ORIGINAL EDITION

Set in Minion Pro
Printed in the United States
Distributed in the US by Publishers Group West

Publisher's Cataloging-in-Publication data

Ferber, Bruce.
    Cascade Falls : a novel / Bruce Ferber.
    p. cm.
    ISBN 978-1-940207-37-7

1. Suburbs—Fiction. 2. Family—Fiction. 3. Judaism—Fiction. 4. Phoenix (Az.)—Fiction.
5. Humorous stories. I. Title.

PS3606.E62 C37 2014
813.6—dc23

For Lyn, who does it all.

"The tragedy of life is what dies inside a man while he lives—the death of genuine feeling, the death of inspired responses, the awareness that makes it possible to feel the pain or the glory of other men in yourself."

—Norman Cousins

"We need wild places. Wild places stir our souls, helping us to see and guiding us without judgment to the wild places within ourselves. I know of no one who has received this kind of wisdom from a sprawling master-planned community."

—Janine Schipper, *Disappearing Desert*

"Welcome to Arizona, where summer spends the winter and hell spends the summer."

—modified from a booster slogan in the 1930s

Smokey

He surveyed the makeshift hillside encampment one last time, reflexively feeling the urge to tidy up before saying goodbye. It just wouldn't be right to leave trash in the rusty frame of the ancient refrigerator that had provided him reliable, if utilitarian, refuge. The puke-green Kenmore's walls had shielded his aching body from blistering heat and cruel winds; even a fluke snowstorm one shivery December night. *Respect that which has sustained you,* he was still clear-headed enough to reason. He also knew that his thinking didn't always work so well these days. In less than a year, he had morphed into a grizzled specimen of indeterminate age, christened "Smokey" by the locals because he smelled like a human campfire. He never minded the name, or the townsfolk for that matter, who treated him with unearned empathy and kindness. *It could be a lot worse,* he always tried to tell himself. The reality was that since he and society had parted ways, he'd been able to survive quite adequately on yucca and weeds and other people's leftovers. But the drill had gotten old quickly, as had he. His number was up. That's all there was to it.

Smokey (he told people his real name was Terrence) squinted through the unforgiving midday sun, taking in the mish-mash of dry mountains, prison yards, and fast-food joints that defined this drive-thru gateway to everywhere and destination for not a soul. If there was a crumb of incentive to stick around, he sure as hell couldn't find it. He figured it must take a special kind of person to be in it for the long haul here in Kingman, Arizona, the town made famous as the last residence of one Timothy McVeigh.

He remembered reading in the papers some years back that the Kingman City Council had made a concerted effort to play down any association with the terrorist by playing up a celebrity from the area. Having only one celebrity from which to choose, the town recognized that perhaps not everyone would get chills down his spine motoring along Andy Devine Drive. The saving grace was that despite Mr. Devine being a character actor from a zillion years ago, at least he had never killed anybody with fertilizer. Smokey knew of him because his dad had been a huge fan of old Westerns and the doughy thespian, with his signature croaky voice, had been in over four hundred of them. On more than one occasion, father and son had watched *Stagecoach* together. ("He's a Cheyenne. They hate Apaches worse than we do!") His dad also told him that Andy had once hosted a kids' show on the East Coast with a puppet named "Froggy," and whenever the old man was in a particularly good mood, he'd go around the house repeating the phrase "Twang your magic twanger, Froggy" for no apparent reason.

It wasn't exactly the farewell he'd imagined. Here he was, about to blow his brains out, yet his thoughts were of frogs, twangers, and Andy Devine. Then something else occurred to him. Once the deed was done, how would the town of Kingman choose to remember Smokey? In truth, what choice was there? He could only be memorialized for the person he had shown them: an addled, homeless bum living on garbage tapas. Perhaps they would name Kingman's Municipal Roving Dumpster after him. Lord knows he'd spent enough time foraging through it.

He felt the beads of sweat multiplying as he lifted the revolver to his head. Lodging his trigger finger in a comfortable position, a revelation

Bruce Ferber

suddenly burst forth. He was someone who had once lived among the living, a man who had loved and laughed and, on more than one occasion, shed tears so powerful he felt like he would combust. And now, he was about to come to an unheralded and ignominious end in the 'hood of the Oklahoma City Bomber.

He knew he had to pull the trigger quickly because sweat was starting to drip from the inside of his index finger, increasing the possibility of a slip-up. *There shouldn't be anything difficult about this,* he reminded himself. With nothing left to consider, no mitigating circumstances to warrant a last-minute suspension of his plan, Smokey's grand finale was a no-brainer. Amazingly, he was still lucid enough to appreciate the irony of such a term in this particular context. A split-second later, he pictured himself on Death Row, releasing a simple, but incisive, farewell statement to the press. Seeing as how there were no reporters combing the Kingman hills, he decided that a reasonable substitute might be to craft a concluding thought. Since this was his last hurrah, perhaps there was a final notion or image he wished to ponder before meeting his Maker.

Wading through possible ideas proved a struggle. He found his brain bouncing back and forth between the need for a Middle East peace pact and Salma Hayek's chest. Each was significant in its own way. Somehow, even this simple endeavor refused to go smoothly. *Why should it?* he then realized. His inability to invoke a clear-headed concluding thought was a drop in the bucket next to this blunder. Contemplating such a thing had been a waste of time, the entire mission rapidly becoming laughable. There could be no more dicking around. He had to end the misery and end it now.

THE GUN WENT OFF with a blast so loud and a vibration so intense, it made the earth rock beneath him, his body hurtling toward the stones that surrounded the fire pit. Bones had surely been broken, blood was splattered everywhere, but unless death ultimately masqueraded as life, something was seriously amiss. Smokey was conscious. His head was throbbing. His lungs were breathing. How could it be? He had finally built up the nerve to fire a .38 revolver directly into his skull, yet he was inexplicably, ridiculously, alive.

There was no doubt about it. His inability to invoke a clear-headed concluding thought was a drop in the bucket next to this blunder. The only thing he could think of to explain the hiccup was that at some point during the trigger-pull, he had panicked and shot the bullet wide. He spotted the gun on the ground maybe twenty-five feet away and slowly began to crawl toward it. It might take him a while, but he'd get there. Having to suffer the embarrassment of not being able to finish the job would only add to the original suffering, which was the reason he'd landed in this place to begin with.

Sliding from the rocks to the dusty ground, it felt as if his left leg was about to detach from his pelvis. As he registered blood running from his pants to his socks, it dawned on him that he'd also peed himself. Soon, it wouldn't matter if he was dry or without limbs. He grabbed the gnarled trunk of the nearby cottonwood tree and pulled hard, which gave him sufficient leverage to advance another few feet toward the gun. Rolling his body over in the dirt inched him further, and with surprisingly little pain. Two body rolls later, the .38 was back in his hand, ready to close it out.

This time, there would be no room for error. He opened his mouth and lodged the gun barrel halfway down his throat. Melodramatic, perhaps, but eminently practical. He proceeded to bid himself adieu. *So long, Smokey. You got a taste of the good life. Too bad the rest was a travesty.*

The sound of the shot reverberated down the canyon. Soon, the powers that be would discover that the vagrant who'd taken his leave hailed from a prominent Arizona real estate family that many considered instrumental in putting the state on the map. There were others who argued that they'd simply made the map more crowded, but what no one would dispute was that if such a thing could happen to a member of this family, it could happen to anybody: a billionaire banker, the pizza delivery guy, a teenager, a grandma. You go about your business putting one foot in front of the other and everything seems to be moving along just fine. Then you make a mistake or two—or maybe you don't. Either way, life could bite you in the ass without the slightest warning. It made a person think. There but for not walking into a shitstorm go I.

Maya

The light glistening off the lake seemed even brighter than usual, Maya thought, as she negotiated the pristine byways of the Cascade Falls enclave. Turning right, past the lawns of Jetty Drive, then left, at the row of date palms on Maritime Lane, she admired the majestic rainbow effect emanating from the army of sprinklers flooding the golf course. For an instant, she pretended her Lexus hybrid was traversing the Carolinas or touring the Florida Keys, but a perfunctory glance at the outside temperature gauge on the dashboard jolted her back to reality. It was 114 degrees, destined to climb to 120 before the end of August. This was home and home was suburban Phoenix, a massive waterless expanse that had been voraciously transformed into an amenity-filled tropical resort. Much the way Disneyland had been duplicated in Florida, it appeared to Maya as if Florida itself had been meticulously cloned, then dumped in the middle of the Sonoran desert.

Waving to Buzzy, the guard at the gate, she surmised that he, too, looked 114, destined to look 120 by Labor Day.

"Howdy, Mrs. Johnson. Beautiful mornin', isn't it?"

"Yeah, if you're a fucking lizard," she snapped, Tourettes-like, immediately regretting it.

"Pardon ma'am?" Buzzy adjusted his earpiece.

Thank God for degenerative hearing loss, she sighed to herself. "It's a wonderful day, Buzzy. Enjoy!"

Maya Johnson (neé Morganstern) and her husband, Danny, had moved to this manicured oasis alongside myriad young families with a common purpose: to snatch their God-given piece of the American Dream at an affordable American price. Everybody seemed to agree that it was a clean, safe environment in which to raise children, but Maya found the uniformity as oppressive as the sweltering heat. During the decision-making process before the move, Danny had done his best to allay her fears, insisting that she would not only get used to their new Arizona life, but infuse it with her boundless creativity. They had been there four years now and Maya had yet to accomplish either.

FIVE HUNDRED YARDS PAST the Cascade Falls exit, Maya turned right onto Hohokam Road, the flat, endless stretch of cotton fields and scrub that always made her want to up her dosage of Prozac. It wasn't that she hated the desert. She hated *this* desert. The elevation was too low for the magnificent saguaro that grew in the North or the primordial Joshua trees of California. Permeating the air was the unmistakable fragrance of ammoniated cow shit, courtesy of the few local dairy farms yet to be swallowed up by home developers. It seemed that this place where she and her family had elected to build their nest was a unique melding of man and nature, the two conspiring to create the joint venture commonly known as hell.

A mile or so further down the road, Maya pulled into the dirt parking lot of the Akimel O'Odham Smoke Shop, one of the many Native American tobacco emporiums lining the East Valley.

"There's my girl," shouted the pony-tailed, three-hundred-pound day manager, Bob, when she'd barely opened the door. (Apparently, names like Running Horse had gone the way of rubbing two sticks together.) "Pack of Merit Lights, darlin'?"

She hated when he called her "darlin'," but didn't dare risk another Buzzy-esque faux pas. "Yes, Merit Lights," Maya smiled weakly, hurriedly handing Bob the cash and rushing off with her smokes.

"Wouldja like a free liter of Diet Pepsi today?" Bob blurted out, just before she made her escape.

"No, thanks. Maybe next time," she nodded.

The fact that the proprietors of this establishment recognized her at all was legitimate cause for concern. She had quit cigarettes in her late twenties, but about six months ago, out of sheer boredom more than anything else, Maya began tentatively revisiting her former habit, limiting herself to two or three ultra lights a day, followed by vigorous gulps of Scope so as to hide her secret/shame from Danny and the kids. If the Indian clerks were now identifying her as a regular did that mean she had officially returned to the fold of nicotine addiction? Adding to her unease was the way they stared at her, and the overly obsequious manner that seemed to accompany it. The sum total of her purchases at the store was maybe a pack a week, but the minute she entered, the staff deferred to her as if she were some sort of Hollywood celebrity.

Climbing back into the driver's seat, Maya reasoned that it didn't take much to be a luminary in this neck of the woods. Heck, the builder of the Cascade Falls subdivision was treated like a fucking god by the snowbirds from Minnesota and Canada, so obviously the bar was set pretty low. She momentarily wondered if being the builder's daughter-in-law had something to do with her superstar status at the smoke shop, but quickly nixed that theory. They were ogling her, plain and simple, mentally undressing a forty-year-old mother of two, who, to her way of thinking, had been drained of any real sexuality years ago. Men were remarkable in that regard. You could emit the most bored, quasi-menopausal vibe imaginable and even that made them horny. You could go without make up, fail to run a brush through your hair, maybe even your teeth, and they'd still be foaming at the mouth, scanning their internal GPSs for the fastest route into your pants.

Approaching the freeway junction, Maya tore open the pack of Merits before heading west on the interstate. The downside of smoking in the car was that she had to drive with the windows down in triple-digit heat, but at the moment, the trade-off seemed worth it. It would be a forty-minute trip to downtown Phoenix and the cigarette would help her relax as she pondered her new project. She had a reasonably clear idea as to the materials she needed, so the shopping itself wouldn't take long once she arrived at her destination. Thankfully, the excursion had been comfortably timed to get her back to school in time to retrieve the kids.

A trip to Arizona Art Supply was always a pick-me-up for Maya, the painterly equivalent of marching into a fine Italian coffee house and ordering a double espresso. The mere act of being amongst the brushes and canvases, the gessoes and oils, filled her with the promise of things to come. Though she didn't know exactly what it was she was about to paint, Maya was certain of one thing: the canvas would be filled with bright, flamboyant color, as far from the desert browns, terra-cotta tile, and ubiquitous white stucco as humanly possible. There would be no cholla, ocotillo, or indiscriminately-placed golf courses in between. Her aspiration was to produce a work that defied her surroundings—a small, but genuine, expression of individuality in environs that reeked of sameness. Inured as she was to the local scenery, it seemed equally pointless to recreate a beautiful vista in say, Tuscany, a place she loved but hadn't seen since graduating college. She came to the conclusion that despite her proficiency at landscapes, this new piece begged to be unleashed in another form.

She proceeded to grab a basket and scoop up tubes of cerulean blue, dioxazine purple, and cobalt green, her mind racing with possibilities of shapes and shadows. In a matter of minutes, she was bellying up to the cash register, giddily handing over her MasterCard for 145 dollars worth of supplies. Unlike the smoke shop transaction, this was a thoroughly joyous affair; the icing on the cake: no oglers.

Maya was brimming with excitement as she hopped onto the I-10 and headed east. It was only after she passed the mall at Ahwatukee that the pangs of nervousness and self-doubt started to kick in. As much as she wanted to begin the new painting, she had been to this well before. How many times had she come up with a brilliant idea and gone to the art supply store for the materials with which to execute it, only to give up midstream? Or worse, never even get started? The truth was, since they'd moved here from California, she had very little to show. A half-painting here, a pedestrian drawing there, for all intents and purposes: nothing. Five years ago, Maya had had her own exhibition at a gallery on Melrose, sold an oil for over five grand, and was regarded by her peers as an up-and-comer. But that was in another life, before she had made this ersatz Florida her home and been sucked into its vacuum.

Maya tried not to assign blame so simplistically. Surely, such a pathetic output couldn't be attributed entirely to one's surroundings. If a computer and the internet allowed people to work from any part of the world, why shouldn't the similarly portable brush and canvas be able to do the same for an artist? Was it marriage that had dried her up? Motherhood? A cruel, earth-toned cocktail of all three? It was a question for which she had yet to find an answer. Maya longed for inspiration and productivity to return so she wouldn't have to keep looking.

Whirring past the Wild Horse Indian Casino, her thoughts drifted to the men at the smoke shop. What specifically was it about her that provoked their fascination? She recognized by now that while her looks were not of the bombshell variety, they consistently piqued the interest of the opposite sex, no matter how unattractive she felt. Her best guess was that it had to do with the inscrutability of her face. Preternaturally smooth, brown, and ethnically welcoming, Italians thought she was from Sicily, Mexicans reflexively spoke to her in Spanish, and the Akimel O'Odham suspected she might be part Pima. In fact, Maya was the product of a Jewish father and Irish mother, her Lodz-Dublin lineage spawning a singularly stunning result. The jet black hair, dark complexion, and blue eyes stood out no matter where she went, particularly so in a world still inhabited by so many white, freckle-faced blondes.

As a young girl she had been painfully shy. Barely able to look boys in the eye, it never seemed to deter them from trying to engage her in innocent play, or the not-so-innocent kind as she grew older. Once she survived adolescence and became more comfortable in her own skin, she learned to accept the attention graciously, even as the target of bold-faced come-ons that made her queasy inside. At those times she summoned the distraught souls who never got noticed, the girls she was sure cried into their pillows because Jimmy De Blasio wouldn't give them the time of day. Yes, it was uncomfortable to be leered at, but it was devastating to be invisible.

In her current stage of life, receiving interest of this sort seemed absurd. The world as she now knew it was all about responsibilities: Danny busy working for his father, she with her hands full parenting Max and Dana while struggling to carve out a precious few hours for herself. If and when thoughts of sex came into the equation, they had to be summoned on a schedule, most likely after the kids were put to bed on Saturday night. As Maya exited the interstate at Hohokam Road, she flashed on Ray Minetta, her boyfriend before Danny, with whom she had traveled across Europe. A charismatic singer-songwriter type, Ray had been wildly obsessed with her body at a time when her body had the will to be obsessed back. Maya couldn't help but wonder if that intensity returned later in life, after the kids were a little more grown up and independent. The urge to feel and hug and devour another had once seemed so primal. It struck her as both remarkable and sad how quickly it had evaporated.

Ted Johnson and Son

His detractors, of whom there were more than a few, dubbed Ted Johnson the William Tecumseh Sherman of Arizona home development. Johnson Homes and Johnson Communities, Inc. had, in their estimation, raped and pillaged untold acres of sacred wilderness, replacing them with horrific environmental and architectural abominations. Riverfront Village, Seaside Harbor, Cascade Falls—the list of idyllically named, resource-sucking subdivisions went on and on. Why was a region with barely eight inches of rainfall per year suddenly awash with pool-happy country clubs and perpetually thirsty golf courses? It confounded Mr. Johnson's foes, but the American Dream at any cost made a heck of a lot of sense to the big-thinking builder. Apparently, the concept resonated with a lot of other folks too, because not only had it made Ted Johnson a multi-millionaire, it turned him into an icon. The outraged environmentalists might get some traction in New York or Boston, but this was Phoenix, by God, and in the Great Southwest it was frontier spirit that carried the day. Arizona was the land of the free and the home of the entrepreneur.

Ted Johnson liked to open with that line when he spoke to the Kiwanis Club or at corporate luncheons. After a few Bloody Marys, he'd admit to anyone who asked that the adulation meant far more to him than the money. For today's address to the Business League of Tempe, he made the conscious decision to focus on the soul-searching epiphanies that had motivated him and his mission.

"A lot of people are capable of amassing a fortune, but how many can say they've made a difference in the lives of others?" As Ted finished the sentence, tears started to well up, the round of applause encouraging him to squeeze every last note out of his self-directed love song.

A six-foot-three, two-hundred-and-twenty-pound man sobbing at the poignancy of his own accomplishments. It was enough to make a thinking man puke, but it played like a Heifetz violin to this crowd. "Many of you own, or know folks who own, homes in the Johnson communities. Some of our Johnson residents never imagined they might one day live a guard-gated lifestyle with an extra half-garage for the cart. And truth be told, I never imagined that I would be able to provide this gift to so many. But I followed my dream so that others might realize theirs. We, as Americans, know no limits and accept no boundaries when it comes to achieving great things."

Then, in a prayer-like trance, the Sultan of Sprawl took a deep breath and closed his eyes. "I'd like everyone gathered here today to turn to the person next to him and shake hands."

Forty-one-year-old Danny Johnson watched in amazement as the entire room obeyed his father's command.

Ted took his voice down to barely a whisper. "Now look into your neighbor's eyes and tell him: 'You can do anything.'"

And with that, a chorus of mid level managers and local insurance agents recited the Johnson mantra in unison. Danny couldn't believe the power his father wielded over these adoring drones. It occurred to him that, as a future partner in the Johnson Empire, he might one day be asked to spout the same capitalist self-help mumbo-jumbo. Where would he find the stomach to do such a thing? Then again, he might never have to. The way the economy was going, there was a reasonable chance that his father's stucco kingdom would crumble, sparing Danny the agony of hawking leisure lifestyle snake oil. Granted, he'd be out of a job, but his dignity would remain intact.

The younger Johnson's preference was to stay back in the office for these dog-and-pony shows, but Ted insisted on having him there to make a point. Strategically placing his son/business associate in the audience and giving him a well-timed shout-out spoke volumes about Johnson Communities, Inc.'s love of family.

"And families are who I was born to serve," Ted intoned, another of his shopworn homilies.

Danny had heard these lines so many times, he could recite them in his sleep. Equally tiresome were the boilerplate Johnson Homes jokes about proud men who loved their Johnsons, and the more ambitious ones who dreamed of a bigger Johnson. Such chestnuts were usually reserved for the hobnobbing that followed the presentation, by which time the assembled group was feeling no pain.

Still, Danny had to acknowledge his father's uncanny business acumen. For someone who had banked so heavily on the real estate boom, going all the way back to the eighties, Ted had weathered the current downturn in remarkable fashion, both professionally and personally. Of course, there were those hapless seniors who had bought high and were now upside down in their loans, desperate to unload their albatrosses. But the majority of residents were thrilled to have bought in when they did, thanked the good Lord for their safe, sun-baked streets, and dutifully genuflected before Ted Johnson's subdivided world vision. Basking in the builder's success somehow made the homeowner more sanguine about the wisdom of his investment. It was an oddly dysfunctional arrangement: bolstering the ego of a narcissistic, self-proclaimed housing prophet in order to deny any possibility that a bad choice might have been made by the buyer.

Ted closed his address with a favorite quote, which he felt summed up his calling as an Arizona developer. "Through many dangers, toils and snares / I have already come; / 'Tis grace hath brought me safe thus far, / And grace will lead me home." Then, the President of Johnson

Communities stepped down from the podium for some face time with his admirers.

Watching Ted hold court with a pair of mesmerized, mortgage brokering good ol' boys, Danny got the signal to make his way over and join the party. He hated the glad-handing even more than the homilies. The only bright spot was that after four years of it, what was once unbearable had simply become tedious; a mindless but necessary tool of the trade.

"You must be thrilled to help carry on your father's legacy," crowed Les Hunsicker of Tempe Home Loans.

"Oh, definitely," Danny lied.

"What's your handicap, son?"

This was always a difficult moment for the junior Johnson. Upon his return to Arizona, he had been ordered by his father to enroll in an intensive golf instruction regimen, but the tri-weekly lessons had done little to improve either his game, or his interest in it. "Working on my strokes, Les. Talk to me in a couple of months."

"Fair enough," the broker slapped Danny on the back, proceeding to dash off and scrounge for brown liquor.

Having been raised by conservative, high-profile parents in upper-middle class Scottsdale, Danny Johnson's young mindset took him in the opposite direction, toward philosophy and the arts. He might not have fully understood Spinoza, but it was gratifying enough to know that Mom and Dad hadn't a clue as to who the man was. He decided to learn the cello, as un-Arizonan an instrument as he could think of. His mom, Jeannie, was a George and Tammy fan, while Ted liked the restorative quality of soft rock, often honing his golf putts to the strains of Poco, America, and Pure Prairie League. The senior Johnson could never understand what his son was doing playing sissy music when he could be out at the driving range, working on his swing.

When it came time to apply to colleges, a local education was off the table. Danny's aim was to be as far away from Arizona, business degrees, and year-round tee times as humanly possible. He fulfilled this wish in the form of Bennington College, a bucolic intellectual refuge where a person could complete both semesters without ever hearing the words bogey or Rotary Club. Relishing the brutal Vermont winters simply because one couldn't find them in Phoenix, he majored in Western Philosophy with a minor in theater arts, writing the one-act play *Up From the Ashes*, which was produced in his senior year. Both a well-reviewed and artistic success, it netted the more noteworthy gain of introducing him to the striking and gifted set designer, Maya Morganstern. The lithe, dark-haired beauty was dating some sensitive guitarist-type at the time, but Danny was as undeterred as he was smitten. He subconsciously channeled his overachieving father, whose entire life had been a love letter to dogged persistence. Danny would bide his time, monitoring the progress of Maya's relationship after they graduated. Then, once he got even the slightest wind of trouble, he would swoop in and make his move. Three years and two of Ray's infidelities later, Maya Morganstern was Mrs. Daniel Johnson.

Danny had always viewed their union as a hard-earned conquest for which he would be rewarded with a prosperous, even glamorous future. As a result, he had enormous difficulty accepting the moment when he and his bride found themselves the unemployed and broke parents of two, scraping to make the rent on their cramped Los Angeles apartment. Despite Maya's taste of success in the art world, she had little time to produce new work once the kids came. Danny wrote screenplays that seemed to get rejected faster than he could churn them out, and his substitute teaching didn't amount to squat, income-wise. After years of struggle, the only alternative was to suck it up and accept the dreaded, ever-dangling carrot from his father. Danny agreed to leave Los Angeles and take a position with Johnson Homes in Chandler, Arizona. He considered the new job a blatant admission of his own failure, but he was willing to be miserable if it guaranteed his family's happiness. They would be given their own three-bedroom Sea Breeze model in Cascade Falls, the flagship Johnson community. That part alone promised to be a refreshing change from their dump in Koreatown.

BACK AT THE WHEEL of his tricked-out Lincoln, Ted seemed pleased with the afternoon's performance. "You know, I just never get tired of giving folks permission to dream," he wistfully informed his son. "I'm sure you feel the same way."

Danny nodded blankly. What qualifications did he have to peddle dreams? And what good were dreams if they were clearly unachievable?

But there was no stopping Ted. Convinced that he was auspiciously poised to meet the future head on, the Johnson patriarch was doubly glad that he now got to do so with his son by his side. He had wanted Danny to join the family business straight out of college, but the younger Johnson expressed little or no desire. The prodigal son's return to Phoenix four years ago filled in the missing piece for a man who had otherwise been abundantly blessed. To have business and family firing on all cylinders was the true definition of success as far as he could figure. Admittedly, there had been lots of bumps in the road before the kid found his way home, but Ted chalked that up to what young folks did. Go off on their own, learn the world isn't so easy, show up with their tails between their legs, finally having realized that their parents knew a thing or two. The elder Johnson quickly forgot the disappointments of the past, eager to embrace a fresh start with his adult son, who was now a husband and father, and ready to start a real career.

Painfully aware of the economic realities Johnson Homes was facing, Danny wondered how his father could remain such a relentless dispenser of optimism. Was it pure self-confidence or deluded idiocy? Even after real estate prices had already started to dip, the man poured millions into Cascade Falls Phase III, which now stood half-vacant and was experiencing squatter issues. "Where do we stand with the Tucson acreage?" the son asked tentatively.

"I'm rethinking Tucson," Ted answered, Danny knowing full well that the deal for the new Johnson Communities Tucson must have landed in the crapper. "I'm flying to Plano, Texas tomorrow."

Wasn't the housing market just as bad in Texas as it was in Arizona? Danny wondered. Maybe it hadn't completely maxed out as Phoenix had, but money was surely tight across the board. As they drove the 101

Loop back to the home office in Chandler, Danny silently bemoaned his own piss-poor timing. Had he bitten the bullet years ago and come back to work for his father during the boom, he would have made shitloads of green and been back in California by now. In this business climate, however, he had hitched his star to a wagon that could sputter off the cliff at any moment, its driver charging undeterred into the 110-degree sun.

Owen

The Mercedes driver on the other side of the stoplight stared at Owen Shea's '78 Ford Ranger, its rough idle sputtering like some terminal emphysema patient. Owen knew it was probably as simple as a bad fuel filter, but he had little time to address his own broken things when he was so busy fixing everyone else's. Just this morning, he had put a new compressor in the Ryman's air conditioner, replaced the Mundy's showerhead, and done some pro bono electrical work for the Boy's Club of Mcsa. Later in the afternoon, he'd be making guest appearances throughout the Johnson Communities, changing the spring on a garage door out at Cascade Falls Phase I, then installing a trash compactor in Phase II. Owen was glad to be busy. Jobs had up and left the county by the hundreds, but you couldn't outsource fixing your house to Mumbai. In a world where most people's concept of working with their hands meant tapping on a computer keyboard, it didn't hurt to know how to snake a toilet. That was a job you could bank on smack through to the apocalypse. While some of the folks in the various Phases weren't exactly free with a dollar, overall, serving the Johnson Communities was getting the bills paid and leaving him with a little to spare.

Finding a good space in front of the school with a view of the exit door, Owen wondered if Brianna was going to have a smile on her face when she saw him. Would his ten-year-old emerge with a cluster of friends, giggling uncontrollably as the group split off to meet their buses and carpools? Would she be tired? Mute? Or would it prove to be one of those infrequent but gut-wrenching after-school confessionals where she revealed that she'd been teased mercilessly, victimized by the cruelty at which schoolchildren excelled. She was waving as she ran to the truck, always a good sign.

Brianna hoisted herself up to open the passenger door and threw her books on the floor, as she did every morning and afternoon since their collective moorings had been shaken. She held out her cheek for Owen's kiss, which she knew was an integral part of the routine for her father.

"Good day today, Monkey?" Owen smiled. "Monkey" was a term of affection he had coined for Brianna when she was a squirmy three-year-old, and she still permitted him to use it as long as it was just the two of them.

"Today was boring," his daughter informed him, in no uncertain terms.

"Something good must've happened," he tried to coax her.

"Oh yeah," she smiled. "They suspended Ricky Rodriguez."

"Okay, now there's something. What'd he do?" Owen's thoughts ran the gamut from spitballs to shooting spree.

"He squeezed Wendy Rogers' boobs."

Owen didn't think ten-year-olds had boobs yet, but he did hear somewhere that kids were more advanced today because of all the hormones in the food supply. Regardless, he didn't want to delve too deeply into the subject. "That was rude of him. I'm glad he got punished."

His daughter shook her head, obviously unsatisfied. "It's not like it didn't happen like a gajillion times. It's just the first time he got caught."

This got Owen's attention. "Brianna, did he ever—"

"No, Dad. He never touched me. He likes fat girls 'cause there's more to grab."

"That's good," Owen sighed. "I mean, not for the fat girls, but good that he doesn't bother you."

"Can we get a Jamba Juice?" Brianna asked, moving on to the next beat as fast as she had gotten to this one.

"Sure," Owen replied without hesitation. He was pressed time-wise, having to drop Bri at home and get to Cascade Falls in time to complete two jobs, but his parental instinct pointed him squarely in the direction of Jamba Juice. It was always such a kick to watch her step up to the counter and pick a "boost" to go in her smoothie. What the hell did a ten year-old know about Omega-3 fatty acids or Flax 'n Fiber? It seemed absurd, yet she always ordered with the supreme confidence of a veteran boost-meister. Owen loved seeing his daughter confident in any aspect of her life, even something as benign as a smoothie purchase. It seemed like these days, there were countless opportunities for a young person to fall apart. A kid could wake up on any given morning and, if the dice happened to roll the wrong way, be reduced to emotional rubble by sundown. One had to be grateful for Jamba Juice and its life-affirming boosts.

The way Owen saw it, these excursions were a cheap excuse for extended bonding. The cups were huge so they took a long time to finish, and whether Brianna drank in the store or the car, they always relaxed her, giving Owen the freedom to talk or listen between sips. There was no doubt that listening to Brianna had become, hands-down, the most important activity in his life. He analyzed each of her sentences, soberly deliberating whether to take them at face value or search for hidden subtext. Was she truly happy, putting on a brave front, or simply too embarrassed to show her real feelings? Knowing the depth to which he, himself, had been hurt, it was unfathomable to him how a young girl could be expected to withstand such pain. All the books said that kids were resilient; you just had to give them the space and permission to go forward. But what if they leapt ahead and fell flat on their faces?

As a newly single parent, Owen felt like he had to do everything right. There was zero room for error, because his wife was no longer around to correct his mistakes. How could he ever be at peace with himself if he were to make the one choice that sent his daughter in the wrong direction? "You have homework?" he asked, Brianna reaching the bottom third of her Razzmatazz.

"Yeah. I may need a little help with my math."

"No problem. Whatever you can't finish while I'm gone, we'll do after dinner."

Owen liked being able to help her with math, especially knowing that in a few years, the problems would be way over his head and render him useless. Given the hand his daughter had been dealt, he considered it his mission to support her in whatever way he could. At the same time, he knew he had to refrain from smothering her with compensatory love, which she immediately saw through, interpreted as pitying, and more often than not, led to a complete shutdown. Buying her three dresses when she only needed one wasn't going to bring back her mother. Yet Owen still couldn't help going to that place because the prospect of a getting an extra smile from his daughter, bought or otherwise, meant an extra few seconds in which she wouldn't have to dwell on what could never be replaced.

The whole thing was fucked up. He owed it to Lucy to continue the exemplary job she'd started, but felt like a parenting rube, abruptly and unceremoniously dumped from the turnip truck. To be frank, the job had been less complicated for Lucy because as the deceased one, she never had to deal with her daughter's grief. Yet Owen knew in his heart that were the situation reversed, his wife would make sure Brianna survived his death with minimal scarring. If only he had that kind of faith in his own abilities. For Owen, being a single parent was like fumbling in the dark for a set of keys that would turn out to open the wrong door.

THEIR MODEST RANCH HOUSE was in Phase II of Riverfront Village, the crown jewel of the Johnson Empire when the builder burst upon the subdivision scene in September of 1982. Over the years, Owen had personally replaced nearly every pipe, wire, wall, and cabinet of the original cheap-shit construction, providing the Shea family with a solid, if far from luxurious, place to call home. As they pulled into the drive, Flora Jimenez was approaching the upgraded maple front door. She'd started taking care of Brianna six years ago, just after Lucy first got sick. A devout Catholic in her fifties, she brought all of her eleven children to the memorial of a nonbeliever, convinced that their prayers would give Lucy a leg up in the hereafter, having been robbed of one in this life. Flora regarded Owen with polite, but reserved, empathy, perhaps because she mistakenly viewed him as the evil instigator of his late wife's atheism. None of that mattered now as he watched Flora hug Brianna like one of her own, and usher her inside to offer a piece of fruit and a cookie. Owen was grateful that his daughter would be safe in the company of an expert nurturer whose only pet peeve was godlessness. *Flora Jimenez, you go and hate my fucking guts,* he thought. *Just keep my daughter happy.*

Backing out the truck to head for Cascade Falls, Owen heard the familiar cell phone chime he'd never bothered to change to something more personal. He glanced at the caller ID, relieved that it wasn't Candy Daniels, one of his late wife's divorcée friends who seemed to take an interest in him the minute she learned of Lucy's Stage Three diagnosis. Candy was an attractive Pilates addict, the kind who still fit into her outfits from high school. But much as his body longed for a woman's touch, her early detection of his future availability made Candy a highly unlikely candidate for the job. The chimes rang again. Owen didn't recognize the number, but decided to live dangerously and pick up anyway.

"Owen Shea," he answered, assuming his most professional independent contractor 'tude.

"Hello Owen," replied the affable voice on the other end. "This is Jeannie Johnson. I got your name from the De Lucas' over on Theodore Springs Drive."

Holy fucking shit, he thought. *Ted Johnson's wife is calling me to fix the crap he built for his own family.* "Hi Mrs. Johnson. Pleasure to meet you. At least on the phone, anyway," he volleyed lamely.

"Suzie De Luca says such wonderful things about your handiwork, and I was wondering if you might have some time to take a look at my decking."

"In need of a little sprucing up?" he asked, certain that the original shoddy workmanship had wreaked the same havoc it had on all the other units.

"A lot of sprucing. I have broken stones and all the grout is crumbling."

"I'd be happy to take a look, Mrs. Johnson."

It was no mystery why her, or anyone else's backyard, was falling apart. Ted always insisted on hiring the cheapest day laborers from across the border, eager but clueless novices who knew nothing about masonry or proper grouting technique.

"Is tomorrow afternoon okay?"

"Whatever's good for you, Owen."

"Thank you, ma'am. I'll be there at 3:30 sharp."

Since his layoff from the IT division of Motorola eight years ago, Owen had worked for lots of homeowners who, while outwardly effusive about Cascade Falls, privately bitched and moaned about the quality of Johnson Homes' construction. This, however, would be his maiden voyage into the world of the man himself, a special assignment from the first lady of Arizona master planning. While she sounded unexpectedly down-to-earth and nice, he was nevertheless intimidated by the prospect. On the other hand, given the sameness of his daily routine in this sleepy Land of Leisure, the idea of venturing out of his comfort zone was strangely exhilarating.

Domestic Life

Three o'clock. The mother's witching hour was upon her, the decisive curtain on the alone time she so cherished. In a matter of moments, Max and Dana would materialize with their extensive lists of needs and wants. The funny part was that no matter how much Maya longed for more hours to herself, the witching hour always came as a welcome relief. She had her theory as to why. Caring for young children, though extremely demanding of one's time and resources, presented a refreshing lack of ambiguity: Give the kids a snack, start them on their homework, attend to the business of preparing a simple, but edible, dinner. From three o'clock on, she had license to run on automatic pilot until her duties were completed. Then she'd pour a glass of Chardonnay, her reward for having excelled at the mundane, and her permission to abandon all deep thinking until tomorrow. It wasn't a bad deal, really. Alone time, liberating as it was, gave Maya carte blanche to question everything. *Could I actually paint that painting? Suppose I learned to like golf? What if the guy at the smoke shop suddenly whipped out his penis?*

How unhappy am I? Is my unhappiness really the worst it has ever been? Is this an exaggeration? Am I being overly indulgent even letting myself have these thoughts? Shouldn't I be thankful that my kids are healthy and have a roof over their heads? Would a giant cinnamon bun fix everything?

Perhaps this whole notion of having time to think was overrated. If you were too busy to worry about being unhappy, maybe you couldn't be unhappy. It seemed far-fetched, but you never heard of a strawberry picker who complained of being creatively stifled.

Seeing the children burst out the school doors brought her back to Mommyland with the velocity of a Six Flags vomit-coaster. Dana seemed particularly excited as she jumped into the Lexus, some unidentifiable goop dripping from her backpack. "There's going to be a potluck on Friday and everyone's mom is baking a dessert."

Maya would be happy to oblige. She had a box of brownie mix in the pantry, plus, if she decided to get ambitious and make them from scratch, it would mean an extra hour of not questioning her arguably pitiable existence. And if this weren't sufficient cause for celebration, Max proudly chimed in that he'd been cast as a giant mushroom in the school show and needed a costume. That was something that could effortlessly eradicate contemplation for an entire day, maybe two. Since it was a good bet that the local Walmart received little demand for giant mushroom costumes, time-sucking design and sewing talents would be called into play. The responsibilities at hand would facilitate a seamless transformation from frustrated artist to metaphorical strawberry picker, leaving no brain space for unsettling thoughts of any kind.

As THE KIDS DESCENDED upon the kitchen, she saw three messages on the machine, one certain to be more annoying than the next. The homemaker's landline was reserved for such choice reminders as Orkin Exterminators asking when she'd like to schedule the annual termite check. *How about never? Wouldn't it take years for the little fuckers to eat through the wood in a way that anyone actually noticed? By that time, God willing, our family would be out of the state.* Message two: her father-in-law's secretary, Barb McDermott, wants to make sure they hold the date of November seventh for Jeannie Johnson's surprise sixty-fifth birthday party. Barb's screechingly grating voice and aggressive perkiness always made Maya want to crawl in a cave, or go deaf, or both. As far as her mother-in-law went, Maya was genuinely fond of Jeannie, the only questionable component of her character (and it was a big one) being that she had married Ted. Since the man's ego was large enough to accommodate two full-size adults, Jeannie's insistence on standing by him made her, first and foremost, an enabler. How could you completely love someone whose devotion was so toxic? The thought of going to the party made her want to get started on the mushroom costume ASAP. And besides, why didn't Ted just tell Danny about it at the office? They saw each other every day, for Christ's sake.

Message three was difficult to decipher. She vaguely recognized the voice, but couldn't quite make out the name. Whomever it was seemed familiar with Maya, going on about how she had to call because it had been way too long since they'd spoken. As the recording went on, it dawned on Maya that she was listening to Judith Aronson, owner of the Meteor Gallery where she had shown so many years ago. "I was at Campanile for lunch and who do I run into? Jay Blackstein." Blackstein was the pediatric oncologist who'd purchased Maya's "Autumn of Our Discontent" for 5000 dollars. Apparently, he wanted to know what Maya was working on these days, which gave Judith the impetus to track her down.

Maya let out a rapturous scream, momentarily oblivious to the fact that she hadn't one new thing to show. This wonderful man, Dr. Blackstein, had placed such a high value on her talent that years later, he wanted to know how he could see, and possibly buy, more of it. Why had she fucked around all this time when the good doctor had been waiting for the next big thing? Of course, Maya had had no idea he'd been waiting, but had she the confidence to imagine such things were possible, she surely would have been motivated to start filling up canvases. How fortuitous it was that she'd just purchased a fresh batch of supplies. She would call Judith first thing in the morning, give her a brief overview of the new antidesert series, and start churning out paintings, thoughts of Jay Blackstein and his impeccable taste dancing in her head.

Cutting up different varieties of apples for each child (Max liked Granny Smith; Dana, Fuji), Maya had to remind herself that this phone call wasn't any kind of slam dunk. Just because Blackstein had bought one painting didn't make him obligated to buy, much less like, whatever she did next. And even though Judith was inquiring about another show, if she didn't respond to the new work, it all amounted to nothing. But to Maya, *this* nothing was head and shoulders above the nothing she had called a life since their move to Arizona. This nothing came with hope, a far better platform on which to operate than resignation. Yes, hopes could be dashed in an instant, but if they served as a call to action, at least something would be ventured. Regardless of the ultimate result, Judith's phone call was Maya's ticket out of stagnation.

DANNY WALKED THROUGH THE door, surprised to find dinner already on the table. More striking was that it wasn't the unadorned chicken breasts that appeared on his plate with dull regularity. Also unusual was that, while the kids would be having their pasta with marinara sauce, Mr. and Mrs. Johnson would be dining on organic Beef Bourguignon, accompanied by a Stag's Leap Estate Cabernet that had been saved for a special occasion. The phone call from Los Angeles had spurred in Maya a spontaneous culinary drive that she hadn't experienced since the beginning of their marriage.

"What's this for?" Danny asked.

"I just felt like doing something for us," Maya told him. It was true. When something nice happens to you, it motivates you to do something nice for someone else. At least, that's the way it had always been for Maya.

"That looks like poop," Max announced, pointing to the meat on his parents' plates.

"Maybe to you, but it's the best thing that's happened to me all day," Danny answered, kissing his wife gently on the forehead.

Maya had seen for some time that the job was wearing on her husband. If she had stagnated in their new life, he had been roughed up by it and set back more than a few steps. Everywhere they went he was

Ted's son, heir to the Johnson Homes Corporation; scion with a legacy to uphold, even if that legacy was becoming more dubious by the day. Danny never wanted to be a fucking heir, certainly not to someone who equated selling cookie-cutter cardboard boxes with delivering salvation.

"What went on at work today?" Maya asked, more concerned than usual. When nice things happen, you tend to be more concerned as well.

"Nothing different than what goes on every day," Danny said, sampling a cube of the wine-infused meat. "Very good. Tender."

"Thanks." She was excited to tell him the news about Judith and Jay Blackstein. He would be happy for her and feel a little less guilty about having moved her to this land of strip malls and big-box stores. "I got a call today," she smiled.

"I know, from Barb. The sixty-fifth birthday party. She nailed me right after she talked to you because she didn't trust you to give me the message."

"Are you kidding me?" Maya felt herself starting to get pissed.

"Nope. And she seemed pleased as punch to tell me that. Yeah, I can't wait for that party," Danny groused.

"Are we invited?" Dana asked.

"Of course you are," Maya told her. "It's your Grandma's birthday."

"I am so tired of these goddamn celebrations," Danny simmered. "Everything has to be a spectacle."

"What's a spectacle?" Dana asked innocently enough.

"It means like a show," Maya told her, not sure if this made sense to a nine-year-old.

"I like shows," Max piped in.

Danny shook his head. "Birthdays, anniversaries, Christmas, it all winds up as some twisted Johnson Homes promotion."

"You know your father," Maya reminded him. "To his way of thinking, there is no Ted Johnson or Mrs. Ted Johnson without Johnson Homes."

"Fuck Johnson Homes!"

"Danny!" Maya shushed him.

Dana's mouth was suddenly agape, her eyes wide with fear as she burst into tears.

Max managed to keep his composure, even though he was equally frightened by his father's outburst.

Maya hugged Dana and moved to further diffuse the situation. "Your father and I are going to eat out there. You guys finish your dinner and we'll all have dessert together." She kissed both kids and proceeded to carry her plate into the dining room.

Stung by his wife's appropriately disapproving look, Danny followed and quietly sat down. "I'm sorry," he said softly. "I don't know what came over me."

"I understand you're unhappy. I haven't exactly been Miss Smileyface around here. We just can't take it out on the kids."

"That was really stupid of me. There's no excuse."

"Forget it."

He was grateful to Maya for understanding. They finished the meal in silence, Maya having lost the will and enthusiasm to reveal her good news. Afterward, Danny cleared the plates and thanked her for the extra effort she put into the dinner. Then he asked if she wouldn't mind tucking in the kids tonight, explaining that he just didn't have it in him to present the kind of positive parental image he deemed essential to the tucking-in process. Maya said it wouldn't be a problem, patting him on the shoulder in a way that was intended to be affectionate, but read as condescending.

HE WAS CURLED SIDEWAYS with his back to her, snoring lightly but erratically. Even in sleep, Danny managed to voice his lack of contentment. Maya, wide awake, ping-ponged between brainstorming for the new painting and stressing over how they had boxed themselves into this black hole of a life that neither of them wanted. At least she had Judith Aronson and Jay Blackstein to remind her of what she once was and might again be, but what light could Danny see at the end of the tunnel? It was a fact that lots of men were forced to relinquish their dreams to provide for their families, but watching Danny submit to it was unbearable. He had always tried to keep a smile on his face, managing it rather successfully for the first couple of years. He was the one who went out of his way to lift her spirits, but now he just shuffled through the days like some anemic suburban zombie. Maya scratched his back tenderly, remembering the gusto and determination he'd exuded in his mad pursuit of her at Bennington. She also recalled the moment she realized that all the passion had been extinguished. It was right around their first Labor Day weekend in Phoenix. She had casually asked whether he'd ever revisited a promising short story he had started in Los Angeles, and he replied that he was never going to write anything again. At this point in his life, he saw no purpose in wasting time on whimsical diversions that would never yield financial gain. Better to keep his nose to the grindstone, learn his father's trade, and become successful at something, no matter how much it bored him.

Maya moved her hand down his back to his ass, which had seemed to loosen and widen the minute they hit the Arizona state line. She stroked it gently but firmly, slowly gearing herself up to offer what could only be described as a mercy fuck to the father of her children. Knowing that she felt nothing sexual toward him, and hadn't for at least a year and a half, filled her with guilt. Then, she considered the situation from a different perspective. Danny hated his job but did it anyway, ostensibly for the happiness of his family. She might lack sexual desire for him (or anyone for that matter), but she could certainly make such a sacrifice for her husband's happiness, with the added bonus that, should he actually *become* happy, he might regain the qualities that had attracted her to him in the first place, and she would want him again.

Maya directed her fingers toward his inner thigh, lightly grazing his balls in the way that always drove him crazy. She saw his eyes open, but a smile was not forthcoming.

"What are you doing?" Danny snapped. "I've got a 7:00 a.m. breakfast meeting." He rolled back over, resuming his mouth-breathing snores within minutes.

Maya admitted to herself that she was never really good at mercy fucks. Just because Danny was her husband didn't mean that was going to change.

Author, Author

As the landing gear scraped the asphalt of Runway Seven, Ted Johnson anticipated his first meeting of the day, confident that it would pump up the adrenaline before his grueling, back-to-back lender conferences in Plano. In the past, achieving such a rush meant picking from his stable of adrenaline-pumping blondes in the Dallas-Fort Worth area, but this time, Ted decided to forgo the pleasures of a Kerry/Carrie three-way for something of far greater import. After snagging his rental car, he would head for the rural enclave of Prairieville, Texas to meet not with a hooker or a banker, but an author. And not just any author, he reminded himself. Harley Mason was a well-respected journalist and biographer, having chronicled the lives of former Texas Governor John Connelly, musician Shooter Jennings, and the late Mrs. Billy Graham. If all went according to plan, Mason's next book would be *The Ted Johnson Story: How One Man Subdivided and Unified America.*

No one else had been informed of Ted's intention to hire his own personal biographer. He didn't see the point in spoiling such a glorious surprise, especially since Harley Mason was not yet officially on board. The Johnson business philosophy had always been "First make the deal, then make the announcement," although Ted had, in fact, strayed from this tenet whenever it served his interests. The bogus press release boasting a new, 7,000-acre master-planned Johnson community on federally appointed Indian land had undoubtedly ruffled a few feathers, but it had also gotten him a photo spread in *Arizona* magazine, highlighting Johnson Homes' unrivaled selection of amenities. Ted had another business philosophy: "There are trade-offs." That one came in especially handy because it justified any road taken, regardless of the moral implications. To Ted's mind, any questionable action on his part was simply a trade-off.

The town of Prairieville, roughly an hour and forty-five minutes from the airport, was situated in the dusty heart of Kaufman County. Like certain other places in Texas (e.g.: Lyle Lovett's hometown of Klein), the name had kind of a Jewish ring to it, but one gathered from its remote location that no Jew had ever driven by the place, much less set foot there. In fact, Ted would soon learn that the county, established in 1848, was named after David Spangler Kaufman, the first Jewish Texan ever to serve his state in Congress. The Jew news made Ted happy because it supported his theory that America was a country full of pioneers you never heard about. And it made him even more excited to think how the new biography would change that up for a pioneer named Johnson.

As he reached the barren junction of Farm Market Road 1836 and Farm Market Road 90, he couldn't imagine why a talented writer like Harley Mason had planted himself in this shit little piece of nowhere. He had heard that writers sometimes needed isolation so as not to be distracted from the daunting task of filling blank pages with original words and thoughts. But hell, that's what Rockies and Tetons and Berkshires were for. You never heard of anyone going to find inspiration in Kaufman County. *To each his own,* Ted supposed—*whatever it took to make these creative types tick.*

The address he had scribbled down led him to an ill-maintained Airstream trailer situated maybe a mile and a half or so from a rusty mailbox on the main road. Ted pounded on the front door, but there was no answer. He looked at his watch to double-check whether he had arrived early, but no, he was right on time for the appointment. Someone had also told him that writers didn't place a high value on punctuality, a trait that never sat well with Ted. After thirty-odd minutes and a vigorous series of unrequited door knocks, he felt himself starting to get agitated. He had taken a major detour and a massive chunk out of his morning to meet this Mason fellow, but it now appeared as if he was going to get stood up. There was no way to call the guy because he didn't have a landline, and claimed to have lost his cell phone on a fishing trip with Shooter Jennings.

Ted had to concede that it would have been a hell of a lot easier to hire a writer locally. The locksmith, Wade Timmons, who had always done a stellar job crafting the church newsletter, had been Ted's number one candidate before the Harley Mason idea got hatched. While Ted would readily admit that the authorized Schlage dealer was a bit of a milquetoast who wore black socks with sandals, the man never once missed a deadline, even at the height of burglary season. And because writing was a hobby for Wade, he'd have no qualms about working cheap.

Before formally admitting defeat and doubling back to Plano, Ted decided to walk around the camper to try and peer in the windows, just in case the guy was sleeping or something. He had also heard that these types of people kept odd hours. There was little Ted could see through the crack in the dark brown curtains, the only clear images being empty Scotch bottles and three packages of vanilla wafers. What if the guy was dead in there? Should he break a window just to make sure everything was okay? On the other hand, if he did, and found a corpse, there was the possibility that he could be implicated in some sort of foul play. Then again, maybe he was overdramatizing the situation. Just because somebody didn't show up for an appointment didn't mean his body was decomposing in a sea of vanilla wafers. And even if that were the case, it certainly wasn't Ted's responsibility.

As he trudged back to the car, Ted checked the contacts in his phone to make sure he still had Wade's number. He imagined the look on the locksmith's face upon hearing that he'd been given the nod. *Fade in: Wade is installing a new deadbolt out at Cascade Falls Phase II. His cell phone suddenly rings and bingo, he's a paid biographer. Fade out.* The picture gave Ted chills. He always took pleasure in making folks unexpectedly happy, which, to his mind, was both a key to his success and worthy of mention in the book's prologue. And, now that he thought about it, what could be more gratifying that putting money into the local economy rather than outsourcing it to Kaufman County?

Opening the driver's side door and getting into the rented Fusion, he nearly squealed with delight as he autodialed the locksmith. Then, at the same moment that Wade's voicemail picked up, the door to the Airstream opened, revealing a vaguely human form, hell bent on taking a piss. As it scurried behind the trailer, a scratchy male voice made its presence known.

"Be with you in a minute, Señor Johnson."

A highly unorthodox way to introduce oneself to a prospective employer, Ted thought.

The mess that had to be Harley Mason unleashed his bladder for what seemed like an eternity, moaning throughout the entire ordeal. When it was finally over, he walked back around to the front and with nary a wash basin in sight, extended his hand to shake Ted's. He was out of luck there, because the Master Planner was a notorious clean freak (that would go somewhere in chapter two, Ted figured), and abruptly recoiled.

"I didn't take a shit or anything," was the author's response, oddly hurt by the rejection.

"I've been knocking on your door for a half-hour," an understandably exasperated Ted informed him.

"I know," Mason replied casually, proceeding to release a gargantuan fart.

"What do you mean 'you know?' And where are your fucking manners?"

"I apologize for the gas. Out here in Prairieville, we're not all that big on Emily Post."

"Or hygiene, or showing up on time," Ted added. "You knew I was out here and you just decided not to open the door until now?"

"Guilty as charged," Mason smiled.

This was just too damn much for Ted. "Well, I wish I could say it's been a pleasure meeting you, but that would not be truth in advertising." Ted walked back to the car.

"As opposed to the 7,000 acres on Indian land, or your love of family values? We use the same hookers in Dallas, by the by," Mason informed him.

"You are a rude and vile man," Ted shot back.

"I don't have a problem with that. As a writer, all I care about is telling the truth."

"You're full of shit."

"Have I said anything untruthful to you, Señor Johnson?"

"My name's not Señor. Cut it out."

"I stayed in the trailer because I wanted to observe my subject," Mason explained. "How does a powerful man respond when things aren't going his way? Is he patient? Is he curious about things he can't analyze with a snap of his fingers?"

"What is wrong with you?" Ted bellowed. "I certainly hope you didn't piss and fart in front of Mrs. Billy Graham."

"I did not. Each subject determines its own process."

"I'm not your subject. I think we're done here, Mr. Mason."

"Suit yourself. But I can tell you right now that nobody is going to get Ted Johnson the way I do."

"Bullshit. You don't know anything about Ted Johnson."

"I know he likes to screw black women from behind."

"You got no proof," Ted fumed.

"I also know that there's nobody else who has the balls to talk to you the way I do."

"You can say that again."

"Think about it, Ted. Anybody you hire is just going to kiss your ass because they're cashing your checks. I will never do that."

"You'll just take my money and write shit about me."

"I'll write what is. It's your dime, so you can edit out what you don't like. But at least you'll have given yourself the opportunity to be evaluated for the whole of who and what you are. None of us is perfect, dude. The best biographies encapsulate the man, 'warts and all,' as Oliver Cromwell said."

Ted wasn't sure who Oliver Cromwell was, though he recalled passing a Cromwell Chevrolet one time in San Antonio. He did, however, recognize that something strange was happening. Much as he hated to admit it, he felt himself beginning to buy into the guy's argument. "You know I could hire a really good writer for probably a third of your price," he informed the author.

"Party down. Go for it." Mason headed back toward his trailer.

"He may be a locksmith, but he knows how to turn a phrase," Ted called out.

"Good deal. No different than turning a deadbolt, right?" Mason replied.

Ted knew it was a lot different. Sure, the locksmith was gifted, but this foul jumble of a man was a professional. The thought of working with someone who stood up to him had never even occurred to Ted, and while it caught him completely off guard, it nonetheless piqued his curiosity. Maybe this pig was onto something.

"Assuming I was crazy enough to get into business with you, how soon could you start?" Ted asked.

"Hard to say," Mason replied. "I guess it would depend on when I get my first installment."

In between whiskey-soaked boxes of vanilla wafers, Ted found himself scribbling out an advance of 1,500 dollars. Mason agreed to arrive in Arizona the next week to begin immersing himself in Ted Johnson's world. Then he lit a cigar and farted again.

The First Lady

O wen had made maybe a thousand trips through the hallowed gates of Cascade Falls Phase II, but this time he had butterflies in his stomach. It seemed silly. He was a knowledgeable craftsman, meticulous with every project he took on, and there was no reason why repairing bad decking at the Ted Johnson house should be different from repairing it anywhere else. His wife couldn't have been nicer when they spoke on the phone. Still, working for the Big Cheese somehow had an uncomfortable feel to it, like being called to the principal's office only to find out that he considered you an ally. The other kids would hear the news, brand you a traitor, and you'd be doomed, spending the rest of your academic life between a rock and a hard place.

But there were no kids and this wasn't high school. The minute Jeannie Johnson opened the door and welcomed him into her home, any trace of nervousness disappeared. He liked the woman instantly, her soft-spoken manner reflecting a modesty and grace that suggested what his dear, departed wife might be like had God given her another twenty-five years. As Mrs. Johnson offered him freshly brewed iced tea, he could tell that she must have been quite beautiful as a young girl, but probably never thought of herself as beautiful. That was Lucy, too.

Jeannie escorted him out to the decaying patio, Owen making a mental note of the cracking drywall in the family room and buckling floorboard in the media center. Ted Johnson had sunk a lot of dough into this place, just not on skilled labor. Circling the deck, Owen could tell immediately that it was a major job. The stones had been laid in a precarious fashion: uneven, aesthetically unappealing, and lacking in proper drainage. He wanted to be as polite and upbeat as possible with Mrs. Johnson, but he wasn't going to lie to her, either.

Jeannie took the news rather matter-of-factly, explaining that, while she didn't know much about the details of actual construction, she was smart enough to identify stuff that looked like shit. Owen told her he would be happy to work up a proposal and fax it over to her, his assumption being that she would show it to Ted, he'd deem it too expensive, and instead hire however many illegal immigrants he could sneak in from Mexicali. Yet, the impression that Jeannie gave was that she had carte blanche on this one. Ted would be happy to let her do whatever she wanted.

What was strange to Owen was that she didn't seem at all excited, either about having been granted that power, or the improvements themselves. Maybe it was the idea of having to deal with a bunch of workmen around her house. Nobody liked that kind of disruption. But Owen got the impression it was something else. Surely, he couldn't know much about the woman after one brief phone call and a walk around the pool, but perhaps the fact that she reminded him of Lucy led him to inferences he wouldn't normally attempt. His gut feeling was that Jeannie Johnson had no interest in the house whatsoever. It was possible that she hated it, or, even more significantly, hated her life. But it wasn't the contractor's place to determine such things, Owen's longtime policy being to steer clear of clients' personal affairs. All he needed to be concerned with were materials and hard numbers.

Bruce Ferber

He finished off the iced tea and shook Jeannie's hand. As she led Owen to the front door, her grandchildren and daughter-in-law came rushing in, the mom apparently dropping off the kids so she could get some work done.

"Maya, this is Owen Shea. He's going to be doing some remodeling around here."

"Pleased to meet you," Owen responded, surprised by Jeannie's proclaiming him "hired" before seeing an estimate. He also thought he knew her daughter-in-law from somewhere.

"You look familiar," Maya offered, before he had the chance to.

They soon realized that their kids were in the same school, Brianna in the grade directly between Maya's two kids. They had probably seen each other in the parking lot, or school assemblies, or some volunteer parent meeting.

"Would I know your wife?" Maya asked, innocently enough.

"I don't think so," Owen responded, not wanting to get into the details. "She hasn't really been around." He turned to shake Jeannie's hand. "So long, Mrs. Johnson."

Owen climbed into his truck, happy at the prospect of more work, but devastated by never-ending thoughts of the woman who deserved to be at those PTA meetings, the woman who was supposed to be his partner for life.

Art vs. Life

It was a seven-minute drive from Phase II to Phase III, where the pride of the homeowner's association, the almighty gates, would release and receive her. Today Maya made the trip in five minutes, anxious to get started on her painting. She had had an encouraging phone conversation with Judith Aronson then spent the rest of the morning sewing a half-assed mushroom costume that was, in its current state, unrecognizable as either mushroom or costume. She was well aware that her work would have to be revisited before her son could be seen in public, wearing the thing. Tonight, however, the kids would be staying at Jeannie and Ted's for dinner, Danny had a late meeting, and the business at hand was to begin her first original work in over three years. It was time to start making good on her promise to Judith, and more importantly, on the one she'd made to herself in those pre-motherhood days, back when she believed she had insights that, once visualized, would illuminate the human condition. This was the engine that drove her and every young artist, the sense of possessing unique perceptions which one felt obligated to share with the world. The naïveté of youth also fostered the belief that a unique voice would forever remain unique, leaving Maya clueless as to how quickly it could be silenced by real life. In the course of her journey into adulthood, she'd seen aspiring rock musicians become insurance agents, future Scorseses reborn as accountants, painters like herself surrender it all to motherhood. Most never knew what hit them and didn't look back, too overwhelmed by day-to-day struggles to bemoan their lost passions. Maya was determined to buck that trend, ready to dig deep into the soul that was still hers. It had been reconfigured, to be sure, but perhaps compellingly so by the adult experiences she'd logged along the way.

What was compelling about being a mom stuck in a listless marriage, in a place she hated? It was a question Maya knew she had to answer with her brushes if she ever intended to send work back to Los Angeles. What was more, even if she never sent off one canvas, it would be impossible to work without believing that she had something of value to say. Looking out the window at the monotonous sea of stucco and tile roofs, she couldn't imagine where the spark would come from.

Perhaps music would open the creative pores. She booted up her laptop and clicked on Pandora, creating a Thelonious Monk station. In the past, listening to jazz had helped her mind wander and encouraged her to experiment. Ray Minetta had taught her that back in college. He'd captured her virginity to the strains of "A Love Supreme," took sex to frenetic heights with "Goodbye Pork Pie Hat," and shared post-coital smokes to "Kind of Blue." The freedom this brought out in Maya gave her the impetus to take the music into the college art studio, where she blissfully worked to geniuses like Monk, Cannonball Adderley, and Charles Lloyd. Now, thanks to streaming radio, she had all of this great jazz and more at her disposal. But would it be enough to get the job done in a Phoenix subdivision, all these years later?

The opening piano chords of "Well, You Needn't" made Maya smile. It was an eleven-and-a-half minute song and Ray had gone down on her for the entire length of it in her dorm room at Bennington. Never mind that the man who swore he was the real Next Bob Dylan was now selling term life for Allstate. Just recalling those unfettered days relaxed her into thinking she still had possibilities. She mixed some red with brown, dipped her brush in, and ponied up to the canvas, no clue as to where the colors might take her. Before long, she found herself painting the very terra-cotta roof tiles she had grown to despise, followed by the characterless stucco on which they rested. The last idea Maya had ever considered, she was suddenly painting the sights of Phase III in all their homogeneous glory. It made no sense, since there was nothing about the place that remotely interested her. She gave in to her stream-of-consciousness, encouraged, if not by the subject matter, then by the speed with which a picture was coming together. Replicating the house directly across the street, she impulsively added a ground-to-ceiling crack in the outside wall. Somehow the crack made it less prefab to her, suggesting that there might be something out of the ordinary lurking behind the monotony. Then she started to play with the crack, making it less uniform, more jagged, transforming it from vertical to diagonal. What would be revealed if the crack opened up, she wondered?

Much to her surprise, the break in the stucco seemed like the opening for which she'd been searching, both artistically and metaphorically. What emerged from this crevice might well be her perspective on the desert lifestyle into which she'd been reluctantly thrown. After hours of inserting, then removing, a strangled coyote, a phallic saguaro, unrecyclable plastic bags from Walmart, what wound up seeping out of the crack was an ugly, green liquid. Was it tainted tap water? Loose, ammoniated cow shit? Some sort of fetid, green goddess salad dressing? Maya didn't quite know the answer. Which somehow felt right. If it wasn't apparent to her, it couldn't be an obvious artistic choice. Abstract color, grounded in emotion, something for the viewer to consider and the artist to continue pondering. Maybe it was the blood this place sucked out of you, having been extracted with so much force that it turned green.

Maya always felt connected to art that commented on the lives of the bourgeoisie, whether it was Manet's denizens of Paris, Grosz's Berliners, or the gay revelers of Paul Cadmus. The difference here, was that her commentary on Phoenix middle class life contained no human beings. Which, she reasoned, summed up how she felt about her tenure in this most suburban of suburbias. You rarely saw anyone walking. Bodies were hidden in family rooms, then shuffled into golf carts and automobiles without ever setting foot on pavement. If you wanted to say hello to your neighbor, your best bet was out on the links. This got her to thinking. While she always hated the idea of painting a golf course, that was before she'd discovered the crack in the wall. If there were secrets to be mined behind stucco, who knew what might be lurking on the seventh green?

She looked over at the clock and saw that it was nearly nine. Danny should have picked up the children and been home by now. She was about to get out her cell phone when she heard the garage door open. Putting down the brushes to greet her family, Max and Dana raced upstairs, beating her to the punch. They had a great time at Grandma's, eating homemade pizza and learning how to play Mexican Train dominoes. They were happy with so little, it seemed. Maya kissed them, grateful to have been blessed with such good, easy kids. Then Danny trudged up the stairs, looking worse than he had the night before, his breath reeking of alcohol. He threw her a quick "hello," and excused himself to the bedroom.

Maya began to feel the evening's momentum drain out of her, much like the stucco house discharging its blood or bilge or whatever it might be. It occurred to her that while these cookie-cutter dwellings were lifeless by design, marriages devolved into a dormant state suddenly and unexpectedly. When you bought into a Johnson Homes Community, you knew what your unit was going to look like because the floor plans were standard. The deteriorating bonds between husbands and wives, however, were a custom deal, each marriage crumbling at its own sickening pace. Sure, after ten years with the same partner, it was only natural to fantasize about a different set of lips or breasts, or a bigger penis. Those were the healthy marriages. In the doomed, moribund unions, the ones where spouses regularly retreated to separate sides of the bed with no interest in restarting the conversation, the ultimate fantasy was not being miserable. Both partners would have strong opinions about how it had gotten so awful, yet be at a loss to remember how the trouble started. One might feel angry, the other hurt, neither wanting to make the first move toward a truce. That was sad in itself, Maya thought. The goal of a truce was simply peaceful coexistence, a clear admission that romance and passion had been irrevocably lost on the battlefield. Maya and Danny had been living in truce country for quite some time, and were equally incapable of enacting change. They came at their stalemate from different places, though, Danny wishing things could go back to the way they were, Maya seeking a path forward. She had made her most recent effort with the Beef Bourguignon, but Danny's outburst and subsequent shutting down would not inspire her to further action.

As she tucked in Max and Dana, Maya dreaded whatever was awaiting her in the master bedroom. Maybe she would postpone her entrance and go back in the studio. She could get her mojo back and continue painting, which might then motivate her to do even more tomorrow. Chances were, Danny wouldn't bat an eye. It was a horrible feeling, this urge to avoid the man whose single happiest thought had been of her bearing his children, not so much because he loved kids, but because the progeny would be half-Maya. While Ray Minetta had taught her about sex, Danny had been captivated by the totality of her, examining every curve and fold of her body with the fervor of an Orthodox Jew studying the Torah. He had discovered marks on her skin she never knew existed, most notably a tiny mole, a dot really, on the edge of the left nostril. Despite its microscopic size, he pronounced it quintessentially beautiful, a bonus enhancement to her more obvious attributes. She would blush when he spoke this way, perhaps because it made her feel inadequate in her ability to see such special things in him. Even had she been capable of identifying similar qualities, she couldn't imagine voicing such praise in the unabashed way her husband did.

About to reenter the studio, Maya found herself pulled toward Danny so she could check on him. She opened the door to the bedroom and heard the shower running from the bath. Maybe if she talked to him from outside the glass door, it would invite some sort of intimacy. She had long given up on such notions, but felt she should try again, for his sake. It was the mercy fuck all over again, stepping up to the plate one more time in a game that was surely over.

Maya marched into the bathroom, attempting a smile he couldn't possibly see through the steam. "How was your day?"

"Sucked."

"Feel like talking?"

"What do you want to talk about?" he barked.

Maya pressed onward. "I don't know. Anything on your mind? That you might want to share with me?"

"Like what?" Now he sounded pissed off.

"Forget it. I'm going to be in the studio."

She had made the effort, but what had she gotten for her troubles? A passive-aggressive response that put the onus on her. Danny knew damned well that she was trying to reach out to him, but rather than accept her offer, he chose to project annoyance, like she was invading his space. He could just as easily have said: "Not tonight, honey," which would have at least conveyed appreciation of her concern. Instead, he had decided to cut her off and make her feel stupid for asking.

Maya didn't feel stupid, though. She felt sad and trapped, convinced that the only way out of her despair was through her painting. She went back into the studio more determined than ever, but the minute she picked up the brush, she felt herself starting to break down. Thinking about how their relationship had come to this turned sniffles into sobs. Her body collapsed onto the futon and curled into the fetal position, certain to accomplish nothing more for the remainder of the night.

Johnson Pride

Ted Johnson was visibly tickled as he hovered over Barb McDermott's desk, watching the whirling dervish of a secretary book a hotel room for his newly minted biographer, Harley Mason. The making of reservations squarely in her wheelhouse, Barb snagged a triple-A rate at the Extended Stay Suites off the I-10, shaving off an additional twenty dollars a night by dropping the name Ted Johnson. She was thrilled for her boss's good fortune. If ever there was a man who deserved to have his story told, it was Ted, who, to her way of thinking, had brought more joy to folks than anyone, except maybe the blessed Jesus. Admittedly, the home developer wasn't exactly generous when it came to salaries, her last raise coming five years ago after lobbying for it the previous two, but the man was loyal, and his love of life, specifically his own, was inspiring to her. Ted's enthusiasm made others enthusiastic, even if there was no good reason for it.

"Mr. Mason is booked starting Monday at three hundred and ninety-eight dollars per week for as long as you need him there," Barb happily announced.

"Thank you, dear, that's fantastic. This guy is something, I tell you what."

"He'd have to be for you to pick him. I imagine they're lining up to write your story, sir."

Barb knew as little about the book business as she did about housing, finance, or world affairs. The concept of vanity press was completely alien to her, so Ted having a biographer was no different from Lyndon Johnson (no relation) having his life chronicled by Robert Caro. And should Barb be informed that Ted was paying the author out of his own pocket, she would assume that the other Johnson paid his guy as well. She was a proud executive secretary who rewarded her boss's loyalty with a fierce devotion of her own, doing whatever needed to be done within, and occasionally outside of, the legal limits. When someone once called her the Rose Mary Woods of Johnson Homes, she took as it a compliment without bothering to find out who Rose Mary Woods was.

"Have you seen my boy this morning?" Ted asked.

"No, sir, not yet. Do you need me to get Danny on the phone?"

"No, just book the small conference room for four o'clock. I need to go over Plano with him, and James, and Dusty."

"Food or beverage service?"

"Just coffee will be fine. Thank you kindly, Barb."

Ted retreated to his office, where he set to thinking about his two best lieutenants, James Dalton and Dusty Sprague. They had been with him since the beginning of the dream, way back when he stole all of Del Webb's ideas, took them to K. Tarkanian, and proceeded to bastardize both business models to start Johnson Homes. Fine soldiers, both of them, sticking by him through thick and thin. He wondered how they must feel now that young Danny Johnson had swooped in and become the heir apparent. If they were unhappy they never let on, having gleaned from the master the ability to mask anger and annoyance with a vapid, shit-eating grin. The plus was that a positive affect made them more successful in business; the negative, that Ted could no longer decipher what they were really thinking. Obviously, the guys couldn't be pleased that they had lost out to nepotism, but if they had learned anything about

Ted Johnson, it was that family always came first. Even on their road trips, cavorting in the cathouses of Pahrump, Nevada, James and Dusty had witnessed firsthand how he always gave Jeannie a "safe arrival" call. Ted made a mental note to sweeten the pot for those boys, even as that pot seemed to be getting emptier with each passing day.

DANNY COULDN'T THINK OF anything more depressing than sitting alone in Applebee's, waiting to meet with a discount supplier of Chinese faux terra-cotta roofing materials. He'd been sipping watery coffee for nearly an hour, having gotten the call that Kim Lee, the tile distributor, was hung up at the golf course by the slow-moving foursome in front of him.

"Just meet with the Chinaman," had been his father's call to action. "I'm not saying we have to buy the fake tiles, but the potential profit margin begs a thorough investigation."

As it turned out, the "Chinaman" wasn't Chinese at all. This Kim Lee fellow he saw sauntering through the doors of Applebee's was a tall, pasty-white, card-carrying Southern Baptist whose last job was hawking Japanese water filtration systems that claimed to prevent cancer. Kim's shtick was that he considered himself to be in the business of helping people, whether limiting their intake of carcinogens or putting plastic roofs over their heads. This self-serving worldview struck Danny as the sub-contracting version of his father's, a twisted savior complex operating at full bore. It seemed inhumane that in addition to having to suffer Ted Johnson, he would now be forced to suffer the sub-Ted Johnson. As Kim pontificated on subjects ranging from per capita consumption of dog meat in Shanghai Province to his affinity for "churchy-type" people, Danny's eyes glazed over. He found himself floating in some foggy Applebee's purgatory, where consciousness subject-hopped between the meaningless chatter and the gluey cherry pie.

"So, what do you think?" Kim asked, after a long rant on something to which Danny had paid zero attention.

"I'll run it up the flagpole," Danny smiled, understandably noncommittal.

Kim looked perplexed. "You'll run what up the flagpole? That the price of gas is too high because the freakin' Saudis are sticking it to us?"

"No, of course not," Danny covered lamely. "I'm talking about the tiles."

"I haven't told you anything about the tiles."

"I get the general idea—cheaper and lighter than real clay—less breakable."

"We haven't even broached energy efficiency—"

"I'm sure they're very efficient. That's okay."

It wasn't okay with Kim Lee. He had photos and spreadsheets and graphs to haul out and nobody was about to cut short his presentation, especially someone as unassertive as Danny Johnson. Kim dived into his pitch with Ted-like gusto, swelling with such pride that a stranger might think he was boasting about his children rather than roofing materials. Danny used the opportunity to focus on their twenty-something waitress, tagged Katie B., who managed to look fetching in her man-tailored Applebee's polo shirt. She was perky, fresh-faced, and wore no make-up—possibly a cheerleader at some point, Danny figured. Katie was exactly the kind of girl who had held no interest for him when he was younger, having always preferred the dark, ethnically mysterious types. But at this moment, it was far more satisfying to imagine what was underneath the Applebee's uniform than to try and give a shit about how fake tiles would save the typical Johnson homeowner three dollars and eight cents a month. He could tell that even though Katie B. was thin, she was full-breasted, the loose-fitting polo not loose enough to hide her femininity.

Danny found it a workable plan. If Kim wanted to obsess on energy tax credits, he would hypothesize as to what type of underwear the waitress might be wearing. All signs pointed to conservative, but you never knew. There were more than a few women who looked traditional on the outside, yet were full of surprises once the outer layers peeled off. The nice part was, this being Danny's fantasy, he was free to put together whatever ensembles he liked. Kim's verbosity afforded him the opportunity to imagine Katie B. in white cotton panties with pink polka dots, then a skimpy purple lace bra and thong set, and finally, au natural, waxed smooth as a baby's bottom. Picturing the waitress in so many different guises somehow made him feel as if he'd gotten to know her. It was an absurd thought, he knew, but was it any less absurd than a white Baptist having orgasms over Szechuan plastic? The more Kim Lee talked, the more Danny wanted to say something to Katie B., no matter how silly or impertinent it might sound. Considering possible opening lines filled up additional time, which was always useful in zoning out a blowhard like "the Chinaman."

When Kim Lee finally finished his spiel, Danny nodded quietly.

"I'll run it up the flagpole," he reiterated.

The tile distributor realized, at long last, that forty-five minutes of pitching his heart out had gotten him nowhere. After a sad handshake, Kim gathered his wares and shuffled out the door. Once he was gone, Danny homed in on how he would approach Katie B. Watching her take an order for boneless buffalo wings, he pulled a fifty out of his wallet and smiled at her, reasonably certain that he was about to reward the waitress with the largest tip of her nascent Applebee's career.

Fix You

Jeannie Johnson was finishing her morning coffee as she opened the door to greet Owen. She appeared happy to see him, something that couldn't be said about most homeowners when a workman and his crew showed up early to invade their space. The developer's wife offered him an espresso from her recently purchased Gaggia machine, which he graciously accepted. Jeannie then volunteered that she had gotten the espresso bug on her trip to Italy, taken with some friends from an Italian class at the community college. Apparently, Ted Johnson wasn't big on leaving the US of A, one of his pet peeves being Americans who spent their money on things and countries that weren't red, white, and blue. Ironic, considering he spent his money on illegal Mexicans and was fully prepared to buy roofing tiles from Mainland China. Despite the misguided patriotism, Ted was fine with Jeannie exploring the world, maintaining that his wife pursuing her own interests would be beneficial to them as a couple.

"I've always believed it was healthy for married people to branch out on their own occasionally," Owen agreed. He had spoken from the heart, but instantly regretted it, remembering the rumors he'd heard. Throughout the Phases, it seemed to be common knowledge that every time Jeannie decided to "branch out," Ted extended his central limb to any female who would grab onto to it. Owen wondered how much Jeannie knew, suspected, and overlooked. She seemed too smart to be oblivious to such things, yet too self-possessed to allow herself to be humiliated by them.

"We're going to start ripping out flagstone," Owen informed her. "If it gets too noisy for you, just let us know and we'll go work on some other stuff."

"You have a lot to choose from," she laughed.

"Nothing wrong with a little sprucing up." He thanked her for the coffee and headed out to the pool area.

Owen and his men spent most of the morning removing what never would have needed to be replaced had it been installed properly the first time. His two helpers, Juan and Roy, were eternally grateful for the Johnson Homes brand of substandard workmanship. The sheer number of abysmal building decisions, combined with Owen's stature as Cascade Falls' top fix-it man, provided them with a respectable means of feeding their families. Owen could handle the small stuff, like wiring, by himself, but a big job like this required extra manpower. Their sense was that the Johnson homestead was a goldmine in terms of what needed to be repaired, and that Owen had the charm and credibility to convince Jeannie Johnson to move ahead with all the work.

By noon, when the guys took their break, the temperature was hovering around 105 degrees. As they sat down under a tree too thin to yield any decent shade, Jeannie appeared with a pitcher of lemonade. Juan and Roy happily gulped it down. The ever-gracious Mrs. Johnson then asked Owen if he had a moment to take a look at the master bath, where she thought there might be some sort of leak. He was more than happy to oblige, hoping, for Jeannie's sake, that it was something small like a corroded washer.

Owen worked in people's bathrooms all the time, but there was just something strange about being in the place where Ted Johnson took his morning dump. They always said that if you were in awe of people who were famous, or successful, or beautiful, you should imagine them sitting on the toilet to remind yourself that they were human. But since Owen thought Ted was slightly sub-human to begin with, a man who made an undeserved fortune at the expense of others, picturing him in a full-on squat only made it even more unpleasant.

Jeannie directed him to a spot on the ceiling. Owen didn't like what he saw, and his initial suspicion proved correct. Ted's house, like every other structure in the Johnson Homes Communities, had been outfitted with the cheapest polyethylene piping—fine for some uses, but deadly in a place like Phoenix, where the soaring temperatures could cause it to burst, melt and in many cases, decompose. For a few pennies more, you could get PVC, and if you wanted to do it right, you used copper. The Johnson's pipes were in serious decomposition mode and needed to be ripped out and replaced as soon as possible. While it obviously meant a lot of work for Owen and his crew, he felt bad about the circumstances. Here was a woman who continually bore the brunt of her husband's character deficiencies, now having to be inconvenienced by his wretched professional decisions.

As Owen gave Jeannie his recommendations for the repair, he detected a sadness in her eyes. It was nothing like the normal disappointed reaction he got when a homeowner was faced with unanticipated expenditures. This was the empty gaze of someone who had endured a lifetime of disappointment and resignation. *Why had she stayed with Ted Johnson all these years?* he wondered. He knew that there were plenty of women who would put up with just about anything in exchange for homes, and jewelry, and country clubs, but from what he could gather, Jeannie didn't fit into that category. Somehow, Owen saw her situation as far more tragic than his own. He had married a woman he loved so deeply that he could never imagine losing her, and while there was no getting her back, he could temper the pain by reminding himself how privileged he was to have gotten the time with her that he did. Were Ted Johnson to drop dead tomorrow, he doubted Jeannie could make the same claim. She wouldn't be losing a remarkable spouse like Owen had. She would be freed from the burden of a shitty one.

"Are you able to do all this work, or do you have other jobs lined up?" Jeannie asked politely.

"We're here for whatever you need," Owen smiled. He wanted to say more, to let her know that the foundation of his life had been rocked and was also in the process of a major remodel. He wanted to tell her that she reminded him of his sweet Lucy. He did neither, opting instead to help Juan and Roy break up more pool decking. Still, Owen sensed that in time, their experiences would be communicated to one another, and that sharing how life had weakened them would make both of them stronger.

Surprise

A quiet panic starting to set in, Maya sat frozen at the sewing machine, wondering if it were even possible to make a person look like a mushroom. One false step and your kid would be a giant penis. Why couldn't her son have been cast as something normal, like a doctor or a superhero? She was totally stumped. How much more time would the mushroom situation take away from her burgeoning artistic resurgence? Maya thought about calling the teacher and lobbying to change Max into a tree or something similarly identifiable. But for whatever reason, the boy was genuinely excited about the idea of playing a mushroom. How would you play a mushroom, anyway? Would you convey a different sort of emotion than, say, a bell pepper? She was wasting valuable time deliberating such matters. There had to be an easy fix. She thought back to when she was a young girl, watching reruns of silly sitcoms like *Alice* and *Laverne and Shirley*. On those shows, whenever they had a character do something out of the ordinary—sing opera, for example—they'd have him wear a T-shirt that read: "Opera Singer," just in case the audience didn't get it from the aria or the line: "I sing opera." As an artist, Maya hated hitting an audience over the head with a message, but at the moment, she was ready to swing the giant hammer and emblazon the words "I'm A Mushroom" across the costume's chest area.

She needed to decide what to do about dinner. There was little food in the house, and it had been a while since she'd cooked anything fresh or healthy for the family. How was one supposed to shop for groceries, drive kids to school, make costumes, and still have the energy for serious creative expression? It was cliché mommy dilemma stuff, the pesky obstacles that stood in the way of getting back to work. Maya knew some people who were really good at compartmentalizing. Her friend Cathy Janelli, back in Los Angeles, could shop, bake a pie, play piano for an hour, then sit down write a short story. But as many times as Maya had attempted that kind of productivity, she wound up being lucky to get one non-kid-related thing done in a day. And those were the good days. There had been entire weeks of nothing but dishes and laundry. She'd gulp down her five o'clock Chardonnay, clueless as to how all those hours could have been pissed away. With a few days left to modify Max's costume and no answer in sight, Maya wondered if her time might be better served going to the supermarket for necessities. She could return to put away the groceries and still have an hour in her studio before she had to pick up the kids.

PHOENIX HAD THE CLEANEST supermarkets in the known universe, and there seemed to be one on every corner. The closest was Basha's, named after a Lebanese businessman who was to the Arizona grocery business what Ted Johnson had become to home development. Yet while the housing market had tanked, food still seemed to be very much in demand. Maya barreled through the produce aisle and grabbed apples, broccoli, and lettuce, barely bothering to examine their condition. There was a time when she enjoyed such excursions, relishing the challenge of obtaining the finest ingredients for the best price. These days, grocery shopping was pretty much "wham, bam, ring me up ma'am," the task executed with the enthusiasm of a gas station fill-up.

This particular supermarket was a sea of white people, which Maya always found odd given the grocery chain's roots and the state's large population of immigrants, legal and otherwise. She found it doubly odd when she heard the man who had stepped up behind her in line greet her with a "Hey, darlin." It was Bob, the overly friendly Pima clerk from the Indian smoke shop who evidently bought his personal Pepsi at Basha's, where it was cheaper. "Haven't seen you in a while. You quit smokin'?"

"I don't really smoke," Maya answered, instantly aware of how lame it sounded since she usually stopped by once a week to buy a pack.

"I understand," Bob sympathized. "We sell cigarettes to lots of people who don't really smoke. How ya been?"

"Fine," Maya answered, taken aback by the man's unsolicited familiarity.

"I don't really know you," Bob declared, "but I always like when you come into my store."

"Thank you," Maya managed a smile, sure that she would never again set foot in the Indian smoke shop.

"What do you do, anyways? I know you're a mom, but you seem like you got a career, too."

"I do?" Maya hated herself for it, but she was flattered.

"You an actress or something?"

"No," Maya laughed. "I haven't been anything for a while. I paint."

"Me, too. I also pick up drywalling work when they need me over in Cascade Falls."

"No, I mean I paint …paintings."

"So do I," Bob chirped. "Mostly, I do sculptures, but I have a few oils. I'll show 'em to you next time you stop by the store."

"I'd like that," Maya lied. Luckily, she was next up at the check stand so the conversation could come to a natural end.

"Nice seeing you," Bob nodded.

Maya silently nodded back and proceeded to check out as quickly as possible.

IN ADDITION TO BEING a Pepsi addict, it seemed the Indian cigarette guy was also an artist. As she transported her haul back to Cascade Falls, Maya thought about how easy it had been for him to volunteer that information. It was always like pulling teeth for people to get her to tell them that she was a painter, even back when she was getting paid for it. Wasn't it disingenuous to call oneself an artist if one hadn't made a consistent living at it, or at the very least, accumulated a significant body of work? But for Bob the cigarette guy, the statement had been as natural as tying his shoes. She allowed for the fact that he was an amateur, but so was she at this point. Turning off Hohokam Road and into the gates of Phase III, she imagined what Bob's oil paintings might look like: no doubt the ubiquitous geckos, coyotes, and ocotillos, infused with plenty of turquoise. As Buzzy waved her through, she considered that she had, perhaps, made a racist assumption. What else would an Indian paint but standard, southwestern motel art? Maya hated herself for thinking that way, but, in truth, her prejudice had less to do with Bob being Native American than him coming from a region she considered a creative wasteland. Which wasn't racist but elitist, and had no basis in fact. Statistically speaking, there had to be lots of talented folks in this part of the world. It occurred to her that maybe she had never sought them out because discovering the brilliance she lacked would have made her feel even worse.

Maya shoved the groceries into the refrigerator and pantry, then went upstairs to review the previous night's work. To her surprise, she wasn't repulsed by it. The crack in the stucco seemed like a good catalyst for further exploration. Images started flashing through her head: fake beaches; chlorinated lakes; sprinklers operating full force, wasting the water that would one day become more precious than crude oil; golf courses, brown and brittle, parched so dry that one live cigarette butt could set all eighteen holes aflame. With barely fifty-five minutes before she had to pick up the kids, Maya decided to put aside last night's painting and greet a fresh, blank canvas.

On a whim, she dipped her brush in the black. The strokes instinctively took her to the wrought iron gate that she had just passed through. Subdivision-as-prison was perhaps where she was headed. Fences seemed to be a theme in these parts: extended, multiplied, yet never able to keep out those determined to find their way in. Maya felt herself starting to loosen up, once again entering the zone of possibility that had long been so foreign to her. It felt good last night, and the fact that she could pick it up again today was a positive sign.

She wasn't going to answer her cell phone, but the ringtone was Danny's. Perhaps he was calling to say he was sorry for his terseness and cranky behavior.

"Hey, what's going on?" She tried to sound enthusiastic.

"Don't wait up for me tonight. I have to meet with a client."

"Okay. Anything exciting?" It never hurt to be encouraging.

"Same old shit."

She waited for him to elaborate, but no new information came. "Sorry. Well, see you later, I guess."

"Whatever."

She threw her brush across the room, spraying the beige wall and carpet with shocks of black. How much longer could this marriage survive? What was the alternative? That one of them move out and rent an apartment they couldn't afford? They could try taking the family back to California and hope things got better. Los Angeles might have wounded them, but this place had sent them to the conjugal ICU. Maybe returning to the southland would stop the bleeding.

It was a dicey proposition. The kids were comfortably ensconced in schools that were newer, cleaner, and, for the time being, better funded than their Los Angeles counterparts. And even if that problem could be solved, what made Maya think that she and Danny would be able to make ends meet now, when it had been impossible before? Wouldn't they just take their misery with them? And what about Ted, who never failed to remind them how he had stuck his neck out to bring them here so they could have a better life. Maybe if they were happier with each other, they would have a better life. You couldn't blame Ted for everything.

She picked up the brush from the floor, but it felt different now that her thoughts had drifted to Danny and what wasn't working. Her imagination might have been reignited, but it wouldn't necessarily prevail over her despondency. As she forced herself to finish painting the gate, the brush that once seemed like a spirited extension of her soul had now been reduced to an inexpensive tool bought in a store. The gate had, for all intents and purposes, become the giant mushroom: complete, but crying out to be reworked.

Connections

He knew the prospect of attaining great wealth was likely out of reach, yet Owen was grateful for the career he had carved out for himself. While tight-lipped about the particulars of his personal life, he religiously informed his clients that he needed to leave every day at 2:30 to pick up his daughter from school. He would bring her home, then once she had settled in, he'd return to resume his work. If the homeowners didn't approve, they were free to hire another contractor, no hard feelings. More often than not, Owen's skill and honesty won the day, and his reputation as a craftsman who took pride in even the smallest of jobs put him in great demand. The only downside of his business was that occasionally he'd get hired by assholes, at which point he'd have to make an executive decision regarding how much shit he was willing to take in exchange for a paycheck. It had never been Owen's nature to put up with abusive people, but thousands of dollars in overdue medical bills had a way of making you grit your teeth and suck it up. Luckily, as each year proved more successful, the amount of gritting and sucking waned and he became freer to choose the projects he liked as well as the clients with whom he wanted to work.

If only he could figure out the job of being a father with similar efficacy. He had read countless self-help books on single parenting, but wound up getting most of his learning in the field, after making the unavoidable mistakes most parents make, single or otherwise. Owen had witnessed firsthand that you could humiliate your kids with nothing more than a benign look or casual comment in front of their peers. He wondered when, if ever, this feeling of being on pins and needles would go away. Even though he saw two-parent families having the identical difficulties, he remained convinced that making decisions for Brianna would have been far more navigable with Lucy by his side.

As the Ranger pulled up to the entrance of the school, he could see Brianna looked sad, like she'd been crying. For a brief moment, Owen took solace in not being the source of whatever had made his daughter unhappy. It was a reaction only a parent could understand, the illusory satisfaction of *Hey, this one wasn't my fault.* The feeling, of course, disappeared the minute his daughter leapt up onto the front seat and started sobbing, telling him that another girl was mean to her because that girl likes a boy, but the boy likes her, and she doesn't know what to do.

This one was problematic on so many levels. First and foremost, Owen hated to see Brianna upset. When your kid hurt, you hurt, that's all there was to it. Then there was the matter of the other girl. Lucy had always told him that at that age, girls were much meaner than boys. And what about this boy? Who was he, and what did he want from a ten year-old? What did Brianna want from him? Owen decided not to push. He simply asked her what was wrong, his heart breaking as he watched her unleash the tears she'd probably been withholding all afternoon. Rather than rattling off the twenty questions that instantly came to mind, Owen pointed the truck in the direction of Jamba Juice, his go-to therapy venue. *What kind of boost would be on the docket today?* he wondered. *Soy Protein? 3D Charger? Maybe the Energy Boost would be the answer to this particular dilemma.*

She threw him a curve with Flax 'N Fiber, but he figured it was probably good to get the roughage thing going at an early age. As they headed back out to the car, an attractive woman, at a table with her two kids, gave him a friendly wave. She looked familiar and he waved back, but he couldn't put together the connection. After Brianna saw them and called out one of the kids' names, he realized it was Jeannie Johnson's daughter-in-law. They went over to say hello, Brianna intently slurping her Razzmatazz.

"Hey, how're you doing?" Owen smiled. "This is funny. I'm going back over to your mom's after I take Brianna home."

"I hear there's a lot of work," Maya smiled.

"Hey, you know, normal wear and tear—"

"You're very kind. I'm aware of how those things were built."

The woman was obviously well-versed in Johnsonian construction. She didn't pull any punches, that was for sure.

"This is my daughter, Brianna," Owen told her, Brianna failing to remove the straw that seemed permanently wedged between her lips.

"I've seen Brianna at school. Max and Dana say she's a really good kid."

Both her children nodded in agreement, which made Owen especially proud.

"You spend a lot of time with her," Maya remarked. "Most dads don't get to do that. Or don't want to."

"Well, I've got a bit of flexibility in my job," Owen explained, not wanting to get any deeper into it.

"That's a great thing. She'll always remember that you were there for her."

And who wasn't there for her, Owen thought to himself, programmed to invoke loss at any provocation.

Maya turned to Max and Dana. "You guys almost done? Mommy's got a lot to do." The three of them stood up, the kids proceeding to take their cups to the trash can.

"Well, it was nice running into you," Owen told her. "Maya, right?"

"Yeah. Good memory."

"Owen," he reminded her, since she probably hadn't remembered. "Maybe I'll see you at the house sometime. Or school."

"I'm sure you will. Nice running into you, too."

OWEN SHEPHERDED HIS DAUGHTER back into the truck. Miraculously, the Jamba Juice had worked its magic once again. Brianna willingly volunteered that she and the coveted boy, Kyle, were just good friends, and that the other girl, Melissa, was known as a problem kid. The more Brianna talked about it, the more confident she seemed that it would work itself out.

As they drove home, Owen thought about Maya in relation to the other Johnsons he had met. Of course she, like Jeannie, was a Johnson by marriage, but in Maricopa County, the families of developers were elevated to the status of southwestern Kennedys. These people were the blood, or in Maya's case, blood by marriage, of the movers and shakers, and for whatever bizarre reason, were perceived to answer to a higher calling. For years, he had wondered why people cared so much about the inner workings of the Johnson family, but now here he was, posing questions of his own as to what made these folks tick. To Owen, Jeannie and Maya seemed like warm, nice people who appeared to have survived the slippery slope of becoming Johnsons. While he couldn't pretend to know any more about Maya than he did about Jeannie, she struck him as possessing an inner strength her mother-in-law either never had, or had abandoned long ago. He couldn't pinpoint why. It was just a vibe he felt. Since Lucy's death he was far more attuned to such things. His wife's hunches about people had always been spot-on, while he'd never paid enough attention to really care. Perhaps this was one skill he had unconsciously learned from her, as opposed to the countless others that would forever elude him.

Convening

Having precious little else in common with Woody Allen, Ted Johnson firmly seconded his theory that "Half the battle is just showing up." Of course, in typical TJ fashion, he couldn't just accept someone else's homily at face value. He had to top it. To Ted's way of thinking, if half the battle was showing up, imagine the possibilities if you showed up early. The result being that while today's meeting was scheduled for 4:00 p.m., he would show up at 3:30 to get a jump on nothing. With in-house confabs of this sort, it was a particularly pointless exercise, because James Dalton and Dusty Sprague had worked for him for so long that they knew to get there at 3:30, and would sometimes arrive even before Ted. Today, the three of them entered the conference room simultaneously, around 3:25. Danny Johnson, for his part, was well aware of his father's scheduling peculiarities, but in what was perhaps his boldest act of rebellion, chose to ignore them, taking the position that 4:00 p.m. meant 4:00 p.m.

Ted and his lieutenants gathered at the conference table, exchanging pleasantries and comparing golf scores as they'd done hundreds of times before. But this afternoon, there was something weightier hanging over them. Through the bogus smiles they had mastered, thanks to Ted, James and Dusty felt claustrophobic, the bulk of the oxygen being hoarded by the elephant in the room. As Ted regaled them with tales of the new sand wedge he'd recently purchased, they could only think about Plano. Had the boss once again defied the odds and pulled a huge deal out of his ass? Dusty wondered about the absence of Danny. Would Ted really vamp for thirty-five minutes until his son showed up, or would he spill the beans and fill in the younger Johnson privately? The commander himself wasn't completely sure what his soldiers might be expecting out of this session. He could bullshit just about anybody into thinking whatever he wanted him to think, but he couldn't bullshit these guys. The news he had for them, good or bad, had to be delivered straight, no chaser. Ted segued from the sand wedge to a riff about the resodded fairway in Phase II, then looked at his watch and buzzed Danny's office. Luckily, his son had returned from his lunch meeting and was currently onsite. A quick anecdote about Buzzy the guard's newly widowed, eighty-one-year-old girlfriend would be all the filler Ted needed until his son arrived and they could get down to business.

DANNY TOOK HIS PLACE at the conference table, exhibiting none of the enthusiasm, phony or otherwise, of his Johnson Homes colleagues. In some ways, he found the in-house meetings even more unbearable than the networking luncheons, where he could at least disappear into the crowd for a breather. James and Dusty were always pleasant enough to his face, but God knows what they said behind his back. Worse, was that Danny didn't give a shit what they thought of him or about anything they had to say. He had tuned them out for months, which had turned out to be good practice for today's Kim Lee meeting at Applebee's.

"So, how was the Chinaman?" Ted bellowed.

James and Dusty knew all about the meeting as well and did their toady best to appear interested.

"Not Chinese," Danny corrected his father.

"What are you talking about?"

"Kim Lee is whiter than rice, Dad. He teaches Sunday School at First Calgary in Mesa."

"No shit," James chimed in, "those are some major-ass Baptists over there."

"I sold Pastor Higgins his first house in Phase II," Ted wistfully reminded them, neglecting to mention that the good pastor had taken him to court for a recurring sewage problem. "So what's your take on the Szechuan roofing product," he asked his son.

"It's definitely cheaper than real tile," Danny replied. "According to Lee, it does everything except prevent cancer. He took care of that in his previous job."

"You think Lee knows what he's talking about?" Dusty asked earnestly.

"Hard to say," Danny answered. "He's got all the statistics to back up his spiel, but I don't think we can really know anything until we work with the stuff. It'd be great to try it out on one of the new model homes. Put the material to the test."

"Point taken," Ted nodded. It was true that Danny didn't approach his work with James and Dusty's gusto, but he had done a good job with the task at hand, even making a helpful suggestion as to how to implement what he had learned. The boy was coming along.

James and Dusty also appreciated Danny's idea, not because they cared a rat's ass about roofing, but because it begged the question of what came next. Testing out a new product on a model home made perfect sense, but to do that, one needed a new model home on which to do it. Nobody built a model unless they had a new development and they couldn't build a development unless they had the land and the money. It all hinged on whether or not the boss had closed the deal in Plano.

"I like your thinking, Danny," James piped in. "How about you, Ted?" He knew the boss's answer would reveal the road ahead. Dusty took out a piece of gum and James fidgeted with his tie as they waited for Ted's response. If Plano was a no, there needed to be a serious discussion about options. Danny found himself daydreaming about the waitress at Applebee's and what she might have thought of his fifty-dollar tip.

After a big swig of water and a deep breath, Ted let loose. "I know you're all bursting with anticipation about what the future holds. What's at the end of the rainbow for Johnson Homes? Well, I'm here to tell you that it's looking very bright."

"Plano's happening?" Dusty blurted out.

"The elements are all in place," Ted smiled.

"That's fantastic!" James cheered. Maybe now he could buy the wife that new Ford Edge and get her off his back.

"Everybody loves the idea of Johnson Homes coming to Plano," Ted crowed. "First Texas Bank and Oilstar, a Houston consortium, are both fully prepared to fund us. Once things start to loosen up, of course."

Once things start to loosen up. The words cut through James and Dusty like a cheap electric knife. This was Ted Johnsonese for not having a pot to piss in. They were screwed plain and simple, newly ordained casualties of the Great Housing Bust. The crazy thing was that in Ted's mind, he wasn't bullshitting them. He fervently believed that a deal would come together, his track record as a businessman making it impossible for him to think otherwise.

It wasn't totally unrealistic to imagine something happening somewhere down the line. The big question was when. With all the cash he had squirreled away hiring cheap labor, Ted could personally ride out the dry spell till the next millennium, but his brain trust didn't have that luxury. "The Boys," as he called James and Dusty, were already in their mid-fifties, and even were they inclined to cut their losses and hang it up, Ted had neglected to provide them with any kind of retirement plan.

While Danny could see the apprehension in their eyes, his personal view of the situation was far different. For him, the disappointments at Johnson Homes were a natural progression from the failures he had been racking up for most of his adult life. It was strange, though, to see James and Dusty with their guards down, bereft of the Ted-schooled effervescence that had become their stock-in-trade. Odder yet was his father's cluelessness as to the repercussions of the bombshell he had just dropped. Not only did he see the Plano trip as an unqualified success, he was practically foaming at the mouth to broadcast the icing on the cake.

"Gentleman, I have major news," Ted beamed.

James wondered what now. Was there some other under-the-radar land deal he hadn't told them about?

"I have enlisted the services of a biographer."

"A what?" Dusty looked confused.

"A prominent author has signed on to tell the Ted Johnson story. I'm sure you boys will get a big shout-out. Maybe your own chapter."

James couldn't believe what he was hearing. Johnson Homes was generating no new business, on the verge of going down the toilet, and this guy was boasting about having his life documented? Dusty seemed to be hyperventilating, stunned by the ease with which Ted could ignore the company's financial state and celebrate himself.

"Harley Mason, that's the fellow's name," Ted informed them. He'll be arriving soon to poke into things. So if you boys see a strange face walking the halls, give him a 'howdy,' and show some Johnson hospitality."

Johnson hospitality? The Boys suddenly had the feeling of being junior officers on the Titanic, the chamber orchestra playing blindly into the night as they headed for the iceberg. James considered handing in his resignation on the spot, but ultimately thought it better not to do anything rash until he had researched other options. Dusty bemoaned having stayed at the party too long. He had known from the start that Ted was an egomaniac, and with people like that, it was only a matter of time before they came unglued.

"Are we done for today?" Danny asked. He was curious as to whether the Applebee's waitress was still on duty.

"That's all the business I have to discuss," Ted answered. "Anybody else?"

The Boys sat in stone silence.

"Why the glum faces?" Ted implored. "Have I ever let you down?"

Even though they believed Ted was delusional, they couldn't hold him responsible for the entire mess. One builder, no matter how successful, couldn't be expected to turn around a dead housing market.

James and Dusty did feel like they had let themselves down. While nobody could have predicted such a quick downturn, it had certainly been within their power to be less greedy. But they had followed a man of dubious character down the primrose path, only to wake up in a field of dust devils, and now faced the possibility that the land would be forever barren.

As they adjourned the meeting and stood up, Ted gave each of The Boys a hug, which, to his way of thinking, was just the encouragement they needed. After all, a pension plan was merely numbers on paper, but a message of hope transcended dollars and cents. Danny found the moment ludicrous, at a loss for how he would react when his father moved in to hug him. Thankfully, Barb buzzed in with a call from the biographer before that could happen, and Danny and The Boys were free to leave.

DAZED AND REELING, JAMES and Dusty decided to retire to the Red Lobster for drinks, as they had done so often in success. The bottom line was that Scotch was Scotch, and whether one used it for reveling or comfort, it got the job done. The only unexpected part of the plan was that James invited Danny to go with them. The younger Johnson was shocked, given that he had never made an attempt to bond with either of The Boys, turning down every opportunity to fraternize. Then there was the matter of The Boys needing to talk about Ted's bad news, which would surely be awkward with his son present. For whatever reason, James wasn't thinking about the details and had acted purely upon the instinct to commiserate. Dusty didn't seem to mind either, his eyes now on the sole prize of getting shitfaced. Surprisingly, Danny found himself flattered by their offer, though not quite enough to forgo Plan A. He thanked them for the invite and said he would join them another time.

WHERE DANNY THOUGHT PLAN A might lead was anybody's guess. He had told Maya he wouldn't be home for dinner because he couldn't face being around his family in his present state of mind. At the time, he had no idea what he was going to do after work, but during the meeting, he hatched the notion of stopping by Applebee's. *Stopping by Applebee's. Checking in on a girl in her twenties.* This is what it had come to. What could this girl possibly have to say to him except "Thanks for the tip, old man?" It was like being in high school, when there was a girl he liked, but dared not speak to. Merry Carnahan. He would drive by her house three times a week, hoping to catch a glimpse of her, but had no idea what he would do or say if she saw him. Now, Danny was a grown man with a wife and kids. He loved his family. Why did he feel compelled to cruise Applebee's, hoping to make small talk with Katie B.? Even in his deflated state, it seemed absurd.

DANNY HAD NEVER THOUGHT about who might frequent an Applebee's bar at happy hour, which in itself seemed like an oxymoron. Tonight's roster was composed of Danny Johnson and several secretaries from the local business park. Mostly Mexican, he found it both sweet and sad the way they cradled their cosmopolitans, mimicking an all-white television show set in New York City. He couldn't afford to waste time on such ironies, his mission being to impress a ridiculously young thing, who, more likely than not, lived with her parents. He'd done the math, figuring that if Katie B. had started serving in the morning, she would now be close to finishing for the day and he would try to talk to her on the way out. If she had started later and was working the dinner shift, he would request a booth in her section and eat slowly.

He positioned himself at the bar so she would have to pass by on the way to the kitchen. Drinking at a leisurely pace, he managed to finish two vodka gimlets before Katie B. came anywhere near his spot. He ordered another, figuring it could only make him more relaxed for whatever was about to go down. *What in God's name did he expect to happen?* The only frame of reference he had was high school, where he would fantasize about Merry Carnahan blowing him during orchestra practice, giving new meaning to the term "woodwind section." But Katie B. was less an object of lust than one of diversion. He had projected lust onto her to secure a temporary reprieve from a life he felt he'd botched beyond repair. What could easily be mistaken for a mid-life crisis cliché (Guy seeks affair because he's bored in his marriage and wants to feel young again) wasn't nearly so pat. Danny didn't care about feeling young. He just wanted to be around someone he didn't disappoint.

DANNY STILL BELIEVED MAYA was the most beautiful woman he had ever seen, sexier than any sun-baked blonde the Grand Canyon State had to offer. He had spent their entire courtship trying to prove to himself that he was good enough for her, and considered winning her heart the great achievement of his life. Now, he felt like it was an honor he never deserved. He had succeeded in charming the girl of his dreams, but what had she gotten out of it? A shell of a man forced to work for his self-important father just so he could feed his family. Maya deserved so much better. Realizing this made it more and more difficult for Danny to go home and face her. And, for whatever reason, he believed that getting to know an Applebee's waitress would somehow alleviate his pain.

Danny struck up a conversation with the young bartender to dig for information. "So who's your favorite server around here?"

"I never eat at this place," the bartender answered, "but they say Gayle's the best." He indicated the other side of the restaurant, where a heavyset brunette was doling out giant baskets of cheesy fries.

"How about Katie?"

"I don't think I know Katie."

Danny nodded his head in her direction.

"Oh, the new girl. Today's her first day."

Danny couldn't help but smile. A fifty-dollar tip on her first day of work. She must be loving the whole Applebee's experience right about now. "She was my waitress at lunch," he told the bartender. "I thought she was very good and I'm thinking about sitting over there again. You know if she works the dinner shift?"

The bartender shook his head. "Like I said, I don't eat here."

A lot of help he was. Mixed a decent gimlet though, Danny had to admit. He made up his mind to roll the dice and request a table at Katie's station. He would order a plate of sliders, and if she suddenly cut out for the evening, so be it. Downing the remainder of the third gimlet, he suddenly felt a tap on his shoulder. Standing before him, polo shirt protruding in all the right places, was Katie B., who had apparently recognized her Applebee's White Knight.

"Hi," she said, lacking the warmth one would expect from a recipient of such generosity. "I think you made a mistake this afternoon." She pulled the fifty-dollar bill out of her jeans and handed it to him.

"It wasn't a mistake," Danny informed her, giving back the money.

"I don't understand. Why would you leave a fifty-dollar tip on a twenty-five dollar check?"

"I don't know. Because I thought you were a good waitress?" Danny smiled.

"I totally suck," she replied. "This is my first day and I got like six orders wrong."

"I was very happy with mine."

"That is really nice of you. I know you must be rich and all, but I feel weird taking this."

Katie B. had a sense of ethics. Now that was a genuine turn-on. "Please. It was my pleasure."

"I'm going to be leaving now, but if I should get fired, I just want you to know that I'll never forget this. Thank you so much."

Danny felt like taking her in his arms and hugging the fear out of her. She was too young, pretty, and decent to think she didn't have what it takes to work at Applebee's. He thought about asking her to go out for a drink, but didn't want to risk tainting the moment with anything that could be interpreted as a come-on. Let this poor girl, still reeling from her shaky first day on the chain restaurant assembly line, feel something positive. Allow her to be validated rather than made to feel like a piece of meat. "I'm sure I'll see you, again, Katie B.," Danny nodded.

"I hope so," she smiled, waving and heading off into the desert night.

Bruce Ferber

By THE TIME HE got there, The Boys were already three sheets to the wind. Never in his wildest dreams had Danny pictured himself walking into a Red Lobster to knock back a few with the likes of James Dalton and Dusty Sprague. These were Ted's people, staunch conservative Phoenicians who had both done weekends as Minutemen, scouring the border for the "wetback leaf blowers who were ruining our country." It hadn't dawned on them that Johnson Homes and, by association, the two of them, had profited handsomely from employing these individuals. All they saw now was a country going to shit and taking them along with it.

That said, the minute James and Dusty saw Danny enter the bar, they jumped up with excitement. Why? Danny had to ask himself. He supposed there was something to be said for turning down an invitation and then making a surprise entrance. People were so shocked when you walked in, they forgot they invited you just to be polite.

"You bastard!" Dusty cried out. "You showed up after all!"

"Set your ass down and tell the man your pleasure," James ordered him.

"Vodka gimlet," Danny shouted, curious as to how the Red Lobster version compared with Applebee's. It occurred to Danny that he couldn't remember ever having gone anywhere in Phoenix that wasn't a chain. It was disturbing on a certain level, but luckily, chain alcohol went down the same as hip, independent entrepreneur alcohol. The Red Lobster bartender was confident and fast, perhaps sensing that the Johnson Homes triumvirate was in it for the long haul tonight.

James raised his glass. "To getting screwed in the ass."

"By your crazy old man," added Dusty. "No offense."

"None taken," Danny assured them as they clinked classes. As little as he had in common with these guys, they were now on the same page, Danny taking it upon himself to offer a toast of his own: "To the Tucson deal that went in the shitter, and the Plano deal that started out as crap."

James and Dusty laughed heartily. They had no way of predicting that Ted Johnson's son would take their side. It remained a possibility that Danny was bullshitting them and would run home to tell Daddy, but what difference did it make now? The boss could dream as big as he wanted, but barring some miraculous economic turnaround, Johnson Homes was finished. After all the years they had put in, the ever-reliable cash cow of selling folks the American Dream had blown up in their faces. Now they would need to seriously reboot just to pay for the dreams they had sold themselves.

Danny flashed back to his time at Bennington when he had understudied for the role of Shelley "The Machine" Levene in *Glengarry Glen Ross*. After a long and storied career selling tract houses, Shelley had been reduced to a puddle of Jell-O, scrounging for the good leads on would-be buyers. It was all very theatrical in that delicious, profane, Mamet-esque way, but here it was, sitting across from him in real life. James and Dusty had become Shelley Levenes. And Danny, while too new to the game to have attained the status of a successful Shelley, slid very comfortably into the character of a desperate one.

THAT THEY COULD DRINK and vent freely was a blessing, not just for James and Dusty, but for Danny, as well. The younger Johnson didn't go into the troubles of his home life, but allowed himself to share how difficult it was to be the son of a local hero. He wasn't born outgoing like his father. He didn't care for golf. The whole idea of being a salesman was anathema to him. He told them that he had come back to Arizona because he needed the gig, which conveniently coincided with his father's romantic vision of the family business carrying on for generations. They found it ironic that he'd made a deal with the devil to support his wife and children, only to have the devil be on his last breath, with no life support in sight.

James and Dusty were surprisingly sympathetic to Danny's plight. In the course of their long association with Ted, they had worked alongside many a novice who quickly discovered that he didn't have the salesman gene, quitting after a few months in the trenches. What with Danny's admitted lack of interest and sales ability, it seemed a reach for him to assume the Johnson throne when the time came. They all agreed it was a moot point now.

Bruce Ferber

"Still, I'm sure your dad isn't going to let anything happen to you and your brood," Dusty said, patting Danny on the back.

"Ted always takes care of family first," James seconded, without a trace of bitterness or envy.

"I know," Danny replied, dreading the eventuality. Being bailed out by a job in his father's company had been bad enough. Becoming a welfare family on the Ted Johnson dole was too unbearable to fathom. Getting this kind of support was a foreign concept to people like James and Dusty, who didn't have a safety net. Danny got the impression that their pride would prevent them from accepting any backup whatsoever, no matter how well-intentioned.

Dispirited as he had become about his own situation, Danny found his heart going out to these guys, who were older and deserved something more for their servitude. Yet, as he watched them employ alcohol and gallows humor to get through the evening, he realized that even without help, they were far better prepared for whatever came next than was he. All those years of selling and refusing to take no for an answer had turned them into the kind of men who would find a way to survive calamity, even rise above it. Maybe James would start selling cars. Dusty might open a foreclosure business. But they would surely do something, and do it pretty damn well. What would forty-one year-old Danny Johnson, with his bachelor's degree in philosophy, do to support his wife and children?

"I just had a lightbulb!" James shouted, the fifth or six Scotch talking. "Let's start our own business."

"Excellent idea!" Dusty concurred. "We've got three capable minds here."

Danny was suspect, but nevertheless touched, to be included as a capable mind in whatever drunken pipedream his father's subordinates were about to cook up.

"A drive-thru something that's never been drive-thru before," was James's first thought.

"That's good," Dusty nodded. "Like you never thought there'd be a drive-thru Starbucks, then boom, they're selling pumpkin-ass lattes by the thousands."

Although Danny didn't see himself partnering up with The Boys, he had to admit that anything involving driving was a decent starting point in Phoenix, where the car was second in stature only to the gun. After James and Dusty pitched a few questionable businesses like drive-thru cell phone store, and drive-thru tattoo shop, Danny threw in one of his own. "What about a drive-thru pet supply place? Why should you have to get out of your car just to buy dog food?"

James gave him the thumbs-up. "That's so good! We've got to write these down!"

AND ON INTO THE night it went, the alcohol-induced ravings of men without jobs, or soon-to-be without jobs if one wanted to get technical. The drunker they got, the more grandiose the schemes. Danny welcomed their enthusiasm, a refreshing break from his daily, ever more bleak, ruminations. The only problem was that fantasizing about Katie B. or drive-thru pet shops brought him no closer to fixing that which was really broken. It was nearly midnight and he was in a Red Lobster getting drunk, while the most beautiful woman in the world was home in his bed, perhaps even worrying about him. He wanted to excuse himself, but James and Dusty kept buying rounds, refusing to let him pay for anything. They were really good guys, despite their dreadful politics. It occurred to Danny that there were probably a whole shitload of Shelley Levenes that had been created in this housing bust, thanks to the business dealings of a few Ted Johnsons.

Sleepless in Cascade Falls

Though her life would not be viewed as stressful by most people's standards, Jeannie Johnson hadn't slept well for maybe fifteen years, stricken by feelings of anxiety the minute her head hit the pillow. She had tried all the quick fixes: the Ambiens, which were too strong, the Melatonins, which weren't strong enough, hot tea, warm milk, television, chick lit, even soundscape CDs. Finally, she realized that her restlessness would never be cured by pills or short-term external remedies. It had become clear that the things keeping her awake were legitimately worth worrying about. Looking over at her husband, who, in addition to snoring like a feral hog, was currently sporting a goofy grin, she found herself mystified as to how he could block out every complexity life had to offer. Perhaps this was the lone positive in being an egomaniac. If all you thought about was yourself, there was only one source for worry.

Jeannie had never managed much interest in tracking the monetary ups and downs of Ted's company, but she did read the papers and knew about the financial misfortune befalling friends and neighbors. Though her husband had remained upbeat through the economic downturn, she noticed that there'd been less talk of replicating the Johnson Homes experience in Las Vegas, phase by glorious phase. Yet even with his Walt Disney mindset abated, humility hadn't followed suit. He was simply more distant, choosing a quieter brand of self-involvement over his typically boisterous ego stroking.

Taking in the sight of this four-time Rotary Club Man of the Year happily wheezing, while she struggled for any semblance of rest, Jeannie went back to the history books, as she had done on many an insomniac night. How had she wound up becoming Mrs. Ted Johnson? What had enticed a bright and attractive young woman with her whole life ahead of her to join forces with an ambitious narcissist, a self-appointed mover and shaker who treated her like an afterthought? She attributed her actions to naïveté, the novelty of being an eighteen-year-old girl driving around in a Mercedes SL with a young, but already successful, businessman. (She later learned that, at the time, Ted was broke, the Mercedes leased, and he was kiting checks from seven different bank accounts to pay his bills.) Still, Jeannie was not a girl easily impressed by money or showiness. All she could figure was that, in spite of the obvious negatives, there was something inspirational about showy people. You might not covet their money, but you wanted their confidence. It was like the Rat Pack. Driving to Palm Springs in their Cadillacs and sharkskin suits, they'd drink like sieves and hang out with gangsters, but they always had a blast doing it. Ted Johnson was a Rat Packer in Baptist clothing, a wheeler-dealer sprung from a strict Christian family whose priorities had been church and more church.

AT 2:45 IN THE middle of the Phoenix night, Jeannie Johnson had an epiphany. The man she married was a tent preacher, the only difference being that his god was the approvable mortgage, and he healed his flock with amenities like Jacuzzis and RV hookups. Ted had successfully sold his message of hope to thousands of "congregants" who were eager to become part of a community that transcended who they were as individuals. It had once been exciting for Jeannie to see him bring joy and comfort to others, much like being the wife of a minister or a rabbi, she supposed. The folks in the Phases showed Ted royal deference, and, by association, treated her like their queen. But as novel as it had first been, she became uncomfortable watching her husband start to believe his own press, and horrified as she saw him venture into Jimmy Swaggart territory. Why was she surprised? If a man believed he was responsible for delivering salvation, there were no limits to where his braggadocio might take him.

Though it had certainly crossed Jeannie's mind, the last thing Ted Johnson wanted was a divorce. Aside from the obvious public liability of appearing to those in the Phases as less than a family man, Ted truly enjoyed having Jeannie by his side. She had been with him from the real beginning, predating James and Dusty by more than a decade. They had raised a fine son and also a daughter, who, while currently estranged from them, stood a far better chance of returning to the fold with the family unit intact. From where Ted stood, they were the all-American Johnsons, the dream couple living large, Arizona-style. How do you chuck all that? And for what?

He was talking in his sleep now, muttering something that sounded like "Esmerelda." It certainly wasn't the first female name Ted had cried out in the night. For years, Jeannie had heard the murmurs of her friends and felt their incredulity as they watched her stick by a man who, at Sunday services, had goosed the pastor's wife right in front of her. And the pastor. Ted naturally attributed his faux pas to an accidental slip of the hand and Pastor Stevens was in the forgiveness business, but anyone who knew Ted Johnson could put two and two together. Jeannie was certainly not fooled.

It wasn't that she enjoyed public embarrassment. The truth was, she didn't view Ted's idiotic behavior as a reflection on her. It didn't surprise her that people formed opinions about the wife based on the husband's exploits, but that was their problem. She hadn't been the horse's ass. Jeannie Johnson would continue to go about her business with head held high, no matter what anybody thought. The key to her empowerment was that nothing she valued interested Ted. She was an avid reader, enjoyed gardening, had become increasingly proficient at Italian, and had recently taken up the piano. And she was equally bored by his passions, which were basically Johnson Homes and sex.

Jeannie did sometimes wonder whether or not her weak libido was a result of aging or being married to this particular man. After all, Betsy Frederickson, the sixty-seven year-old leader of her book group, claimed to be enjoying sex more than she ever had. Sally Krantz over in Phase II, who had just turned seventy, privately admitted that she had recently taken it upon herself to become a blowjob queen. Apparently, it was entirely possible for a woman her age to be sexually motivated. Yet, it was so much easier not to be. Things functioned quite smoothly as they were, two Johnsons existing alongside each other as roommates. Ted had his flings, while she bonded with the brightest women in Cascade Falls. People with whom she could discuss world events and the arts, as well as join on vacations, thanks to Ted's liberal travel policy. It wasn't such a bad life, she would remind herself.

Still, the need for constant reminding revealed rumblings within. Occasionally, Jeannie would find herself trying to pinpoint when it had all gone south, the specific moment where it became clear that her role had switched from wife to roommate. It seemed as if they had been stuck in this particular groove for at least twenty years. To be fair, it wasn't as if the man she married had ever shown signs that he would ripen well with age. At her suggestion, the couple had seen various therapists, but Ted never saw the point. The Johnsons were rolling along just fine, thank you very much. They didn't need a repairman tinkering with their innards. The end result, of course, was that there were few remaining innards to speak of. To Jeannie, they were an empty chassis, marking time until they made it to the junk heap.

AFTER A FULL DAY of manual labor, preparing dinner, and helping with homework, Owen rarely had difficulty sleeping. Lately though, he found himself waking up in the middle of the night, pondering every possible crisis. "What would Brianna do if I suddenly dropped dead?" was a recurring theme. Sometimes, he'd obsess about whatever job he was on. Were they doing the best work they could for the price? Would they finish in a timely manner, and to the satisfaction of the client? It wasn't a bad thing to be dedicated to your daughter and your work, but he wished his conscientiousness could rear its head at more convenient moments. In truth, his days and nights were so busy, there was little time for contemplation, so it got forced out at three in the morning. Or appeared in dreams.

He had been dreaming nonstop since Lucy died. As might be expected, she was often the focal point, which made it only more gut-wrenching when he woke up alone. He had scattered her ashes himself, yet it still seemed inconceivable that he would never again get to see her brushing her long wavy hair in front of the mirror, or hear the laugh that made everything okay. He had read about the "magical thinking" that often overtakes people in grief. Against all logic, they convince themselves that if they're really good, if they make all the right choices, and if they exhibit exemplary behavior, their loved one will magically reappear, exposing their presumed death as a lame practical joke. Owen had participated in his share of magical thinking, imagining that he would turn down an aisle at the supermarket where they shopped and suddenly run into Lucy. "There you are," he would shout, taking her into his arms. "I've missed you so much."

"I've missed you too," Lucy would say, as he inhaled the sweet Lucy-essence of her skin.

Then they'd go on with the shopping. Husband and wife would comb the cookie aisle for those pinwheel things Brianna liked so much, and proceed to the produce section, where Lucy would fill the cart with fresh fruits and veggies. They'd load their take into the car and head home, after which they'd address their separate tasks until dinnertime. Neither of them would stop to acknowledge the outing as noteworthy. They were just going about the business of living their lives. It all seemed natural.

This wasn't natural. Waking up alone in the middle of the night, drenched in sweat, filled with anxiety. People told him that the intensity of his grief would lessen over time as the "the healing process" kicked in. Thus far, Owen had not identified any sort of process, and couldn't imagine the wound ever going away. Deciding to cut his losses rather than face hours of tossing and turning, he reached over to the nightstand, turned on the light, and grabbed the book he had started probably six months ago. Owen had little time for reading, yet Lucy had left an extensive library, assembled over a lifetime in passionate, if random, fashion. His wife had been a voracious reader with wide-ranging tastes: everything from Joseph Campbell, to Anthony Burgess, to Kurt Vonnegut, to one-hit wonders like John Kennedy Toole. She loved the earthy novels of the Southwest like *The Milagro Beanfield War* and Edward Abbey's books. Toward the end, she fell in love with Latin American literature, devouring the entire Garcia Marquez oeuvre, then exploring the canon of his Peruvian rival, Mario Vargas Llosa.

INHERITING LUCY'S LIBRARY HAD been a gift of significant value. Owen knew there was a lot to be learned from reading the books themselves, but more importantly, there was something to be learned about Lucy. *Why had she chosen these volumes? These authors?* He doubted that he would ever be able to finish the contents of the shelves in his lifetime, but he knew that each time he opened a new book, he would wonder what it was about the work that spoke to her. Sometimes he would imagine himself as Lucy, lying next to him and extolling the virtues of a sprawling novel she had started, like *The War at the End of the World*. This was the book he currently had on the nightstand, an epic tale of warring Brazil centered on a mad Messianic figure and his carnival-like sect of worshipers. It was a dense nine-hundred pages, loaded with fifty or so major Latin American names whose characters he completely forgot whenever he put down the book for too long. Yet he could vividly picture Lucy glued to the pages, looking up at him and describing how the journalist in the story had fallen in love with a beautiful girl, Jurema, who suffered the misfortune of being raped four times in the course of the novel. Lucy had appreciated the harsh complexity of life, relishing the art and literature that helped define it for her. This book was filled with cruelty, yet there were rays of hope that managed to seep through. It had been one of the last books Lucy read, at the point when she was rapidly succumbing to the cruelty of her own illness. Owen knew that he and Brianna were her rays of hope. Sometimes remembering that made him feel better, but mostly it made him sad. That she could no longer see them. That they could no longer shine for her.

Now he was crying. It was difficult to give full attention to warring nineteenth-century Brazilians while he was imagining Lucy in the here and now, talking about them. He closed the book and grabbed the TV remote, thinking a sitcom rerun would be easier to swallow in this state of mind. Lucy had always liked *Friends*, and even though it had never been one of his favorites, he considered the possibility that it might be more interesting now because, as with the books, he could try to decipher what about the show might have appealed to her. It was a series in which two characters out of six were dumb, or perhaps in that television way, just said stupid, clueless things when it facilitated a joke. He supposed it was amusing enough, though he never found himself actually laughing along with the studio audience or the laugh track, whichever it was. What he did notice, was that the females in the cast did nothing for him. They were attractive, but their characters projected a kind of sitcom neurosis that was neither overly funny, or relatable enough to make him give a shit. It seemed as if the women he knew, Lucy first and foremost, were so much funnier and more interesting than the neat freak, fashionista, and daffy naïf featured there. What was one to make of Rachel: "Well, excuse me, my fashion-impaired friends. I am here to tell you that hats are back," or Phoebe: "And this time they've ganged up to form one giant, super hat!" To Owen it was like white noise, chatter that could easily be replaced by a car alarm or jackhammer. Still, he admired Lucy's ability to segue from the grueling terrain of Vargas Llosa to Joey asking Ross "How you doin'?" Why couldn't he have an ounce of that? Without Lucy, Owen felt like he was half of something. And the more time he spent alone, the more he realized how much he liked the other half better.

According to the clock on the nightstand, it was 3:45 when the sound of the garage door woke her up. Maya buried herself under the blankets, partially disappointed that her husband had even decided to come home, the other part hoping that he would at least have the decency to stop off in the bathroom to remove his vodka-soaked stink with soap and toothpaste. Either way, she would remain absolutely still, feigning sleep because she had no interest in confronting him. What would it accomplish besides keeping her up for the rest of the night? Danny had always been hypersensitive to criticism, so reprimanding him now for his behavior would be nothing but wasted energy. She felt herself trying not to breathe as he stumbled into the room, but a bouquet of cigar smoke suddenly overpowered everything, an unwelcome if unsurprising addition to the liquor stench. In a matter of seconds, he stripped off his clothes, fell onto the bed, and put his arm around her, proceeding to clumsily stroke her back and shoulders.

Maya's instinct was to register no sign of consciousness. Just play dead and hope the bastard fell asleep or blacked out. Danny didn't seem to be headed in that direction. His hand was rapidly moving southward and pawing her ass as if she were some barmaid he had hooked up with after closing time. Maya couldn't believe it. Two innocent children fast asleep in their beds and their drunken father, the man who had stopped bothering to come home for dinners, had barged in at an ungodly hour to solicit sex from their mother. She was appalled, but made not a sound, hoping against hope that her silence and lack of response would impel him to switch gears. When his hand stopped moving, Maya breathed a quiet sigh of relief. Then, before she had even a moment to process what was going on, she felt his hand plow deep between her legs and head upward toward her clitoris. Her head turned with a start, and for the first time ever, she slapped her husband across the face. "What the hell is wrong with you?" Clearly, the mercy fuck offer had expired.

"I'm sorry," he blurted out, "I thought you—"

"You thought I wanted to fuck a stinking drunk at four in the morning? You thought 'no woman could resist a piece of this,'" she pointed at him derisively.

"I was just…I was thinking about you all night," he slurred, not helping his case.

"That's nice to know. What about Max and Dana? Any room for thinking about them? In between gimlets?"

"The company's in the crapper, Maya," he moaned, reaching out for a shred of sympathy.

"I don't care about the fucking company. I want to know what you think you're doing. What kind of man are you?"

It was a good question, one to which Danny had no ready answer. He really had been thinking about Maya all night, how lucky he was to have her, how he wanted to show his appreciation for all she had meant to him. Yet much like his failed attempt at assembling a career, he had botched this chance to acknowledge her. "I'm sorry I woke you," was all he could manage now.

MAYA ROLLED OVER WITHOUT a word. As bad as she had previously felt for her husband, she was now starting to worry about the well-being and safety of her children. Was there anything that could undo the mess? The alarm would ring in a couple of hours and the kids would need to be fed and gotten off to school. The best that could be hoped for at this moment was a calm before the storm, a brief respite before facing the day-to-day tasks of tomorrow and the deeper issues of a lifetime. Maya tried to think of something peaceful to take her mind off Danny. She pictured herself sunning on an island beach—St. Bart's maybe, or Turks and Caicos.

It is high tide, the water creeping up to where she has laid out her towel. She knows she should move, but the warmth of the sun keeps her affixed to the spot. She feels the ocean water travel up to her toes, so gentle and welcoming that she can't imagine being anywhere else.

Maya sank into her pillow and felt herself starting to relax. About to drift off, she was suddenly jolted by a succession of sharp, adenoidal proclamations emanating from the body next to her. She turned her head to see Danny, totally zonked out, his snores loud enough to travel down the hall and wake the children. Maya considered elbowing him but thought better of it. Waking him might reawaken his awkward pursuit of sex. The best solution was to let him snore and ride it out.

SHE TRIED GOING BACK to the beach at St. Bart's, but the moment had passed. Out of sheer desperation, she attempted to visualize Ray Minetta in her dorm room at Bennington. Slowly, her hand began to explore the territory Danny had just entered uninvited. The volume of his snores, combined with the certainty that she would never be able to fall asleep, gave her the will to let go, touching herself with abandon as she conjured up the memory of Ray's tongue inside her. She recalled him trying to estimate how many gallons of her juices he had swallowed, telling her that it was never enough, then helping himself to more. As her drunken husband wheezed away, Maya felt herself starting to come. She pictured Ray not being satisfied with her output, then came again and again, completely soaking herself. Maya took this as a positive sign. If this much juice could still flow out of her, there must be some life left inside.

In the Light of Day

Danny was still asleep when Maya rose to wake the kids. After feeding them breakfast, she ran upstairs to get her keys before shuttling them to school. She heard the shower running, which cut to the bone like needles piercing her skin. This time, she would not address what lay on the other side of the bathroom door. Had Danny been interested enough to talk about last night's debacle, he could have gotten his ass out of bed earlier to apologize, or to at least let her know he recognized what had gone down. She grabbed the keys and bolted, convinced that lingering would only make her angrier than she'd been last night. It was a new day, another chance to move forward. As she drove Max and Dana to school in the cool, soon-to-be stifling air, she found herself in a good mood. How could that be? Her circumstances were no better than they'd been yesterday. In truth, they were substantially worse.

It was only after she kissed the kids goodbye that Maya began to connect the dots. While masturbation had certainly never been taboo for her, it had been a while since her last exploratory visit. Lately, even when she daydreamed about sex, the urge would be overtaken by a list of a mother's chores. Back when she actually had time to masturbate, the primary venue was the shower, and it was never done in the presence of Danny. Last night's autoerotic pleasure had been aching and intense in a way she had never before experienced. She wondered if getting off while lying next to her snoring husband made her cruel, or even sadistic. But those qualities were not in her nature. More likely, the act had been her way of daring Danny to snap to his senses and feel some sort of outrage. Was he so far gone, so lost in his despondent, drunken haze, that he couldn't see what was happening right next to him? In his own bed? His dream girl, the unattainable goddess he had fought with all his might to win, was inches away, literally oozing sex while picturing another man's tongue deep inside her. The louder he snored, the bolder she became with her thoughts and fingers, ultimately matching his decibel level with her cries of ecstasy. And still, there was no reaction from the buzzing mass at her side.

By all rights, Maya should have been depressed, yet as she pulled into the Starbucks parking lot, she found herself feeling downright giddy. The output of last night's multiple orgasms now seemed like a clarion call, the physical manifestation of her creative renewal. Didn't the phrase "juices flowing" imply a logical connection between sexuality and creativity? It made perfect sense. As her paintbrush had once again become active, her vagina didn't want to be left behind. Both benefited from imagination and neither had any limits as to where that imagination might take them.

HEADING HOME, MAYA SUDDENLY felt the urge for a cigarette. Ironically, her car was only a few hundred yards from the Akimel O'Odham Smoke Shop, the den of unwanted familiarity she swore she'd never set foot in again. Right now, it didn't seem like such a big deal. She needed cigarettes, what difference did it make where she bought them? So what if Bob was overly solicitous and his ogling annoying? She was on a roll.

Bruce Ferber

As Maya parked the Lexus and got out of the car, she caught a quick glimpse of her reflection in the driver's side window. It was then, for one fleeting moment, that she saw what it was men saw. Her features were unique, her smile readable as friendly or beckoning, depending upon the light and the viewer. She wore no make up, but her dark, slightly tousled hair presented a wild, fuckable look that the male of the species seemed to love.

There was no one at the cash register when she walked into the shop. Maya saw her old pal Bob over by the hard liquor, talking with a customer. She grabbed a copy of the local Pima newspaper, content to bide her time until his tobacco dispensing services became available. According to the paper, the tribe was about to simultaneously expand their casino and open a new medical clinic specializing in nutrition and diabetes prevention. Out of the corner of his eye, Bob saw her reading and rushed over.

"Yep. The white man takes our land, makes us poor, and gets us addicted to fast-food. Then, to patch things up, he lets us open casinos so we get addicted to more shit."

Maya couldn't argue with that. She hated the Indian casinos as much as she hated the mentality that bred them.

"Come here. I want to show you something," Bob commanded. As she followed him toward the liquor aisle, Maya saw that the customer, bottle of Dewar's firmly in hand at 8:30 a.m., was admiring an oil painting, most likely one of Bob's.

"Reminds me of the last time I did acid," the man declared.

"Thanks," Bob replied, electing to interpret this as a compliment. The clerk then turned to Maya. "Glad you happened in. I've been wanting to show you my stuff. This one's called *Mi Casa es Su Casa*."

The title was horrible, but the painting, something else entirely. Bold and surreal, not at all desert-like in its color scheme, it was thematically as dark and twisted as classic Münch. Not only was the piece well executed, it had a strangely eastern European look to it, the skeletons suggestive of Nazi Germany rather than southwestern O'Keefe-like animal carcasses.

"It does jump out at you," Maya declared, sincerely impressed. "Where did you learn to paint like this?"

"I don't know," Bob shrugged. "I got a lot of weird shit in my head."

"Amen," the customer nodded, raising the now open bottle of Scotch. "Who was it who said that beauty springs from the loins of the weird? Oh yeah, me."

Bob chuckled enthusiastically, Maya more politely so, having noticed the customer checking her out as he recited his witticism, which she sensed was part of a well-rehearsed repertoire.

"Maybe I'll buy the thing after I get some more cash," the man told Bob. "We'll see how long this gig lasts."

"She's an artist, too," Bob explained, indicating Maya. "This fella here's an author."

"Harley Mason," the man announced, extending his hand to her. "I'm in town to write a biography of a guy named Ted Johnson. Ever hear of him?"

Maya burst out laughing. The book was news to her because Danny never had the chance to tell her about it, having only learned of this latest wrinkle the previous afternoon, before his little bender.

"I guess you have heard of him," Mason said.

"He's built practically every house in the area," Maya quickly covered, deciding it best to withhold her relationship to the man and hoping Bob didn't already know the connection.

"I'm aware he's a big developer," Mason continued. "But what's funny about that?"

Maya struggled to come up with something. Something other than *my father-in-law's a self-deluded jerk, why would anybody want to write one word about him?*

"Ted's a bit of a larger than life kind of a character, if you will," Bob stepped in, giving Maya time to gather her thoughts.

"I've met him," Mason informed them. "He doesn't seem much different from anybody else who commissions his own biography."

"He's paying you to write a book about him?" Maya spit out in disbelief.

"It's actually not that unusual among successful entrepreneurs," Mason explained. "They feel like they're an important part of the human fabric; that their contributions need to be memorialized for future generations. I take it you've never read the *Stephen J. Poplawski Story*."

Bob and Maya looked at him askance.

"Four hundred and fifty-six pages chronicling the man who, in nineteen twenty-two, invented the blender. Believe it or not, kind of a fun read. Hey what's your name?" Mason abruptly asked Maya.

She wanted to say Harriet, or Nicole, or Annie, but she just wasn't any good at lying. "Maya," she answered as quickly as possible, looking at her watch and informing Bob that she had to be somewhere and needed her Merit lights ASAP. The Pima Edvard Münch was, as always, happy to oblige.

Mason didn't take his eyes off her. His was a true ogle, which, in retrospect, made her realize how innocent Bob's had been. "It was a pleasure meeting you, Maya. I hope I get the opportunity to look at your art someday." The smarminess was palpable.

"Yeah, well, I'd like to get a look at it, too," she replied. "At the moment, I've got nothing to show." Maya wanted out of there as soon as possible, which made it doubly maddening when she found herself in an argument with Bob for refusing to accept his offer of free Diet Pepsi. She finally managed to break away with her cigarettes, feeling the weight of Harley Mason's leers the entire way to the car. She hopped in, lit up, and peeled out of the parking lot, thoughts going back and forth between Ted hiring an oily biographer and Smoke Shop Bob's undeniable talent.

Bob's paintings were evidence that you couldn't make assumptions about anyone. It was as if she had walked into a 99 Cents Store and found Monet showing his water lilies to a guy buying cleaning supplies. She chalked it up to another of life's wonders, another spark she could use to rev her own engine. Bob's talent filled her with excitement, her mind racing with ideas on how to exploit her own. Then, seemingly out of nowhere, she came up with the fix for Max's mushroom outfit. What about a headdress that could be put on separately from the body of the costume? It would be kind of like a footstool for the head, stuffed with foam, round enough and wide enough to rule out any form of penile comparisons. Two holes for the eyes and *bada bing*, Max would be ready to deliver the fungal performance of a lifetime. Maya set off for the local Michael's, which would have the foam stuffing and any other craft accessories she might need to get the job done. "Thanks, Bob," she whispered softly.

As hangovers went, Danny's proved manageable, a low-impact throbbing in the back of the skull that didn't interfere with his driving ability. Heading for the office, he wondered how James and Dusty might be faring after having closed down the Red Lobster. Today was being touted as a "big event" at Johnson Homes, celebrating the arrival of Ted's biographer. Employees had been briefed by Barb McDermott that they would each be required to spend a half-hour with the author, extolling their boss's achievements. The junior Johnson would surely be expected to donate more time, not just today, but throughout Harley Mason's stay in Chandler. To Danny, it seemed like a personal horror movie in which a nightmarish domestic scene, like the one last night with Maya, dissolved into an atrocious work scene featuring an office full of sycophants kissing Ted's ass for a hack writer. Add in a montage of his gloomy financial prospects and hatred for the job itself, and the Danny Johnson story became a full-on fright fest. Suddenly he was hyperventilating, unable to make the turn on Dobson Rd. that would lead him to the office. He kept driving, only half-suspecting where he would end up.

As Harley Mason marched through the Johnson Homes main entrance to a balloon-filled hero's welcome, Danny sat in his car,

Bruce Ferber

alternately sweating and shivering. The parking lot was half-empty, surprising in that Applebee's normally did a big breakfast business. He had gotten out briefly and scouted the room for Katie B., finding out from the host that she didn't start her shift for a couple of hours. After making a few more unsuccessful attempts at motivating himself to go to work, he decided to wait, hoping that she would get there a little early so he could talk to her before she began serving customers. What he planned to say was unclear, as big a question mark as when he had initially sought her out the night before. The difference now was that she knew him. She would see his face and be happy to reconnect with the nice "rich guy" who had made her first day of work so memorable. This recognition would naturally ease them into a conversation on any number of subjects. Maybe they'd talk about her major in college. Or if she never went to college, what it was she saw for her future. Perhaps he'd ask if she had a boyfriend. He would act supportive if she did, and if she didn't, he would tell her that she was too pretty not to have one.

Where was this headed? And what were these hypotheses but the pathetic musings of a man trying to figure out how to flirt in a situation where he had no business doing so? Aside from it being inappropriate, given his marital status and their age difference, the entire crush had been fabricated as a reaction to a boring tile salesman, and used as a diversion from his own desperation. He was running on phony adrenaline, but it was adrenaline just the same. Fantasizing about his imminent interaction with this young waitress made him remember what it was like to feel excited and hopeful. The anticipation of Katie B. allowed him to exist in a pre-failure state of mind, and that was worth something.

WATCHING VARIOUS APPLEBEE'S CUSTOMERS and employees come and go, Danny's thoughts drifted between what kind of movies Katie B. might like (Rom-coms? God, he hoped not.), her underwear du jour, and her honest opinion of Arizona politics. The truth was, any white girl born in Maricopa County had, more likely than not, been raised by staunch conservative parents whose idea of tolerance was deporting

Mexicans as opposed to hanging them. So whatever Katie B.'s political bent, he couldn't hold it against her. And what difference did it make? They weren't about to get married or live together. They were simply going to run into each other and have a conversation, into which Danny would read all sorts of portentous things, while Katie B. would continue being an Applebee's waitress. He was self-aware enough to realize the folly of it, but that didn't make him savor the opportunity any less.

He ducked a couple of cell phone calls from the office, moving on to check his empty email box, then his Facebook page, which informed him that Ted Johnson "Likes" Walmart. It occurred to Danny that had he known what Katie's "B." stood for, he would be able to wait productively, checking out her wall, photos, and relationship status. That was the way people got their information these days, as opposed to looking for it in half-empty parking lots. Since she wasn't due to show up for some time, Danny weighed the idea of a quick snooze. He could set the alarm on his phone and check out for an hour, which would still leave him plenty of time to stalk the Sweetheart of Applebee's. It sounded like a sensible enough plan, and he was prepared to pull the trigger when he heard a knock on his driver's side window. Suddenly, he was face to face with the tile-peddling, faux Chinese Baptist, Kim Lee. Danny forced a smile and rolled down the window.

"How you doing, Junior Johnson?" Kim belted out enthusiastically.

"I'm good, Kim. Ran your stuff up the flagpole yesterday. Lot of interest."

"That's super, Danny. Thank you."

"My pleasure."

"Hey, can I buy you a cup of coffee? I've got an hour to kill before my meeting with the Roofers' Association."

"That's very nice of you, but I have to get going," Danny told him. So much for his nap, at least in this parking lot. He'd have to drive away and come back in an hour, once Kim Lee was safely nestled amongst his fellow roofers.

"Gee, that's too bad. I was hoping to tell you a little more about the chemical composition of the material. Didn't really have the time to go into detail yesterday."

"That's okay. I know in my heart that it's a good product." Danny was certain he'd nailed it, throwing in the word "heart." It reeked of the earnestness these religious types had coming out their asses.

Kim Lee was visibly moved. "I really appreciate you saying that. Because you know, I wouldn't steer you wrong."

Just like he hadn't steered anybody wrong with those exorbitant water filtration systems, which were later found to have no antioxidant effect whatsoever. The truth was, Danny thought the Chinese tile might actually be a decent product. He just didn't like having anything, be it roofing tiles or spirituality, jammed down his throat by born again hucksters. "Maybe we can talk chemicals another time, Kim."

"I'd like that," the Baptist smiled, extending his hand to shake Danny's. "You have a blessed day, my friend."

"You, too," Danny replied, watching Kim stride purposefully through the hallowed doors of Applebee's. He knew it was another born again thing, this wishing people a "blessed day." But how was one supposed to respond to that? "Thank you, I will do everything in my power to have a blessed day?" I'm not the one in charge of handing out the blessings, so how could I be expected to make that happen? Perhaps it was a shortened way of saying: "I hope you have a blessed day." Which would mean that the well-wisher hopes God shines his light on you and things go swimmingly for the next twenty-four hours or so. But what if they don't? Does that mean that God has decided not to bless you, even if you did nothing wrong? Why even bring up such a thing? What passed for a simple goodbye struck Danny as maddening and nonsensical. He hoped Katie B. wasn't a fan of this phrase.

Kim safely inside Applebee's, Danny considered staying put for a while, but then figured it best not to risk being rediscovered by the tile man after he finished his coffee and came outside. It was easy enough to pull into the parking lot across the street. Better yet, he could find a residential neighborhood with a park or, at worst, a lone shade tree to beat the heat. Turning onto Frye Road, he drove a few blocks down in the direction of Harter Park. As he slowed at the yellow light, his eyes were suddenly drawn to a figure walking on the right side of the street. Striding down the sun-baked sidewalk, in this land where pedestrians were as rare as rain, was the inimitable Katie B. To the chagrin of a semi driver and a blue-hair in a vintage Crown Vic, Danny swerved over two lanes in order to make contact with the waitress cum goddess. Reaching the curb, he tapped his horn and Katie B. saw him smiling through the windshield. She gave it right back, rushing to the passenger side door as Danny rolled down the window.

"It's you," she said adorably, clueless that she was being stalked.

"Need a ride?" he asked, thinking he must sound like some sort of predator on the ten o'clock news.

Katie hopped right in. The girl was obviously not a big news watcher.

"Where to?" Danny asked, mock pretending not to notice the Applebee's shirt.

"Puerto Vallarta. Do you think we could get there in time for cocktails?"

Danny laughed. Just the fact that she could joke with him this way lifted his spirits. It also seemed like a pretty fearless thing to say to a strange man nearly twice her age. "Vamanos, Señorita B. I'm Danny J., by the way."

This time Katie laughed. "Pleased to meet you, Danny J. I guess we should make a stop at Applebee's, seeing as how I've got this job and all."

"Not a problem. Unless maybe you want to grab coffee somewhere else beforehand." Danny knew she was early, and he couldn't risk walking back into Applebee's with the tile man ready to pounce on him at the slightest provocation.

THEY AGREED ON STARBUCKS, where he bought her a whipped creamy iced frappucino thing that must have had 1,800 calories. Danny sipped his nonfat latte, welcoming the opportunity to observe someone still at the age where fat and cholesterol were non-issues.

"So what's your deal?" Katie B. asked, point blank. "Wait. Let's get the B/J thing out the way first."

"The B/J thing?" Danny nearly did a spit take.

"My last name's Barrett. What's yours?"

"Johnson."

"Wow. That's like even more boring than Barrett."

"Thanks."

"I know, right? Hey, not our fault we have boring names. How long have you been married?" she continued, homing in on his ring.

"Be fourteen years in May."

"Very cool. Kids?"

"Two. Boy and a girl."

"Nice. I swear I thought you were gonna say: 'Three. One of each.'"

"I always liked that one."

"I know, right? It's funny but it doesn't really make sense."

"Maybe that's why it's funny." Danny liked the way she said: "I know, right?" A youthful affectation that was redundant, yet somehow endearing.

"Okay, so what else?" Katie went on. "Why would you leave a bad waitress a fifty-dollar tip?"

"It's complicated," Danny replied sheepishly. He knew that the complexity of the issue wasn't the problem. Rather, he feared that she would find his explanation pitiful. Then the thought occurred to him to simply tell her the truth. Suppose he systematically laid out for Katie B. what it was that the Kim Lee moment represented in the larger scheme of things? That sitting through the tile man's pitch had been, perhaps, the crowning mortification in a life gone terribly wrong. And that when he looked up and saw her fresh face and supple curves in Applebee's, he saw salvation. Honestly, what was there to lose? He hardly knew the girl, and if his rationale came off like the ravings of a lunatic, she was free to thank him for the frappuccino and be on her way. He did wonder, for a moment, whether or not it was morally acceptable for a married father of two to voice such intense feelings to someone who was still basically a kid. Just because he had projected this vast power onto her didn't mean she was obligated to relieve his unhappiness.

Katie Barrett was sharp enough to sense the turmoil brewing in her former customer's head; that when he explained his reasoning as complicated, she wasn't dealing with a bald, fifty-dollar come on. She also knew it was well within her rights to politely excuse herself, but there was something in Katie's nature that made her want to hear the man's story. She had already come to the conclusion last night that Danny wasn't dangerous, plus, she had time to kill before work. What could be the harm? "So, Mr. Johnson, tell me what's complicated about leaving a large tip for a horrible waitress?" She called him Mr. Johnson not to make him feel older, but as a way of injecting lightness into an encounter destined to enter territory that was raw and uncomfortable.

Danny smiled, acknowledging her munificence. Then he fired away, starting with how he hated growing up as the son of Ted Johnson and was later forced to come back and make his living being the son of Ted Johnson. He told her about Maya, the passion he had felt upon meeting her in college, and how that passion had deteriorated into nothingness, thanks to his inability to adequately provide for her and the family. He found himself speaking to this twenty-two-year-old (her exact age came out in the course of the banter) as if she were his therapist, or at the very least, someone interested in, and capable of, understanding his troubled condition. Why was he unloading on a perfectly innocent young girl sipping an 1,800-calorie beverage? He felt a bit ridiculous, first for burdening her with his shit, then for expecting the poor girl to offer some kind of enlightenment.

"Okay, let me get this straight," Katie started in. "You're having financial issues and you're worried about letting down your wife, so you go and leave me a huge tip."

Danny shook his head. "It makes no sense."

"Actually it kind of does," was Katie's unexpected response.

"How do you figure that?"

"I don't know. You feel like your life sucks, but you still want to be a hero…to somebody."

Danny nodded, impressed by her perceptiveness. "And boy, did I pull that off. I make this flashy, magnanimous gesture, then I blow the whole thing by telling you who I really am."

"I know, right?"

"I never have been much of a salesman."

"Danny—"

"What happened to 'Mr. Johnson'?"

Katie put her purse on the table and unzipped the top. Danny knew what was coming, or at least he thought he did. The money he had left to impress was about to be returned to him, along with whatever pride he had taken in fashioning the idea in the first place.

"I want you to have this." Katie scribbled her phone number on a piece of paper and handed it to him. "If you ever need to talk, call me."

"Thank you, Katie." Danny carefully placed the phone number in his wallet, way in the back where it would be hidden, properly protected, and unable to fall out. "You're very sweet." She was also smart and had bowled him over with everything she said.

"I like you, Danny."

Suddenly he felt like he was twenty-two, and blushing uncontrollably. "I like you, too."

"Please don't think that means I'm going to fuck you. I'm not into the older, married man thing. Plus, I have a boyfriend."

"That's fine. I mean it's great, actually. I'm not looking to cheat on my wife." He meant it, too, at least in the sexual sense. As attracted as he had allowed himself to become to Katie's polo-clad torso, what he had really been after in his hero's quest was intimacy. The closeness he no longer shared with Maya had created a hole so deep that he had spontaneously attempted to fill it with the companionship of a twenty-two-year-old waitress. And for thirty-two minutes at Starbucks, he had succeeded. Perhaps all was not lost. Maybe there were still some fragments of the life force that had yet to be stripped from Danny Johnson.

Katie went on to share some personal details of her own. She was dating Steve, her premed high school sweetheart, going on six years. Her parents adored him. The future neonatologist was madly in love with her, Katie loved him, but wasn't sure she was *in* love. She conceded that having had only one serious boyfriend, it was hard to tell. Danny recounted his own experience meeting Maya, telling her that when the right person came along at the right time, one knew it.

"So you're telling me I should break up with him?"

"That's not what I'm saying. Maybe he's the right guy, but it's not the right time yet. You've got to trust your instincts." Look who was giving relationship tips. Danny couldn't help but see the irony.

To the outside observer it might seem like a midlife crisis at full throttle, (a married man listening with rapt attention to a beautiful young girl's trite romantic dilemma and offering equally trite advice), but to Danny it was a heavenly balm. The content of their interaction, his own story included, was secondary to the undeniable fact that a connection had been made. Danny had reached out to another human being, who had not only responded, but hadn't bailed after learning the truth about his situation. She was one little miracle, this Katie Barrett.

As Danny drove her to work, he contemplated trying to arrange the next meeting while they were still in each other's presence. On the other hand, it might be better to let things marinate a bit, then casually call her for coffee, or maybe even lunch. Then again, what if the novelty of meeting him had subsided by the time he made the call? But hadn't she been the one to volunteer her phone number without his even asking? Of course she wanted him to call her.

They pulled up to Applebee's, Danny praying that Kim Lee had already gone off to commune with his fellow roofers. "Well, you have a great day, Katie B.," Danny smiled. "Who knows, maybe you'll get another big tip, and this time you won't have to listen to a long, boring story about it."

Katie laughed, and gave him a hug. "You have a good day, too. And don't be so fucking hard on yourself."

"Thanks. That's nice of you to say."

"I didn't say it to be nice. I'm just not wild about giving my phone number to a walking time bomb."

"You think I'm a time bomb?"

"Its possible. I don't know you that well."

"I'll try not to implode until you get more information."

Katie laughed appreciatively. As she closed the car door and walked toward the coffee shop, he noticed that this twenty-two year-old with the most womanly of bodies, still walked like a kid. It was a loping, bouncy sort of gait, reminiscent of a middle schooler on her way to soccer practice. He lingered on the picture for a while, that is, until he saw the dreaded Kim Lee emerging from the restaurant. Danny quickly threw the car into reverse, then headed for the office with a smile on his face for the first time in as long as he could remember.

As HE MADE HIS way toward Johnson Homes headquarters, or "Bullshit Central," as he and Maya often referred to it, Danny's thoughts were with the "Lieutenants of Bullshit," Dalton and Sprague. How might James and Dusty be holding up under the glare of the biographer's arrival, fresh off last night's descent into a Red Lobster stupor? As Danny vaguely remembered it, the three of them had proffered a slew of brilliant moneymaking schemes, all of which, in the light of day, had as much chance of succeeding as a Phase III caviar bar. The hard truth was that when James and Dusty woke up with thumping hangovers, they would still be men with families whose mortgages weren't being subsidized by the Ted Johnson personal nest egg. Danny wondered if they might have been so distressed that they decided to stay home, boycotting their boss's delusional self-promotion. Or had they, like the loyal soldiers they had always been, trudged into the office and sucked it up, no matter the damage it would inflict on their already wounded psyches?

Seeing their cars parked in the usual spaces made Danny sad. At least he had been able to bridge the transition from nighttime drunkenness to morning drudgery with a brief, but extraordinary, diversion. As far as he knew, there were no Katie Barretts in their lives to take them to unexpected destinations, even if those destinations were fantasies. Fantasy, at least, got the blood circulating. Johnson Homes was offering them nothing but blockage. The way Danny figured it, at least he was showing up for support—to let James and Dusty know that they were not alone in their struggle.

To THE UNTRAINED EYE, the whirlwind of activity Danny witnessed upon entering Bullshit Central suggested a company about to overtake Google or Apple. In addition to the excited buzz and the balloons (Were the tech giants equally big on mylar inflatables that said "Wow?"), Ted had ordered up a catered spread, replete with omelette bar and waffle station. It seemed a bit much, even for Danny, to take in. His father, whose career was on a runaway train to nowhere, felt the need to shower lavish perks on a new toady who was already being frivolously compensated.

"What an auspicious day!" Barb McDermott crowed, proceeding to grill Danny as to why he had been late for the biographer's arrival. "I know your father can't wait for Mr. Mason to meet you," she announced, throwing in an accusatory look for good measure.

"He looks like he can wait," Danny answered, seeing Ted and the man who was surely the author clinking glasses of Scotch, well before noon.

"Oh, and The Boys are looking for you," Barb informed him. She called them The Boys because Ted did, even though they were a good ten years older than she.

Danny welcomed the opportunity to meet with James and Dusty in their offices, the perfect excuse to duck out of a party he had no interest in attending. Unfortunately, before he was able to make his exit, Ted happened to look up from his Scotch and see him. He grabbed the biographer by the arm to shuttle him over.

"The heir to the dream," was Ted's way of introducing Danny, who, at the moment, felt like he'd rather be a peanut vendor at Chase Field. Working the Diamondbacks games would afford him the chance of scoring some actual peanuts, as opposed to the figurative ones that would be left him by Johnson Homes. As his father went off to score a Belgian waffle, Danny found himself alone with the dubious honoree of this senseless bash.

"DJ, son of TJ, I've heard a lot about you," the author declared, shaking his hand. "Harley Mason." Mason's handshake was weak and clammy, his eyes awfully beady for Danny's tastes. He saw that the author was looking past him, his gaze fixed on Vanessa, the receptionist, who had purchased a tight black miniskirt for the occasion. "I'm sure your dad has told you all about me as well."

"Not really. I know he hired you to write about how great he is."

"Good one," Mason laughed. "Your dad is understandably proud of his life's work, but I'm here to tell the truth."

"And what's that?"

"You tell me. I just got here. How the fuck would I know?" Mason laughed again, going off to refill his Scotch glass.

WHATEVER TRUTH DANNY MIGHT have to tell, Mason obviously had no need to hear it right away. Why should he? The longer it took to get to the truth, the more of Ted's checks he would be cashing. It all seemed par for the course in the Ted Johnson way of doing business. Bullshit begot more bullshit, the mass increasing exponentially until it became its own entity, something that could no longer be distinctly identified as bullshit. Assuming this Mason guy was capable of thinking clearly enough to get the job done, and Ted had the means to keep bankrolling him, there would be a Ted Johnson biography where there had been none before. The self-published tome might summon mild interest from only the hardest core Johnson homeowners, yet it would create a new reality for Ted, which he would then employ to create all new bullshit, which would beget more bullshit, and become something else entirely. The more Danny thought about it, the more he saw it as a genuine talent, beyond the grasp of ordinary human beings.

The merit of such talent was another story. It seemed to create an environment of verbal and psychological clutter, both of which Danny believed had chipped away at his childhood and damaged the adult he was to become. At face value, he couldn't blame his father for every fuck-up. It wasn't Ted's fault that he and Maya couldn't make ends meet as writer and artist. On the other hand, there was the bigger picture of having to grow up in the man's shadow. There was something about being the son of a kingpin, whether it be a politician, renowned surgeon, or stucco magnate, that put undue pressure on the child who had never asked to be born into such a world. It had turned him into a shy boy who felt too intimidated by his father's confidence to ever measure up. Even at Bennington, he never possessed the self-assuredness of Ray Minetta, whose full court press of Maya met with spectacular results. For Danny, it took every ounce of courage he could muster to even speak with her, and he viewed his ultimate success as a by-product of patience, persistence, and Ray being a cheater.

Danny supposed that just as bullshit begot more bullshit, confident men could conceivably beget confident sons, but it just didn't happen in his case. His disposition had been more like his mother's, which at first pleased him, but later proved disheartening, once he realized the woman had relinquished her entire being to assume the role of Ted's wife. Where had James and Dusty gotten their confidence, he wondered? Certainly they had learned their salesmanship skills from Ted, but their belief in themselves had to have been there to begin with. It was unfair, Danny thought, that this once proud and confident pair of winners now found themselves on the same sinking ship as the shy boy who had never known pride or confidence to begin with.

DUSTY'S DOOR WAS OPEN and the office empty, so Danny figured they must be in James's. Not only were they there, they seemed as happy to see him as they had been last night, and this time it wasn't even a surprise. For whatever reason, their smiles were relaxed and happy, unlike the "We're fucked anyway, let's tie one on" smiles of the previous night. Did they have some unexpected good news to share? Danny wondered. When Dusty locked the door behind him, it was clear something was afoot. Danny prayed it wasn't the drive-thru pet shop.

"We made a few calls," James announced. "We may be able to fix this yet."

"You figured out how to turn around the housing market?" Danny asked, hoping that somehow, they had.

"We can't solve the whole country's problems," Dusty explained, "but maybe we can make our situation a little better, and yours, too."

Danny had to love these guys. They were always thinking, programmed to deal with the here and now, as opposed to seeking answers from an Applebee's waitress. "What did you guys come up with?"

"We haven't moved forward on anything because we wanted to get your approval," James told him.

Danny was shocked. "My approval? I don't really have much authority over anything at this point."

"You're the future of this place," James continued, "assuming there is a future, which there isn't unless we do something, but still, we wouldn't feel right about pushing any buttons without your blessing."

"Are you shitting me?" Danny couldn't believe what he was hearing. Was it possible that there were people working for his father who actually had ethics? That, they surely hadn't learned from Ted.

"Johnson Homes is a family business, and we respect that. Ted did right by us for a lot of years, and we want to do right by you."

"That's really nice of you." Danny was moved, and at the same time mystified, as to what would come next.

Dusty cut to the chase. "We talked to some of the upper management guys at Tarkanian. They think the boss might be open to a purchase."

"Tarkanian wants to buy out Johnson Homes?" Danny was incredulous. "Do they know what kind of shape we're in?"

"According to these guys, the talk there is that despite the downturn, our brand is still strong. That if they come in while the Johnson name still stands for something, the deal might make sense. And, of course, we could put ourselves in the position of either joining the reconfigured company or receiving our own buyouts." James cautioned that these were purely off-the-record talks, but nevertheless thought they had the potential to lead to a significant development.

While Danny didn't know nearly as much about the business as The Boys did, he was reasonably sure Tarkanian would make an offer that Ted would consider well below the company's value. "You do know that Ted is going to be insulted by whatever number they throw out?"

Dusty nodded his head. "That's where we come in. We have to be proactive by massaging, greasing the wheels, putting your Dad in a frame of mind where he's open to change."

"In other words, kissing his ass ad infinitum," Danny interpreted.

"Whatever it takes," James agreed. "Dusty and I can put it all in motion, arranging breakfasts, golf dates, and such with the Tarkanian team, but we need to know you're on the same page."

"Absolutely," Danny assured them. The end of Johnson Homes sounded like a great idea to him. Ted might find himself at a loss for what to do with his life, but maybe it would finally force him to get one, and acknowledge the existence of a world that didn't revolve around real estate as religion. As far as Danny was concerned, shedding his father's baggage and working for another company might actually allow him to enjoy the business. He doubted it, but how could it be any worse than it was now?

"Thank you, Danny," James smiled, proceeding to give him a hug.

Dusty followed suit, and Danny suddenly found himself with new respect for the two men. They were stucco warriors fighting to the last breath, determined to make lemonade out of one sorry-ass batch of lemons.

Working On a Building

It was supposed to be an annoyance, yet Jeannie Johnson was happy to see workmen around the house, tending to the broken aspects of her life that could be fixed with tools and raw materials. The constant noise had become her comfort, a welcome sign of life in a place devoid of it for so long. She recognized that the true source of her appreciation was Owen Shea, the handyman/general contractor whose skill and demeanor had impressed her from the start. Not only was he intrinsically trustworthy, it seemed that once Owen took on a project, he would become personally invested, attending to details as if he were remodeling his own home. What was more, he saw his job as a full-service operation that included bringing in newspapers, putting out trash cans, even picking up a quart of milk for the client when necessary. Having heard that Jeannie belonged to a book club, he'd taken it upon himself to buy her a copy of *The War at the End of the World*, the novel he was currently reading. Owen hoped that once she caught up to where he was, they could talk about the story and he would be spurred on to finish the darned thing.

Jeannie found herself looking for excuses to make contact with Owen at various intervals during the day. It wasn't sexually motivated (he was the same age as her son, Danny, for God's sake), but an honest, effusive reaction to having found someone capable of making intelligent conversation. Plus, he was a good listener, a quality that seemed to accrue in value as one got older. How many years had she spent trying to talk to Ted about books, or sculpture, or native plants, only to be met with a glassy-eyed stare, making it clear that he'd rather be chugging cold ones down at the Elks Lodge? To her way of thinking, she had only become more interesting with age, while her husband had narrowed his worldview to subjects he could easily understand, his favorite being big, young tits. Jeannie couldn't picture Owen ever acting like Ted. In truth, she knew nothing of the handyman's personal life other than his having a daughter around the same age as her grandchildren. But she needed to believe that there were good men out there, too, and Owen Shea seemed as likely to fill the bill as anybody.

AT LUNCHTIME, OWEN CAME in to show her some different options for the decking grout. Rather than go with the standard gray, he proposed tinting the cement a shade of brown to complement the new flagstone they'd be laying down. Jeannie liked the idea, as she seemed to like every suggestion the contractor threw at her. It wasn't just that he had good taste. He took the time to weigh the options himself before presenting them to her, always keeping an eye on quality versus price point.

The two of them were comparing a piece of stone with various tint colors when Owen's cell phone rang. He told Jeannie he thought he should take the call, and she assured him it wasn't a problem. She could hear a young girl crying on the other end, no doubt the handyman's daughter. Owen listened patiently. Jeannie thought he might move into another room for privacy, but he stayed put, obviously comfortable with her hearing his side of the conversation.

"I'm sorry she was mean to you," Owen said. "Are you going to be okay for the rest of the day?... You want me to pick you up now?"

Jeannie could see that while he remained composed, the contractor was feeling frustrated. She couldn't be sure, but it appeared as if the responsibility for the girl's welfare rested solely on him, however that situation had come to be. She attempted a nod in Owen's direction to let him know that should he need to leave, it was okay by her.

Owen didn't notice Jeannie, his focus on solving his daughter's problem. "Brianna, listen to me. Remember what we talked about at Jamba Juice?" Then he recalled that they hadn't talked about anything at Jamba Juice. Brianna had come to the conclusion that things would turn out fine purely on her own, with no mention of the problem. Miraculously, though, the gambit worked. Based on whatever wasn't said at Jamba Juice, Brianna decided that she would be able to survive the next few hours without her father having to stage an early intervention. Maybe just hearing her dad's voice had been enough to calm her fears.

Hanging up the phone, he breathed an audible sigh of relief. It was then that Jeannie looked Owen in the eyes and spoke to him in silence. Though he couldn't be sure, he interpreted her gaze as: *I would like to be some small part of your life. I want to hear your story. Begin at the beginning.* He took a seat at the kitchen table, ready to address subjects of even greater import than grout and flagstone.

"I have no idea what I'm doing," he sighed. "I don't know what to say to my own kid."

"You think anybody knows?" Jeannie replied. "It's all a crapshoot. If people had any idea what was really involved in raising children, nobody would ever have them."

PER HER UNSPOKEN REQUEST, he began at the beginning, recounting his rustbelt childhood in Buffalo, New York, the only son of a steel worker who became an unemployed steel worker when the factory shut down. His parents had saved every penny so he might go to college, and he rewarded them by choosing a school nearly three thousand miles away, not for academic excellence, but climate. They weren't particularly fond of Buffalo winters themselves, but it was all they knew. Nobody in their family, or anyone they'd ever met, had just picked up and moved to Arizona. Dave and Sandi Shea were happy for their son, but sad for themselves, now that they would have to spend all but a few days a year a world away from him. When Owen met Lucy at Arizona State and brought her home to meet them, his parents immediately fell in love with her, secretly hoping that she would fall in love with the charms of Buffalo. They realized it was a lot to ask, and weren't surprised that it never came to be. The Sheas made only a few trips to Phoenix (his mom had a fear of flying), once on the occasion of Brianna's birth, the last, for Lucy's memorial. Owen brought Brianna back East whenever he could—most recently, for his father's funeral.

He pointed out the strange parallels between his parents' life and his own. Just as they had lost their blue-collar jobs to a company's relocating, Owen's tech sector position in Phoenix had become a casualty of outsourcing. Luckily, his mother and father were at retirement age with decent pensions when the shit hit the fan. Owen, on the other hand, was still in his late thirties, and faced with a massive stack of medical bills. He was forced to reinvent himself in a hurry. He found it ironic that all the Saturdays when he had been pulled away from playing sports and video games to help his father in the garage were the reason he could now support his daughter.

JEANNIE LIKED HIS STORY. Not the hardship he'd been forced to endure, but the breadth of how he'd responded to it. "I'm so sorry you lost her at such a young age," Jeannie said, immediately feeling as if she had spouted an empty cliché.

"Me, too," Owen replied. It had already been three years, but his tear ducts had never gotten the memo.

The phone rang. Jeannie ignored it. "It's okay, let it out." She fetched him a box of tissues.

"Thanks." Owen dabbed his eyelids. "I'm sorry, Jeannie."

"Nothing to be sorry about. Tell me. As you've been dealing with your grief, have you made any sort of attempt to…go out with anyone?"

"No time for that. I've got my hands full with work and my daughter."

"I'm sure." She didn't want to press, but still, she could see that he had adopted a bunker mentality which would cut off the possibility of any new, and conceivably positive, human interaction. She decided to make one more stab. "So you never feel like, I don't know, just maybe talking to a woman your own age?"

He shook his head. "Too much work."

"I assume you know a few."

"I do. But nobody I want to know better."

"All I'm saying is, it's important to get yourself some adult time. That's what I do with my book group and when I travel."

THEIR WHOLE CONVERSATION HAD been centered on him, but now Jeannie had made a striking admission of her own. Being married to Ted Johnson did not constitute "adult time" as far as his wife was concerned, so she had to seek that out anywhere she could. It occurred to Owen that for all intents and purposes, he and Jeannie were both widowed. And regardless of past relationships, wonderful or shitty, each of their futures was a blur.

Jeannie told him he could take a relaxed approach. "You don't have to get serious with the first woman you talk to, you know?"

"I know." His new client had made a fairly standard observation, but the kindness with which it had been delivered touched him.

The phone rang again. This time, Jeannie checked the caller ID. "It's my husband's office."

She didn't seem thrilled about taking the call.

"Hi Barb, what's up?...Where?...Fine, I'll see him there at 7:30... Tell him not to worry, I know what to wear."

The minute Jeannie hung up, Owen could tell she was stressed out. She explained that Barb McDermott had just handed out marching orders: she was to be at the Phase II Country Club Dining Room at 7:30 in order to meet and greet her husband's biographer. The entire family had been summoned to engage in the equivalent of a two-hour photo op, the MO being to hail the patriarch and ooze Johnson pride.

It sounded dreadful to Owen, but still, he wanted to be positive. "How bad could it be?"

"How well do you know my husband?"

Well enough, Owen thought, but kept his mouth shut to be polite.

"At least my grandkids will be there," Jeannie reminded herself, searching for some kind of silver lining.

"There you go. Hey, I forgot to tell you, I ran into them and your daughter-in-law at Jamba Juice the other day. They seem like a really nice family."

"They are," Jeannie smiled. "Although after tonight, I think they'll wish they were living in Buffalo. Hey, who knows? Maybe they'll take me with them."

Owen laughed. "Well, I guess I should be getting back to work."

"And I've got to go find a dress. I have no idea what to wear to this thing. It was nice talking with you."

"You, too," Owen smiled. Then he headed out to the pool to help Roy and Juan clean up more of Ted Johnson's mess.

Mushrooms, Surf, and Turf

Max paraded around the house in full mushroom regalia for over an hour, a testament to Maya's motivation and handiwork. Despite his sister's pronouncement that he looked "dumb and goofy," there was no denying the boy's enjoyment. For whatever reason, this eleven-year-old was proud as punch to be a fungus. And as was often the case with children, the joy was infectious, filling Maya with a lightness normally absent inside these four walls. Even Dana, the identifier of her brother's nerdiness, found comfort in his silly behavior. For a moment, Maya remembered the days when the four of them could disappear into that cocoon of silliness so specific to young families. She and Danny would get down on the floor with them, playing with blocks, building wooden train sets, reading picture books like Pat the Bunny and Goodnight Moon. They would lose all track of time, sequestered in a rarefied place where the only demand was being with each other. Max's present enthusiasm meant that such moments were still possible.

Maya's guess was that in her husband's current condition, he would view Max's mushroom mania as little more than an annoyance. This made her mad, even though she understood the reasons for his unhappiness. She believed that when children were still young enough to have a sense of wonder, parents needed to find a way to recall theirs. No matter how many curves life threw you, there were always windows that allowed in bits of light. Maya had known this even during her darkest hour, when she felt like nothing more than a walking baby machine. If she could just hang on, she would once again be able to find the openings. Now they were coming at her from unexpected places: the out-of-the-blue call from Judith Aronson; the out-of-the-box art from Smoke Shop Bob; the carefree clowning of her son, the mushroom. Individually, they weren't life-changing, but if one could put together enough of these disparate rays of light, they might add up to something.

FOLLOWING HER FUNGAL TRIUMPH, she summoned the inspiration to figure out what she wanted to place behind the gates in her second new canvas. After completing the wrought iron portion of the piece, she would paint not only what existed inside the gate, but whatever she imagined might be outside. Channeling Cadmus and adding a dash of WPA populism, canvas two became *Aliens at the Gate*. A crowd of non-threatening Mexican immigrants peered through the bars of Phase II, hoping to enter, but exhibiting little optimism that they would actually gain admittance. Too obvious? Perhaps, Maya thought, but it was not the time to edit herself. She proceeded to inject the same green liquid from the first painting into the body of this one. One had to look closely, but whatever this stuff was, it could be found oozing from the bottoms of the men's pant legs. Maya wasn't positive she liked it. Was she ready to have her first new series of work in years defined by slime?

ONE OF THE PERKS of productivity was that it made a person more tolerant of normally dreaded chores and obligations. This was why, when Danny called to request her and the kids' presence at the Phase II dining room, it rolled off her like water. She would be eating a tasteless dinner at a boring country club, yet she felt positively jovial. Maya even toyed with the idea of putting on a nice dress and make-up for the occasion, thinking it might be a kick to look fabulous when she walked in. There seemed to be no limits to the places self-worth might take you.

Surf 'N Turf Night at Phase II was a bit of culture shock, even for a well-traveled mercenary like Harley Mason. While the would-be gonzo writer was certainly no stranger to pasty-white America, having immersed himself in the world of Mrs. Billy Graham before settling in East Bumfuck, Texas, this seemed to be a whole new brand of bland. The Phase II bar's idea of premium booze was Old Crow, and the surf part of the evening appeared to be glorified fish sticks in silver-plated chafing dishes. The diners to whom the author was introduced were mostly older people who, from what he could gather, rarely left the Cascade Falls compound, touting the variety of tomorrow's Italian buffet and the spiciness of the following night's south of the border fajita station. These were hardcore Johnsonites, who put more miles on their golf carts than their Tauruses. And they all seemed delighted to be in the presence of Ted and his official biographer.

The developer was in his element, deftly negotiating what could have been an awkward moment between Harley Mason and the number two candidate for the job, Wade Timmons. Somehow, Timmons had found out that he'd been in contention for the biographer's position, and while he knew there was no shame in being beaten out by a professional, he was devastated nonetheless.

"Harley, I want to introduce you to the greatest living locksmith slash church newsletter writer in the free world," was Ted's opening line.

Timmons was a modest man, certainly not used to this kind of flattery. He turned beet red and mumbled some nonsensical approximation of "thank you" in the developer's direction. The biographer looked right past him, checking out every female under the age of seventy.

Danny and The Boys were huddled by the bar, talking Tarkanian strategy. Apparently, James and Dusty had already sprung into action, setting up a golf date for next week with Ted and the potential buyer's senior VP.

"You don't think he suspects something's up?" Danny asked.

James shook his head, no. "The man loves any excuse to golf, especially when he gets to show off the Phase III course. He believes the Tarkanians know their greens are inferior, and welcome the chance to enjoy a first-class golf experience in the Johnson Communities."

"Damn, you know my father well," Danny smiled.

"We've been here a while," Dusty answered. "Back when you were doing thee-ayter up at that fruity college in New Hampshire, me and James were gettin' schooled in Johnson 101."

"Actually it was Vermont," the younger Johnson corrected him. "But you're right. You two know him far better than I do at this point."

Danny looked up and saw his mother enter the dining room, as she had done so many times before. She never enjoyed coming here, having long ago developed a deep hatred of Surf 'N Turf Night. Jeannie Johnson not only swore the steak was liver, but remained convinced that the fish filets were day-olds from McDonald's. Her disdain for Surf 'N Turf Night wasn't merely relegated to the food. Practically a parody of itself, the first thing she saw upon walking in was her husband drooling compliments on Vanessa, the receptionist, whose topaz necklace was resting comfortably in her ample cleavage.

"Excuse me a second, guys." Danny extricated himself from The Boys and went over to greet his mother. The two weren't especially close these days, but they would always share the bond of having to suffer Ted.

"Hi, sweetheart."

After she kissed him on the cheek, he saw the familiar *How-soon-can-I-get-the-fuck-out-of-here* look in her eyes.

"Where are Maya and the kids?"

"They should be here any minute. I came from the office. Can I get you a drink?"

"If you don't, I may shoot someone," Jeannie replied.

"Don't make me guess who." Danny walked across the room to make the bartender aware of his mother's presence, implicit license to break into Ted's private stash of high-end alcohol. As he waited for his mother's double margarita, to be made with nothing less than Patron

Silver, he failed to notice Max and Dana scamper in, nor the vision that accompanied them.

MAYA, WITH WHAT HAD amounted to very little effort, had put together a look that cut through the sea of human mayonnaise in stunning fashion. Her long, Sonia Braga-like tresses, more often than not pulled back, now flowed freely, halfway down the open back of a simple, but fetching, black cotton dress. Blue sapphire earrings matching her eyes completed a picture that, to her mind, celebrated her permanent status as an alien at the Cascade Falls gate. She projected none of the "bootylicious" qualities of the twenty-something receptionist, yet it was somehow far more threatening to this group when a woman her age, a mother for God's sake, could walk into a room and turn so many heads.

The ladies smiled politely as they watched their husbands assume the neck-craning position. Maya's presence had made a roomful of aging males start to wonder how they had gone from commanding lovers to men in plaid pants. A gaggle of them began heading in her direction, the pretext being that welcoming their builder's daughter-in-law was just the neighborly thing to do. They were beaten to the punch, however, by the man who had met her earlier that morning in the Indian Smoke Shop.

"I guess Surf 'N Turf Night must be some kind of artists' salon," was the witty opening line.

Maya hadn't noticed the biographer approach, and found herself startled to see him sizing her up anew. "Oh, hey, how're you doing?" she managed weakly.

"Real good now, Maya."

She hated that he remembered her name. It made the way he looked at her seem even sleazier.

Luckily, and this could rarely be said about such an occurrence, Ted came over to say hello. "Harley, I see you've met my daughter-in-law, Maya. I hear she's a terrific little painter. Someday, you'll be writing a book about her."

"I'd like that," the author smiled, to Maya's chagrin. "Funny, you didn't mention you were my new boss's daughter-in-law."

"I didn't want to get you nervous," Maya smiled, looking to remove herself as quickly as possible. "Excuse me, I want to go say hello to my husband." As she walked toward Danny, who had been talking to Jeannie and the kids, she saw that he had been watching her, perhaps having witnessed Harley Mason's not-so-subtle advances.

He had. After giving his mother her margarita, he saw Maya and the author speaking, but rather than step up to join them, chose to become an observer. It was a strange sensation, watching his wife interact with another man whose lust for her was palpable. In the past, if Danny had seen Maya walk into a room looking this spectacular, he would have rushed over to kiss her, but now the sense of inferiority blunted his excitement and deepened his jealousy. When she reached him and Jeannie, it was her mother-in-law who greeted her enthusiastically. Danny gave her a hug, but it felt as empty as the blank expression on his face.

If only Maya could realize that what appeared to be disinterest was actually the helplessness of a man overwhelmed. He found her beauty staggering, her intelligence, equally so, her mothering skills incomparable. Danny wanted to shout this to the heavens, but the words would not find their way out. His unspoken fear was that since he lacked credibility as a husband and provider, any compliment sent her way would be neutralized by the weakness of its auspices. He settled for standing awkwardly by her side, finally managing to ask how her day was.

"Fine," she smiled. "Finished Max's costume for the play."

"Play?" Danny asked in earnest.

"'Edible Planet,'" she reminded him with a frown. "I told you about it like a hundred times. It's tomorrow at one o'clock."

"Don't worry. I'll be there."

"That would be nice." She turned away and grabbed Dana's hand, if for no other reason than to feel the closeness with one of her children that she lacked with her husband.

TED STARTED WAVING TO the crowd and directing people to their seats. Barb McDermott had arranged two tables for Johnson employees and their spouses, a third for Ted, Jeannie, Danny and family, and Harley Mason. Having not had the opportunity to eat dinner with their father the last few nights, Max and Dana quickly positioned themselves on either side of Danny, leaving the seat next to Jeannie open. Harley Mason abruptly swooped in, holding out Maya's chair before occupying the coveted place beside her. Had Danny known of her distaste for the author, he might have taken it upon himself to switch places. But the two of them were so out of sync that he assumed she preferred anyone else's company to his.

IT WASN'T LONG BEFORE Ted rose to his feet, giving a rousing introduction to the man who would soon be intruding on his family, as well as the people whose paychecks he signed. "I would only hope that he finds us half as interesting as the Billy Graham clan," was Ted's toast.

For some reason, this garnered wild applause from the employee tables. Danny figured that his father must have instructed them to clap at specific points in the evening as a condition of being invited. Ted, never one to be satisfied with a low-key welcome, then proceeded to introduce the members of his family one by one, making them each stand in their places as their names were called. The kids, of course, got a kick out of it, Max even using the moment to plug the show he would be starring in tomorrow. His spontaneous promo made Danny think that Max could be the natural heir to the Johnson empire, if only it had a prayer of lasting that long. After finishing his spiel, Ted invited Harley Mason to come up and say a few words.

HAVING STARTED DRINKING AT eight in the morning, the author would have preferred to avoid the limelight of a formal Surf 'N Turf Night address, but the die had been cast. After a brief toast to Ted, Mason informed the uninitiated that not only had he written the Mrs. Billy Graham Story, but spent many hours getting to know the woman.

"When I was researching that book, my bedroom was situated directly over hers. It didn't matter what time I went to sleep at night, I could see the light from her window reflected on the trees outside and I'd know when she was up. And if I should slip down to her room, I would always find her on her knees." He paused, then looked over at James and Dusty's table. "Stop snickering, Dusty. She wasn't blowing anybody. The woman was in prayer. Shame on you for thinking such things."

Of course, Dusty hadn't been. Nobody in the room had considered the thought, even as a joke, except Harley Mason. Ted, suddenly having déjà vu of Mason peeing by the Texas trailer, did his best to cover the loud Christian gasps with laughter, then went on to thank the biographer and announce that dinner was served.

"Of course it's served," Mason cried out. "It's a friggin' buffet!"

At least he said "frig" instead of "fuck," Ted sighed. And thank goodness the grandkids were too young to be permanently scarred by the fellatio reference. *You had to be prepared for such hitches with these creative geniuses,* he rationalized, going on to fill his salad plate with iceberg lettuce smothered in Thousand Island dressing.

DANNY WOULD HAVE FOUND the blowjob joke more amusing had it not been at Dusty's expense, but still, the opportunity to see the horrified looks on the Cascade Falls faces, as well as his father's reaction to them, was priceless. From Maya's point of view, she was only offended by dirty jokes if they were bad, and since the kids hadn't understood this one, there had been no harm done. Harley Mason, meanwhile, picked at the glorified cafeteria food while exploring different ploys with which to engage Maya in conversation. It wasn't that he was specifically out to fuck other men's wives, he just always found himself drawn to the most beautiful, interesting woman in the room. And, more often than not, the interesting ones were married. On the nights he got totally shitfaced, he didn't care whether they were interesting. On the nights where he managed to retain some of his wits, like tonight, he didn't care whether they fucked him. It would be enough to see what common ground he could find with Mrs. Johnson (art would be a natural jumping off point), and what he might say that would make her laugh. To Harley Mason, getting to know a woman of Maya's quality was an exercise in intellectual and psychological cocksmanship.

Having negotiated this territory many times before, Mason addressed his initial comments to both Maya and Danny, remarking how beautiful and polite their children were. Danny had little interest in making small talk with the guy, preferring to direct his energy toward bonding with Max and Dana. This, of course, played perfectly into the biographer's hand. He threw a few obligatory questions at Jeannie, praised her responses to Ted, then sat back to concentrate on Maya. He began with his analysis of Smoke Shop Bob's painting, which he had found impressive, but lacking discipline. Maya wondered what made him say that, the thoughtfulness of his answer taking her by surprise. The author explained that while he found the imagery arresting, there was something about the sum of it that seemed mechanical, as if it had been plotted in the painter's head rather than emerging from his heart. It turned out that Mason actually knew a thing or two about art, having written a non-vanity biography of Jasper Johns before the legitimate work dried up and he was forced to become a schlock for hire.

"Shit happens," he explained. "One day you're probing the abstract expressionism of a modern master, the next day you're eating Phase II fish sticks." Maya laughed, perhaps his first inroad. He followed this with a nimble Googling of the Johns book on her iPhone, showing her the many positive reviews for what he deemed his finest work.

MAYA FELT TORN. HERE she was, implicitly allowing herself to be ogled in exchange for stimulating dialogue. Never in her years at Cascade Falls had she imagined sitting in the country club dining room, discussing how the personal relationship between Johns and Robert Rauschenberg affected their individual outputs. Mason talked about a Rauschenberg piece depicting the spot where two had slept together for so many years, appropriately entitled "Bed." Every once in a while Maya glanced over to see Danny playing with the kids, appearing to be enjoying himself immensely. Discussions of art, which she had so missed since coming to Phoenix, tended to bore him anyway, so why not seize the moment and share her ideas with someone who might appreciate them?

What Maya had no way of knowing was that while Danny loved playing hangman with Max and Dana, another part of him was self-destructing at warp speed. Each time he, or one of the kids, added a new letter, Danny snuck a peek at his magnificent wife, in awe of her ability to converse knowledgeably on any number of subjects. Beauty seemed to radiate from every pore of her, which obviously had not been lost on Harley Mason. He could hear the two of them talking about some Rauschenberg show at the Modern in New York, but the image fixed in Danny's mind was of his wife giving this loquacious drunk a blowjob. Slowly and soulfully, the way she used to do it for him, back in the days when he still had the capacity to turn her on. In Danny's experience, there were certain types of women who hated performing oral sex, others who tolerated it to shut their husbands up, and a third group who actually loved it, taking pride in their proficiency, and pleasure in bestowing it upon the worthy. Maya, when she was excited by life, fell into the third category. Bennington smarts and porn-star talent. An unbeatable combination, as far as Danny was concerned, which made it nothing short of unbearable to picture Harley Mason sampling it.

Danny didn't really think she wanted to blow the guy, yet when he was feeling this vulnerable and insecure, it was easy to imagine such a scenario playing out. Her motivation might be that her husband had failed to satisfy her sexually, or that he had been such a bust in general that she longed to exact revenge. Danny saw Mason elicit a full-throated laugh from his wife, Maya throwing her head back and giving the biographer a peek at her small, but indefatigably perky, breasts. Making matters worse, Ted suddenly felt the need to start up a conversation on the feasibility of using the Chinese tiles. Jeannie begged her son to switch seats so she could talk to the kids, rather than have to listen to Ted. This put Danny next to his blowhard father, and directly across from the man attempting to seduce his wife. The more miserable he felt listening to Ted's yammering, the more captivated his wife seemed to be by the raconteur sitting next to her.

THE HEIR TO THE dream started to become lightheaded. It was as if Danny were on some kind of psychedelic drug, the voices melding into an indiscernible drone as he became lost in his own murky thoughts. Each time someone at the table spoke, it felt like he was being poked in the skull. Unable to remain in the chair any longer, he politely excused himself and headed out to the hallway, continuing outside for a breath of fresh air. Unfortunately, upon opening the doors and inhaling, his nasal passages were greeted with the stench of ammoniated cow shit. He quickly retired to the men's room to wash his face, letting the water stream into his nostrils in the hope that it might dissipate the odor. Even in his muddled state, he knew that noxious, dairy farm smells were the least of his problems. Danny Johnson was in a bad way. He hated his job, resented his father, and felt inadequate as a parent and lost as a husband. What was there left that might give him a glimmer of hope? Then he remembered Katie Barrett.

HE STARED AT HER phone number for a minute or two before daring to punch it in. Reminding himself that she had offered it up willingly, specifically instructing him to call her should the need arise, he started to feel a little better about the prospect. Then, he considered that Katie might have just said that to be polite, humoring an old man who happened to be nice to her on her first day of work. Either way, he had no choice in the matter. If he didn't make an effort to connect with the one person who had yet to form a negative opinion of him, what were his alternatives? Danny looked at his watch and wondered what his Applebee's friend might be doing at 8:47 p.m. on a weeknight. There was the distinct possibility that she'd be working, in which case she could always call him on her break. But where would he be able to talk when she called back? It would be great if he could get a hold of her right now. Throwing caution to the wind, Danny dialed away, conjuring up an image of Katie Facebooking on the computer in her parents' house. By the third ring, he knew he would have to settle for her voicemail.

"Hi, I can't come to the phone," she announced adorably. "Your loss."

As the tone sounded, Danny realized that he was completely unprepared for what came next. What kind of message was one supposed to leave when in so dire a state? He didn't want to scare or alienate her. As a result, he wound up going the complete opposite route. "Hey, it's Danny, nothing important, just checking in."

What would Katie Barrett think upon hearing his casual tone? Perhaps that it was a call not worth returning. He couldn't risk such an outcome. Missing that opportunity on account of cowardly messaging skills was not an option. He had to follow up the first call with something weightier. He swiftly hit redial, realizing that taking a little break might have given him the chance to compose his thoughts.

Too late for that now. "Hi. Me again. Listen, Katie, I really want to talk to you. It's kind of important. Call anytime. Bye."

Perhaps not the perfect wording, but at least it conveyed some sense of urgency. He checked his look in the mirror, then, after realizing there wasn't much he could do about it anyway, prepared to reenter the dreaded dining room. The evening would last maybe another hour tops, during which time he'd be able to feel his phone vibrate and duck out to talk to Katie. It was amazing to Danny how quickly he had gone from pumped up to falling apart. As much as his brief encounter with Katie Barrett had soothed, if not quite renewed, his spirit, the experience of watching his beautiful wife charm, and be charmed by, another man had negated all of it.

Danny gingerly made his way back into the dining room. He had never been the victim of a heart attack, but the sight of both Maya's and Harley Mason's empty chairs seemed like it might facilitate his initiation. Jeannie was laughing with the kids, Ted deep in conversation with his cherished locksmith, Maya and the biographer, nowhere in sight. All he could think of was that while he was dialing Katie in the men's room, they had slipped out to Mason's car so she could orally pleasure him.

Between palpitations, he tried to discern the difference between his calling another woman on the QT and his wife blowing another man. Calling obviously wasn't blowing, but perhaps it was a prelude to it, despite Katie's previous assertions. Then again, his overtures had never really been grounded in sex, while Harley Mason, for all his bullshit art talk, was after one thing only.

As Danny waded through the possible alibis for Maya being missing in action, he suddenly noticed Mason by the bar, having just bent down to tie his shoe. Then, Maya entered from outside with a jacket for Dana, who apparently had felt cold. It turned out that the earth-shaking, five-star blowjob had all been in his mind. Relieved though he was, the minute Danny reclaimed his place at the table, he felt as far away from Maya as ever. Not because of anything she said, but of how little they had to say to one other. She reminded him that the kids had to get up early for school in the morning and should probably be taken home. Cheerfully volunteering to drive them, she explained that she was ready to go, anyway.

The kids, however, said they wanted to ride home with Daddy. Danny might have been flattered if it hadn't started the jealousy churning all over again. Daddy driving left Maya here alone, giving Harley Mason more time and motivation to hatch his prurient plan.

"You sure you want to ride with me, guys?" he asked lamely, which only annoyed Maya further.

"Do you not want to take them?" she blurted out.

"No. I mean, I do. I just thought that since they came with you, some of their stuff was probably still in your car."

He knew the words sounded ridiculous as they came out of his mouth, the realization confirmed by Maya's *What the fuck is wrong with you?* look. Danny said his goodbyes to Ted and Jeannie, then gathered Max and Dana to shuffle them out. Maya, with nary a glance in Harley Mason's direction, followed them to the parking lot and got in her car to head home.

In a normal person, the scales would have tipped back, away from jealousy. But these days, Danny's thought processes were imbued with paranoia, spurring him to the conclusion that there had been no goodbye between the biographer and Maya because they wanted to appear casual and disinterested, when in fact, they had made secret plans to consummate a liaison at a future date. As he watched Maya's car following them home in the rearview mirror, he made a mental note to ask Barb McDermott where the biographer was staying, just in case he needed to do some spying. Suddenly, Max started to sing the song he would be performing for the school show. The predepressed Danny loved these kinds of spontaneous kid moments, but tonight he was off in his own world, simultaneously wondering if Harley Mason had a big cock, and why Katie Barrett hadn't returned his call.

It took everything he had to keep the car from swerving off the road. Horrible things were going through his mind, the most notable of which was that his kids would be better off without him. He hated himself for thinking such a thing, but it was becoming clear that the biggest favor he could do for his family would be to get as far away from them as possible. He allowed for the option of being talked down, but the only person he felt comfortable talking to was Katie Barrett. Which meant that his future rested in the hands of a twenty-two-year-old Applebee's waitress. Danny decided that he would keep the phone on his nightstand. The minute it vibrated, he would go off to the bathroom to decide his fate.

Good Night and Good Luck

Turning off their reading lights, Danny and Maya assumed what had become the default bedtime position, facing away from each other at a great enough distance to thwart any possible physical contact. Their now-lifeless marriage had also terminated a ritual they had once savored, the Couples Post-game Show. After attending a party or gathering, husband and wife would share impressions of the evening, formulating a Zagat-like analysis on the basis of the company, the conversation, the food and drink. The first topic discussed was always which of the other couples looked good, and who seemed miserable in their relationships. Now it didn't need to be stated. Danny and Maya were the miserable ones.

MAYA CLOSED HER EYES and thought about Harley Mason. While she wasn't physically attracted to the man, she had been fascinated by his stories and impressed with the caliber of friends and acquaintances he had cultivated. Equally remarkable was that he had polluted his body with massive amounts of psychotropic drugs, yet, at least for the time being, lived to tell the tale in entertaining fashion. She reasoned that if he could stay sober enough to do the work, he might be the one person capable of making something interesting out of Ted Johnson.

On the other side of the bed, Danny felt his heart racing with anticipation. Rather than leave the phone on the table where the buzzing might awaken Maya, he gripped it tightly in his hand, ready to silence it at first vibration. He alternated between wanting to nap for a bit before the phone rang and trying to stay alert so he could make the quickest exit to the bathroom. The end result was that as the hours ticked by, he found himself neither alert nor asleep, just fidgeting anxiously. One a.m., two, four, five-thirty. In an hour he'd be waking up to start his day. But what kind of day it would be had been predicated on a conversation that hadn't taken place. He dragged himself into the shower, feeling a combination of agitation and exhaustion that didn't bode well. He was pissed at Katie Barrett. Even had she been too busy to talk, couldn't she at least have texted him to let him know she got the message? To assure him she'd phone as soon it was feasible for her to do so? That was just common courtesy, an unwritten rule of friendship. What kind of a friend was she? His only contact with the young woman adding up to maybe fifty-five minutes, he really was in no position to ascertain such a thing.

By 7:00 A.M., DANNY was dressed for work, but as soon as he opened the car door, he knew he would never get there. His time at Johnson Homes had come to its necessary end, well before the implosion, or the sale, or whatever it was the future might hold. He went back into the house, not quite knowing what his next move would be. Then, upon hearing Maya start the shower, he entered the bedroom to pack a small suitcase with the essentials: underwear, socks, some T-shirts, and jeans. He could always stop at a Target somewhere to pick up the toiletries. Where he intended to go was another matter entirely. The destination wasn't important. He just had to get away for a while so he could gain some perspective on what to do with his life. He knew that had he been more communicative, Maya would have understood his need for self-examination and encouraged him to take a sabbatical. Now, it would just be another reason for her to get pissed off. The notion of trying to explain this to her when she had to get the kids ready for school was a nonstarter. The bigger picture was that any kind of talk seemed like too little, too late.

Rummaging through the sock drawer, he found an old 4x6 photo of the family in California, arms around each other, smiling, in obviously happier times. He shoved it into the suitcase, thinking it might be helpful for him to have at his disposal, some visual proof that happiness had once been his. He zipped up the bag and headed for the door, stopping by the kids' rooms to find them sleeping peacefully. Unable to leave without saying goodbye, he ran in and kissed them each on the forehead. Then he wheeled his suitcase out to the car to embark on whatever it was people embarked on when they got lost.

Goodbye

The plan was in motion. Fill up the '07 Accord and get on some freeway going somewhere to do something. He had a few credit cards to max out while he filled in the rest of the pieces. Topping off the tank and pulling out of the Mobil station, he eyed the thirsty cotton fields of Hohokam Road, which always struck him as what the surface of the moon would look like had it decided to be pedestrian rather than breathtaking. That's when the terrifying thought hit him. Danny Johnson bidding a final adieu to this haven for dust devils carried with it the possibility that he might never see his kids again. Mercifully, his despair was tempered by the feeling that he'd been injected with a massive dose of cerebral novocaine. All things are equal in the land of the numb.

Armed with a past he needed to forget and a future with no promise, Danny occupied a here and now that could veer off in any direction, depending upon what entered his consciousness at a given moment. He had fully surrendered to instinct, leaving him bereft of the critical thinking necessary to grasp the ramifications of his choices. This became evident the minute he got on the ramp for the I-10 West, when a voice in his head told him to take the next exit for Applebee's. He hadn't said goodbye to his wife before departing for God knows where, yet somehow it was important to get closure on a relationship with a twenty-two-year-old who'd been in his life for less than an hour.

To his blank canvas of a brain, it made perfect sense. Katie Barrett had empathized with his situation and reached out to him, inviting his telephone call at any hour of the day or night. He had taken her at her word and allowed himself to be vulnerable; his reward, another rejection for his fast-growing collection. Yet it seemed wrong to lump this one in with the rest. This rejection was fresh and new, courtesy of a person who hadn't known him well enough to treat him like shit. Katie needed to understand this. Giving her a pass was unacceptable because it would encourage egregious behavior in the future.

WAITING FOR THE NON-RETURNER of his phone call to show up for her shift, he parked the Honda in his usual space, inspecting the lot for any sign of the plastic tile man. He had no interest in perusing his phone for email messages, or turning on the radio to find a decent station that wasn't in Spanish. Today, Danny just sat there, breathing in the stifling smog of his last Maricopa County morning. Across the way at the Home Depot, men were gathered on the corner, smoking generic cigarettes and angling for day jobs. If they hit the jackpot, they'd get to spend eight hours nailing two-by-fours in 110-degree sun. To Danny, their situation seemed like a step down from the hookers, who got to leave their corners and work in air-conditioned cars, for a better hourly rate. For a moment, he wondered if there might be an intersection someplace with Home Depot guys on one side of the street and hookers on the other—kind of a one-stop shopping idea in the spirit of the other night's brainstorming at the Red Lobster.

The reverie was broken by a rap on the glass. He looked up and saw Katie Barrett smiling at him, her youthfulness like coarse sea salt about to be poured on his open wound. Danny rolled down the window, not about to smile back.

"Hey, I was going to call you on my break," she said.

"I needed to talk to you last night." His tone was that of a dismissive father.

"My battery died, so I didn't get your message till this morning."

Did she really expect him to believe that? Maybe it was a plausible explanation. He wasn't thinking all that straight, so it was hard to tell.

"You sounded stressed. Are you okay?"

"Do I look okay to you?"

"I don't know. Yeah. I mean, I haven't like seen you that many times so for me to be able to—"

"I just came to say goodbye."

"I see." She walked away, and as far as Danny figured, out of his life forever. He certainly didn't expect her to open the passenger door and sit down next to him. "What's the deal?" she wanted to know. "Why are you being so tight-assed and weird?"

"I'm done with this place."

"Preaching to the choir. I fucking hate Applebee's."

"I'm leaving," he spelled it out, with as much gravitas as he could muster.

She stared at him, at last grasping weight of his words. "No fucking shit? You're getting out of Dodge?"

Danny nodded his head.

"Awesome. So where are we going?"

"This isn't a joke."

"You see me laughing?" She wasn't.

What in God's name was this girl trying to prove? The last thing he needed was somebody else to fuck with him. "I'll call you in a week or something. So long."

"Bye." She didn't budge.

"Here's the deal, Katie. I'm about to put my foot on the gas and keep driving until I need to fill the tank again. It won't be a round trip."

"And?"

"And I'm glad I met you, thanks for listening the other day, you're a nice kid, but—"

"Start the fucking car."

"Katie—"

She tossed her purse in the back, hit the recline button, and stretched out.

"You can't do this. You have a life here."

"Really? Seems like someone else does, too. How's that working out for you?"

"You have parents."

"You have children."

"Fuck you."

"You should be so lucky. Wake me at the first rest stop." She closed her eyes, bracing to establish her assertiveness with a nap.

Adding insult to injury, Danny just knew she was the type who had no trouble falling asleep wherever and whenever she chose. "Look, you're not making any sense," he tried to argue, "and I can't be respons—" His eyes suddenly widened, a nightmarish vision appearing in the distance. "Hang on." Popping the transmission into reverse, he gunned the engine, nearly flattening two Mexican ladies lugging shipping container-sized baskets out of the laundromat.

"What's the hurry?" Katie asked. "You see a bunch of zombies or something?"

"Worse." He pointed to his right, where Kim Lee was waving and preparing to descend upon them. Danny might be down, and inching toward out, but he refused to have his last conversation in Maricopa County be about plastic tile or born-again Christianity. He left the faux Chinese Baptist in a cloud of exhaust and, in a matter of seconds, was back on the I-10, now with company.

No Show

T he buzz in the auditorium made her think of those Johnny Cash concert recordings at Folsom Prison—the difference being that these inmates were not murderers, but grade school children, released from their academic cells to watch other children dress up as vegetables. Scattered about the room were the stay-at-home moms, the working ones who had to get back before the end of their lunch hour, two or three unemployed dads, and the usual smattering of doting grandparents. Maya took a seat in the back, where she could save a place for Danny without being subjected to the pruney stares of the school übermoms. As onerous as that group was on normal school days, they were doubly irritating when their kids were on stage, morphing into Stepford talent agents. Cathy Carlson, stage mom of the lead broccoli stalk, had threatened to yank her daughter from the production if she wasn't allowed to sing her precocious original song, "Green with Envy."

Ironically, the one thing Maya had looked forward to about the Phoenix move was people being more normal than the Hollywoodinfected LA crowd. No such luck, because apparently all of America now suffered from Creeping Show Business Syndrome. Thanks to reality TV, everybody thought they, or at the very least, their offspring, were celebrities. Entering one's kid in the school show was like buying a lottery ticket that came in the form of an underage human being.

As more children and parents filed in, she caught a glimpse of Dana, who had already informed her that she would be sitting with the class, rather than with her mother. Glancing around the room, Maya noticed the handyman who worked for her mother-in-law—the guy she had run into at Jamba Juice the other day. Owen-something-or-other. He was alone, which made her wonder what kind of fancy, important job his wife had that she never seemed to be around.

The principal, Jane Mallory, called the assembly to order, announcing that the play had to begin promptly because teachers needed to get back to their classes and responsibilities in a timely manner. She went on to explain that this afternoon's show, "Edible Planet," had been the brainchild of third grade teacher Missy Butler, who believed that students needed to know where their fruits and vegetables came from— not the local Bashas or Safeway, but the ground. A reasonable, if obvious topic, Maya thought.

THE LIGHTS DIMMED AND the prissy Missy Butler took a seat at the piano, striking the opening chords of a syrupy ballad destined to be rendered cute by a phalanx of wide-eyed elementary school kids. Then, as the center-stage spotlight came up, the audience applauded the entrance of a lone broccoli stalk, inside of which was nine-year-old Heather Carlson. One could barely see through the hole that had been cut for her face, but her soprano, young and soft though it was, hit all the right notes.

I'M NOT A BUSH,
I'M NOT A TREE,
I'M YOUR DINNER,
I'M BROCC-O-LI.

It was strangely affecting, Maya had to admit. The girl didn't push it like a lot of those American Idol wannabes. She let words flow naturally, which actually made you want to listen. Maya's concentration was suddenly broken by people standing up to let in a new arrival. It was just like Danny to show up after the thing had started. Lucky for him, Max hadn't yet come onstage for his part. She soon realized that the "excuse-me's" of the man about to take the seat next to her weren't Danny's at all, but the hushed intrusions of Ted's biographer, Harley Mason.

"I thought I saw the lovely Mrs. Johnson," he smiled, helping himself to the empty chair to her left.

"Hey," she whispered. "What are you doing here?"

"Research for chapter twelve. The Ted Johnson grandchildren."

"Going to a grade school show is research?"

"What can I say? I'm dedicated."

"And, the only person here getting paid to watch."

"Touché." He looked up at the stage. "Mercenary or not, that's some talented-ass broccoli."

Heather Carlson was winning over the crowd and she hadn't even started her original song. Other broccoli stalks stumbled out to join her, looking limp and wilted in comparison. That was always the rub with one kid being so much better than the rest. Parents now had to sit in anguish as their "normal" children decimated the major scale, as normal children did. Maya prayed that the broccoli delegation would be offstage by the time Max and the mushrooms came on, which would make the talent contrast less glaring. With no sign of Danny, she took her phone out and looked for a text, feeling the wandering eye of Harley Mason checking her out as he pretended to watch the show.

Maya saw there was no message. "What's Ted up to?" she asked, thinking it might shed some light on Danny's whereabouts.

"Emergency Elks Luncheon. But Jeannie just walked in."

Maya spotted her mother-in-law standing by the door. She was always good about coming to see the kids' performances, calling them a level up in quality from her husband's dog and pony shows, where she was often required to make an appearance.

"Where's Danny?" Mason asked, doing his best to sound like he gave a shit.

"Working probably."

"I didn't see him at the office."

"Maybe he wasn't there when you went by."

"I was there all morning."

"He's out in the field a lot." Maya had no idea if that were true, but it sounded plausible enough, and she knew he had had a meeting off-site the other day. Still, Danny had never missed one of the kids' shows, no matter how busy he was, or how badly things were going, personally or professionally. She texted him again. "Max about to go on…where are you?" Her phone buzzed back almost immediately, but the message turned out to be from Judith Aronson.

"Just wanted 2 chk in. How goes it?"

"Grt," she texted back, tossing the phone into her purse.

The root vegetables then came out to do a slow blues, cheerfully mangling the key of C while bellowing "Orange You Glad You're a Carrot." Maya looked back at the doors for a sign of Danny. Mason registered her anxiousness, smiling as if to say, *But I'm here.*

EVERYTHING ABOUT THE MOMENT felt wrong. Attending a school show was usually Maya's opportunity to relax, a welcome respite from the suburban grind. This afternoon, however, she felt anything but calm, her anxiety provoked by Heather making the other kids look like shit, Danny being late, and Harley Mason enjoying his role as a seat filler just a little too much. Even if Danny still planned on making an appearance, he was now sure to miss the introduction of the fungi, which, according to Max, included a kid dressed like one of those skinny, white enoki things that always reminded Maya of sperm.

MISSY BUTLER HIT "PLAY" on the boom box, the room filling with the opening chords of "Born to be Wild." The crowd burst into applause as Max led the charge, launching into a spastic mushroom dance that elicited enough laughs to circumvent the talent issue. It seemed odd to have Mason sitting next to her rather than her husband, and even more bizarre when he whipped out an old digital camera and started snapping pictures of Max the mushroom.

"Do you really think anyone who reads Ted's book is going to be interested in this show?" she had to ask.

"What makes you think anyone's gonna read Ted's book?"

The man had a point. It was a vanity biography. You could do a whole chapter on Ted's last colonoscopy if you felt like it. Still, it was weird to have this stranger taking pictures of her son. She tried to return her focus to Max, whose awkward gyrations seemed to make the other parents feel less self-conscious about their own kids' lack of ability.

DESPITE FEELING UNCOMFORTABLE ABOUT Mason snapping away, she was present enough to realize that the biographer was capturing a unique moment in time, that period in a young life where exuberance has yet to be obliterated by the judgment of others, before the fear of failure has set in. Goofy Max could still be himself without worrying that the act of goofiness might be perceived as a negative. Eventually, he would cross the line as everyone did, his freewheeling spirit diluted in a sea of standardized tests, compromised by the agony of peer pressure, silenced by the odd reversal of having to compete against classmates who had once been playmates.

"Would you mind you printing up some of those pictures?" Maya asked Mason.

"Just give me your email address, I'll send all of them."

The biographer detected that his suggestion of a correspondence had made her uneasy. "Or I can just give 'em to Ted," he quickly covered. "Bill him as a business expense," Mason chuckled.

THE CABBAGE AND LETTUCE now graced the stage, proceeding to rap the gastrointestinal benefits of roughage. Then Heather Carlson returned to lead the ensemble in the grand finale, "Green With Envy." Against all odds, Maya found it a moving thing to witness. Rather than appearing jealous, the other kids seemed to enjoy backing her up, somehow believing that this little girl's talent elevated theirs. Even though their parents were fiercely competitive, these children wanted no part of it, at least for this moment in time. They were all on the same team, Heather their quarterback and they, her supportive offensive line.

FROM BROCCOLI TO STRING BEAN,
WE'RE HEALTHY AND WE'RE LEAN,
CONSUME US OR BE GREEN…
…WITH ENVY.

IT HARDLY MATTERED THAT the song made no sense. The audience jumped to its feet, cheering the performers like they were Broadway stars. Watching them take their bows, Maya marveled at the priceless looks on the their faces. Her joy quickly evaporated. The minute Max took off his mushroom head and scanned the room for his father, who was nowhere to be seen, his smile disappeared into the void. *Was this it?* she wondered. Could the moment have arrived where her son, in the blink of an eye, had unwillingly advanced from the innocence of youth to misery-laden adulthood? That milestone which offered no possibility of return? Maya hoped with all her heart that it wasn't the case. She wanted Max and Dana to keep their spirits intact until the last possible moment, perhaps because she was so keenly aware of how hers had been shattered.

What Do You Want?

He had stepped on the gas to get away from the cloying tile man, never imagining that three hours later, Katie Barrett would still be sitting next to him. But each time he'd asked where she lived so he could take her home, she'd given him the wrong directions. He couldn't figure it out. What was the allure of riding shotgun in a beat-up Honda with a fucked-up married man almost twice her age?

"You think you have a monopoly on wanting to escape?" she explained. Being twenty-two didn't mean she could abide this big-box wasteland any better than he could. "For all you know, I'm a step ahead of the game for bolting now."

"They say you bring your shit with you wherever you go," he reminded her.

"That didn't stop you."

"I'm doing it for my family."

"I see. You're abandoning them out of a sense of nobility?"

"Who the fuck are you to talk to me like that?"

"Sorry, I was just trying to understand—

"Tell me where you live, or get out of the car."

"Wow, listen to you, all in control."

He was nowhere near in control and she knew that full well.

"Katie, I really don't know what you want from me."

"How about a ride?"

"To where?"

"We already discussed this, don't you remember? Puerto Vallarta."

Danny rolled his eyes. "You might have reminded me before we drove north for two hours."

"Forget why I'm here a second. You're supposed to be concerned about your family, but you leave a fifty--dollar tip for a terrible waitress you don't even know. Then, you bottom out, and who's the one person you absolutely must speak to? Hello? I'm right here. Your go-to sounding board just gave up a promising career at Applebee's to sit her ass down in your car and listen to you, and all you can think of is how to get rid of me."

"Katie—"

"Are you going to lecture me now?"

He was. "I don't want you to do anything foolish. People are going to worry that you're missing."

As soon as the words left his mouth, he knew they applied to him. "It's just—I'm the last person you should be entrusting your life to."

"My life? Dude, it's a ride. And besides, who says I trust you?"

"You're too smart to get in a car with someone sketchy."

She smiled and patted his cheek. "You're attracted to me, am I right?"

"You love throwing around that power, don't you?"

"Sometimes. But that's not what's happening now."

"What do you call it?"

"Looking at somebody beating up on himself who deserves something nice."

"I don't exactly know what you're offering and frankly, I don't want to know."

"My bad. So what's your next move?"

"The same one I tried three hours ago. Taking you home."

Suddenly, she grabbed his hand. It was as if the answer to everything had just come to her. "Let's go to Meteor Crater."

"What's that?"

"We're gonna go find out."

HE KEPT DRIVING, WHICH would have been against his better judgment if he still had any. Forty-three miles east of Flagstaff, Danny found himself paying sixteen dollars apiece for them to stare at a giant hole in the ground. According to the information packet, the hole had been formed by a fifty-four-yard nickel-iron meteorite at an impact energy of ten megatons. It was a nice enough pit, but, to his mind, didn't come close to justifying the tourist trap admission price. Katie, on the other hand, seemed thrilled to be there. She told him she'd been a geology major, who, while unable to find a job in her chosen field, still got a rush from the sight of sandstone and dolomite. She explained to Danny how the impact of the meteor created an inverted stratigraphy, so that the layers immediately exterior to the rim were stacked in reverse order. It all looked like dirt to him, yet it was a kick to see this girl excited by geology. It had been so long since he'd seen anybody excited about anything of substance, the only enthusiasm in recent memory being his father's zeal to bastardize the American landscape.

LEAVING THE CRATER, THEY were naturally directed to exit through the gift shop where, inexplicably, Danny found himself overcome by the urge to buy Katie a Meteor Crater refrigerator magnet. It seemed an absurd choice, as both of them had just fled any kind of domestic scene that might render such an item useful. Just the same, he handed the magnet to the cashier and presented it to Katie as a memento of their first, and probably last, sightseeing trip. It was gifting in the best sense because it had not been motivated by the previous intimations of sex, but by the scientific passion she had shared with him. And although it was a nothing trinket, it seemed to mean something to its recipient.

Danny was more relaxed now, and he could see that Katie was taking a certain amount of pride in having gotten him there. He held the door for her as she got back in the car. In a moment they would be driving again and one of them would pop the only question that mattered. *What now?*

Fallout

T hanks to the principal's insistence that everyone rush back to the classroom, parents nearly trampled one another getting to the stage to congratulate their kids. Harley Mason hung back and watched Maya home in on Max for a hug. It took a certain kind of woman to be dressed in mommy sweats at a school assembly and still exude world-class sexuality. Especially when her task was to explain to her kid why Daddy didn't show up. Ted Johnson's daughter-in-law was miserable in her marriage, Mason knew that much. He was also sure that she had enjoyed his company at the Phase II surf 'n turf dinner the other night, which might've made her feel guilty afterward. That would explain why she seemed so threatened by his casual offer to email her the pictures. The bottom line was that he wanted her. Was it too much to ask for one measly night? Where he could see her art (which he sensed was good) and her body (which he knew was), and celebrate the fuck out of them both? For a second, it occurred to him that banging his employer's married daughter might not be the best course of action if he wanted to continue to work and get paid. But Harley Mason didn't live the way other people lived. The secret to his success, sporadic though it might be, was that he followed his own gonzo code. Rule Number One: a great writer must submit to the random pull of the universe, whether it be the power of a fine single malt Scotch, the feel of a well-made firearm, or the scent of an irresistible woman. He knew there had to be a more sensible way to deal with such urges, but being sensible held little interest for him. The more he'd been told "you don't shit where you eat," the more it made him want to do it. One night, in the throes of a Scotch and ether binge, he had dined at Ruth's Chris Steakhouse in Dallas and finished off the evening by taking a giant crap on the same plate that had previously housed his bone-in ribeye. He just wanted to know what it felt like to literally shit where he ate. Other than being hauled away by the Dallas PD and spending a night in the slammer, he could honestly say that it felt good. Anybody could play it safe, but when had important things ever been accomplished by the head-nodders of the world?

EVEN FROM THE BACK of the room, he could see how upset little Max was. Jeannie kneeled down to talk with the boy, and that seemed to help. Mason felt odd standing by himself, observing a troubling scene into which he could offer no comfort. He headed for the exits, convinced that future contact with Maya was all but assured by the digital media sitting in his pocket. As he got into his car, the thought occurred to him that maybe he should put together some kind of slideshow. He could add music and present her with an edited DVD. Mason quickly recognized how odd it was to be bandying about such ideas. The "Fearless Shitter of Ruth's Chris" had, at least for the time being, become an awkward adolescent, angling to impress the girl he wanted to take to the prom.

"You need to change and get to class," Maya told Max.

"I want Daddy."

"He's working with Grandpa," Jeannie chimed in, her skill at making excuses for her husband effortlessly repurposed.

"Give me your phone." Max grabbed it from his mother.

"Honey, stop it. You have to get out of that costume."

"I want to talk to him." Max dialed, growing more frustrated with each unanswered ring. When his father's voicemail came on, he gave the phone back to his mother and ran off, not bothering to leave a message.

Jeannie was as perplexed as Max. "I don't get it. Ted's the fuck-up in this family, not Danny."

"Danny's had a lot on his plate. He's pretty stressed out." Maya was surprised to hear herself defending him, considering all that had gone down.

"I know things have been tough at the office. But he always shows up for the kids."

"He's been unhappy for a long time," Maya said.

"Me, too. But here I am." It was true. Jeannie was the undisputed queen of stoicism, having lived her entire adult life in the shadow of a man who made her unhappy.

Jeannie's frown quickly dissolved at the sight of Owen Shea coming over to greet them. Apparently, his daughter had played a non-speaking brussels sprout in the legume chorus.

"We could have driven over together," he told Jeannie. "Hi, Maya."

"Hey there."

"Max was terrific," he said, giving Maya the thumbs up.

"Thank you. He's no Heather Carlson." It was important to let people know she wasn't one of those moms who believed her mushroom was the next Laurence Olivier.

"That'll probably save you some therapy bills down the line," Owen smiled. "I'll see you back at the house, Jeannie."

"Sure thing."

As Owen went off to greet Brianna, Maya remarked that she had never seen his wife at school. Jeannie gave her the bullet points—how Owen had lost the love of his life, pledged to devote the future to his little girl, and built a small business that could function profitably while he focused on what mattered. The chunk taken out of him had been replaced with duty and purpose, she told Maya. Jeannie said she admired the man's resolve and hoped he would find a way to fill in the missing piece someday.

As her mother-in-law told the story, Maya couldn't help but make comparisons. Her own husband, whose spouse was still alive, albeit no longer in love with him, hadn't bothered to show up or even call. But when was the last time Danny had really shown up for anything? "Do you think it takes some sort of tragedy to have resolve?" she asked Jeannie.

"Maybe. But if there's no strength in there to start, you've got nothing to work with."

What did this say about Danny? He had brought them to Arizona with the finest of intentions—to provide for his family. But resolve? However much of the stuff he possessed seemed to dissipate with each sales meeting and Kiwanis Club roundup. Owen Shea, on the other hand, was the kind of man who faced tragedy by pulling himself up by his bootstraps and moving forward. According to Jeannie, his devotion to his daughter had taken on a maternal urgency, which he accepted as part of the package. It struck Maya that her family situation was not that dissimilar. She had felt alone for some time. If she only had a little resolve of her own, she too, might be able to cobble together a life for her broken family, not to mention herself.

AS THE DAY WORE on with no word from Danny, Maya's thoughts veered from the mundane (*What do I cook for dinner?*) to the psychotic (*If you don't call and explain to Max why you weren't there, I'm going to grind your balls to a bloody pulp.*). Too agitated to paint anything, she just wanted answers for the kids by the time she picked them up from school. When none were forthcoming, she tried to divert them from the subject by buying silly, low-tech novelty gifts to have ready in the car. Dana seemed to like her wood paddle with the ball attached by a rubber band, but Max was having no part of his Groucho mustache/glasses combo. He said he was going to be really mad at Dad when he came home for dinner. What made him think his father would be there tonight, as opposed to the last five nights? As she tried to diffuse the boy's anger, she became more agitated herself, finally announcing that all talk of Daddy's absence was officially off the table.

TWENTY MINUTES OR SO into their macaroni and cheese, the landline rang. Max looked hopeful, momentarily willing to trade rage for the comfort of knowing that his father was on his way home. He ran to the phone, and saw from the caller ID that it was Jeannie.

"Hi, Grandma. Did you talk to him?"

"Not yet, hon," Jeannie sighed. "Can I speak to your mom?"

Max handed the phone to Maya and ran upstairs leaving half his dinner, while Dana continued to pick at her macaroni.

"No calls or messages," she told her mother-in-law. "Nothing on your end?"

"No, I talked to Ted, who, apparently was on the golf course all day. He said that according to The Boys, Danny never came into the office."

"Did they know if he had meetings?"

"There wasn't anything on the books. Where else do you think he might have gone?"

"I have no idea." She really didn't. They'd been so disconnected for so long, she barely knew who he was anymore. He could be in Tokyo or New York or Maui, or, just as easily, browsing the shelves at the local library. In any scenario, Danny was continents away.

"Well, we can't panic, no matter how worried we might be," Jeannie reminded her.

"I agree." Though she would never admit it to her mother in-law, Maya was neither worried nor panicked, just fed up. It was true that something awful could have happened to Danny. For all she knew, his lifeless body was lying in a ditch somewhere, getting picked at by coyotes. Yet the only picture she saw in her head was a giant sign neon sign, flashing the words "Fuck-Up. Fuck-Up. Fuck-Up."

"Let me know if there's anything you need," Jeannie offered. "And keep me posted."

"I will." The minute Maya hung up, she knew what it was she needed and it had nothing to do with Danny. She would put the kids to bed and repair to the studio, armed with new brushes and a decent bottle of Sauvignon Blanc. Crank up Thelonious Monk, get a buzz on, go wherever the night took her. She was aware that anger plus alcohol was a crapshoot combo, equally capable of producing brilliance or stupidity. But in this case, it was no-lose. Either result would divert her from the guilt she felt, knowing that, at this moment, she didn't give a shit what might've happened to her husband.

Now What?

Fresh off the high of Meteor Crater, Danny pulled into the nearest truck stop so they could grab something to eat. After placing their order with Bobbie, a bleached-blonde waitress with pumpkin-colored nicotine stains, Katie took out her phone for the first time since their escape from Applebee's.

"You first," she told Danny.

"Me first what?"

"Tell me how many messages you have."

His phone was still in his pocket, turned off. "I don't really want to look."

Katie smiled, her theory being that their situation might not be so troubling if they could make it into some sort of game. "Here's the thing. Should we count voicemails and texts only? Or do we throw emails in the mix? I'm guessing I've got you beat either way."

"Let me get this straight. You want to make a contest out of seeing who has more people worrying about them?"

"Sure, why not?"

"Seems kind of sick."

"I say I have a minimum of three from my boyfriend, four from my parents, and two from work. Think you can top that?"

"Katie, I'm not proud to have put the people I love in this situation."

"So you concede?" She was determined to keep it light.

"If that what's you want, sure." He picked up the napkin under his silverware and waved the white flag.

"Aren't we Mr. Party Pooper?"

"I just don't get how tallying up who we've hurt is cause for celebration."

"I'm not celebrating. But I'm not crying over it, either."

"What if they're crying?"

"Everything happens for a reason."

"That's a cliché. And on the off-chance it's true, the reason they'd be crying is that you disappeared."

This didn't sit well. "Look, do I believe my boyfriend is going to be devastated by this? No, I don't. In fact, he'll probably just go and fuck my best friend, Leila, who he's been obsessed with since forever. Do I think my parents will freak out because they haven't heard from me? Sure. But maybe that's their own fault for being up my ass about finding a real job and marrying some guy because he's gonna be a doctor. Oh yeah, and they'd also like grandchildren, in case we're making a list."

Her point of view made some sense. Katie felt entitled to bail from an unsatisfying life, stifled by unfair expectations. But Danny? What gave any man permission to abandon children who loved him? Or even ones who didn't? Did a rationalization exist that could justify a father skipping town? He wasn't some kid in his twenties who'd mistakenly gotten a girl pregnant, but lacked the maturity to see it through. He had made a conscious, adult choice to become a husband and father. Now he was damaged and didn't want his children to see him this way, but there were options he could have sought to get help. Had he checked into some sort of a facility, Maya could have explained that Daddy went away for a little bit and, while awaiting his return, they could have visited him wherever he was. But Danny had never considered such a path because his descent hadn't been predicated on logic. And, from where he stood now, the cure for misery was freedom, not confinement. As reprehensible as his choice was, he finally had the space to figure things out. It was up to him how, or if, he wanted to deal with the people who were looking for him.

"Is your plan to listen to the voicemails and read the messages, or just count the number?" he asked Katie.

"Just count. But you can do whatever you want. Whoever has the biggest combined number is the winner."

"Winner?" He shook his head. "You're not going to feel the least bit bad when you see all these people worried about you?"

"I don't know how I'm gonna feel. Part of the deal with what we're doing is not knowing everything that's gonna happen. Right?"

That was an understatement. Danny was certain, however, that whatever surprises lay ahead would not be good ones.

"Turn on your phone," Katie instructed. "Check emails, voicemails, and texts from anyone you think is looking for you, count 'em, and call out the number."

Danny powered up, dreading what he would see before him. Then a thought popped into his head. What if nobody was looking for him? Wouldn't that feel even worse?

The home screen came on, indicating that he had ten voicemails, twenty-two emails and fifteen texts. After weeding out the unblocked spam and depressing Groupons, he added up Maya, Max, Dana, Jeannie, Ted, and the office, winding up with a grand total of thirty-three. Katie counted eight from her boyfriend, ten from her parents, and two from work.

"Wow!" she cried out. "You killed it."

"I'm so proud," Danny replied, the sarcasm dripping. "So what do I get for being the winner?"

"I don't know," she giggled. "A blowjob?"

That wasn't where he'd been going at all. It was true that, initially, he had been physically attracted to her, but everything changed once she became his de facto fugitive companion. This new adventure had redefined the connection, the boldness of it negating lighthearted notions such as crushes and casual sex, at least from Danny's end. It had all happened so suddenly that neither of them had an inkling of what came next, the difference being that Katie seemed empowered by their actions, while he was desperate to justify them.

She could tell from his eyes that her flirty joking hadn't landed in the slightest. Danny was lost in fear and panic. "Hey," she nudged him. "You could be sitting here by yourself. If you're unhappy, at least you have someone to talk to."

"We're going to have to call people back, you know."

"We will. Can we eat first?"

Bleached-blonde Bobbie was headed their way with grilled cheese sandwiches, and Danny hadn't had any food since last night. Perhaps some of his despondence could be attributed to low blood sugar, and he'd be able to think more clearly once there was something in his stomach. Katie dug in with the gusto of a kid, able to enjoy her food and block out whatever portentous clouds might be looming. It reminded Danny of Maya's meditation classes at Bennington, where the instructor's mantra was to be in the moment. He was always terrible at it because what truly constituted "the moment" was never clear to him. What was the essence of this moment? He wondered. Was it about biting into salty, fatty American cheese, or his first day as a deadbeat dad? Contemplating the latter made him queasy. He wished he could be consoled by the sight of Katie's beautiful, pouty lips as she brushed the toast crumbs from the side of her mouth, but instead, he pondered the inevitable tragic consequences of his actions. Guilt trumped beauty by a long shot, in the moment, or out.

HE FELT A LITTLE better after finishing his meal, even managing a smile as he watched Katie dive into a hunk of cherry pie.

"You ready to call home?" she asked.

"No." He couldn't do it. It was just too soon to get into this stuff.

"So I guess we keep driving." She seemed excited.

"And where would you like to go? Disneyland? The Washington Monument?"

"Either one. You pick."

"I guess the bigger question is, how long we do we plan on being gone?"

"And the answer is—'we don't know.'" She grabbed her phone and started texting something.

"I have some credit cards we can use for a while," he told her. "But we probably shouldn't check into a Ritz-Carlton or anything."

Katie didn't answer, face glued to the phone as her thumbs performed their digital pas de deux.

"I think I have a cousin in California who runs a marijuana farm," he suggested. "Up in Humboldt County."

"Juju and Lucky!" she cried out. "They just said we could stay with them."

THE NAMES SOUNDED TO Danny like a couple of rescues from the pound, but they were, in fact, friends of Katie's from college who had moved to Salinas, California, AKA, the "Salad Bowl of the World." Juju, neé Julie Horowitz, worked at a new age crystal and book shop in Carmel, and her boyfriend James "Lucky" Briscoe ran a training school for dogs (many of whom were rescues) out of the property they rented.

"I gotta ask—"

She cut him off, knowing where the questioning was headed. "They call him 'Lucky' because one time he was driving and a giant boulder came crashing down on his truck. The truck was totaled, but he walked away without a scratch. Pretty much his whole life has gone like that, people always telling him how lucky he is. So it just kinda stuck."

"Sounds like he's tempting fate. Still, I'd kill for that nickname." Danny recognized that a lifetime of being lucky was a lot to ask for. "Heck, I'd settle for being called 'Caught a Break'"

"Maybe this is your break," she smiled. "Maybe mine, too."

Danny nodded, not believing it for a second. He looked over in Bobbie's direction. "Check, please."

The waitress stared at them as she came forward. Danny presumed, correctly, that Bobbie had been trying to figure out Katie and his relationship from the minute they walked in. Katie appeared as if she could be eighteen, and he as old as forty-five, so the natural conclusion was father and daughter. But they looked nothing alike, and this "daughter" gave off a decidedly flirty vibe.

"I don't think she likes us," Katie whispered.

Danny grinned as he took the cash out of his wallet. "That's why you got a fifty-dollar tip and she gets four."

Wine and Roses

espite having grown accustomed to being tucked
in without seeing their father, Max and Dana
never failed to voice their protest. Tonight,
however, found them oddly quiet, all traces of
anger exiled to some secret cave in the heart. It was as if they could
sense the rumbling tectonic movement within the family and dared
not risk anything that might increase its magnitude. Even so, Maya
was relieved to see their nightly routine mitigate some of the angst and
disappointment. As for her own state of mind, while she wouldn't be
sending text messages with little smiley faces anytime soon, she felt
pretty damn solid. No matter where Danny happened to be or when he
decided to return, this family was going to survive. It suddenly dawned
on her—if she truly believed everything would be okay, didn't it mean
that the quality she'd been coveting, the one she wished Danny had been
able to acquire by this point in his life, already existed in her? On paper,
at least, it appeared that Maya Morganstern Johnson had resolve.

THE MERE POSSIBILITY OF such a revelation informed her decision to go back into the studio. She would start another painting and fantasize about presenting it to Dr. Blackstein, who would, of course, decide to snap up the entire collection. As she got her materials ready, Maya suddenly found herself wrestling with the situation: Was it reasonable for her to just go about her business without knowing the whereabouts of her husband, a man who had lost his way and whose powers of reason now seemed highly questionable? The honest answer was yes. Cold though it might seem, she had arrived at this juncture only after having done everything in her power to prop him up. If he was determined to fall into an abyss of his own making, her most important task would be to build a protective wall for herself and the children. Danny's issues, whatever they might be now, would need to be addressed by Danny, and could not be allowed to jeopardize the emotional health of his kids.

THE FIRST THING SHE did after kissing them goodnight was change clothes. Loose and free was her preferred creating mode, a reliable catalyst for getting immersed in the work and dispensing of extraneous thought or judgment. She stripped off everything, sneaking a quick peek at her respectably preserved mommy body before throwing on an old cotton dress she didn't mind ruining. Passing on the underwear, Maya realized that she would probably paint naked if she didn't have to worry about Max and Dana barging in.

She picked up a brush, only to find herself switching gears once again. What if something bad had happened to Danny? How could she be in a relaxed place, prancing around without panties, when she didn't know if the person she'd pledged to have and to hold was dead or alive? On the other hand, what, realistically, were her options? He hadn't been gone twenty-four hours. Even if she were truly frantic and decided to call the police, they'd tell her to sit tight and relax. The most positive thing would be for her to do just that, minus the sitting tight part. Once she could find some fluidity and feel relaxed enough to free associate, she would be able to release her emotions onto the canvas.

"Epistrophy," one of her favorite Monk tunes, got things started, spurring an unexpected flurry of stucco and slime. Like it or not, this was fast becoming her signature, the omnipresent green goop now oozing out of Camelback Mountain and winding its way toward a landing strip at Sky Harbor airport. She suspected that as her series progressed, the very same slime would infiltrate the Chandler Mall, one of the 8,000 Phoenix Walgreens, and Rawhide, the fake western town that seemed about as phony as Cascade Falls passing for Florida. Pausing for a sip of wine, she considered the possibility that her patented goop might be nothing more than a gimmick. What if the symbolic leap she had chosen to take was perceived as cheesy, the painterly equivalent of Rawhide Western Town? It was not beyond imagination that her inspiration might be someone else's cliché.

Maya had nothing against self-criticism, but she'd been around the block long enough to know that analyzing midpainting was, more often than not, the prelude to artistic paralysis. The creator's credo was to get the work done now, dissect later, and should the end product turn out to suck, throw it in the trash without beating yourself up. It was equally important to remember that even if ninety-nine-point-nine percent of the piece proved to be horseshit, the point-one percent could well be the spark of something new and brilliant.

An hour and a half into the process, she did not believe that her symbolism sucked. The wine didn't hurt either, the warmth of the alcohol making her feel vital and unfettered as she let the brushes fly. *If only Ray Minetta could see me now,* she thought. They had made love to Thelonious Monk in the dorm, his Volkswagen Beetle with the cassette player, and, in a fit of nerve, the men's room of the Village Vanguard. She considered sending him a Facebook message, but quickly reminded herself that he was happily married to a Celtic harp player, and she adored the Celtic harp. Then she felt guilty for even entertaining such a notion in light of the current situation. Yet she couldn't deny that she was feeling a little frisky, which always seemed to happen when art poured out of her as wine poured in. Over the years, Maya had discovered a unique relationship between creativity and sex. When she was being creative, she didn't need sex, but should it happen, she enjoyed it all the more. When she wasn't thriving creatively, having good sex proved a serviceable way to fill the void. But during those times when neither sexuality nor creativity were in the picture, she felt like a purposeless blob, whose life had been reduced to running errands, paying bills, and going grocery shopping. Tonight she was liking her work and extremely comfortable in the body she'd taken a moment to examine in the mirror. To top it off, the New Zealand Sauvignon Blanc was as smooth as anything she'd tasted in ages. And Monk's piano? That weird syncopation had more than stood the test of time. Where was the old Ray Minetta when she needed him? Or the prebroken Danny, who would do anything to please her? She reached under her dress and felt heat coming off her thighs. Venturing upward, Maya discovered that she was soaking wet. Liberation plus libation equaled lubrication, she deduced, wishing she had someone there with whom she could share her witticism. She wondered whether to dry herself, or finish what she had unwittingly started, when a loud chime signaled a text message on her phone.

IF IT WERE POSSIBLE to feel relief and dread simultaneously, this was such a convergence. She was sure the text would say that Danny was okay—obviously a good thing, but once she knew he was out of danger, she would be compelled to start interrogating him: "Where were you? Why didn't you call? When are you coming home? What if I don't want you here?" Thinking about it made her head throb, the pounding certain to get worse the longer she took to answer her husband's message. She picked up her phone to read and respond, but what she saw defied expectation. The text read: "Did you hear from him?" and the sender wasn't Danny, but Harley Mason. She felt herself becoming flush. How had the biographer gotten her phone number? Was she obligated to text back or should she just turn off her phone? Maya felt like she was back in the sixth grade, her space suddenly invaded by one of those boys she always avoided. The truth was, she hadn't avoided Harley Mason since their first encounter at the Indian Smoke Shop, when he sent her running to her car. She had enjoyed his company at Surf 'N Turf Night, and other than blanching when he asked for her email address, had a perfectly pleasant experience sitting next to him at Max's show. What she couldn't quite wrap her head around was how he had managed to text her at the exact moment she felt all tingly inside.

Maya started to type. "He hasn't called. How did you get my number?"

"Ted," he texted. "I showed him the pictures and he said I should send them."

"I don't see any attachments."

"The files are too big."

"So you just texted because you were concerned?"

"Yes."

There was a long pause. Maya had no idea what to write back. It turned out not to be a problem because Mason sent off another fast one, confirming what she already suspected.

"Could we have lunch or dinner sometime? I'd like to get your perspective on Ted."

"I don't think that's really what you want," her thumbs fired off. She immediately regretted hitting send.

"No, it's not," came the reply.

At least he admitted it. She needed a few breaths before attempting her follow-up text. What good could possibly come of meeting this guy for a meal? If all he wanted was sex, it made zero sense for her to engage. A positive response would serve little purpose other than getting the man's hopes up, so it was imperative that she nip it in the bud before things progressed any further. Finally, she typed…"I'll think about it."

"Good. You know where to reach me now."

"I do." She couldn't believe her own words. Why the fuck had she left it open-ended? How could she now say no after so clearly acknowledging the possibility of yes?

"Goodnight, Maya."

"Goodnight."

As much as she hated herself for it, she enjoyed seeing her name in his text. After all these years of feeling either neutered or harassed, she was suddenly getting a kick out of being pursued. *What would it be like to have sex with a new person?* she wondered in a generic, rather than Harley Mason-specific, way. She then thought it best to postpone such thinking until after she got into bed. For the time being, the green goop had more of metropolitan Phoenix to explore.

Drive, She Said

I t was nighttime now, the two of them having driven long
enough to be done with the pleasantries, as well as who
might be worried about them and when those people
might call the police. Katie was at the wheel, having
relieved him just after they crossed the California border. Danny's
argument had been that Humboldt County would provide a more
remote, and consequently easier, place for them to hide and regroup,
but Katie was averse to rain and the darkness of the northern woods.
Her vote was for Salinas, and, as in virtually all his dealings with the
opposite sex, she won.

They drove in silence, Katie occasionally fiddling with the radio,
happy to find anything that wasn't a right-wing talk show. Every so often,
Danny would reach into his pocket and feel his cell phone, wondering
when he would make the dreaded call. Then he began to question why
he felt so pressured about it. If he truly needed time to reevaluate, why
risk having people trace where he was? He just wanted Maya to know
he was okay so she could at least assure the kids that nothing bad had

happened to Daddy. But something bad had happened. It wasn't that he'd taken off with a twenty-two-year-old waitress, but that he'd been broken so badly that he had no other choice but to take off. Could there be anything less reassuring? Kids could understand if their dad had a bum leg, but a shattered psyche? How do you spin that fucker?

Katie wasn't dealing with this kind of baggage. She also wasn't the registered owner of the vehicle that authorities would soon be tracking.

"What was the craziest sex you ever had?" she asked out of the blue.

"Huh?" The more anxious he felt, the less things like sex entered his thoughts. Of course this wasn't about to stop her from telling her story.

"I once did two guys in the same night—not together—although I've always wanted to try that. Anyway, I had a date with one guy, public policy major, prelaw—but I didn't feel like staying over. Then, after I left, I started thinking about this other guy in environmental science. So I called him and wound up doing him for the rest of the night."

Danny looked at her askance. "Why are you telling me this?"

"It's called having a conversation. People talk to each other, you know."

"About who they fuck and for how long?"

"It's an ice-breaker, okay? Jesus, you're uptight."

"I've got to call home."

"So call."

"I can't—"

"You need privacy?"

Danny nodded. He thought he saw her eyes roll, but a second later, she was swerving over to the shoulder. Throwing the transmission in park, she ordered him out of the car. "Take as long as you need."

As Danny opened the passenger door, a ridiculous movie trope began to play in his head. He'd step out of his own vehicle, after which, the female companion he barely knew would take off into the night, leaving him alone and shivering on the side of the road. The scene had been done to death. Which meant it would probably be done again. Possibly right now.

Sure enough, the minute Danny was a few feet away, he heard the engine rev. *What was I thinking?* he silently berated himself. *How could*

I allow an Applebee's waitress to come with me? Of all the stupid choices he had made in his life, this had to go down as the all-time stupidest. He wished that he were a lot smarter, or dead. Then he saw Katie flash him a playful grin, similar to the one she employed when offering a blowjob as his reward for winning the voicemail contest. Danny smiled back.

Danny stared down at the phone, aware that thanks to auto-dial, Maya's voice was but one keystroke away. Was it really the right time to do this? It was late. She'd probably just turned off the news, and Max and Dana were deep in dreamland. He hoped to hell they weren't dreaming about their daddy. Danny felt his pulse racing, aware that the minute he touched the screen, Maya would know he had called, even if he chose to hang up at the last minute. Then again, the caller could be someone who had stolen his phone, perhaps after murdering him, and accidentally butt-dialed the victim's wife. Envisioning Maya trying to make sense out of seeing his number was only delaying what needed to happen, yet he couldn't press forward until he was prepared for what he might hear on the other end.

Calling

"You were great in the show," Owen told Brianna as he tucked her in.

"I didn't do anything. I just sat there."

"That's kind of what a Brussels sprout does, honey. Sits there on the plate next to the other, you know, sprouts."

"But broccoli moves around?" she shot back.

The girl cut right through the bullshit. When had his little girl acquired such a developed sense of sarcasm? "Of course it doesn't move on its own," he vamped, "but the stalks sort of look like trees, blowing in the breeze and all."

She wasn't buying any of it, suddenly getting quiet. "You think Mom would've liked the show?"

"Oh yeah. She would have loved it. She loved everything you did."

"I know." Brianna turned to the picture on her nightstand, the one where she was safely nested on her mother's lap. "How come she thought I was so great?"

"Because you are." Owen felt his eyes start to water. Able to count on one hand the number of times he had cried in the first forty-five years of his life, he now wept at the slightest provocation, ferociously so at anything having to do with Lucy. What made him saddest was the thought of Brianna having to go through adolescence without her. Every girl deserved to have a mother, and Owen, hard as he tried, considered himself a feeble substitute.

"I wish I could be little again," Brianna said.

His yearning to go back in time was as strong as hers, but he knew it would be counterproductive to reveal such a thing. "If you stayed little, you'd never get to go to college or drive a car...or get married."

"But she wouldn't be dead."

"I know." He kissed her on the forehead, then on each cheek. "I love you, Monkey." He tucked her in as fast as he could, before the tears burst out of his eye sockets. Quickly turning off the lights, he cried as he sprinted out of the room. Upon reaching the hallway, he felt the phone vibrating in his pocket. It turned out to be Candy Daniels, Lucy's hard-bodied friend, who, despite his unflagging lack of interest, was still on the prowl. Whether it was a moment of weakness or the primal need to speak to someone who wasn't feeling his pain, he decided to pick up.

"Hi, Candy." He tried to sound enthusiastic, but didn't quite get there, critiquing his own affect as, at least, not annoyed.

She was still her perky self. "Just wanted to give a shout and see how you and Brianna were doing."

"I appreciate that. We're good."

"I'm so glad."

"I mean, not that good, but we're hanging in—"

"Of course. Nobody in your situation would be jumping up and down—"

"Unless they were jumping off a building," he chuckled, immediately regretting his dark response.

"You sure you're all right?"

"I am, Candy."

"'Cause if you ever want to talk—"

"Okay." It surprised him how quickly it came out. He did want to talk, just not particularly to her. He knew what he wanted from Candy, and opening the door brought a combination of relief and shame.

"When's good for you to get together?" she asked, the lilt in her voice telling him she'd come over right now if he wanted her to.

"How about a week from Saturday, assuming I can line up a sitter? Dinner at Vitale's maybe?"

"Sounds great."

"Unless you hear otherwise, I'll pick you up at seven."

"It'll be wonderful to see you." The woman was flat-out cooing.

"I can't vouch for what kind of company I'll be."

"No pressure. It's just dinner."

"I guess I can do that. See you then."

He felt like he needed a shower. One minute he was crying over his wife, the next he was conspiring to have sex with one of her friends. He had long anticipated that whoever volunteered to be the first partner since his becoming a widower would be in for a night of raw, animal-like acrobatics. Owen needed his virgin, post-Lucy encounter to be 180 degrees from the caring and tenderness he had felt toward his wife. A good, hard fuck couldn't be mistaken for love, so that was what needed to happen. As he thought about what Candy's expectations of him might be, the phone rang again. Perhaps she'd had a change of heart, though he couldn't imagine it from the eager tone of her voice.

Looking at the caller ID, he saw it was Jeannie Johnson. A *little late for her to be phoning,* he thought, *but perhaps she wanted to reschedule his crew for tomorrow.*

"Hey, Jeannie." He realized that he sounded far more animated than when he answered Candy's call.

"I'm sorry to bother you."

"No trouble. Everything okay?"

"I don't know. I'm worried about Danny."

"Your son? What's wrong?"

"Well, you saw that he didn't show up at the kids' play today. He never called, and nobody's heard from him since."

"And that's not like him?"

"Not at all. It feels strange."

"Do you want me to look for him?"

"Where would you start?"

"Any friends he might be with? Places he hangs out after work?"

"Not that I know of. Neither does Maya."

"That's a tough one."

"I guess it's probably a little early to get alarmed," she reasoned.

"Probably. But still, you're right to be concerned. If he doesn't show up by tomorrow, I'd call the police."

"We will. I just needed to, I don't know, talk to someone."

"I understand." It occurred to him that in one way or another, everybody was reaching out, and while it might appear to be voluntary, it wasn't. People all seemed to be on the verge of something—detonating maybe. Perhaps these attempts at connecting were a last ditch effort before a cluster of internal bombs went off.

MAYA FLOPPED DOWN ON the king bed, her senses reeling with what she had accomplished in just a few hours. Regardless of what Judith Aronson and Jay Blackstein thought of her new collection, pieces of art had appeared where none existed before. She had discussed that feeling of exhilaration with Harley Mason the other night at Surf 'N Turf, Mason mentioning that he'd had the identical conversation with Chuck Close. Her thoughts reverted back to the biographer and his intentions. It was so strange. Most of the time when men came on to her, she found it either laughable or disgusting, and she had experienced both upon meeting this guy. But now that she felt flattered, she realized that she also felt aroused. Maya touched her leg, which seemed to shoot up ten degrees for each inch her fingers traveled north. She allowed herself to continue exploring, things progressing so quickly that she was already coming when the phone rang, moments later.

DANNY WOULDN'T BLAME HER if she didn't pick up. What kind of father is a no-show for his kid's play, then disappears without a trace? Perhaps Maya would listen to the voicemail, learn he was okay, and wait a few days before giving him the satisfaction of a return call. Or maybe she wouldn't call back at all. Then he found another reason to panic—if she didn't pick up, what would he say in his message? Leaving a voicemail was tricky because every word would be dissected for meaning that wasn't there. It had to be short and sweet, something like, "Everything's fine, I'm away for a bit, I'll call you soon." The only problem was that he was a mess, he hadn't a clue as to how long he'd be away, and it had taken every ounce of emotional strength just to dial.

"Hi," Maya answered flatly after the fourth ring.

"Hey."

"And?" She wasn't about to ease him into the conversation with bullshit.

"I'm okay."

"Nice of you to let us know. Is that it?"

"Look—I know you're mad. You have every right to be."

"Me being mad is the least of it."

"I'm sorry—"

"I hope so. You have two very worried children who don't understand who the fuck their father is anymore."

If only I knew, Danny thought. "Look, I just need some time."

"Time for what?"

"I have to decide what I want to do with my life."

Maya felt herself starting to seethe. "Maybe it's just me, but aren't you supposed to figure that out before you have kids?" As angry as she was at Danny, she became angry at herself for saying it. The truth was, he had figured it out. He wanted to be a writer, but stoically gave up that dream for a bigger one—having children with Maya Morganstern, the love of his life.

"I tried my best, Maya."

It was true. He had done everything he could to support them, but collapsed under the weight of living a life he hated. Maya imagined there were probably lots of people like that, even though men were expected take a job in a coal mine if they had to, cheerfully contracting black lung just to put food on the table for the wife and kids. As irritated as she was with him, she didn't feel her husband deserved whatever constituted the emotional equivalent of black lung.

"I'm sorry," he whispered.

"I know. Me, too. What do you want me to do?"

"Reassure everybody. Tell them I'm on a little sabbatical."

"Okay." Her voice got quieter. "Who's going to reassure me?"

He wished he had an answer. He couldn't make up anything because she knew him so well that she'd see through whatever he invented. "Maya—" was all he could manage.

"Yes?"

"I love you." He waited through a pause that seemed eternal, hoping to hear an echo. Everybody who loved anybody wanted to be loved back.

"Danny, I—"

She was about to say it, he was sure, now picturing what she would look like as the words came out of her mouth.

"—I want to know that these kids won't be damaged by whatever is going on here."

Suddenly, he was like a bicycle tire that had run into a nail so big, it got punctured all the way through. It took him a few moments to respond. "I think they'd be more damaged by me being there. At least for now."

There was some truth in that, she had to admit. And young kids seemed to be able to bounce back from just about anything. Plus, she had the whole resolve thing going on. "So, do you have a plan?" Maya asked, if only because it seemed like the right thing to say.

"Remember your meditation teacher at college, Krishna something or other?"

"Debbie Krishnamurti?"

"Yeah. I want to try taking her advice. Be in the moment."

"Debbie's in jail for insider trading."

"Jesus Christ. Is there anyone who hasn't been corrupted?" Suddenly, he looked over and saw Katie in the car, her head bouncing up and down to whatever country tune was on the radio. Perhaps that one still had a chance.

"What about Ted?" Maya had to ask. "Are you going to call to let him know why you stopped going to work?"

"I can't. Not yet."

"So I'm supposed to do it for you?"

"Just say you talked to me and I needed to take some time off."

Maya hated that Danny was laying this on her, but also understood that having to explain himself to Ted would be as demoralizing as his first soul-crushing decision—to capitulate and become his father's employee.

"Done," Maya agreed. She would speak to Jeannie, too. Even though Danny was probably capable of making that call, it wouldn't help his mother to hear the despair in his voice.

"Thank you." Danny was grateful, and also aware that there was nothing else for him to say until he acquired new experiences that might provide some answers.

On some level Maya understood that. "I'll speak to you...whenever, I guess."

"I'll try not to make it too long."

"Okay."

"Tell the kids I love them."

"Of course." She would do that for him, even if it meant having to see their conflicted faces as they asked the essential question, be it spoken or not. *If he loves us, why isn't he here?*

"Bye," Danny said, hanging up just as she said her own goodbye.

MAYA TOOK A MOMENT to process what had transpired, a conversation she never could have imagined having with the man she married. She had just volunteered to be the spokesperson for his disappearance out of empathy for his anguish. And yet, despite knowing how much he wanted to hear it, she had refused him the comfort of saying, "I love you too." At the moment she didn't, at least in the way she was supposed to. The father of her children had become like a brother to her, a former roommate toward whom she felt no ill will, but also no desire. She wanted him to work through his pain, but at the same time, wasn't about to demand that he return home immediately. Danny needed to progress at his own pace, and she was ready to put in whatever extra effort it took to pump up the children. She would find a way to combat their sadness with enthusiasm, and this, in turn, would propel her forward.

Forward

The station playing "God Bless America" by Kid Rock and the Mormon Tabernacle Choir was Katie's cue to shut off the radio. She saw Danny returning to the car with tears in his eyes, the kind of tears she knew she had yet to earn, but would soon enough.

"You okay?" she asked, obviously aware he wasn't.

Danny had no words for her. He was shaking.

Finally, she took him in her arms and held him tightly, as if trying to squeeze the hurt out. "Don't worry," she said. "Be happy."

He broke away, looking at her like she was some kind of insane moron. Then he realized she was joking. He laughed. She laughed back. Katie Barrett might only be twenty-two, but she was smart enough to know that the world didn't exist in black and white, and that sometimes the grays got pretty fucking dark.

KATIE SEEMED TO ENJOY being behind the wheel, and while she took the curves a little too casually for Danny's tastes, she was competent enough for him to feel comfortable nodding out every now and then. He couldn't recall the last time he had driven anywhere through the night, but remembered that strange, heady feeling of existing separate from the real world. At three in the morning you were hurtling into the pitch black, a starship in motion, bound for some unimaginably important destination in the cosmos. Then the sun would come up, and you'd find yourself pulling into a 7-Eleven for a pee.

In between catnaps, Danny glanced over at Katie's young face, wondering what she might be thinking. Every so often he'd ask, and she'd tell him how close they were to Salinas, or how great it was going to be to see Lucky and Juju again. According to her description, they were the kind of positive, non-judgmental people she needed in her life right now, and she was pretty sure Danny could use a dose of the same.

"I believe you that they're nonjudgmental, but still, they've got to react to their friend showing up with this grizzled old geezer who's not her uncle."

"You're not old."

He felt old. Still, it was kind of her to disagree.

"That's why you're on this little adventure," she reminded him. "To get those negative thoughts out of your head."

"Negative thoughts be gone!" he shouted, like that flaming Baptist preacher he used to watch on TV, the one who instantly restored people's hearing by screaming in their ears "Deafness be gone!"

"Feeling old be gone!" she chimed in.

"Everything gonna be all right tonight!"

"Amen, Reverend Johnson!"

She was certainly game, especially when it came to making something fun that had no right to be.

"Tell it, Miss Katie!"

"I left my job! Walked out on my boyfriend! My parents don't know where I am! I'm a bad girl!"

"And you want salvation, do you?"

"Sure. But not if it means becoming a good girl who's dull and bored and has no reason to get up in the morning."

"That's a tough one, sister. I'd have an easier time healing you if you were blind."

Katie burst out laughing.

"Wouldn't it be awesome if life really worked that way?" she postulated. "You go to some church, tell them your problem, and poof, it disappears? 'Excuse me, Reverend, but I have stage four ovarian cancer.' 'No problem, Miss Katie. Stage four Ovarian cancer be gone!'"

Danny agreed it would be really cool if it were that easy. "What about the people who seek out those guys?" he wondered. "What do you think it takes to have that kind of belief? I mean, if we just say 'stupidity,' isn't that a complete rejection of faith?"

"And you don't reject it?"

"I don't want to. I wish I could believe in something that doesn't make sense, or isn't proven by a thousand scientists. Maybe if I did, something extraordinary would happen to me."

"Did you ever think that it might be happening to you?"

"If abandoning my family is extraordinary—" He felt tears welling up again. "Do you have faith, Katie?"

"I do."

"In what?"

"This."

Danny saw she was looking right into his eyes.

"Where we are right now and wherever the fuck we're going. No roadmap for the future, all in for the ride."

He managed a non-committal nod.

"So what are you?" she asked. "Like half-in, maybe?"

"A little more than half. Less than three quarters."

"So maybe an eleven-sixteenths kind of thing?"

"Yeah. Exactly. I'm eleven-sixteenths in."

THEY REACHED THE HILLS of Central California around the same time the sun did.

By dawn, Danny was driving again, Katie working her iPhone's navigation as he tried to picture what kind of home might be inhabited by people named Juju and Lucky. Both sides of the road seemed to be nothing but commercial farmland, ranches, or a combination of the two. Katie said Salinas had a downtown that was mostly poor and Hispanic, which was the reason Juju commuted to a new age shop in Carmel. It stood to reason. This was fieldworker country, home to the descendants of the Joads, the sons and daughters of Chavez. They would naturally opt for a new pair of shoes over a crystal wand. As for the man of the house, Lucky needed space for his dog training business, which was why they lived outside of town. Just how far out was unclear, as Danny and Katie found themselves winding through dusty dirt roads boasting little in the way of housing, much less the Ted Johnson-proclaimed American birthright—amenities.

"I think we're almost there," Katie shouted.

"How can you tell?"

"Lucky texted me. That boulder we just passed was a landmark. Now we take the third right."

"At that Walmart over there?" Danny joked. He was struck by how they had traveled all this way to arrive at nothing in the middle of nowhere.

"You had plenty of Walmarts where you came from, mister. And if I wanted to find myself looking at another Applebee's, I never would've left the first one."

The girl had a point. Plus, this out of the way location would give them what he had sought from Humboldt County—breathing room to figure things out without fear of being hunted down. As far as lodging went, he was curious as to what their little piece of nowhere was going to look like. Per her instructions, he made the third right.

"He said you'll see a bunch of houses coming up."

"Obviously he uses the term loosely," Danny responded, eyeing a bunch of dilapidated shacks on their left.

"Once again. If you'd like to go back, just drop me off and be on your way."

"That wasn't my point. I was just—"

Suddenly he couldn't hear himself talk. The car was surrounded by six or seven barking, snarling pit bulls.

"Now there's something you don't see in Cascade Falls," she shouted.

It was true. Most of the dogs in the Johnson Communities were of the foo-foo poodle or rat-dog Chihuahua variety, as if certain standards of dog ownership had been part of the Ted Johnson Master Plan. "You think that one has rabies?" Danny asked, pointing out the foam dripping from the mangy, brown-and-white dog's mouth.

"I don't think he liked that comment." The dog was now leaping up and scratching the passenger side window.

Just as Katie started to scream, a burly dude around her age, with long, blond hair and a bushy, red beard, ran out, snapped his fingers, and uttered a firm "No." Seconds later, every dog was on the ground, still and cowering, looking to the their master for marching orders. The dude ignored them and walked over to the car, smiling warmly at Katie.

"Sorry about that, darlin'. You can roll down the window now."

She did, and smiled back. "Hey."

"Hey." He gave her a kiss.

A little too close to the lips, for Danny's tastes, but who was he to judge?

"Long time, Katie."

"I know. I missed you guys. This is my friend, Danny."

"Pleasure to meet you, sir. Lucky Briscoe." Lucky extended his arm across Katie to display one of the firmest handshakes Danny had experienced since his move to the Southwest. Which was saying a lot, given the monster shit-kicker demographic.

"Good to meet you, too. And you can lose the 'sir' thing."

"He doesn't want to be perceived as old," Katie clarified.

Lucky nodded. "Age is just a number. It's about how old you feel."

"And I feel old." Danny pulled the car up the drive as Lucky told him to, arriving in front of a structure that looked like a succession of glorified outhouses that had been glued together.

"Suitcases?" Lucky asked.

Danny popped the trunk, and Lucky removed the small bag. Danny then realized that Katie had willfully boarded this train without clean underwear or a toothbrush.

"Maybe Juju has a few things I could borrow?" she asked.

"Of course. Whatever you guys need. We're happy to have you as long as you want to stay. We don't get a lot of visitors."

As they entered the all-purpose living room/kitchen/bedroom/kennel, Danny understood why. There was only one dog crate in the room, but a pungent canine order permeated the place.

"There's a guest bed in the back for you. Close to the bathroom. Make yourselves comfortable."

"Is Juju at work?" Katie asked.

"Yeah, she left early for the shop. They're putting together their Winter Solstice clearance sale. Forty percent off all chakra sticks, FYI."

"Good to know," Danny replied, proceeding to check out what would be his quarters for at least one night. He followed Katie into a room that was roughly the size of his closet at home. A double mattress had been squeezed in between two walls, a small crate with a cat in it serving as the nightstand.

"Are you okay with this?" Danny asked.

"You said we shouldn't be staying in Ritz-Carltons."

"I mean…you know," he nodded politely.

"Being in the same bed? No problem. Sleeping isn't fucking."

"Women are always cooler about that. I forget." Plus, she seemed to be cool with fucking if that was what he wanted. The woman who had no interest in that particular activity was the one with whom he'd been sharing a bed for almost twenty years. And on the rare night when she did seek it out, he refused to give her the satisfaction of calling the shots. None of it made sense.

"Where do you think the bathroom is?" Katie asked.

Danny looked out the window and noticed what appeared to be an outdoor shower with no curtain, across from which rested a toilet and sink, with only a low-hanging laurel tree for privacy. "Not exactly a Phase II floor plan," he chuckled, pointing out the facilities.

"I'm gonna jump in the shower. Think you could get me a towel?" She peeled off her shirt, seemingly as comfortable in the buff as she was in her new rustic surroundings.

"Sure thing." Danny went off to find Lucky Briscoe. It sounded like a name right out of Damon Runyon, yet somehow he couldn't imagine Nathan Detroit living in the Salad Bowl of the World with a bunch of pit bulls. He couldn't imagine Danny Johnson living there either, but that was a matter for another day.

Ted Preoccupied

It was widely known in subdivision circles that Phase III offered the flagship golf experience of the Johnson Communities. To wit, The Boys were flummoxed as to why Ted had insisted on inviting Tarkanian Homes President Norman Lutz to the Phase II course. While all the Johnson fairways tended to be earth tones, as Ted euphemistically referred to them ("Anybody can do green" was the mantra), Phase III was both logical in design and well-maintained. Phase II, on the other hand, seemed like the neglected stepchild, its fairways hardened and cracked, its greens covered with so much sand they were nearly unplayable with a putter. Piles of nasty trash made a permanent home on the fourth tee, catty-corner to the Christmas gnomes on Dorothy Miller's patio. Adding to the mix, sewage runoff from the clubhouse collected along the bunkers of the ninth hole, assaulting one's nasal passages so fully that one could smell nothing else for holes ten through eighteen. James and Dusty's only explanation for Ted's rationale was that he must have gotten wind of their plan and brought Norman Lutz to the sucky course in order to dissuade him from trying to buy out Johnson Homes.

Luckily, Lutz's enthusiasm wasn't deterred by having to stomp on his tee to lodge it in the soil. "Another beautiful day in paradise," he crowed, inhaling the 104-degree-dairy-farm air. "You know, you kinda get used to that cow shit bouquet."

James smiled, channeling his boss. "It reminds us of a simpler time in America."

"When you can smell an animal, it makes you a better man," Dusty chimed in, quoting a Ted Johnson Masonic Lodge lecture from 2004.

Normally, Ted would use these remarks as a jumping-off point from which to expound on the glory of the Johnson lifestyle: all the perks of luxury in an environment of humility, fostering an upscale mindset with middle-American values. To Ted's way of thinking, the Phase II course encapsulated this concept. It wasn't showy, but it got the job done.

IF GETTING THE JOB done meant four hours of nonsensical doglegs, overgrown crabgrass, and an ammonium nitrate high, one might agree with him. None of these annoyances came as a surprise to the rest of the foursome, but one peculiarity did manage to take them aback: Ted's complete lack of boisterousness. Through the first six holes, the stucco kingpin was eerily quiet. Contemplative, it seemed. Odd behavior from a twenty-four-seven sales machine who viewed contemplation as a scourge comparable to men talking about their feelings. He was amiable enough, agreeing to play two-dollar skins rather than his usual five because he knew The Boys were strapped for cash. As far as the game went, his drives were north of adequate, and although he had yet to birdie through six holes, he'd parred all but one.

Ted was well aware that Lutz was a much better golfer, so it made sense that he wasn't fazed knowing the Tarkanian president was already three under by the seventh hole. Traditionally this would be Ted Johnson's cue to seize the moment and get in his rival's head, the preferred tactic being to mutter some negative spin on Tarkanian's earnings report for the previous quarter. Ted was a master of this ploy, able to succinctly pinpoint the one dark cloud in a competitor's two-for-one stock split.

For the time being, however, psyching out the frontrunner seemed to hold no interest for him.

"Very pretty," he complimented Lutz on his 260-yard drive off the eighth tee.

"Thanks," Lutz replied, thrown by Ted's lack of spitefulness. Maybe this was his crafty new plan of attack. Shock the competition by acting like a human being. Two can play that game, Lutz thought to himself. "Hey, how's Jeannie? Any exciting trips planned?"

"I don't know," Ted answered. He honestly didn't, but the Ted people knew would have made up some flashy globetrotting excursion just to enhance his aura of pizazz.

Lutz threw The Boys a *What the fuck is going on here?* look.

Dusty, who had made an avocation of dissecting Ted's idiosyncrasies, told James that perhaps the boss was starting to get a whiff of reality— that contemplation might be his way of processing the imminent end of the real estate dynasty that had defined him.

"I don't think that's it," James countered, certain that Ted's delusions of grandeur weren't about to sail off into the sunset anytime soon.

THEY MANAGED TO MAKE it through the first nine holes without a single utterance of the word "amenities," a previously unimaginable occurrence in a Ted Johnson golf outing. Ted remained deferential and polite, asking Lutz about his family without the usual sniggering reference to Lutz's twenty-four-year-old daughter Brandy, the stripper. The boss's respectful behavior struck the others as major cause for alarm.

At the tenth hole, which abutted a Taco Bell, Ted asked James and Dusty if they'd heard from Danny. Both assumed the younger Johnson was probably back in the office this morning, but Ted informed them that Danny hadn't come home last night, and that no one in the family had heard from him.

"I hope it wasn't something I did," Ted murmured.

This would go on record as the first time James had ever heard his boss murmur, except for dramatic effect at sales presentations. More significantly, it was the only instance he could recall in which Ted had suggested he might be culpable for anything.

"You gave your boy a great career was my understanding." Lutz slapped Ted on the back, going on to birdie hole ten.

"It's a wonderful business we're in," Ted replied, "and the Johnson family considers itself fortunate to be of service."

"I know Danny appreciates that," Dusty assured Ted.

"Have you checked your messages?" James asked. "Maybe he's texted you."

Ted pulled his phone out of his pocket. There were three texts: one from Barb at the office, telling him the utility bills were three months past due, another from Harley Mason, confirming that he would be meeting Ted's barber to discuss the Johnson Empire from a hairstylist's point of view, and a third from Kim Lee, informing him that he still hadn't gotten a roofing answer out of Danny. "Christ that tile guy's pushy!" Ted blurted out. "I should never have saddled my son with a born-again Chinaman."

"He's not Chinese," James reminded him.

"He's a pain in the ass is all."

BY THE FOURTEENTH HOLE, Norman Lutz was six strokes ahead of Dusty, who seemed to have a firm grasp on the number two spot. Ted's game had gone so far south it could have been in Ensenada, his thoughts now occupied with whether or not he had alienated his only son, as he had his only daughter so many years ago. Pondering the big picture of one's life wasn't very good for one's golf, and being new to the concept of pondering didn't help either. Ted had always insisted that questioning the universe was for other people: that Dalai Lama fellow in his cave, Woody Allen and his city of Jews…Ted Johnson was about moving forward, charging headfirst into the future and literally breaking new ground. As he had once told the Knights of Columbus after a few too many whiskey sours, "A person doesn't create a great civilization of subdivisions by worrying if he should have said: 'Let's have a dialogue' instead of 'Tough shit, I'm doing this.'" Nevertheless, he bit the bullet and pored over his history with his son. He couldn't, for the life of him, recall being anything but positive and encouraging, especially when it came to Danny joining the fold.

SOMEWHERE AROUND THE SIXTEENTH hole, Norman Lutz let it be known that Tarkanian was in the process of acquiring Gold Coast Developers, a struggling tract home builder in Kansas.

"Where the fuck in Kansas is there a gold coast?" Ted wanted to know.

"Where are there 'Cascade Falls' in Phoenix?" Lutz shot back with a laugh.

Ted failed to find the humor in this. "Johnson Homes doesn't claim to have created a fucking ocean. We simply acknowledge God's gift of irrigation, and use it to our best advantage."

This sounded a lot more like the Ted they knew.

"The point I'm trying to make," Lutz explained, "is that we've made other companies some pretty nice offers. Of course these are companies that were open to change—"

"What are you trying to say, Norman?" Ted locked eyes with his fellow pillager.

"I'm just putting it out there, friend. I know you're a proud guy."

"I don't really like what you're insinuating."

"That we're friends? Or that that you're proud of your outstanding achievements?"

"The implication was that I'm too proud to see that I shouldn't be proud anymore."

Ted Johnson might be grandiose, he might envision himself a suburban spiritual icon, but he damn well knew a sniff-around when he met one, especially the patronizing kind.

"I didn't mean to bend your nose out of joint," Lutz told him.

"And believe me, you didn't. It would take a lot more than an outfit specializing in C-grade amenities to put a dent in this schnozzola."

There it was. The A-word in all its glory. TJ was back, which signaled to James and Dusty that they were most likely doomed. The dream of a company sold and lives salvaged was slipping out of their collective grasp. And Norman Lutz had just wasted five hours of his valuable time playing a horrendous course with average golfers for chump change. The only upside—he'd been spared the reminder that his daughter once offered Ted a private lap dance. The rest of the round played out in silence, Lutz parring the eighteenth hole after Ted's triple bogey. The stone-faced Tarkanian president then proceeded to collect his cash and walk off, declining Dusty's offer to buy a round at the nineteenth hole. It was just as well, because today happened to be a particularly busy sewage day.

Hold My Calls

S torming his way into Johnson Homes Central, Ted's expression frightened the crap out of Barb McDermott. In her long tenure as executive secretary, she'd only seen this look once before, that time the DNA test confirmed he had a love child on the Indian reservation. Barb deemed it prudent not to ask if another rugrat had been added to his collection, opting instead to employ the first lesson she had learned from the man himself: Always open with good news. Putting forth the biggest smile she could muster, she announced: "*Mamma Mia!* is coming to the Chandler Arts Center!"

"What the fuck is *Mamma Mia!?*" Ted snarled.

"It's this wonderful show about—"

"Hold my calls." Ted slammed the door to his office, as uninterested in a theatrical revue of ABBA songs as he was ignorant of it.

Barb saw James and Dusty coming through the door. Surely they would appreciate such valuable information. "Guess what's coming to town? It involves a wedding, a Greek island, and all my favorite songs."

Dusty just stared at her. "You think I'm gonna spend a dime on *Mamma* fuckin' *Mia!?* This whole company's going in the shitter."

James added that, if he had to hear "Dancing Queen" one more time, he would commit a hate crime against some random Scandinavian, assuming he could find one in the state of Arizona.

"So much for the good news. What in the Lord's name happened on that golf course? How bad did Ted lose?"

"Losing wasn't the problem," James told her. "You may want to sit down for this one."

She got back in her chair slowly, preparing herself for the worst. "I'm listening."

"First off, for practically the entire eighteen holes, Ted Johnson was nice and polite."

Rightfully, Barb was stunned. "To Norman Lutz? That's impossible. The only thing he hates more than Tarkanian Homes is the Democratic Party. And maybe pho."

The other disturbing thing, Dusty explained, was that when Ted finally woke up and became his combative self, he infuriated Lutz to the point where the Tarkanian president swore he'd washed his hands of all things Johnson. "We needed that guy. He could've pulled us out of the slump."

Barb had seen a bad omen of her own and she wasn't about to sugarcoat it. "I hate to say this, but Ted had that look on him when he walked in."

"The DNA look?" asked James.

"The one and only. He went into his office and slammed the door. Thankfully, he's got a ton of calls to return. Some good bullshitting on the phone always puts him in a better place."

They glanced over at Barb's console and saw that none of the lines were lit up.

"Probably on the throne," Barb wagered. "He says that's where he does his best thinking."

Dusty wasn't much of a praying man, but he could still wish for stuff. "Let's hope to hell he takes one enlightening crap."

Ted sat at his desk, staring out the window at the other buildings in the business park. They were so close to identical that he had once parked in front of the wrong cluster and mistakenly entered the Arizona headquarters of Bimbo Mexican Bakeries. He loved to tell the story of how he had walked into the office that mirrored his own and was mistaken for the President and CEO of Bimbo. The fact that he was so intimately familiar with the local bimbo population made the story that much funnier to him. Today, however, Ted wasn't laughing. He was hard-pressed to remember having a less enjoyable time on a golf course. Not that he ever particularly liked being around Norman Lutz, but golfing with his loyal lieutenants always lifted his spirits. Except this time. What was the problem? Yes, he was thinking about Danny, but why should that bug him so much? He'd given his son the opportunity of a lifetime. If the boy wanted to flake out, it was on him. The father had done everything right.

IT OCCURRED TO HIM that a follow-up call to Plano might be just the thing. A little time to digest the deal, followed by some Ted Johnson prodding, was usually all it took for investors to come to Jesus, and a yes from Plano would be sure to get his adrenaline going again. On the off chance they were still teetering, his charm would, at the very least, begin to chip away at their resistance, setting the table for him to close the fucker on the next call. He reminded himself that no matter what transpired in the conversation, he'd be no worse off than he was now.

Ted donned his headset in anticipation of Barb getting Steve Summers on the line. Summers always required extra "smoozing," as Ted liked to call it, and the wireless ear thingies gave him the ability to multi-task, should he need to take a crap or what have you. He got comfortable in his big, leather chair, put his feet up on the desk, and prepared to buzz the most loyal executive secretary to ever come down the pike. Then, just as he was about to push the button, he removed the headset and threw it on the sofa. He just didn't have it in him to proselytize right now. Everyone was entitled to take a little break from selling. Why not Ted Johnson? Having never indulged in such a thing before, he found the impulse disconcerting.

HE CONSIDERED BROWSING THROUGH the little black book, which he used primarily for black women because it struck him as a fun concept. (The other races mingled freely in the brown leather volume that sat beside it in the safe.) He felt like he needed a little encouragement, and there were a few ladies in those pages who were particularly adept at bolstering his ego. According to Ted, none of the women had anything to do with his marriage, which he maintained was actually stronger because his sexual needs were being met. One drunken night, James and Dusty had asked him how he'd feel if Jeannie demanded the same sort of freedom. Ted told them he'd be totally cool with it, later admitting that the answer came so easily because he couldn't imagine Jeannie ever wanting such a thing. Then he wondered if maybe he really would be cool with it. Bibles and Commandments aside, how was anybody supposed to have one partner for forty or fifty years and not get bored? "I don't think it's possible," he told them.

TED HOMED IN ON Stephanie, a full-figured gal of mixed race whom he affectionately liked to call "My Octaroon." Whether she was really an eighth black or a quarter, he wasn't sure, but he chose the nickname because it reminded him of those sweet coconut cookies he got every Passover from the Feinsteins in Phase II. If there was anything sweeter than burying his troubles in Stephanie's haunches, he sure as hell hadn't found it. As he got up to extract the secret cell phone from the safe, Barb suddenly buzzed him over the intercom.

"I thought I said hold my calls."

"It's Maya. She said you'd want to take this."

Not bothering to acknowledge Barb, Ted swiftly picked up Line 1. "Talk to me. Is everything okay?"

Maya proceeded to lay it all out for her father-in-law. Danny was under a lot of pressure and needed time away. The sabbatical was nothing he'd planned, but the stress had become so unbearable that there was no other choice but to get some distance. He promised to check in on a regular basis so everybody in the family would know he was okay.

Ted sat in silence, incredulous that his daughter seemed satisfied with her husband's lame excuses. Finally he had to ask: "That's it?"

"Look, I'm not saying what he did was right...but sometimes people need to recharge. For their own mental health."

"I don't buy that at all. I just took a one minute break from selling and I feel worse than I did before."

"Danny isn't you."

"You're damn right, he isn't." Ted was fuming, but forced himself to dial it down. Maya wasn't the one who needed a slap on the wrist. "I'm just flabbergasted is all."

"This has been coming on for a long time," she tried to explain.

"Is that so? How come he never said anything?"

"Psychological instability is not something you go out and announce. I honestly don't think Danny's been himself since we moved to Arizona."

That was all Ted needed to hear. He spoke softly, but deliberately into the receiver. "Maya, the next time you speak to my son, would you tell him something for me?"

"I'm sure your support would mean the world to him."

"That's too bad, because I'm all maxed out in that area. But do let him know that in my day, when a man felt stressed, he didn't run away like a baby. Nobody even thought to use the word stress. We went to work, got a paycheck, supported our families. We didn't have the luxury of being mentally ill."

"You think mental illness is a luxury?"

"Not in the amenity sense of the word, of course not. But taking care of your own isn't a choice. I don't give a flying fuck what your problem is, you don't just pick up and leave your flesh and blood."

"I know he feels horrible about it."

"I'm not exactly jumping for joy myself. Wait till his mother hears this."

"I already spoke with Jeannie. Obviously, she's not happy. But she's not disowning him either."

"Lemme ask you something, Maya. What about you? The mother of his two children is fine with this kind of behavior?"

"Of course I'm not fine. But I want him to get better. He was miserable here."

"Which I take personally, by the way. So where the hell did he go?"

"He wouldn't say."

Ted felt a vein ready to burst. "Are you fucking shitting me? Not only did he run away like a weenie, he's hiding?"

"He needs some space so he can sort things out."

"Space my ass. I'm gonna call my PI friend on the rez. We'll have him tracked in twenty-four hours."

"Please don't do that."

"Jesus Christ, Maya. He's too fucking old for this 'figuring out your life' shit. What's he gonna do, join the circus?"

Maya didn't want to say what she knew to be the truth. That, for Danny, working at Johnson Homes was the circus, which was exactly what he was running away from. "Please, Ted. Can we just give him a little time?"

"How he could do that to those beautiful little kids is beyond me."

"I don't think any of us is in a position to judge other peoples' track records as parents."

Her pointed response appeared to go completely over his head. "You're a lot kinder than I would be, is all I can say."

"This isn't about kindness. It's about making the best choice we can, given his state of mind."

Ted sighed, having heard enough of this nonsense. "Listen, not to worry. I'm going to deposit some funds in your account."

"Thank you, Ted. I appreciate it."

"You're welcome. Bye-bye."

MAYA WASN'T SUPPOSED TO know it, but Ted had been making these deposits for some time because Danny's income barely covered their expenses. The day Danny broke down and admitted as much, she could see how much it pained him to take his father's charity. He wished there was something else he could do to make more money, but neither of them could figure out what that would be, at least in the short term. A new career might require years of training, so wasn't it more practical just to get better at this one? The truth was, getting better at it wouldn't have done any good because the real estate bubble burst less than a year after their move to Phoenix.

She found herself feeling sorry for Ted. He viewed himself as a person who had triumphed over adversity and was capable of fixing anything, but watching his own son ditch his job and his family? This was new territory for him. It was new for Maya as well, but at least she'd seen it coming. For all of Ted's faults, Maya had to acknowledge that, deep down, his devotion to family was steadfast and pure. The man could fuck a thousand different women, but he wouldn't willingly leave Jeannie for any of them. In his own twisted, self-absorbed way, Ted Johnson wanted to do right by everybody. It didn't matter whether his empire was thriving or on the brink of collapse, he was CEO of the family and the buck stopped with him.

Salinas

Katie was fast asleep on the dog hair-covered mattress, having segued from outdoor shower to afternoon nap without a hitch. Danny continued to be awed by how effortlessly the girl embraced the unknown, diving headfirst into cleanse and rejuvenate mode so she could begin her new adventure fresh. As for his own addled state, he was still carrying around dust and grime from the road, not to mention guilt from the bigger mess he'd left behind in Phoenix. He wondered if a nice, long shower might lift his spirits. He decided it would and summarily nixed the idea. His reasoning: What gave him the right to feel better when he had made everyone else so miserable? He knew this was self-defeating logic. Danny would never stand a chance of cleaning up his mess unless he found a way to feel better about himself.

Despite this realization, he passed on the shower, choosing instead to pick through the ratty paperbacks on Juju and Lucky's brick-and-board bookcase. It made total sense that Lucky was a huge Cesar Millan fan, and the Rumi collection seemed perfectly in keeping with a person who called herself Juju. The other volumes, however, were more curious, appearing to be straight from the library of past Juju and Lucky archetypes. *On the Road, Desolation Angels,* and the poems of Gregory Corso suggested a Lucky of the fifties and early sixties, while the faded brown pages of *Our Bodies, Ourselves* conjured up images of earth mother Juju cavorting in the mud at Woodstock. Filling out the shelves were the complete works of Richard Brautigan, *Beautiful Losers* by Leonard Cohen, and *Been Down So Long it Looks Like Up to Me* by Richard Farina, the Bob Dylan rival who died in a motorcycle accident in 1966 at the age of twenty-nine.

DANNY FOUND IT IMPRESSIVE that these modern day New-Agers seemed to have a sense of their bohemian ancestry. Based on the reading material, they were obviously aware that the Beats begat the hippies who then begat the new age dog trainers and crystal heads. What was more, Juju and Lucky's books seemed to imply that they had researched how they wanted to live and the kind of the people they wanted to be, adding their own modern spin to the canon as they went along. To Danny, the notion of anybody in this day and age being able to live an authentic life was nothing short of miraculous. Maybe these two had actually found a way to pull it off.

It hadn't taken long for him to start playing the comparison game. Why hadn't he been able to engage the world on his own terms and make it work? He had spoken to Lucky for maybe two minutes and hadn't even met Juju, yet he had turned the twenty-something couple into instant heroes, elevating them to a perch so lofty it had no basis in reality. Danny hadn't stopped to consider that they were young and probably naïve, preferring to contrast their commendable choices with his own pathetic ones. Plus, he wasn't of sound enough mind to realize that the achievements of others were always magnified when viewed through the prism of low self-esteem.

"WANNA GO FOR A ride?" The cheerful, booming voice of Lucky Briscoe was beckoning him to hop in the van with him and the dogs for the afternoon run. "We hike up in the hills for a while, let these guys work off their adrenaline, then get back in time for dinner. Sound good?"

It sounded as good as anything Danny might come up with, especially since all he could think of at the moment was how he had been eclipsed in life by people fifteen years younger. "Sure—I mean, if you think the pit bulls are good with a stranger coming along—"

"Fuck yeah. That whole pit bull stigma is bullshit. They're really sweet dogs. It's the people that screw 'em up."

Danny couldn't help but think about the brown-and-white one who was snarling at him in the car. It seemed like that dog had already been screwed up by people, which logically might have the effect of making him dangerous to new people. On the other hand, Danny was in the company of Lucky Briscoe, his new hero. How could he go wrong?

LUCKY OPENED THE BACK of his beat-up Dodge and the pack frantically leaped in, a boxer and pit mix butting heads as they jockeyed for position. Once all the dogs were in, they seemed to calm down instantly, curling up against each other to begin their daily afternoon commute.

"How long've you been doing this?" Danny asked his dog-whispering host.

"Two-and-a-half-years. Left college early when I figured out what I wanted to do with my life."

"Looks like you enjoy it."

"Who wouldn't? I'm outside with a bunch of great animals, and at the end of the day, I know I've accomplished something."

"Not everybody can say that about their work, I can tell you that."

"I guess there are a lot of shit jobs out there."

"I know it firsthand."

"What do you do for a living, sir?"

Danny threw him a look.

"Sorry. What do you do for a living, bro?"

Danny smiled. "Ever hear of Johnson Homes? Cascade Falls?"

"Yeah. That place outside of Phoenix that smells like a dairy farm. My grandma lives around there."

"I worked there for almost four years. My dad developed all those subdivisions."

"Geez. I'm sorry to hear that." Tongue-tied after receiving this information, Lucky figured his best bet would be to change the subject. "Well, at least you got yourself a good woman."

"Oh, no. Katie and I aren't together."

"No need to be defensive about it. Juju and I are totally cool with people being different ages and shit."

"No, really. It's not like that. I needed to leave town, and it turned out she was looking for a ride."

"Well, she's a good girl. And she deserves a good man."

"Which is one of the many reasons we're not together," Danny told him.

"You seem like a good guy to me. Just a little too hung up on how many birthdays you've had."

"That's actually the least of my problems." He saw Lucky looking at his wedding ring. "Yeah, I'm married. It's complicated. Like the stupid Facebook thing."

Lucky had no idea what Danny was talking about. It turned out that he had never used Facebook and avoided computers at all costs. He explained that he and Juju had made a conscious decision to read print books, write real letters on actual paper, and whenever possible, communicate with each other in complete sentences rather than BRB and LOL-style text messages. He went on to express concern over Danny's marital difficulties, guessing that since he was still wearing the ring, he couldn't have left of his own volition. "When did she throw you out?"

"She didn't. But she should have. I mean, I didn't cheat or anything—"

"Then what?"

"She could have done a whole lot better is all."

Lucky shook his head. "Man, if you shit on yourself anymore it's gonna start landing on me—so cut it out, you hear?"

Before Danny could apologize, Lucky had parked the van and was headed to the rear door to release the beasts, who were up and ready to be sprung. The trainer explained that the hills were browner than usual, due to the paucity of rainfall over this particular summer. If the dogs gave a shit, they didn't let on, bolting into the beyond, seemingly without regard for how far they were going or if they would ever come back. Danny mentioned this to Lucky, who just laughed. Of course they would come back because he was the alpha dog, in command of the whole shebang. With dogs, as in most of life, it was all about setting ground rules and establishing hierarchy.

"Once I accepted this concept, things really changed for me," Lucky explained. "Setting ground rules worked with just about everything—except women. They are creatures unto themselves."

Danny laughed, but it pained him to think about what rules he might have invented, or followed, for that matter, in order to make it work with Maya.

"Juju does what Juju does. Part of what makes her so special," Lucky offered.

"I'm looking forward to meeting her," Danny told him, half out of politeness, the other half wanting to put the face with the name, as well as the books he had just thumbed through. All he could picture was one of those zaftig hippie chicks with long, dark curls that cascaded down over huge, braless breasts. She would cook up a vegetarian feast, spiced with curry and served over couscous, after which she'd luxuriate on the floor pillows while Lucky did the dishes. Perhaps she'd take out the bong and introduce them to a strain of marijuana so strong it would make him forget his troubles. Maybe she would want everyone to get naked. How would he respond to that request? He supposed that, if he were stoned enough, anything was possible.

DANNY LOOKED UP AND saw Lucky running with the pack, doing his alpha dog thing. If he turned left, they turned left. If he stopped, they stopped, waiting for their next instruction. Lucky signaled Danny to come join them. He decided to dive in, much as Katie had done the minute she opened the door to his car in the Applebee's parking lot. By the time he reached the group, all except Lucky were frozen in the down/stay position. In an unexpected surge of spontaneity, Danny dropped to the same position as the dogs, confident that it would not only elicit a laugh from Lucky, but show that underneath all the angst, Danny Johnson had a loosey-goosey side. Much to his surprise, the dogs became agitated, some starting to whimper, others growling. Then, as if Danny were one of the pack, Lucky ordered him back to standing position, explaining that you never want to get down on the same level as the dogs because it makes them perceive you as weak. Danny stood up, digesting the irony that his game attempt at joining the party had resulted in yet one more opportunity to expose his ineffectuality.

DESPITE HIS MISSTEP, AS the afternoon wore on, Danny felt the anxiety diminishing, his brain unclogging as a result of the running and breathing air that wasn't a choking 108 degrees. The more vigorous the exercise, the more the dogs seemed to thrive on it, until they were finally spent and breathless from their workout. Danny began to see why Lucky liked his job so much. Sure, it was the same thing day in and day out, but spending a couple of hours on ground that had yet to be taken captive by people in golf pants seemed like a damn healthy way to live. Lucky pointed out some of the local wildlife, as well as the flowers that flourished in spite of the drought-like conditions. There was something sublime about spotting a family of deer while sniffing a bunch of freshly picked mustard. By the time Lucky was ready to load up the pack, Danny felt his neurons firing again, his body looking forward to a shower and hungry for dinner. For better or worse, he had landed in the moment. Now, if he could only scare up the tenacity to hang there a while, he might have a chance of turning things around.

THEY WERE A GOOD quarter-mile from the house, but Danny could already smell whatever home-cooked specialty Juju was whipping up. He now pictured her in one of those sixties peasant blouses, her breasts bouncing freely with every stir of sauce and each sip of Cabernet.

"I'm guessing coq au vin, green beans, and corn bread," Lucky announced, as he sniffed the air. Apparently they were mostly vegetarian, but occasionally treated themselves to chicken as long as it was free-range and raised locally. Lucky explained that Juju bartered chickens for crystals with a like-minded couple in the Monterey area.

The outing having energized his brain, the aromas coming from the kitchen now delighting his senses, Danny was inclined to up his assessment of Juju and Lucky from heroes to saviors. While it seemed over the top to ascribe such power to a couple of twenty-three-year-olds, his thinking was that if these two could continue to inspire him, they might be able to be able to save him. Thomas Edison had maintained that genius was one percent inspiration and ninety-nine percent perspiration, but Danny knew that without the one percent, you were nothing. Any life worth living required inspiration, and Danny needed to reclaim that worth.

AFTER SECURING THE DOGS in the kennel area, the men made their way toward the food. Danny was as excited as he was famished, eagerly anticipating the woman he'd pictured frolicking naked in hippie water. He was not disappointed. Juju greeted him with a warm smile and a hug. She was, indeed, long-haired, large-breasted, and slightly zaftig, as he had imagined. But rather than being a brunette, Juju was a striking redhead with tiny freckles and piercing blue eyes.

"Welcome, Danny."

"Thank you for having us."

"Hey, it's not every man who could get this one to run away with him," she winked, looking over at Katie.

Katie said nothing, laughing a bit too flirtatiously for Danny's liking.

"Apparently, her only criteria are that the guy have a full tank of gas and be really screwed up," Danny clarified.

Juju patted him on the back, put a glass of red wine in his hand, and went over to give Lucky a kiss. "Good day, babe?"

"Excellent," Lucky replied, holding up the goblet Juju had placed before him. "To my new hiking buddy, Danny, and his beautiful lady."

Katie giggled again. Danny had to wonder if this was all some kind of game to her. As a person who appeared to blend seamlessly into any environment, perhaps she was prepared to be his lady if that's what others expected of her. But why was Lucky encouraging this? Hadn't Danny flat-out told him that they weren't an item? Danny wondered if, for all their new age bohemianism, Juju and Lucky were one of those couples who felt safer being with another couple, rather than with two unique individuals. Individuality sometimes threatened people who functioned in pairs, propelling them to seek out clones of themselves for validation. Danny remembered how he and Maya had gone through their couples phase, and then graduated to their friends with kids phase. Now they were in their unable to be around each other phase, which would be the final one, unless things changed dramatically. He started thinking about Max and Dana. What were they having for dinner? What was their day like? Did they have any fun, or had his disappearance put a damper on everything? He then asked himself if it wasn't completely egotistical to believe that his absence could color the whole of their experience.

THANKFULLY, JUST AS HIS brain began to twist back into a pretzel, Juju called them to the table, putting a piping-hot platter of coq au vin in the center. She explained that she used chicken, even though the French traditionally cooked the dish with rooster, or cock, if one wanted to be literal.

"You have something against cock?" Katie asked, always at the ready to veer the conversation toward sex.

"I love cock," Juju replied, matter-of-factly. "Just not for cooking. It's tough."

"Hard in the bedroom, good, hard in the kitchen, bad," Katie felt compelled to add.

"Brown rice pilaf?" Lucky held up the bowl and passed it around.

Danny was grateful for the interjection, relieved to have the conversation switch to something not involving sex or his and Katie's presumed relationship. He helped himself to the steamed broccoli, and a piece of chicken so tender his fork cut through it like butter. "Amazing," he told Juju. "This is best meal I've had in I don't know how long."

"Don't you cook?" Juju asked Katie.

"Not really." Katie seemed to enjoy the ruse, failing to mention that even if she did cook, Danny would never have tasted her food because she lived with her parents and he had a wife. He was about to reiterate the facts he had laid out earlier for Lucky, but was enjoying his chicken too much to make the effort. Thankfully, the conversation drifted first to politics (Juju and Lucky had no use for either party), then religion (Buddhism for Lucky, Haitian vodou for Juju), and finally, the subject of having children. Juju and Lucky both wanted them, probably with each other, Katie was on the fence, and Danny found himself in the position of explaining what it was like to actually raise the little rugrats—not that he should be held up as any kind of role model. He ventured that there was no greater challenge than being entrusted with the shaping of another human life, and no greater fear than the prospect of fucking it up. It surprised him that he was able to talk with such candor, but he could see that his honesty struck a chord with his host and hostess. Juju and Lucky might be young, but they wanted to talk about important things and learn whatever they could from anyone who knew more than they did. They didn't have a TV and rarely went to the movies, gleaning most of their knowledge from books they bought or took out from the local library.

Whether or not this couple would live up to the description of saviors, Danny found their approach to life rejuvenating. Just knowing that there were human beings out there who were determined to make their own choices and mold their own futures was nothing short of a revelation.

AFTER A DESSERT OF homemade apple pie with açaí berry tea, they cleared the table, after which Lucky offered up a home-rolled nightcap. *The perfect coda to the perfect evening*, Danny thought. He didn't have to drive anywhere, and obviously he didn't have to go to work in the morning, so why not partake of some kick-ass sensimilla, or whatever it was the young'uns were smoking in Salinas? By the second hit, he was feeling no pain, stretched out on the floor pillows along with his new, young friends. Juju told him and Katie how glad she was that they had come to stay, and made a point of singling out Danny's wisdom and intelligence. Danny wasn't sure whether it was the pot talking, but Juju seemed pretty flirty herself, albeit more nurturer than hot-bodied ex-Applebee's waitress. Either way, it was an unanticipated joy to be in a place that welcomed him wholeheartedly, with people who thought the things he said were worth hearing. For the first time in as long as he could remember, he felt like he had done something right, and that maybe he had a shot of turning things around.

LUCKY AND JUJU BROKE out their vintage vinyl collection, proceeding to sing along to *Workingman's Dead* and *American Beauty*. Somehow Danny and Katie had managed to time-travel back to the sixties, and it wasn't a bad place to be—at least for him. He had to wonder what Katie made of the whole thing. If the retro hippie lifestyle was somewhat alien to a fortysomething father of two, what must it look like to someone who had been born in the early nineties and spent her whole life in redneck Maricopa County? Danny looked over and saw Katie, eyes closed, grinning from ear to ear, as she listened to her friends belt out "Sugar Magnolia."

After the song ended, Juju sat up and straddled Lucky's lap. She then initiated a long, deep kiss, surely the promise of things to come. Moments later, the couple announced that it was bedtime, Juju giving them both generous hugs before heading off to put the finishing touches on the evening. Lucky hugged them, too, and Danny thanked them both for their hospitality. "Maybe I can come out with you and the dogs again tomorrow?" he felt courageous enough to ask.

"Anytime, my friend." Lucky smiled and went off to join his bedmate, leaving Danny and Katie to negotiate what came next for them.

"You think Juju's sexy, don't you?" Katie asked.

"She's pretty," Danny acknowledged. "And really nice."

"Those boobs. Oh, my God. Are they fantastic or what?"

"They're good," Danny nodded.

"Good? Please. You couldn't stop staring at them."

"What are you talking about? I wasn't staring."

"I mean, I'm not blaming you. You'd have to be blind or a masochist to avoid them."

"I think I'm ready to go to sleep." Danny yawned, making a solid effort to move things along.

Katie wasn't ready to switch it up. "It's not only that she's gotta be like a double D, it's that they look so damn good on her, right?"

"They…fit nicely with rest of her body."

"What about mine? Do they fit?" Katie pulled up her T-shirt and snapped off her bra, revealing breasts that, while smaller than Juju's, were not only full, but the most beautiful Danny had ever seen.

"Jesus Christ. Look, Katie, you're kind of high right now. I don't think it's really the time for a boob-off."

"Boob-off. I like that."

Danny knew that if he didn't put an end to it immediately, he might start it up for real. "I'm going to sleep. Goodnight." He went off to the bedroom, leaving her with the impression that he had no interest in her perfect body, a body he would have readily devoured were he just a touch more fucked up.

HE WENT TO BED fully clothed so as not to make sex any easier for her should she choose to pursue it further. He spent the time before her entrance from the bathroom half-trying to fall asleep, half-formulating a plan for rejecting her possible advances without insulting her. It seemed like a good twenty minutes before Katie raised the covers and slipped in, totally naked and radiating a heat so overpowering that it left him speechless. He felt as if her energy was reaching out to him, making it available on whatever level felt right. Even if he wasn't ready to sign on for adulterous sex, she seemed to be offering the prospect of comfort and healing. He instinctively opened his arms and drew her to him, her flesh and smell enveloping him with a warmth that shot straight through to his bones. It had been so long since had held or hugged anyone beside his kids. This body was not only adult-sized, but intuitive enough to know exactly what he needed at the moment. Katie didn't ask why he was still dressed or try to alter that state. She just held him close, and he, her.

AFTER A WHILE, HE started thinking about Maya, and how proud he was that he wouldn't allow himself to betray her, despite formidable odds. Satisfaction proved fleeting as he realized that he had betrayed her, not by bailing and coming here with Katie, but by failing to deliver on the promise that he would give her a good life. His thoughts then drifted to Max and Dana, and how confused they must be. *They don't deserve this*, he thought. *I don't deserve them.*

HE LOOKED OVER AT Katie and saw that she was asleep in his arms. How was it possible that this young, gorgeous, slightly-geeky goddess felt so comfortable with him? Weighing her physical perfection against the depth of his own failure was a combustible mix, making him want to simultaneously cry out with joy and yelp in pain. He managed to bottle up both urges, but then found himself unable to stop the tears that started streaming down his face. He suddenly felt a strange yet potent urge to let his tears fall on Katie and see what would happen. He had been around her long enough to sense that it probably wouldn't freak her out, but you never knew. As the floodgates opened, Danny reminded himself of everyone he had let down, and how none of them had deserved it. Soon, a torrent of drops began to land on Katie's cheek and neck. He could see that she felt the wetness, but wasn't wiping anything away.

"Let it all out," she whispered, reaching up to touch his eyelids. "You're not a bad guy, Danny Johnson. Everything's going to be okay."

Date Night

He'd spent the better part of the afternoon at Jeannie's, laying copper pipe, and consoling her over the situation with her son. Danny had been gone for almost two weeks now, and while he'd been communicating with Maya, there was no sign that he intended to return anytime soon. Sometimes a man had to disengage in order to see things more clearly, Owen explained, just as he had after Lucy's death. When Jeannie pointed out that Owen didn't run away, leaving an innocent child to absorb the fallout, he reminded her that in this case, there was another parent. And from what he had witnessed firsthand at the kids' school, a competent parent, who seemed more than qualified to take up the slack in Danny's absence.

"Maya's a strong one," Jeannie acknowledged, going on to say that her daughter-in-law was the kind of woman who could have any man she wanted, yet also had the ability to thrive on her own. "I wish I could say the same for me."

"You keep yourself pretty busy," Owen replied, knowing that it would be hard for anyone to feel confident and independent while married to Ted Johnson.

"You're exactly right," Jeannie said. "I keep myself busy as an avoidance tactic. It's so ironic. I mean, why on earth did I hire you to do all these things?"

"Maybe because I know what I'm doing?"

"Of course you do. That's not the point. I hired you to make things more structurally sound, but I'm working on the wrong structure. I can redo this house 'till I'm blue in the face, but it won't fix what's really broken."

"Jeannie, you're going through some difficult stuff right now—'

"Everything's falling apart. You making improvements on this stupid house is just one more distraction."

Owen got it completely. "Do you want me to stop?"

"God, no," she suddenly laughed, telling him his words sounded like lines from a bad romance novel. "If you stopped showing up, who the hell would I talk to?"

"I've got to be honest. This is the first time I've ever been hired for my conversational skills."

"Embrace it. It'll help prepare you for when you're ready to date again. We women do like to talk, you know."

OWEN HADN'T PLANNED ON filling her in, partly because it was his nature to keep his own counsel, more so because he was embarrassed that the plans he'd made for the evening had been based purely on his hunger for sex. Of course he wouldn't have to mention that aspect of the date, but men like Owen had a way of revealing the truth on their faces, no matter what they chose to withhold. All it took was a woman of intelligence to figure it out, and Jeannie had that in spades.

He decided that it didn't make any sense to keep secrets from her. "Um, you know, after I'm done here, I have, uh, a date," he mumbled.

Somehow he'd managed to mangle his words so completely that Jeannie thought he'd said something about the gate, which, along with the entire pool fence, was rusted and in need of refurbishing.

"No. A date. As in I'm going out with a woman."

This news filled her with joy, almost as if she, herself, had been released from marital prison to test the waters anew. "I am so happy for you, Owen." She hugged him, pleased that perhaps she had played a small role in encouraging him to reacquaint himself with the opposite sex.

"It's nothing, really," he told her. "Just dinner."

"It's not nothing. It's a good man who deserves a night out with a very lucky woman." She kissed him on the forehead.

Owen contemplated telling her the whole story, how he had avoided Candy Daniels since Lucy's death, finally acquiescing to her invitations out of pure horniness. But he could see that Jeannie was playing out a sweeping, epic love story in her head and he didn't want to spoil it for her. Here he was, dreading an evening of uncomfortable small talk, but Jeannie had him starring in the Maricopa County remake of *A Man and a Woman*. Her long-lost memory of romance had taken her to a fantasyland where a suffering widower miraculously finds true love again, right under his nose.

By the time he got home, Flora was already there, on the floor, playing a board game with Brianna. They appeared to be having a great time, so much so that his daughter barely noticed his presence. Owen looked down and saw that they were playing The Game of Life. He'd had this version since he was a boy, but hadn't gone near it since he started playing the game of life for real, losing one too many times for his liking. He excused himself to get ready for the evening, feeling the familiar, and in this context ridiculous, butterflies of adolescence. It was amazing how that came right back, just like riding a bicycle. Would the rest of the evening unfold in equally recognizable patterns? And if it did, would that be uplifting or depressing? He really had no idea at this point.

Having sold Lucy's car shortly after she passed, Owen felt a little strange having to pick up a grown woman in his Ford Ranger. He supposed that if he were still eighteen, arriving in a big, macho truck would be a turn-on to a certain type of girl. It was surely less impressive to be showing up at forty-five in the same vehicle one used to haul grout and toilets. As it turned out, Candy didn't seem to mind at all, which actually made him feel even worse. In her undaunted pursuit of him, the woman had been agreeable about everything. It was okay that he hadn't returned calls, or acknowledged her Christmas card, or even confirmed her as a Facebook friend. Who on earth could be that agreeable? Lucy was never that way, even when they'd first started dating. It seemed like his most successful relationships had been with fierce, independent women who had something to say and weren't afraid to let you know when they didn't see things your way.

He had to admit that Candy looked very pretty, and appreciated how she'd transformed a vehicle that smelled like Sonic Burger wrappers to a four-by-four spring meadow. She had a nice smile, too, and it didn't seem phony. He'd first noticed it when she asked him in for a drink before they headed to dinner. He declined, saying it would be cutting it a little close on their reservation, the truth being that sitting in her house felt like too intimate a starting point. She was agreeable, of course, as she continued to be when he told her he preferred to sit inside, rather than on Vitale's patio. He didn't mention that the patio had been Lucy's favorite and that he wanted to reserve that space for his memories.

As the date began to unfold, it struck Owen that so much of it was an exercise in marking time: the setting down of water glasses, the drink orders, hearing the specials, choosing a wine.

"Red or white?"

"Either's fine."

"Cabernet or Pinot? Maybe we should get a Pinot since you're having fish."

"I can just get a glass of white—it's no trouble."

And on it would go until that moment where two people finally looked each other in the eye and had to answer the question: "Who is this person sitting across the table?" Regardless of whether a date was defined by small talk, deep conversation, or hot sex, there always existed that one telling nanosecond in which the judgment call was made, where one concluded if it was or wasn't working.

"Business has finally started to pick up for me," Candy informed him. "What about for you?"

"No complaints." Owen couldn't think of any, except for the fact that he had forgotten what it was Candy did for living, assuming he had ever even known.

"My first quarter was a bear, but little by little, people are starting to spend again."

"And what exactly is it they're buying?" was what he wanted to say, but bit his tongue, hoping the details would emerge organically.

They didn't, but Candy quickly switched off the work talk and charged headfirst into the personal, grilling him with a few perfunctory questions about Brianna before launching into the history of her divorce.

"Ron was not easy," she told Owen, who instinctively had zero interest in the Story of Ron. If Candy read this in his expression, she wasn't letting on, explaining that her ex was a big executive at an even bigger consulting firm that specialized in taking over and revitalizing ailing corporations. "Sure he was brilliant, but the man wouldn't know a real emotion if it sat on his face." According to Candy, Ron was also cheap, passive-aggressive, and an alcoholic, the latter having claimed the remainder of his already-flagging sex drive. The only positive was that they had never had children together, attributable, of course, to a drunk's pathetic sperm count.

Every time Owen wondered how close they were to the moment where their eyes would finally meet, he felt his glazing over. Random thoughts began to enter his head, like the rusted fencing at Jeannie's house, and how he needed to finish reading *The War at the End of the World*. They were midway through their entrées when Candy finally concluded the diatribe on her failed marriage, for which she evidently accepted no responsibility. Owen was pessimistic about whatever was going to happen next, having felt his own sex drive start to go the way of Ron's without the perk of a vodka buzz. Figuring he was at least forty-five minutes from asking for the check without appearing rude, he thought it worth a shot to go into salvage mode, firing off a cliché that might make her feel better about past mistakes.

"Hey, the good news is, you're still young. You've got your whole life ahead of you."

She nodded in agreement. "A lot of men want to date me."

"Why wouldn't they?"

"You didn't."

Suddenly she wasn't so agreeable. "Candy, you know what I've been dealing with. You can't be offended."

"I'm not offended. I just that—I don't reach out to everybody, you know."

"I'm flattered. I really am. I just wasn't ready."

Suddenly she softened, taking his hand. "I'm glad you're ready now."

The moment had arrived. She was looking into eyes, and unless all his receptors had suddenly gone haywire, the message was that once the check came, she expected him to take her home and fuck the shit out of her. Returning her gaze, he felt only distance and emptiness. Why couldn't he just be flattered and enjoy the offer? Was his disinterest rooted in guilt over betraying Lucy? Or himself? Was it simply that he didn't want to hurt Candy, or did he just plain not like her? He wondered what happened to all the testosterone that had spent years building up inside him, the stuff that had been bursting at the seams, demanding an audience. Perhaps, once Candy's clothes came off, desire would again emerge from the shadows and he'd be able to perform as planned. At the very least, it would be a warm body, something that had been absent from his life for too long.

Candy segued from patting his hand to stroking the individual fingers, as if each was a penis unto itself, from which she would extract five separate ejaculations. As Owen wondered if Candy had been sex-deprived as well, or whether she was just obsessed, the hostess wandered over to ask how they were enjoying their meals.

Normally he would just say "Everything's great" and send the hospitality person on her way, but in this instance, he needed a diversion. "Do I taste tarragon in the chicken?" he asked, completely uninterested in whether or not this was the case, "I know there's rosemary, but I could swear I detected a hint of tarragon."

"I actually don't know," the hostess admitted. "We do grow all our own herbs, so the flavors are very distinct."

"I could tell they were fresh."

"Would you like me to ask the chef?"

"Oh, yes. Please."

"I'll be right back," she smiled.

Candy was naturally confused as to why her dinner date had directed the talk to tarragon as opposed to what she was laying on the table. "I didn't know you were interested in cooking."

"When you're a single parent, you've got to have options," he replied, knowing any mention of children would cool the sexual temperature in a hurry.

Understandably perplexed, Candy turned her attention back to a meal she would have preferred not to finish. Owen picked at the remainder of his chicken, noticing that a couple at the bar was starting to attract attention from the other patrons. The bartender was pouring Glenlivet for a boisterous, somewhat disheveled man, who seemed to be pontificating about something Owen identified as sports-related. Upon closer listening, it appeared that he was dissing one of the Arizona State teams, firing up the men around him. Owen couldn't see the face of the martini-sipping woman next to him, but even without a full frontal, he could tell that she was too beautiful for this guy. *The guy's got money,* Owen thought. *Everything is available when wealth comes into the picture.*

CANDY SAW OWEN EYEING the couple in the center of the brewing fracas. She suggested that unless he wanted dessert, it might behoove them to get out before there was a scene. Owen agreed, after which the banter coming from the bar got louder. The restaurant owner sprung into action, telling the couple that their patio table was ready, and that he would gladly escort them to it. Following a few choice profanities directed at the ASU fans, the man and his companion followed the owner. As they headed in the direction of Owen and Candy's table, Owen saw that the woman was even more stunning from the front. A split second later, he realized that he knew her. The couple was about to move past them when he spoke up.

"Maya?"

"Oh. Owen. Hey, how're you doing?" She seemed extremely uncomfortable, which made perfect sense since she appeared to be out on a date, two weeks after her husband had abandoned the family.

"I'm good. This is my friend, Candy."

"Nice to meet you. This is Harley Mason, my father-in-law's biographer. He wants to talk to me about what it was like, you know, being Ted Johnson's daughter-in-law."

"Hey," Mason grunted, barely looking them.

This was a business meeting? It seemed all wrong to Owen. Granted, the man needed details for his book, but he couldn't imagine that most authors solicited such things on a Saturday night over Glenlivets and martinis. And why, in God's name, was Maya all dolled up for this hobo? He wondered if Jeannie knew about the meeting. He doubted it, certain that it wouldn't sit well with her at all.

"It was nice seeing you," Maya smiled awkwardly. Mason tugged at her arm to guide her out to the patio.

"She's pretty," Candy noted. "I had no idea Ted's daughter-in-law was such a looker."

Owen had certainly thought Maya attractive the numerous times they had run into one another, but never realized that she was a flat-out beauty. Taking this in, along with the circumstances under which he had just encountered her, seemed to shake his equilibrium. What was going on in this crazy fucking county? He had lost his wife, Jeannie was in a miserable marriage, Maya's husband disappeared, and now, two weeks later, she's on a work date with some loudmouthed writer. Owen couldn't make sense of any of it.

"It is tarragon," the chipper hostess returned to announce.

Owen had no idea what she was talking about, now lost in trying to connect a Cascade Falls jigsaw puzzle for which none of the pieces seemed to fit.

"Check, please?" Candy finally had to ask.

Owen craned his neck so he could see out to the patio, and observed Maya smiling at something the writer had just said. Even though it was none of his business, and his credo had always been to not get involved in others' affairs, this one bothered the shit out of him. Suddenly, his passive emptiness had been replaced by something dark and driven. As if dropped from the sky, his testosterone was back and open for business. He would take Candy home and do everything she wanted. And more. As they left the restaurant and headed for the shopping center parking lot, he drew her to him, his kisses deep and hard. "Sneak preview," he whispered in her ear.

THE MINUTE THEY GOT in the truck, it became clear that she was ready for the main attraction, and determined to be the star of the first scene. Candy unzipped his jeans and began going down on him as people walked past to pick up their Walgreen's prescriptions. While she proved excellent at the task, Owen was still distracted enough to be checking out the folks in the parking lot. Ironically, he found himself waving to Pastor Higgins from Phase II at the same moment that he was about to blow his load. "Praise the Lord!" he shouted, killing two birds with one stone.

HAVING MADE A RELATIVELY smooth transition from brown liquor to Cabernet, Harley Mason now sat on Vitale's patio, imploring Maya to hop in his Jeep and accompany him to the desert, where he would instruct her in the art and craft of handgun usage. He was inclined to put her into a Glock 19, but conceded that you could never go wrong with a .38 Special. Maya listened in disbelief, wondering what made this man think she'd be interested in such an invitation, as well as when he might deign to mention her father-in-law, if only to pay lip service to the premise of taking her out.

"Why is it so important to you that I have a gun?" she asked.

"You're going need it for your protection. Especially with your old man MIA." He downed his glass of wine like it was a shot, then lifted her arm. "This hand is so beautiful. Imagine what it's gonna look like wrapped around cold steel."

Maya could see it in his eyes. Somehow the image of her wielding a firearm was getting him off.

"You seem to have a thing for women and guns," she said.

"Nothing hotter," he affirmed. "A man hasn't really had sex until he's done it with a barrel to his head, you know what I'm saying?"

"I do, and yet, I find it very disturbing."

"Think about it, Maya. The dude's got no choice but to give it his best."

"Harley, do you want to talk to me about Ted?"

"Sure. That's why we're here, right?"

"I don't think it's why you're here, but irrespective of that, you do have a contract."

"Understood. Okay, let's get started." Mason took a deep breath, then launched into his opening question. "Maya, what do you think Ted Johnson's like when he's banging all his babes?"

"That's gross. First of all, the man's my father-in-law. Second of all…it's gross."

"Maybe so, but for a lot of businessmen, sex and money are inextricably bound. It's all one big swinging dick contest, if you get my drift."

"You just want to talk about sex. Sex and guns, sex and business—'

"Sex and you—"

"Not gonna happen."

"Really? Then why'd you come out?"

It was a fair enough question. She was completely aware of what Mason was after, yet accepted his invitation anyway. "Why am I here? I don't know, maybe I've been home with a nine- and an eleven-year-old, doing the same thing every fucking day… I just needed to get out. Talk to somebody new. I'm sorry if that disappoints you."

"No, ma'am. I am here and ready to talk. I know you've been going through some hard times. God knows when the last time you and your husband had—'

"Jesus, Harley. When I sat next to you at Surf 'N Turf Night, I thought you were actually interesting. You talked about art. And writing. Tonight's nothing like that."

"You always want to mix it up or it gets boring."

"Here's what I want to know. Do you have any reservations at all about coming on to a married woman who's the daughter-in-law of your employer?"

"My only reservation would be if she didn't like it."

"She doesn't."

"I disagree."

"You have a really inflated ego, mister."

"Not true. Most days, I fucking hate myself. I'm just honest about what I'm feeling."

"And the reason I won't sleep with you is because I'm not being honest?"

"I think you will sleep with me even though you're not being honest."

CANDY'S BEDROOM LOOKED LIKE the master suite in a nineteen-eighties dollhouse, one of those pink and fussy numbers that made a man feel like a prisoner of war in a country where lace was used for currency. It didn't matter how beautiful or sexy a woman was, just being in a place that girly was testicularly challenging from the get-go. It proved especially uncomfortable for Owen, who was summoned to join Candy on hot pink sheets, under a satin comforter, and beside big, poofy pillows on top of which sat her two Bichon Frisés, who would be watching them as they had sex. Despite the contractor's request that she remove the dogs or at least turn off the lights, Candy was used to doing things her way. The animals seemed so nonchalant about what was going on that it made Owen think it must happen all the time.

As he dutifully went through the motions, he had to wonder: Doesn't it bother her that I could be a robot? Strangely, she didn't seem to mind opening herself to a sexual cyborg, whose every thrust was as mechanical as a rep in a workout session. As long as she was on board, he decided to maximize his own gain, getting his heart rate up while making every rep count. In a certain sense, fucking Candy was the emotional equivalent of riding a stationary bike. No matter how fast or for how long he pedaled, it was a journey to nowhere. As encouraging as it was to know that he still had the stamina, he wished there were a way to make it pleasurable. As Candy turned over, demanding it from behind, he started to think about whether he should replace some of Jeannie's wrought iron fencing with lighter-weight aluminum. Plowing into the divorcée with yeoman-like aplomb, he priced out the different materials in his head, opting for the gates with the highest-quality springs and latches. Even though he didn't want to save Ted Johnson a dime, it was important to make sure Jeannie got the best value for her money. She was such a nice lady, she had beautiful grandchildren, and her daughter-in-law...

IT WAS AS IF a switch had been pulled. Suddenly, he was picturing the Johnson grandchildren running into Jeannie's house, followed, of course, by their mother. But in this picture, Maya looked like she had tonight in the restaurant, long, dark hair shimmering as she walked, body swaying in the summer dress that revealed just enough to turn every head in the place. She was smiling awkwardly and avoiding eye contact because she had been seen with the biographer. Still, she sparkled.

Before long, the contractor was thrusting not only forcefully, but with purpose. Totally unbeknownst to her, Candy Daniels was now receiving her pleasure courtesy of the woman she'd just met at Vitale's. The only raw materials on Owen's mind now were the ones comprising the essence of Maya Johnson. He conjured up her body, losing himself in each nook and cranny. So long in the the widower mindset, Owen had forgotten that it was even possible to fantasize with such abandon, and what an important function that served in releasing one's demons. When he finally came, he felt like he had released enough sperm to make both his real and his fantasy partner pregnant with twins.

THEY WERE THE LAST ones on the patio, and as far as Maya could make out, the only customers left in the place. The wait staff seemed to be watching them and fidgeting, as if their entire existence depended on getting rid of the two remaining stragglers. Having gotten nowhere with his flirtations, Harley had moved on to other subjects, currently expounding on the proper way to hunt and skin an alligator. He explained that the process began with slowly pulling the animal to the edge of his boat or onto the bank, then killing him by shooting or clubbing him in the head with an axe or hatchet.

"And why is it that you feel I need to know this?" Maya asked, gulping down the last drops of her Cabernet.

Harley Mason wasn't in an apologizing mood. "Look, sweetheart, you've been puttin' a lot of subjects off limits tonight. Truth is, unless you tell me what you want to talk about, I'm gonna jaw about what's interestin' to me."

"Sex, guns, and killing alligators."

"I'm sorry. What are the acceptable topics here? World Affairs? Which I hate. Yoga? Which is a boring crock of shit. Art? Which we can dance around all night, but you need to make the next move there."

"What's that supposed to mean?"

"It means it's time for you to give it up. Show me your work."

"Oh—I don't know that I'm ready to do that."

"You're afraid?"

"No. I'm not afraid."

In fact she was, for myriad reasons. First off, she had evidence that he could be a harsh critic. Secondly, since he wanted to sleep with her, his reacting positively might only be in the interest of procuring sex, so how would she be able to tell if it was a true response? Lastly, the two of them alone in her home studio, looking at her art, suggested an intimacy that made her nervous. She wasn't about to bring him over and introduce him to the babysitter, or let him anywhere near the place where her kids slept.

"Contrary to what you might think, I don't bite," he told her. "Unless it's asked of me."

Over the past weeks, Maya had given some thought to whether or not she wanted to show Harley her paintings, and if so, how and where that might take place. She had actually taken the step of formulating a plan for the least invasive way in which to accomplish this, should she decide to vote yes.

WHEN THEY FINALLY LEFT Vitale's, Maya could've sworn she heard cheers coming from inside. Mason was unfazed, assuring her that this wasn't the first time people had been ecstatic to see him go away. He took her home, negotiating the roads remarkably well for someone whose alcohol intake would soundly betray him in a breathalyzer test. The only reason Maya let him drive was because she had figured out that his tolerance was gargantuan. The ride proved uneventful, Mason having run out of small talk and grown tired of his big talk being met with disdain. He pulled up to Maya's driveway and held out his hand to shake, a mocking admission that he'd thrown in the towel on having sex with her, at least for the evening.

Maya laughed, pleased that he'd received her message with such clarity. Flush with victory, she then informed him that the evening wasn't over. Mason didn't flinch. He had been around enough women to know that you could never underestimate their ability to surprise and confuse.

"Follow my car," she said, getting out of his and opening the door to her own, which was parked in the driveway.

MAYA EXITED CASCADE FALLS AND turned onto Hohokam Road, Mason hopeful that a late-night liaison was in the cards after all. They weren't far from the freeway ramp, where a Days Inn, EconoLodge, and Marriott Courtyard would be eager to accommodate. Suddenly, she cut a hard left into the Akimel O'Odham Smoke Shop parking lot. She probably wanted to pick up a bottle of vodka to help her get loose, he surmised, naturally, all for the idea. The next thing he saw was Maya popping the trunk and pulling out canvases. He walked over to help, realizing that she intended to show him her paintings within the brightly-lit confines of an all-night liquor store.

WHEN SHE'D FIRST CONSIDERED this as an option, Maya had called the store to confirm that Smoke Shop Bob would be working the night shift. Perhaps she was hedging her bets, because she had a feeling that Bob would like her work as much as Mason would hate it. As she and the biographer hauled in a dozen or so oil paintings to an ad hoc gallery better known for its displays of Lucky Strikes and Beer Nuts, Maya noticed a surprising number of shoppers for this time of night. Unconcerned about keeping his customers waiting, Bob dropped everything upon seeing Maya, immediately clearing a place by the boxed wine for her to prop up her canvases. Harley Mason had to admit that he got a kick out of her ingenuity. While her intent had been to show him her work in a safe space devoid of a bed, she suddenly had a store full of Phoenicians stopping by to get a look at her work.

THE REACTIONS WERE VARIED, but pure, Maya thought. These were the sort of critics who bought their Old Crow and Kool 100's at eleven o'clock at night. They had no preconceived notions of what constituted fine art or what might be considered derivative, they just knew what they liked. Eighty-five-year-old Pima carpenter Leonard Travers seemed to enjoy everything about the paintings but the green goop, which he thought were mistakes Maya had made, spilling something on the canvases at the last minute.

"I've got some thinner in my truck works real good," he told her, offering to donate a pint as his way of supporting the arts.

Cassie Wyatt, a waitress at Denny's, elicited an understanding nod as Maya explained that the green paint hadn't been a mistake, but an attempt to comment on her life in Arizona. Leonard Travers scratched his head and wished Maya good luck, proceeding to load three boxes of Almaden in the passenger side of his pickup. Cassie seemed quite interested in the paintings, inquiring as to what they cost, and whether or not the prices included a frame. Maya explained that nothing was for sale at this point; that she was still finding her voice as she continued to work on the collection. Cassie said she didn't know what that meant. Why, if the stuff wasn't for sale, was it on display in a store?

"She's got a point," Harley Mason smiled. Neither he nor Bob had voiced their critiques, having acceded the first round of opinions to the unwashed masses, which numbered roughly eleven. Unsurprisingly, Bob studied every inch of the canvases intently, while Mason ADD-ed his way through the bunch, eyes darting from one to the next, intermittently stealing a glance at the row of Macallan Scotches. For Maya, anticipating their reviews felt like a return to elementary school, as if she were seated at a little desk, biting off her nails as she waited for the teacher to hand out the graded tests. Examining Bob's face to get a sense of what he might be thinking, she saw the typically jovial cashier looking solemn, depressed even.

"Well," was all he said, emitting nothing close to a smile.

"You hate them. This is like the worst art you've ever seen," she quickly apologized.

"I didn't say that," Bob replied.

"You didn't have to."

Mason felt compelled to interject. "I don't think it's so terrible. I can tell you right now that these are, hands down, the best oils I've ever seen in a cigarette and liquor store. Not to take away from your work, Bob," he chuckled.

What a dickwad thing to say, Maya thought to herself.

"The paintings are really good," Bob piped up softly.

Maya thought he might be crying. "What's wrong?"

"I don't know. They just seem so…sad."

Maya knew her canvases weren't exactly packed with frivolity, but they seemed to have turned the habitually jovial Bob into Arizona's gloomiest Gus. "Like I said, they're kind of a commentary on my life here, which hasn't been all that perfect—'

"I guess not," Bob nodded. "I'd never have known things were that hard for you."

Maybe she was a better artist than she thought. How else could she explain the Indian cashier taking one look and intuiting the struggles she had lived with for so long? "I have been unhappy," she confessed, "but I'm getting it out in the work. Not a bad thing, right?"

"No," Bob replied. "As long as you feel like you're still in control."

"The best work comes when you're *out* of control," Mason interjected. "You've got to unbuckle the safety belts." He thought the paintings were good, but that there was even more pain to be mined. Maya needed to allow herself to come unglued in service to her vision.

Smoke Shop Bob took umbrage with this. "Do you have children, Mr. Mason?"

"Probably," the biographer answered, the range of his smart-ass persona directly proportional to the amount of alcohol he'd consumed.

"Ah, so you're proud of being an obnoxious, amoral asshole?"

"I'm in the truth business," Mason replied.

"Are you now? Well, here's a truth for you. Mrs. Johnson here, actually knows who her kids are, and my guess is they're pretty young. So wouldn't you say it's highly irresponsible of you to encourage a young mother to lose control?"

"My bad. I thought we were talking about art, not babysitting."

"You're drunk and your advice is a load of hackneyed shit. Don't listen to this idiot, Maya."

"Believe me, I don't," she assured the Indian. "If I go off the deep end, it won't be because of him."

Bob was staring at her. "I just gotta tell you—your stuff moves me."

Maya could see he meant it. She gave him a kiss on the cheek, grateful that she had chosen his store for that initial nicotine craving. "I'm going to paint something for you."

Bob beamed from head to toe. "I would love that, Maya. Can I get you a liter of Diet Pepsi for the road?"

"Sure," she smiled. "And a pack of Merit Lights."

Bob went off to fetch the goodies, which Harley Mason took as his cue to reinsinuate himself into the conversation. If he felt like the odd man out at this love fest, he wasn't letting on. "Want to go get a drink at the Biltmore?" he asked Maya.

"I'm done, Harley."

"I figured. Doesn't hurt to try."

"Doesn't hurt to try a little less sometimes. Thanks for dinner."

As SHE BEGAN GATHERING paintings to take back to the car, Bob quickly bagged the soda and cigarettes and rushed over to help. Mason grabbed a canvas as well, a disappointing ending to a night he was finally ready to declare a failure. Usually, after a first date that hadn't come to fruition, he felt some possibility of converting the second time around. Not so with Maya Johnson. He'd thrown her his best stuff and hadn't even been offered the goodbye kiss granted the three hundred pound Indian guy. He wondered if it had just been an off night, or whether he'd lost it completely. Luckily, a fresh bottle was waiting at the hotel room and he and the Glenlivet would be able to figure it out together.

Ted's Bed

I f anyone were to ask Jeannie Johnson if she had any areas of expertise, she would reply that, no, she was just a regular person, trying to lead a good and honest life. But since such a life was a fantasy as long as she remained married to Ted, Jeannie filled in the blanks by becoming a master of learning new information; accumulating a wide variety of knowledge that happier folks might never get the opportunity to know about. Tonight, she was starting a one thousand piece jigsaw puzzle of the unfinished Basílica of the Sagrada Família, the Gaudí cathedral in Barcelona, which she hoped to visit someday. She'd read about the ornate facades: Passion, Nativity, and Glory, which made her Church of the Good Shepherd look like a low-end Circle K. Some critics had found the Basílica over the top ("Gaudí too gaudy?"), but unlike the Good Shepherd, it would never be mistaken for the architectural equivalent of Wonder Bread.

At around 9:30, as she was finishing the second portico of the Nativity facade, a weary Ted Johnson trudged through the door, uncharacteristically early for a weeknight. These days, she was almost always asleep by the time he stumbled in and he, over time, had become considerate enough to spare her the smells of alcohol and sex by crashing on the living room sofa. Tonight, he seemed subdued, which Jeannie interpreted as a bad day at the office. Normally, the man could always find a way to spin shit into gold, but there were times when even a Pollyanna like Ted had to admit that turning scorched earth into Orlando wasn't as glamorous as it was cracked up to me.

If his affect seemed listless, his behavior was even stranger. After greeting her with a quiet "hey," he quickly glanced at the puzzle, picked up a random piece, and proceeded to fail miserably in his attempt to connect it.

"What's going on?" Jeannie asked, as concerned as she could be about someone she considered a stranger at this point.

"Same ol' same ol." He tried another puzzle piece, getting closer this time, but striking out nonetheless. "You hear from Danny or Maya?"

"Not today. We just have to take it one step at a time."

"That's what people always say, but it's a crock. Never worked for me."

She added a piece to begin the third portico. "When was the last time you tried it, Ted?"

"Not interested. I've got to be passionate about everything. Ted Johnson doesn't do half-assed."

"This isn't about you. If you really want to help your son, maybe the best thing you can do is have a little patience."

"I've been plenty patient. I waited for him to get a career. Then, when he couldn't succeed at anything, I offered him a new one. After that, I waited patiently for him to figure out how to capitalize on the tools I gave him. I don't figure I'm the one at fault here."

"Why does someone have to be at fault? Assigning blame isn't going to make Danny get better any faster."

Ted sighed. "I just hate feeling helpless is all. It's not my nature."

"Nobody likes feeling helpless, but some things are out of our hands."

"I don't accept that. I mean, none of us is God, our creator, et cetera, et cetera, but that doesn't mean we should throw in the towel when we have the ability to keep fighting."

"So what do you propose we do?"

"Find him wherever he is and talk some fucking sense into the kid."

Jeannie looked him straight in the eye. "Did it ever occur to you that you might be the reason he left?"

Ted started to erupt. "I thought we weren't playing the blame game. What in the hell do you call that?"

Jeannie realized that her response had been as unproductive as Ted's suggestion. "I'm sorry. You're right—'

"But you really believe I'm the problem, don't you?"

"All I'm saying is that sometimes you two push each other's buttons—"

"He doesn't push my buttons. I don't even know what that means. What the hell are my buttons?"

"You like to be in control—"

"Of course I do. It's my fucking company and I hired that boy so he could support his family. I have given him every opportunity to do that. Now, why is it so complicated?"

"Because not everybody can fit into your cookie cutter vision of how the world works."

"Then what's *his* vision? That's what I want to know."

"He's still trying to find it. People are different, Ted. Sometimes they're going to think and behave in ways that you wouldn't. You only see things through your own eyes."

Ted took a moment to take this in. "They're the only ones I got."

FOR PERHAPS THE FIRST time ever, Jeannie found herself feeling sorry for the man she wished she'd never married. Yes, he had cheated on her with scores of women; projected such braggadocio in public that it made her blanch; alienated both of their children, as he had his only daughter, so many years ago. But just as Danny could never be like Ted, Ted simply didn't have the skill set to see beyond his subdivided worldview, and on some level this pained him. In order to be the good guy and make people happy, you had to be able to understand where they were coming from.

Whether it was out of pity or kindness, Jeannie began rubbing his shoulders. He used to like that, back in the days when they were still touching. The sensation was eerie to her. It had been so many years since their flesh had made contact that his no longer felt familiar. Perhaps it had been so long that her husband's physiological makeup had actually changed. Ted received her kneading passively, considering what he might do to fix his inability to appreciate how other people saw the world. The potential sensuality of the moment was lost on him. Neither did it do anything for Jeannie, whose sole motive had been to temper his sorrow over Danny's situation. As far as what she was doing with her hands, she could be volunteering at the local hospital, or stroking somebody's injured pet. This was a service call.

FOR WHATEVER REASON, TED felt the urge to turn back to the jigsaw puzzle. With the same determination that had made him the only Arizonan to complete three 400-unit home developments in two years, he picked up a piece and placed it correctly into the third portico. Then he smiled and did something completely unexpected. He kissed his wife. It was nothing more than a peck, really, but it landed on the lips, as opposed to the cheek or forehead, and Jeannie was mystified by it. Was it his way of thanking her for the shoulder rub? Or was this man, known for patting himself on the back at the slightest provocation, merely celebrating his jigsaw puzzle accomplishment? Perhaps it was a goodbye kiss? Maybe he intended to sit with her all night. The most distasteful possibility was that he wanted to take her into the bedroom and replicate the moves he'd acquired in the course of his carnal travels. This seemed unlikely, but she couldn't chance it. "What was that?" she demanded to know.

"What was what?"

"You just kissed me. On the lips."

"Yeah?"

"Why'd you do that?"

"You're my wife. I don't think it's all that strange."

"Come on, Ted."

"Geez. It's just a kiss. When did you become so uptight?"

"Do we really want to get into this?"

Ted didn't look at her, choosing instead to try his hand at another piece of the puzzle. "I don't know what you're saying, Jeannie. I'm sorry if my kiss offended you."

"That's it?"

Ted looked confused. "As you were nice enough to point out, I'm only capable of seeing things my way, so I'm having some trouble figuring out what you're asking."

"I'm asking what's the point?"

"The point of what?"

"How much longer are we going to do this? Pretending to be together? Who are we pretending for after all these years?"

"Come on. Stop talking crazy. Nobody ever said being married was easy."

"Really, Ted. If you showed up at the next surf 'n turf dinner without me, would it really make a difference to anyone?"

"It would make a difference to me. I like having you there."

"To present your homeowners with the image of a happily married man."

"This may shock you, Jeannie, but I am a happily married man."

"And what about me? Do you think I'm happy?"

"Not from the way you're speaking right now."

"Jesus, how could I be? We never talk, we don't like the same things, I have my own set of friends, and you have your…relationships."

"They are not relationships. Please don't dignify them with that word."

"Excuse me. What I should have said was that it's not particularly fun being married to a man who fucks anything that moves."

"That's not true—"

"You're right. You also did Sally Wentworth in Phase II, who's paralyzed on the left side."

"Right side. But that's irrelevant."

"Fine. If you have any insight into what is relevant, I would love to hear it."

"Fair enough." Ted took a deep breath. "While it is true that I've had my share of…dalliances, shall we say, they don't mean anything. It's just my way of working off steam."

"You want to work off steam, you run a marathon. You don't stick your dick in four hundred hookers and a lady who had a stroke."

"I never meant to hurt you, Jeannie."

"I'm not hurt. Not anymore. I'm just fascinated by what kind of ego thinks it might be enjoyable, on any level, to be your life partner."

"Then lemme ask you something. How come you're still here?"

"Because I'm an idiot. I got into a routine and I began to feel paralyzed. Please don't take that as a turn-on."

He was having a hard time processing what she was saying. All he knew was that regardless of past carryings-on, it sickened him to think that his marriage might be on the verge of blowing up. "We got a lot of history together, Mrs. Johnson."

"Bad history," she reminded him. "Most of it, anyway. The first six months were fun."

"We were happy when the kids were born."

"And then we went and fucked them up."

"You're being too hard on yourself."

"Mostly, I'm being hard on you."

Ted shook his head. "Okay. I give up. What exactly do you want to do here?"

Jeannie couldn't figure how, but the reply just rolled off her tongue. "I want to toss this puzzle in the trash and go to Barcelona to see the real thing."

Ted broke out in a smile. "Are you asking me to go with you?"

"No, I'm not. Would you have wanted to come with me?"

"Seems kind of silly to spend double the airfare. Hell, I can see what the place looks like on the puzzle box."

"Our loving marriage in a nutshell. Do you want to move out, or should I?"

"Come on, Jeannie. Is that really necessary?"

"I think it is."

Ted pointed to a stack of drywall in the corner. "What about all these improvements you're making on the house?"

"It was just something to do. This place doesn't mean shit to me. You can have it."

"Look, maybe we need to stop and digest everything. You never want to make hasty moves in these situations."

"I've been trying to digest this for forty years. My system can't take it anymore."

"Okay, then." Ted stood up and started for the door when a thought occurred to him. "One question. If hadn't kissed you, would we be having this discussion?"

"Probably not. So thank you for that."

"I'll find myself a place in one of the rental properties," he told her. "You get the work finished here and we'll decide what to do with the house when it's done."

"Fine. And you should probably contact an attorney."

"For God's sake. Do we really need to get lawyers involved?"

"It's generally what people do when they file for divorce."

"I always thought we were better than those kinds of people, but whatever—Let me know if you hear from Danny."

"I will."

"Oh. What about your big birthday party? I assume it's still on?"

"Hmm. Let's try and imagine what kind of celebration that would be. Missing son, newly separated birthday girl, unhappy daughter-in-law, sad grandkids—"

"So that's a no?"

"Sorry, Ted. You'll have to come up with some other gala to promote Johnson Homes."

"Don't be so cynical. That party was for you."

"I appreciate the sentiment. If it makes you feel any better, not having to pretend to enjoy myself will be the greatest gift you've ever given me."

"You've got a truckload of anger in there, don't you?"

"A fucking convoy."

"Alrighty then. It's been real."

As Ted walked out the door, Jeannie found herself feeling sorry for him for the second time in one night. The only difference was that this time, she felt happy for herself.

Inspiration Nation

Having recognized that it would be impossible to move forward until he stopped castigating himself, Danny surrendered to his new environment, making the commitment to stay put for as long as it took to feel whole. He became a little more acclimated each day, the Juju and Lucky compound serving as part Betty Ford Clinic, part boot camp. It was a hub of positivity, infused with the spirit of idealistic kids who didn't shy away from hard work. Since their arrival, Katie had put herself in charge of replanting and mulching the garden, while Danny studied Lucky's dog training techniques. Was he now considering a career in canine rehabilitation? He couldn't think that far ahead. The goal for the time being was simply to do something of value. Compared with his previous job of selling false hopes, helping troubled animals work through their aggression seemed like a huge step up. And as for Katie, she was learning how to cultivate beets and broccoli, instead of stuffing folks with carb-busting Applebee's food. Plus, they both felt good about pitching in, their small way of repaying Lucky and Juju for the kindness they'd shown.

IT WAS A FINE arrangement. Danny discovered that spending a good portion of his day outdoors left him happily exhausted at night, which somehow made him more at ease in the platonic bed he shared with Katie. As his anxiety diminished, he began to appreciate how fortunate he was to have her around. The girl was a protective wall of flesh and blood, whose irrepressible heat reminded him that he still had the ability to feel. She also made him see that he was making strides, and encouraged him to establish a routine, which included a regular schedule for calling home. He soon got into the rhythm of phoning Maya at the same hour every other night, if only to let her know that he hadn't fallen off the face of the earth. One time, he'd even felt bold enough to ask to speak with the kids, quickly realizing that he'd overreached when the plaintive sound of their voices began to tear him apart. In spite of this one arguable misstep, he was able to detect his anguish slowly giving way to hopefulness. His sense was that if he could stay in it for the long haul, he would come out on the other side.

HOST AND HOSTESS SEEMED to take pleasure in watching their guests get more comfortable. Earth mother Juju continued to be complimentary of Danny, and was particularly excited to find out that he'd been a playwright. One night, after a hearty veggie paella and a little too much wine, she cajoled him into reciting a monologue from *Up From the Ashes*, his "hit" back at Bennington. Danny had pledged to forget that part of his life the minute he'd moved to Arizona, yet the eighteenth-hole soliloquy came back to him like it was yesterday. It was the speech that closed the last scene of Act I, when the main character, Dennis, explains to his father, Todd, why he hates golf. The father wonders how he could have failed so badly as a parent and human being, likening his son's abandonment of the game to joining the Communist party.

DANNY TOOK A DRAMATIC cleansing breath, then faced Juju as if she were playing the role of Todd.

Bruce Ferber

"I hit a three-hundred-forty-yard drive, you tell me it's spectacular, but I feel nothing. I don't want to feel nothing. That's just how it is. I try to picture myself as Tom Watson, or Nicklaus, or even your hero Arnold Palmer, hoping that their love of the game will spark some enthusiasm in me. But it never happens."

Juju hung on his every word, loving the concept of a theatrical performance taking place within the confines of her living room. Katie was also impressed, seeing a confident, charismatic side of Danny she hadn't known existed. He continued.

"Do you know what golf is spelled backwards? Flog. So maybe it's no accident that every time I get out on the course I feel like I'm entering eighteen separate torture chambers. You say: 'What could be better than spending a day on acres of manicured lawn and ending it with two martinis in the clubhouse?' For me, a colonoscopy. Really, I can finish two under or eight over. Either way, it bores me to tears. Now, I'm fully aware that this brands me a freak in the state of Arizona, but before you start calling me 'Elephant Man,' there's one thing you need to know. This is not a choice. It's the way I'm wired. And after finally accepting that it's just not in me to like this sport, all I ask is to be able to not like it in peace. Dad, please know that my rejection of golf is not a rejection of you."

Danny bowed, to generous applause, after which Juju initiated a discussion about the ritual of sports. She was pretty much clueless about anything athletic, but loved tradition and ritual. Katie hated ritual, but had enjoyed cheerleading at high school football games. Lucky, it turned out, had grown up playing golf and been passionate about the game, but now had neither the money nor the time to pursue it. His take was that Danny would have actually liked golf had it not been foisted on him by his father.

THEN THE BONG CAME out, as it did many nights. Danny found himself wondering how this couple financed its marijuana habit. They weren't spending their money on home remodeling or expensive jewelry, so perhaps pot was their one luxury. For tonight they'd hauled out a freshly purchased strain called Pink Lady.

As the spicy, lemony mix kicked in, whatever inhibitions Juju and Lucky had (and there weren't many) flew out the window. Completely unprovoked, Juju blurted out that she'd had an intense lesbian relationship in college with an Aussie girl named Olivia. This came as a surprise to Katie, since she and Juju had been roommates. Katie also remembered Olivia having a prelaw boyfriend. Juju explained that the clandestine affair, in addition to being more erotic than a D.H. Lawrence novel, had been so transformative that she thought she would wind up settling down with a woman.

"So what happened?" Katie asked.

"Olivia brought a guy into bed with us one night. Unlucky for her, Lucky for me."

Lucky smiled, having obviously heard this line many times before.

"That is amazing," Katie remarked. "The woman who took you away from one man led you back to another."

Lucky took this as his cue to chime in with an out-of-the-box sexual experience of his own. Apparently, he had once been kissed on the lips by a male clothing store owner who mistakenly thought he was gay.

"What did you do?" Danny asked, thinking a big dude like Lucky might have hauled off on the guy.

"I told him that I didn't have those kind of feelings for him. Which I didn't."

"Wouldn't have it been easier to just say you're not gay?" Katie asked.

"I guess. But I was young. I thought, what if, down the road, it turned out that I did have those kinds of feelings for someone of the same sex? Then I would be gay, right? It seemed more truthful to speak to the individual experience happening right then and there."

"Wow," Katie nodded, helping herself to another hit of Pink Lady.

There was no denying this couple's uniqueness. Each evening's conversations, cannabis-injected though they might be, seemed to be chock full of insights and epiphanies. Danny suddenly realized that the four of them had had dinner together every night since their arrival. He started to think: *Don't these people have other friends? What did they do for entertainment before Katie and I showed up?* This notion either hadn't occured to Katie, or she was just going along with the program. Danny made a mental note to bring it up once they were alone.

AFTER THEIR FIRST FEW days in Salinas, Katie had made the wise decision to inform her parents of her whereabouts. Since they knew Juju from Katie's college years, they agreed to give their daughter some breathing room so she might examine what it was she wanted to do with her life. Katie had left out the tidbit that she was sharing a bed with a forty-something married man, regarding it as unnecessary information since they weren't in a romantic relationship. She was, in fact, feeling closer to Danny all the time, which she proudly announced to the others once the Pink Lady took front and center in her brain cells.

The news seemed to please Juju and Lucky as much as it discomfited Danny. While it was true that he'd grown increasingly fond of the girl, she was still a girl. And he was still married to Maya. Danny was also worried that Katie would interpret her hosts' sexual confessions as an invitation to publicly chronicle her own history in the bedroom. It wasn't that he thought her stories would be shocking or damaging. He was afraid that hearing Katie speak intimately would make him want her in all the ways he had worked so hard to suppress.

MUCH TO HIS SURPRISE, Katie went a whole different direction. She was excited to tell Juju and Lucky about having experienced something new and amazing that, literally, had nothing to do with sex.

"Don't keep us in suspense," Juju squealed. "What do you want to share with us?"

Katie smiled. "What it feels like to sleep with a man, night after night, and not fuck him."

"Do tell," Lucky nodded, his eyes bulging from a little too much Pink Lady.

"It's been otherworldly," Katie said. "Spiritual." She looked over at Danny. "This man, who, a month and a half ago, was nothing more than some guy leaving a big tip, has become the person I trust more than anyone in the world."

Lucky gave Danny a pat on the back. Juju started tearing up as Katie described how she'd been so unhappy with her life that she hopped in Danny's car on a whim, and now, she felt like she'd known him forever.

At first, Danny was speechless. Then he was blown away, as he heard Katie telling their hosts that she hoped, someday, to find a husband as faithful and devoted to her as he was to Maya. "I can't understand why she didn't try harder to work things out."

"It's a lot more complicated than that," Danny replied. "Most of the blame falls on me."

"It's hard for me to believe that." Katie turned to Juju and Lucky. "I lie next to him every night. I want to do whatever I can to make him happy. He says that just having me there makes him happy. How amazing is that?"

Juju and Lucky smiled, now looking at Danny as if he were their savior.

WAS SHE REALLY IN love with him? Or was the pot just magnifying everything, ascribing life-changing import to each thought and feeling? Danny was having trouble deciphering it all, especially the outpouring of love being directed his way. Juju hugged him for a good thirty seconds, her fiery mountains heaving as they pressed into him. Lucky gave him a hug as well, after which he let everyone know that as of now, he was still not gay.

Then Danny looked at Katie, the rare and beautiful creature who had lavished him with caring and respect he never presumed he'd earned. "You think I'm special, don't you?"

"I do."

"Why?"

"Why not? You ever hear of the phrase 'innocent until proven guilty?'"

"So you believe that people are special until proven ordinary?"

"No. I believe you are. So far you haven't let me down."

On the surface, it was strange to be having this talk in front of other people, but in fact, the night had evolved into a free-form group therapy session, starting with Juju's college lesbian experience and building to the joy of no sex.

Lucky looked at Danny. "I gotta ask. What do you think is so fucking wrong with you?" He had picked up on his houseguest's low self-esteem from the beginning, but had yet to find any good reason for it.

"I bailed on my family," Danny explained.

"You were in a lot of pain," Katie reminded him.

"What about their pain? That I caused and have no clue how to stop? It's my responsibility to support my wife and kids. I need to know how I'm gonna do that."

"You don't need to figure it all out tonight," Juju offered.

Danny was miles from any kind of strategy, but he knew she was right. He felt tears coming on, but managed to fight them back. "I just want to say that I really appreciate how nice you've all been."

"We love you." Juju kissed him on the cheek, her lips hot and loaded with suction.

"Maybe it's time to go to bed," Katie suggested.

The others agreed. Danny followed Katie to the back, whereupon she sat him down on the mattress and began rubbing his shoulders.

"Man, you're tight. When was the last time you had a massage?"

"Let's see. It was before the last time I had sex, and that was at least two years ago."

"So...which would be your choice tonight?"

"Katie, you just went on and on about how great it was to sleep next to me without fucking. Why would you want to change that?"

"I don't know. Basis of comparison?"

"You're not making this easy."

"Which means..."

"I'm still going with the shoulder rub."

"You got a shitload of willpower, sir."

"That doesn't make it any more fun," he assured her.

She was digging deep into his rear deltoids when he suddenly remembered—"Hey, I've been meaning to ask you. What do you think went on before we were here?"

"I don't know. Dinosaurs roamed the earth?"

"I mean here with Juju and Lucky. Do they have other friends?"

"I'm sure they do."

"Then why don't they hang out with anybody but us?"

"Because we're fascinating?"

Danny had to laugh.

"I'm serious. We're like these two random particles that wound up being part of the same atom. You don't meet a couple like us every day. I mean, we're not a couple, couple, but we showed up as pair, and we're a pretty odd combination."

"But still, you don't think being only with you and me is a little strange?"

It didn't seem strange at all to Katie. "If I'm them, I want to know more about us."

"We told them the whole story."

"No, we haven't. Because we don't know how the story turns out."

Danny was curious as to what she meant by this. "Are you thinking we might wind up…together or something?"

"How would I know? I just work with the facts on the table. One of which is that I'm going to need a power tool to get this knot out of your neck."

"You know, Katie, I don't know what I ever did to deserve being around someone like you."

"You left your passenger door unlocked."

He looked up at her soft blue eyes, open wide as a California poppy. "You are so fucking beautiful."

"I don't think you want to start that up."

"You're right." He did, though. Badly. But as much as he was dying to kiss her, it was more important that he find a way not to. He pictured Maya, in the early days when she truly wanted him, and how she would look today, in his fantasy of her wanting him back. Then he pictured the kids hugging him as he burst through the door.

"Thank you, though." She smiled.

"For what?"

"For saying I'm beautiful."

"Can't be the first time you've heard it."

"But you really meant it." She kissed him on the forehead and turned to shut off the lamp. "Goodnight, mister."

"Night." As Danny closed his eyes, he felt the knot in his shoulder breaking up, and the one in his brain beginning to loosen.

Ted Johnson and Company

While not big in the self-awareness department, Ted Johnson freely admitted that displays of affection were not his strong suit. Still, it boggled his mind to think that one four-second smooch devoid of tongue could blow up the whole goddamn playbook. Hiccups of this sort weren't part of the Master Plan, and master planning was supposed to be his raison fucking d'être. Walking through the doors of Johnson Homes at 8:30, as he did every morning when he wasn't on the road, Ted felt a wave of ambivalence sweep over him. It threw him for a loop, because it was the first time he had ever been less than a hundred and ten percent enthusiastic about being there. This was the utopian work environment that had been his brainchild, the corporate Eden where he gave other decent folks the opportunity to be fruitful and make a killing off their fruit.

NORMALLY, HE DIDN'T PAY attention to the details of what the office staff did, content to soak up the routine adulation, but this morning he saw before him a roomful of drones, immersed in pointless busywork, marking time until they got sprung at five o'clock. Ted knew they weren't to blame, because without him being able to fund development, what crucial tasks were they supposed to be handling? Whatever it was these employees were doing, they made sure to put on a good face, going through the motions as if each was a key player in a Fortune 500 company. Since "Putting on a Good Face" was step two in the Ted Johnson manual, *Building Blocks for Success*, they were, in fact, honoring him by showing pride in doing nothing.

One sideways glance from her boss was enough for Barb McDermott to figure out that something was amiss. This wasn't the *I got an Indian girl pregnant* look either. Ted's countenance seemed almost thoughtful, which surely spelled trouble in a man for whom step three was "Don't Think, Do."

"Morning, Barb," he greeted her in a near whisper.

"Goooooood morning, Mr. Johnson!" she shouted back, her strategy being to counter cogitation with spunk.

"Is the large conference room booked this morning?" he wanted to know.

"I'm not sure, Mr. Johnson. Let me give it a check-see."

"Buzz me when you find out." Ted zipped into his office and quickly shut the door behind him.

To Barb, whatever was brewing smelled like something big. As for the large conference room, checking its availability was just a formality because the place hadn't been booked for the last three months. Why would it be? There'd been no business, large or otherwise, on which to confer. But out of Johnson deference (she forgot whether that was step eleven or eighteen), she behaved as if the matter warranted investigation. Just for the heck of it, she checked the books anyway and discovered that the large conference room had sat completely unused for five months, with the exception of an employee baby shower during a Wednesday lunch hour.

"Yes, Barb?" Ted answered her buzz.

"I shuffled a few things around so it's yours whenever you want it. What time are you thinking of?"

"Now." His voice had an urgency that was at once sexy and frightening.

"I can work with that. I assume you'll be wanting coffee service. What kind of food would you like brought in?"

"No coffee, no food."

"Anything at all you need?"

"Yes. The entire company."

"As in everybody who works here?"

"That is correct. And call Harley Mason to wake his ass up out of bed. He should be there, too."

"Will do. I'll let you know when we're ready to go." Barb hung up, certain that the bomb about to dropped would seriously affect the livelihoods of the forty or so people Ted Johnson considered his extended family. Her first move was to check the room to make sure there were enough chairs. Upon opening the door, she found Pete and Joey from the mail room on either side of the conference table playing a makeshift version of air hockey. To add insult to injury, they used a commemorative Johnson Homes coaster for their puck. Barb was outraged. As penance for their unprofessional infraction, she ordered the young men to help arrange the seating so everything looked neat and tidy. If Ted Johnson had something to impart to his flock, he deserved to do so in the style to which he'd grown accustomed. Suddenly, she felt a primal urge to ignore her boss's edict and order up some homemade Mexican pastries. A platter of tres leches cakes and pan dulce would not only buoy the troops, but be a welcome diversion for Ted, should his message be less than cheery. Yet something told her that this morning, he had no interest in being diverted. Barb acceded to his initial command, sad that she couldn't sweeten or soften whatever it was that was about to go down.

THE WORDS "LARGE CONFERENCE room" and "everybody needs to be there" set off a ripple effect throughout the cubicles. It quickly mushroomed into a game of telephone, starting with the rumor of Ted cutting salaries, and leading up to him having contracted some rare affliction that was the male equivalent of cervical cancer. Barb did her best to quell the speculation, but in truth, she was as curious as anybody. Most confused by the call to assembly were James Dalton and Dusty Sprague. Never in the history of Johnson Homes had a general meeting been initiated without The Boys being consulted ahead of time. James was ready to bust into Ted's office and demand an explanation, but Dusty held him back, maintaining that it would be more valuable to hear what Ted had to say independent of their input. Even though the man had flat-out rejected the idea of a Tarkanian takeover and continued to strut like a peacock in public, he was smart enough to know the bottom line. This meeting might give them an indication of how he intended to move the chess pieces, provided he still thought he had any left.

TED LOOKED AT HIS watch. Twenty minutes or so had passed since he'd given Barb the order to gather the faithful. He'd spent the wait time quietly admiring all the awards that had been bestowed upon him by small business organizations and various Chambers of Commerce. Ted knew he'd been blessed, and made a mental note to mention as much in his speech. He mused on what the mood might be like in the hallways, hoping that he hadn't incited any sort of mass hysteria. One thing he knew for sure—they couldn't be expecting bonuses.

AS BARB SCURRIED ABOUT to find everyone a seat, the conference room buzzed with nervous joking about the dozens of company pep rallies they'd been subjected to over the years: The time Ted handed out the lyrics to a Johnson Homes fight song he'd written for everybody to sing as they drove to work; when he announced he was recruiting cheerleaders for the company softball team and everyone had a good idea how each Johnsonette would be selected. Lighthearted banter seemed like a much more positive approach than pondering salaries getting cut, or what exactly male cervical cancer might look like. Only Harley Mason, who still reeked of last night's Glenlivet, was grumbling about having to be there, mystified as to what could be so important as to warrant him being wrested from a sound sleep. The last thing Barb intended to do was apologize. Over time, she had come to view the alleged author as nothing but a drunk getting a free ride. She had seen no manuscript pages, and as far as she could tell, neither had Ted.

"Could I get some coffee?" Mason asked, regarding her like she was his lackey.

"Ted says no coffee," she snapped back. "Not even hangover coffee."

Mason realized that he wasn't on a great roll. Getting rejected last night by Maya, now getting reamed by the secretary. He found himself pining for simpler times, those nights when he'd down twelve mint juleps after joining Mrs. Billy Graham in her evening prayers.

"How y'all doing?" boomed the voice of the man who once crowned himself the Profit Prophet. Ted was smiling as he charged through the door, and the group responded in kind, doing their best to bullshit about how great their lives were.

"Well, we've always been in the happiness business at this company, haven't we?"

The response to this was substantially more feeble, one or two people nodding their heads so as not to appear rude.

"In that spirit, what I'm here to tell you is that Johnson Homes is forging ahead."

As far as Dusty, James, and Barb could see, this looked just like the old Ted, but perhaps he needed to get some posturing out of his system before going in for the kill.

"Now, some of you have heard me speak about the importance of Nexting."

They'd all heard it up the wazoo. Nexting was the obvious and unnecessary term invented by Ted to emphasize that people had to be ready for the next deal, or the next week, or the next football season, or whatever happened to fit the thing Ted was trying to sell. Odder still, was that he took great pride in inventing concepts where none were needed, anointing them "verbal gravy."

"Your humble president has been doing his own a bit of Nexting lately," he told them. "While that shouldn't surprise you, the specifics have been somewhat out of the ordinary. Since I consider you all family, I want to share them with you."

Had he come to his senses and sold the company? James wondered. Dusty just didn't see how a deal could've gone down without them getting wind of it.

"Folks," Ted began solemnly, "what I've learned in the past month or so is that there's no greater motivation for Nexting than when others have nexted you."

"What the hell is that supposed to mean?" James whispered to Dusty. "Now he's making up new contexts for his made-up word."

"It's no secret that you all haven't seen Danny Johnson around here for a while. I know there's been lots of whispering about drugs and rehab and what have you. Not true, I'm happy to report. And no, he's not living on one of them kibbutzes in Israel, the birthplace of drip irrigation, you'll be interested to know. They tell me my son is taking a little break to figure out the next chapter of his life. Fair enough. You can't force somebody to love a dream job, am I right?"

Dusty remarked how the hubris was still there, comfortably wedged between sanctimony and delusion. James wanted to shout out the truth about the company's dire straits, convinced that perpetuating the sham was a disservice to the employees who were still in denial. But per Dusty's request, he forced himself to stay silent, waiting along with the others for the latest avalanche of bullshit.

"I don't pretend to know the inner workings of the human heart," Ted continued. "But I now know that changes of the heart can have monumental consequences. Not just for other folks, but for yours truly." He stopped and took a breath. "And so, it is with deep regret that I tell you of another misfortune to befall the House of Johnson."

There it was, James shook his head. He was finally coming clean about having taken the company in the shitter.

"My beloved Jeannie and I are going to separate."

Barb let out a gasp. "But the birthday party—"

"We'll deal with that in due time, Barb. It's the least of our worries right now."

Easy for him to say. He hadn't ordered four thousand turkey pinwheel sandwiches from Costco.

To the rest of the workforce, the only surprise was that it had taken Mrs. Johnson this long to wake up and smell the infidelity. Ted's womanizing had been as legendary as Jeannie's niceness. Yet, while the majority of employees thought him deserving of comeuppance, they nevertheless found it troubling to see their boss in such a state.

"I guess you never really know what the future is going to bring," Ted sniffled. "Jeannie's Nexting has kind of thrown me for a loop. That said, we have to press on. "Get up, stand up," as the Jamaican marijuana guy used to say. No matter what gets thrown in our faces, we find a way to move forward."

Lorena Alvarez from accounting, a sixty-five-year-old grandmother who'd worked with Ted from the beginning, stood up. "I just want to say how sorry I am. I'm going to pray for your marriage to heal."

Ted thanked Lorena and conceded that he had entered uncharted territory. He'd been wed to the same woman for forty years and didn't know anything else. Maybe, somewhere down the line, reconciliation would be possible, but it was nothing he could count on. "The truth is, all I have left now is Johnson Homes."

A good forty-five seconds of silence followed, suggesting that while the group empathized with his marital troubles, they were even more disturbed to see an entire life defined by a company that conducted no business.

"And where exactly is Johnson Homes? You're probably asking. I think it's common knowledge that this hasn't exactly been a great quarter for us. Financing's been tight, the market's down, and we're still looking to close on our next development. When will it happen?

Will it happen? I can't answer that. What I can tell you is that we, as a company, have arrived at our Nexting moment. In light of the changes affecting my personal life, I've made the business decision to go all in and put the whole stack o' chips on the number Tucson. I plan to return there, spend a little time hunkering down with my potential funders, and do everything in my power to make Cascade Falls South a reality. If, somehow, it turns out that the stars fail to align, there's a fella over at Tarkanian Homes who I'm pretty sure wants to be your boss. The long and the short of it, friends, is that I love this place. I've put my entire soul into it. Maybe my problem is that part of it needed to go somewhere else. Time will be the judge of that. Thank you all for listening, and…go Johnson Homes! At least for now."

AND WITH THAT, THE subdivision magnate made his exit to a weak smattering of applause. To the majority of the group, it seemed like they had just been given front row seats to Custer's Last Stand, Ted's final skirmish sure to be as bloody as the Battle of Bighorn. Yet there remained an optimistic few who clung to the belief that the Profit Prophet would pull it out of his ass one more time.

"I don't think there's anything to worry about," Barb announced, starting to think of places where she might send her résumé. She then noticed Harley Mason fast asleep in his chair. She was about to rip him a new one for snoozing through a potentially key dramatic moment in the book, when the conference room phone buzzed.

"Hell-o, large conference room," Barb chirped. "Absolutely, sir, no problem." She hung up and glared at Mason. "He wants to see you in his office. Right now. I only hope, for your sake, that he doesn't ask for pages."

"It's all on my computer," the disheveled writer replied, convincing no one.

TED'S FEET WERE ON the desk, eyes staring into space as Mason stumbled into the office. "Good morning, author. Is that how you like to be addressed?"

"It's a little formal, but whatever." As hungover as the biographer felt, it appeared to him as if Ted were stoned, or on some megadose of Valium. "Nice speech in there, sir. Very dramatic."

"Glad you thought so, since it's probably the penultimate chapter of your book."

"Exactly what I was thinking."

"You were asleep, jerk-off."

"I'm sorry. I had a rough night."

"Not interested. Pack your bags and be ready to go in two hours."

"Huh? Where are we going?"

"Wow. You really were out like a light. The Johnson Express is bound for Tucson. I'm staying at the Ritz-Carlton, you're at Motel 6."

Mason couldn't tell if the man was joking or hallucinating. "You know, as much I want to go along, maybe I should stay here and work on my notes. I need to organize the first six chapters."

"And I need my ball and chain to come to her senses. Doesn't mean it's gonna happen, does it now? Start packing."

"You're serious, aren't you?"

"You bet your ass I am. The do-or-die moment is about to reveal itself. You, my friend, are going to witness firsthand, the future of Arizona tract housing."

"The Yalta Conference of it all," Mason mumbled under his breath.

"You know, one would think that such an accomplished writer might recognize a great story when it presented itself, but it's hard to do that when you're snoozin' through act three."

"Oh, I know it's a great story. After all, you're a pioneer. An icon—"

"Jesus Christ. I hired the one bastard who's more full of shit than I am. Let me spell out the drama for you. First off, my wife of forty years just walked out on me."

"No shit?" the biographer cried out. "Your secret's safe with me."

"Mason, I just told the whole fucking office while you were dreaming about pussy or some such thing. "

"Sorry. My bad."

"Here are your bullet points, son. Up until two years ago, Ted Johnson was one of the most successful businessmen in the Grand Canyon State. Today, my son's left his family, my wife's left me, and my company has been reduced to a precariously positioned dingleberry, inches away from making the toilet bowl its final resting place. My point is, the whole enchilada hinges on Tucson. All that I've worked for and the only thing I have left. That enough drama for you?"

"The stakes are high. I got to admit."

"I'm not a writer, but heck, I think it beats that dead salesman show I saw at the dinner theater."

"You saw *Death of a Salesman* at a dinner theater?"

"Excellent chicken Kiev. And Tony Danza was fucking fantastic. God, can that man tap dance."

As VISIONS OF A jitterbugging Biff danced through the biographer's head, he realized that his source material had actually become interesting. What more could a writer ask for than a protagonist who'd once been on top of the world, but was now on the verge of losing everything? Even in his hungover state, Harley Mason was able to grasp the awesomeness of a universe that was capable of turning fluff into substance. He then considered that he hadn't written a book with authentic drama in at least fifteen years. Shooter Jennings' homemade fishing lures and Mrs. Billy Graham's praying habits weren't exactly life or death situations, so the cliffhangers had to be manufactured artificially. This was a second chance, his opportunity to graduate from vanity to red meat. The question was, after having spent so many years as a shill, did he still have anything left in the tank? He supposed he was about to find out. "So when do we leave?" he asked the boss.

"Be outside your hotel in two hours. I'm not going to wait around for you like I did in Texas."

"I apologize for that."

"Write me some good shit and we'll call it even."

Deconstruction

Jeannie watched through the upgraded plantation shutters of the guest bedroom as Owen's truck pulled up to the house. It seemed fitting that he should be the first to know about her decision to leave Ted, since he had opened up to her and expressed the depth of his grief. She also felt like she'd played a part in getting him back into the dating world and wanted to hear all about his evening out. Then there was the small matter of her curtailing further work on the house, thereby ending Owen's term of employment. This part didn't really worry her, so confident was she that a man with his skills and reputation would never suffer financially.

As soon as she opened the door, she saw that Owen looked different. She couldn't tell if it was in a good or bad way, but something had changed. This made her even more interested in talking to him, rather than wasting oxygen on Ted.

"How you doing, Jeannie?" He looked concerned.

"I'm doing great. Come on in."

Owen hauled in his tool box, paint brushes, and spackling tools. Today was a drywall finishing day, to the best of her memory.

"I'm glad," he told her. "Because I heard some things—"

Jeannie couldn't imagine that word was already out on the street. Then again, it was no secret that news traveled fast in Cascade Falls, especially when the breaking story pertained to the Johnsons. Apparently, the minute the meeting in the conference room ended, Verizon's cell phone network was flooded with calls to spouses, friends, and neighbors about Jeannie having given Ted the boot. Like most others, Owen viewed the move as positive, but he also knew that the man, no matter how vile, had been her husband for decades. They had a past. Had raised children who had borne them grandchildren. Jeannie's life had been entwined with Ted's for so long that the news demanded deeper circumspection than: "He's an asshole, she's better off."

She assured Owen that even though she had made the choice in a split second, the wheels, however slowly they'd advanced, had been in motion since her honeymoon. She compared her emotional composition to that of the earth on which her husband had built his empire—scorched, dry, and battered from years without nourishment. "But eventually, it rains. Maybe only small drops at first, but enough to see growth and new life taking form."

Owen said he was happy for her new opportunities. She thanked him, then gingerly broke the news about wrapping up whatever projects that were left so the house could be put on the market. He said he was fine with that, and asked where she was planning to go once the residence was sold.

"Who knows? Maybe Prescott. Maybe Barcelona."

"Like in the jigsaw puzzle?"

"Why not? Be a hell of a place to celebrate my sixty-fifth."

"I'll say. Man, I'd love to meet the general contractor on that church."

"I think there's been about fifty of 'em. They'll probably go through a couple more before the thing's finished. They're shooting for 2026, which would bring the construction time to a hundred forty-four years."

Owen pointed out that building had begun forty years before Arizona had even become a state. "They should let Ted finish. It'd be up and running by June."

They both laughed. Still, Owen wondered if it was a cheap shot, in light of their separation.

Jeannie, at least outwardly, didn't seem fazed. She admitted that she probably didn't want to travel out of the country until she could be sure Danny was in better shape.

Owen said that sounded like a good idea. The Barcelona cathedral would still be around, and the longer she waited to go, the closer it would be to completion.

"So now let's hear about you," she smiled.

"What do you want to know?" The real question was: *What could he possibly tell her?*

"I want to know everything. How it felt. Were you relaxed? What was she like? What were you like interacting with her? Was there a spark?"

The truth was, virtually nothing of what transpired last night was fit for her ears. Owen was suddenly filled with shame, imagining what she would think of him if she knew the lurid details. He certainly wasn't proud of his actions, and recognized that it had been within his power to abstain. Just because Candy Daniels was horny and he had been without sex for so long didn't mean he was obligated to fuck her, and worse, fantasize about someone else in the process. Oh, and by the way, Jeannie, the vision that brought me to ejaculation was your daughter-in-law. That would go over great, wouldn't it?

"I'm waiting," Jeannie tapped on the table.

"I don't know. It was…pleasant."

"You're lying. You had a miserable time, didn't you?"

"In some ways, I suppose I did. In other ways, it was…liberating."

"Do you want to elaborate?"

He didn't at all, but still, he needed to come up with something that sounded credible. "It was just kind of freeing to be able to—"

"Have an adult conversation with a woman your age?" she interjected conveniently.

"That's it!" Just as he tried to think of where to take the conversation next, he was saved by a knock on the door. His sense of relief was fleeting. Jeannie's visitor turned out to be Maya Johnson, who had spontaneously decided to swing by after hearing the separation news.

"Hi." She waved awkwardly at Owen.

He felt his insides starting to churn, as if she somehow she knew that he had pictured himself inside her as he was pounding Candy Daniels. Then he remembered how uncomfortable she had seemed when she made her entrance with the bigmouth biographer. Maya averted his gaze even now, maybe because she was concentrating on Jeannie, more likely because she was embarrassed about last night.

Owen kept looking at her, hoping to convince himself that it was merely the liquor, combined with his need to block out Candy, that had fueled his fantasies. But the more he observed Maya, the more taken he was. He wasn't getting hard, or imagining her naked. For no good reason and completely without evidence, he now found himself thinking, *I could love this woman.* He managed to snap himself out of it, telling Jeannie that he needed to get started in the back. "Nice running into you again, Maya. We seem to do a lot of that."

"Yeah, we do." Maya smiled nervously as she watched him go off to the master bedroom.

WHAT A STUPID THING to say, the handyman berated himself. She surely didn't want anyone to know she was out with that guy. Then again, if that were true, why would she let him take her to a restaurant that was so close to Cascade Falls? Owen could barely concentrate on the work, his energy consumed by the object of sexual fantasies he shouldn't be having in the first place. On the other hand, people said that fantasies were healthy as long as nobody got hurt. And Candy Daniels couldn't have been hurt by the thoughts in his head because she didn't know what they were.

He steeled himself into a spackling and sanding groove, and after twenty minutes or so, had settled down enough to forget about Maya and whatever it was about her he found so alluring. He was making considerable progress when he looked up and saw her standing in the doorway.

"I just wanted to say goodbye." She was grinning. Apparently, she wasn't mad at him for the gross infraction earlier.

"Well, it's not goodbye for long, considering our history."

"True. Did you have a nice time last night?"

Why was she asking this? Did she know Candy Daniels? Was she trying to draw him out about seeing her with Harley Mason so she could explain her presence there?

"It was fine. I thought the food was good. You?"

"The food was okay. Company was kind of weird."

If she could have said one thing to make Owen's day, boy, had she nailed it. "Actually, my date wasn't that great," he told her.

"I'm sorry."

Not only did Maya say the right things, she had empathy. "She was very nice," Owen explained, "but I don't know…just didn't click, I guess."

"Been there. Well, I should go. Guess I'll see you around."

"I've got money on it."

She smiled and waved goodbye.

Owen shook his head, knowing that the ability to concentrate on work would elude him for the rest of the day. Now he would begin fantasizing about her in whole new ways. When would their next chance meeting be? After school? In Jamba Juice? At the stoplight in front of Phase II? What would he say when he saw her? Perhaps if he started composing his words now, he wouldn't feel flustered when the time came. Then he had another thought. Why did their next meeting have to be by chance? If she could go to dinner with the sleazy writer guy, she could certainly have a coffee with him. Her cell number was in the school directory.

Jeannie walked in and broke his reverie. "Now what were we talking about?"

"Nothing important. I'm almost done with this wall."

"I remember. I was asking you about your date last night. Oh, before I forget, I just gave Maya your number. She said there were a couple of things around her house that needed fixing."

Now he had a whole new bunch of stuff to think about. After coming back specifically to say goodbye to him, she then asked her mother for his number. That meant she was going to call him. But when? What if she had a change of heart and didn't bother? Worse yet, what if her real reason for wanting to contact him was to fix a toilet or something equally mundane? What was he thinking? This was a married woman with two kids and she was way inside his head. Meanwhile, her mother insisted on pumping him for information about someone in whom he had absolutely no interest. "The date was fine," he told her. "Really."

"You don't want to talk about it. I understand. It must have been difficult."

"It was. Thank you, Jeannie."

"I can only imagine. Being out with one woman and thinking about another the entire time."

Owen turned beet red.

"You don't have to be embarrassed about it. You still miss your wife."

That was true. But it was also true that he was currently so obsessed with Maya that he had completely misinterpreted what Jeannie was getting at. Now he felt guilty not only for thinking about Maya, but for not thinking about Lucy. Everything seemed so much easier before he answered Candy Daniels' phone call. His life had been divided between caring for Brianna and going to work so he could pay for the things she needed. With those parameters, there was no room for entertaining his own "What ifs?" Actions and responses revealed themselves clearly when performed in the service of others. Thinking about his own needs just mucked everything up.

Downtown

Simplistic though the daily tasks were, Danny had managed to fill his life in Salinas with purpose. Whether he was helping Lucky erect a block wall to keep the dogs out of the garden, feeding the pack at dinnertime, or dirtying his hands in the pungent mulch, it felt good to be making a contribution. What was more, his burgeoning sense of self-worth seemed to foster another component that had long been missing: clarity. All of a sudden, he didn't feel the need to second-guess every thought or instinct. Yesterday there had been a freak thunderstorm followed by a double rainbow. For fifteen minutes, Danny allowed himself to just stand there and take it in. Like the ground at Meteor Crater, the colors of an outer rainbow always presented themselves in reverse order. Had Cascade Falls Danny witnessed the identical phenomenon, he would have stopped himself from enjoying it. The rationale: on what basis did a failure of his caliber deserve to experience joy of any kind? Salinas Danny had made the big step of being able to appreciate beauty without guilt. Soon, he might even be able to tell right from wrong, which would be a major plus given the choices he needed to make.

TODAY HE HAD DECIDED to go into town. He'd pick up the sacks of dog food for Lucky, some worms and kelp meal for the garden, and swing by Home Depot for hardware supplies and low-energy light bulbs. The outing would also be his excuse to see Downtown, which, according to Juju, was in restoration mode. As in countless other American cities, an area teeming with scum, blight, and little-mentioned character had been given the full Disney treatment and christened the reliably cutesy "Old Town."

Choosing to make Home Depot his initial stop, the first thing he noticed were the day laborers standing on the corner, just as they did in Maricopa County. Perhaps it was his imagination, but the men seemed less desperate here. Maybe the cool marine layer that wafted in from Moss Landing just made people more relaxed. The stakes were identical to those in Phoenix—if these guys didn't get picked up, they'd go home with empty wallets. But at least here they weren't developing melanoma in the process. The bodies that loitered outside on those stifling Phoenix summer days reminded Danny of exposure victims in Somalia. He wondered if anyone had ever done a test study comparing workers doing the same job in wildly different climates. Danny then considered the possibility that the men of Salinas appearing happier might have nothing to do with the weather. Perhaps these guys seemed less like tragic figures because he had finally stopped seeing himself as one.

CLARITY BROUGHT WITH IT the courage to dream, freeing him to imagine future possibilities without berating himself for doing so. As Danny gathered S-hooks and light bulbs into the shopping cart, he pondered the idea of going back to school and maybe teaching. Granted, the pay wasn't the best, but there were benefits, which he had a hunch might supersede anything related to medical insurance. His logic was that if training a dog could be so satisfying, imagine what it would feel like to teach a kid how to write a play? Or simply to analyze one? Of course his father would be apoplectic, but who was Ted Johnson to judge? Teaching children was certainly more noble than selling deeded snake oil, or bragging ad infinitum about an empire that had crumbled into nothing. The way Danny saw it, jumping in some guy's truck and clearing brush for eight bucks an hour was more noble.

In the spirit of embracing the new, Danny bellied up to the self-service line to pay for his things. Holding the bar codes over the light box and hearing the beeps as the items rang up seemed like fun, until he made the egregious mistake of lifting a plastic bag off the metal rack too soon. The screen began flashing: "Please see attendant." This being Home Depot, there were, of course, no attendants in sight. Behind him, he could hear Spanish grumbles growing into Spanish curses. Clarity kept him calm. As a first-time, self-service shopper, how could he be expected to know all the quirks of the system? The attendant would come over, explain how it worked, and give him a mulligan. When the young, heavyset manager, Rosarito Gomez, finally did arrive, he proceeded to scold Danny for keeping the other customers waiting. Danny politely explained that this was his first time doing self-service. Gomez replied that if he didn't know what he was doing, he should have gotten into the regular checkout aisle. Danny wondered how anybody was supposed to learn the new technology unless somebody was willing to teach it. He was about to ask whether they had a Genius Bar when he quickly realized that Gomez has already answered that question.

HARDWARE, KIBBLE, AND GARDEN shopping completed, Danny headed downtown and pulled into a metered space by Sherwood Park. He was surprised to learn that the highlight of the city's main greenbelt was a collection of Claes Oldenburg sculptures in the form of giant cowboy hats. Apparently, they had been commissioned in the early eighties to show the world that Salinas had art and culture in addition to lettuce and broccoli, but the mega-Stetsons had since fallen on hard times. When kids weren't climbing their crowns, gangbangers sprayed them with graffiti and homeless gathered under their brims for shelter. Danny supposed that if you thought of it as interactive art, it might not seem so depressing. He suddenly wondered whether he had unconsciously started to adopt a glass-half-full mindset. That, thrown in a blender with purpose and clarity, would undoubtedly point toward a brighter future.

HE CONTINUED HIS WALK, truly impressed by the manner in which Old Town had been restored. Even the additions seemed architecturally sound. Most significantly, there was a fourteen-theater movie complex boasting the largest screen in Monterey County. Then, as if he'd landed in a movie of his own, he looked up and saw that he was standing in front of an entertainment complex known as the Maya. What were the odds of that? Was this a sign? Was it time to go back home and try to work things out with his wife? His recent telephone conversations with her had been pleasant enough, if brief. But he had never believed in signs or karma or any of that new-agey stuff. Just because he happened to be staring at her name in giant letters didn't mean his marital problems were ready to be solved. Coincidence couldn't repair a life.

THERE WERE BILLBOARDS EVERYWHERE advertising a Victorian home that had been the birthplace of John Steinbeck. Having fond memories of playing George in a high school production of *Of Mice and Men*, Danny decided that a visit might be a soothing antidote to the neon reminder of his busted marriage. Seeing the literal cradle of populist literature would jumpstart his brain, and perhaps advance him a few more spaces on the game board. He was convinced that the road would reveal itself based on these sorts of moves, rather than the prodding and teasing of random signs.

He spotted the building on the southwest corner of Central and Stone. There was a placard out front, but he couldn't quite make out the smaller words underneath Steinbeck House. Venturing closer, he saw that the place from which he had sought some kind of inspiration had been turned into the Steinbeck House Restaurant and Gift Shop. In an effort to realize maximum tourism potential, the author's birthplace was now a cafe featuring malibu chicken and a knick-knack emporium hawking souvenir mugs and cookbooks. Danny felt his heart sink.

He had planned on spending the entire day in town, but after seeing someone buy a thirty-dollar *Grapes of Wrath* lunch box made in China, he wanted out as quickly as possible. An extreme reaction, perhaps, but the right one, he was certain. Clarity.

Despite the disappointing denouement, Danny felt positive about the crux of his day. Plus, he was looking forward to dinner, having heard rumblings of Juju fixing organic steak fajitas. In truth, he would be pleased with whatever was put before him because he loved sharing a table with people who valued and respected him. Though the awe he'd felt in Juju and Lucky's presence had diminished as his sense of self began to return, his admiration for them remained steadfast. So what if they were younger than he? That they had learned lessons early rather than wait around, only to find out that they'd wasted twenty years? More power to them. He fiddled with the radio dial, landing on a station playing Dave Matthews' "Crash Into Me." As he began grooving to the beat, Danny wondered how many people had gotten into car wrecks while listening to this song.

He was just about home and headed down the dirt road when he heard the sputtering. The old Civic was gasping for air and eventually stalled out. After a few minutes, he managed to restart it, only to have the engine cough and die again a yard or two later. Danny recalled the car having had this problem once before when the alternator blew. With that in mind, he made the decision not to try again and risk flooding the engine. He opened the trunk and grabbed the Home Depot bags to walk them up to the house. Once there, he'd get a hand truck for the big stuff and ask Lucky to come down and take a look under the hood. Being a car guy, he'd likely be able to diagnose the problem on the spot. Figuring he was less than a half mile from home, Danny decided to enjoy the walk and take in the crisp afternoon air. The sage and lavender smells proved so intoxicating that by the time he reached the house, memories of the dreaded Steinbeck Café and Gift Shop had given way to gratitude—just to be in this place, inhaling its promise of renewal.

He'd planned to go in through the kitchen to drop off the Home Depot bags, but stopped when he heard odd sounds coming from inside. Seeming to emanate from the back of the house, he put the bags down and tiptoed forward to scout for intruders. The closer he got, the more clearly he identified the noise he heard as the grunts and moans of sex. Inching toward the window of Juju and Lucky's bedroom, he saw a naked Lucky engaged in Olympic-level thrusting. The dog trainer's efforts appeared to be well received, as the moaning beneath progressed into screams. Danny wondered how, after four-odd years, the couple's sex life could have remained so vital that they were still having wild sex in the afternoon. He saw Lucky suddenly pull out, signaling that he wanted to be attended to in a different manner. As Juju sat up to oblige, Danny realized that it wasn't Juju at all. *Of course it isn't. It's still the afternoon and she's at work.* Lucky was fucking Katie.

Danny felt the blood draining from his head. Everything that had been good about the day mutated into a toxic blur. In broad daylight, Katie Barrett and her gorgeous, perfect body were submitting in full to her best friend's husband. It was awful on so many levels. Yet, he kept watching. Aside from a brief teenage porn addiction, Danny had never been privy to seeing other people have sex, but all of a sudden, he was a voyeur. Lucky, as Danny might have suspected, was extremely well endowed, and Katie, intensely sexual creature that she was, seemed to have no problem accommodating him. Part of Danny's fascination, as well as his disappointment, was that he was observing an intimacy that could have been his. Katie had been generous and loving toward him from the get-go, but he'd turned her down because she was young and he was married. Now, his role reduced to nothing more than a spectator at an expertly performed carnal ballet, he regretted declining the offer. It wasn't so much that he wanted the sex, but that by refusing her, he had driven her to Lucky.

He considered the possibility of Juju and Lucky having an arrangement. That maybe there was some dude at the crystal shop who was burying his face in her heaving chest during lunch hour. Or even the notion that Lucky sleeping with Katie was designed as a prelude to Juju asking to sleep with him. The possibilities were dizzying, but to Danny, none of them purported to end well.

Clarity came in handy in a situation like this. He knew right away that he didn't want her anymore, either sexually or as a platonic bedmate. It wasn't that he was a prude, and now considered Katie a slut, simply because she'd had sex with Lucky. It was more that he had idealized this particular living situation and its inhabitants. It turned out they were human after all, with flaws that would likely multiply once the shit hit the fan. And he didn't want to stick around for the fallout. Besides, if they were flawed just like he was, why should he be in Salinas dealing with the consequences rather than in Phoenix, confronting the consequences of his own flaws?

He heard Lucky let out a gasp as he spent himself in Katie's mouth. Danny watched her finish, after which she stuck out her tongue to show Lucky his handiwork. The two of them laughed, then fell back down on their pillows as if there wasn't a marriage to consider, or a friendship to respect.

DANNY TRUDGED BACK TO the car, which, to his pleasant surprise, started right up. Pumped to leave the premises as quickly as possible, he dumped the garden supplies and dog food bags on the side of the road. Later, when he was well on his way to points unknown, he would text Katie as to their whereabouts. Whatever possessions and clothes he'd left at the house could be replaced at the nearest Walmart. Avoiding the drama that the new domestic configuration would surely cause was worth the price.

As he sped down the hill, he had to wonder: *Was this the sign that it was time to go back home?* Perhaps the Maya Cinema marquee, followed by what had just transpired, was the telltale combo. But he didn't believe in signs before. Why should he believe in them now?

Road Warriors

Despite their mutual fondness for hard liquor and hookers, Ted and Harley Mason proved uneasy travel companions. For the "Stucco King," the bloom of being in an author's presence had come way off the rose, his mission now simply to corral his mercenary so he could recoup something from his investment. Mason, for his part, recognized that he had been exposed as a hack, and feared he was too burned out to exhume whatever talent he'd once possessed. He did, however, have enough long-term memory to recall that if a writer wanted to realize his potential, he had to think about something other than cashing his subject's checks. Harley Mason knew he needed to get inside Ted and feel his plight. Since this wasn't easy for the author to do with a subject he liked, inhabiting the soul of a man who symbolized everything he despised about America would be a near-impossible task. Still, the biographer was astute enough to recognize that through an unanticipated roll of the dice, he had a story that was at once larger than life and intimately tragic. When would he get the opportunity to write such a thing again?

As the star of his future opus gunned the town car to ninety-five in a seventy-five mile an hour zone, Mason had to wonder what the man was thinking. Was he wistfully reflecting on his defunct marriage? Castigating himself for the hubris that had sent him charging willy-nilly into Phase IV construction? Perhaps his mind was on Danny, and how to get him back. Then again, there was a better-than-even chance that Ted was simply going over his pitch for the upcoming meetings. This was, after all, the deal that would make or break him. The author saw no reason to beat around the bush. "So what's going on in the mastermind's noggin' right now?"

"You can cut the mastermind crap, Mason. You already got the job."

"Duly noted. Just tell me, are you at all nervous?"

"Why the fuck would I be nervous?" Ted snapped. "You think I haven't been through this a zillion times before?"

"With all due respect, you've got an awful lot riding on these meetings."

"Which is exactly what's going on in my head. So write that."

Mason explained that good biography was about character exploration and demanded more detail than *The dude's got a lot of shit he's thinking about.*

"What do you want me to tell you? That I had an abusive childhood or whatnot? Should I whine about how my dad called me Teddy-Wetty when I peed the bed? Or that I paid for seven abortions that I know for a fact I had nothing to do with? Bellyaching's just not my style."

"I take it you don't want those examples in the book."

"If you need to pad the thing, fine. Be my guest."

Thinking he might be starting to get somewhere, Mason pressed on. "Tell me what you're thinking about right this moment."

"Oh, Jesus."

"Come on. Free associate. Even a bunch of disparate thoughts are good."

"If you really want to know, I'm thinking about a Two-Finger Peek-A-Boo."

Mason was surprised and somewhat impressed to hear that even as Ted stood firmly at the brink of corporate annihilation, he was thinking about pussy. "I thought I was obsessed with sex, but you're off the charts, sir."

"It has nothing to do with sex, you idiot. Lindy's Diner, baby. The Two-Finger is the best burger in Tucson. 'Course some folks prefer the Dirty Sanchez."

"Okay, so you're not thinking about sex. Yet, with your life on the verge of going in the shitter, you're thinking about burgers that sound like sex."

"They're fucking great burgers, man. And, by the way, sink or swim in Tucson, my life does not go in the shitter."

"Tell me how that one works," Mason wanted to know. He hoped Ted's response might peel back a layer or two.

"If I don't get my funding, I pack up and move my ass to a nice golf community that's never heard of Ted Johnson. They say Hilton Head's a pretty nice place to close out act three."

"It'd be that easy for you to just leave town? With your family here?"

"Who knows where the fuck my family's gonna be? Or who still considers themselves my family?"

The first crack in the armor, the biographer thought. "I know you'll say it's irrelevant, but did you have a happy childhood?"

"Not really. We were poor and it sucked. Which was my whole motivation for creating a better life. And for making that dream available to others." Ted's eyes started to get misty. "It'd be hard as fuck to walk away from that."

It fascinated Mason how the thought of not being able to share a dream with strangers made Ted weepy, yet he couldn't get emotional about the near-liquidation of his family.

"You ever been married, Mason?" Ted asked, completely out of the blue.

The biographer nodded. "Three or four times, depending on whether you count Vegas. Not sure the Pope Benedict impersonator had a license."

"Three or four times? So you're a way bigger fuck-up than me." This gave Ted something to smile about.

"You could look at it that way," Mason countered. "Or, you could say that I wasn't with anyone long enough to actually hurt them."

"And I stayed until I ruined people's lives is what you're saying?"

"No—" It was exactly what Mason was saying, and it was too late to take it back.

"Lemme ask you something, Mr. Author. You've written a boatload of biographies. In the grand scheme of things, am I that horrible a person?"

Mason knew he was not in a position to judge, but his silence was interpreted as an affirmative.

"You know," Ted continued, "I never wanted to screw up anybody's life. It just kind of happened, I guess."

It was hard to believe, but Harley Mason felt for his subject. Not just Ted, but all the Johnsons. Jeannie, who'd trudged at her husband's side for forty-odd years, had certainly put forth her best effort. Danny had tried like hell to make the wheels turn smoothly, but never found a tolerable way to balance work and family. And his misery trickled down to Maya. It struck the biographer that the Johnson family, whom most would agree possessed the means with which to be happy, had somehow been robbed of the vital connectors that brought human beings together; that the sum total of their Cascade Falls existence had been a series of misfires.

"You know, sometimes you just gotta drown your troubles in a hamburger," Ted proclaimed.

"That place serve beer?" Mason asked.

"Nah, but no worries. I got a cooler in the trunk."

Mason smiled. "You're not concerned about me being drunk in the meetings?"

"Not at all. Most of these guys are shitfaced before noon. Plus, I can always leave you at the motel."

Mason laughed. "I have to tell you, you've got a pretty good attitude, under the circumstances."

"It's that attitude that got me where I am today. Would you like to hear a little secret from the Ted Johnson archives?"

"Off the record or on?"

"To be determined after we're through. I've never told anybody this, but when I first got into the business, I made a little deal with my myself for motivational purposes. I decided that for each Johnson home constructed, I would treat myself to…a lady."

"Let me get this straight. You gave yourself bonuses in the form of prostitutes?"

"I suppose, if you want to take the narrow view. To me, each encounter was a beautiful celebration unto itself."

"You've built hundreds of units, Ted."

"And right there's the reason why."

"Holy fuck." It suddenly dawned on Mason. "How many units are in the Tucson plan?"

"Four hundred and twenty-three. That thing goes, I'm a busy boy."

HARLEY MASON, WHO ONCE, on a cocaine and nitrous oxide holiday, ordered up seven hookers, had never seen the likes of this. The man behind the wheel was, for all intents and purposes, the white, Baptist Wilt Chamberlain of home developers. "I've got to ask," Mason began, "as a churchgoing man, how do you reconcile your sex life with your religious beliefs?"

"Apples and oranges, my friend. I keep my spiritual orgasms out of the bedroom. You should try it sometime."

"I've never had a spiritual orgasm," Mason confessed.

"Gotta work on that, pal. Godlessness is what's killing this goddamn country."

Mason felt himself starting to hate Ted Johnson all over again. He decided that this conversation was on the record, whether Ted wanted it to be or not.

School's Out

Somehow he'd managed to do a near-perfect job smoothing the drywall seams, a formidable task given that every thinking moment of his day had been preoccupied with Maya Johnson. Now, as Owen got back in the truck to pick up Brianna from school, his heart pounded at the prospect of spotting a white Lexus in the parking lot. He chastised himself for being so weak as to indulge in such counterproductive fantasies. Had he simply been able to enjoy the sexual pleasures offered by Candy Daniels without adding an extra component, he'd be completely focused on his daughter, rather than hunting down a Japanese SUV. The more salient truth was that if Lucy had been given the chance to accompany him into old age, Candy Daniels, ergo Maya, would never have been an issue. But death had fucked up everything. All he'd wanted in its aftermath was some measure of stability so that Brianna would feel safe and loved. And it had been working pretty well until he did what everyone said widowed people were supposed to do: "Be good to yourself." "Recognize your own needs and take steps to fulfill them." "Go out and date." "If it's all about taking care of others, you'll burn out."

Now that he'd opened the "What about me?" can of worms, the ramifications seemed far more perilous than burnout.

THE MINUTE HE PULLED up to the front entrance, he got a glimpse of Maya loading Max and Dana into the Lexus. His truck was a few cars down and she was too busy to notice him in the line. Owen, on the other hand, saw enough to confirm that whatever it was this woman had stirred in him, wasn't about to go away anytime soon. Out of every possible female, he'd become fixated on one who was not only married with children, but whose husband had recently suffered a breakdown.

The brain trust of advice givers always recommended that the newly single seek out people in similar situations, preferably ones who were relatively unencumbered. Yet as he studied the way Maya interacted with her kids, he realized that sometimes the things that encumbered people were what made them attractive. Candy Daniels presented as a page out of *Fitness Magazine* and had absolutely nothing tying her down. The experts would undoubtedly give two thumbs up, but to Owen, Maya's tousled ponytail and paint-stained sweatshirt was far more enticing. This was a woman deep in the trenches, unafraid of getting her hands dirty, and, at least for now, taking care of business with a smile on her face. Still, he wasn't the kind of man who snatched married women from their husbands. And Maya didn't seem like the type who'd want that, certainly not for her children. The shitty part was that you couldn't pick who you were attracted to. The pheromones would kick in, start to do their thing, then the tough choices had to be made.

OWEN REALIZED THAT IF nothing else, his ill-fated adventure with Candy had forced him to identify what he'd been lacking—apart from sex. He missed having a talking partner, someone next to him whose conversation compelled him to listen. Just from observing Maya, with little in the way of logic or evidence, he had convinced himself that she was a kindred spirit; that should they be given the opportunity to dine together as he and Candy had, the two of them would instantly realize that they were soul mates. It was crazy thinking. On the other hand, didn't every romantic fantasy start with grandiose assumptions?

The next thing he knew, Brianna was knocking on the passenger-side window. She opened the door, but didn't hop in or put down her backpack. "Hey Dad," she called out sweetly. "Would it be okay if I stayed after school to work on my science project with Jenna?"

Jenna Martinson was the best science student in the class, so Owen happily agreed to her request. "No problem, honey. When do you want me to come back?"

"Like four-thirty, maybe?"

"You got it." Owen held out his cheek for a kiss, his daughter still at the age where she happily complied.

Watching her run back into the school, he suddenly realized that he had an hour and a half to kill and needed a plan to occupy his time. Then he remembered something Jeannie had told him.

It was not only brazen, but flew in the face of everything he considered appropriate under the circumstances: that would have been to stay as far away from Maya's house as possible. Yet here he was, parking at the curb and getting ready to ring her doorbell. He checked his look in the rearview mirror, ran his hand quickly through his hair, and got out of the truck.

By the time he reached her front door, it was already open. Maya stood there waving. "Hey there." It seemed like she was glowing. One thing was for sure, his unannounced presence hadn't made her unhappy.

"Your mom said you might need some stuff done around the house. I just happened to be passing by and wondered if it might be a good time to take a look."

"Um…yeah, sure. Come on in."

He walked into a typical suburban after-school tableau, Max and Dana finishing their milk and cookies and about to start in on homework.

"You guys remember Mr. Shea?" she asked the kids.

"Yeah," Max piped up. "You're Brianna's dad. Sorry about your wife."

"Thanks, Max," Owen smiled.

Maya turned beet red, but Owen was appreciative. Not only did it show that she'd raised her kids to care about other people, the blushing revealed her own sensitivity about how the mention of Lucy might affect him.

"I'll show you around. Start your homework, kids."

ONE UNIQUE ASPECT OF Owen's profession was that the work drew him into the most private of spaces, affording him a rare window into how human beings lived among their things. What did a crystal chandelier, or stuffed walk-in closets, or a douching toilet say about a person? Had he the time and the gumption, he could compile a book of short stories based on the oddball environments he'd visited over the years. No living space, however, had piqued his interest the way this one did. His curiosity, of course, had nothing to do with the woefully standard features of the master bath. Owen was transfixed because he was in her bathroom, looking at the shower stall where Maya Johnson stood naked each morning to prepare her body for the day.

She pointed out some water leaking under the sink and into the vanity. He assured her that it was just a hose, and that he had a bunch of spares in the car. Then they went back into the master bedroom, where he did everything in his power not to stare at the California King and imagine her smell on the sheets. What needed fixing there was a GFI behind one of the nightstands. Whose nightstand was it? he wondered. His or hers? Just as Owen was about to tell her that he'd have to go to the hardware store to pick up a new receptacle, Maya's cell phone rang.

Her face seemed to turn pale upon seeing the name of the caller. "Would you excuse me a second?"

"Take as long as you need."

MAYA OPENED THE SLIDING doors and stepped onto the patio, leaving Owen alone with no place to sit other than on the bed. He concluded that since Danny had been gone for so long, the nightstand with the pile of books and magazines was most likely Maya's. He had to look. What people read usually gave you a pretty good insight into who they were. Unfortunately, this particular stack proved difficult to quantify. Joyce Carol Oates shared bedside real estate with *Us Weekly*, a compilation of Chuck Close portraits, the latest *Bon Appétit,* and a Sudoku book.

Her eclecticism made her inscrutable, the sense of mystery exciting him all the more. He looked outside and saw Maya pacing the patio and gesticulating animatedly. Part of him wished he knew what she was saying, but he also appreciated the beauty of not knowing. You didn't want to hear everything about a person's life in one sitting, especially someone as captivating as Maya. Details were to be savored in small bites, the better to appreciate each flavor.

"It's not just your decision," Maya argued into the phone. "You can't just pick up and leave, then show up whenever you feel like it without considering how it affects the rest of us."

"So you don't want me to come home?" Danny asked.

She didn't, but for the sake of the kids, remained open to the idea. "I only want you here if you're ready to be here. Really be here."

He grew silent.

"Are you prepared to go back to work or get a different job?"

"I think so."

"Can you promise me that whatever it is you wind up doing, you can be a positive and cheerful role model for the kids?"

He tried to say yes, but in his heart, Danny knew that even with all the progress that had been made, he couldn't respond with a hundred percent certainty. It didn't help that she seemed to have little desire to see him, much less offer anything in the way of comfort. While he ached to see Max and Dana, he felt incapable of meeting his wife's conditions. "Maybe I do need some more time," Danny told her.

"I'm sorry."

"I'm the one who should be sorry."

"We're both allowed," she reminded him. "We'll keep talking."

Hanging up the phone, Danny wasn't so sure they would.

OWEN PRETENDED TO BE absorbed in an *Us* magazine article on Hollywood midwives while he peeked up to read Maya's expression. He could tell it had been a difficult conversation and suspected that she'd been talking with her husband. He wanted to ask if everything was okay, but deemed it too intimate a question given the fact that they were alone in her bedroom. "What else needs looking at?" was his substitute line.

"A bad light socket in the family room and some baseboard in the studio."

As soon as he entered the studio, Owen realized that he needn't have worked so hard trying to analyze her reading material. The canvases told a much bigger story about who she was. While he didn't know much about art, he could see from the first painting that this was someone who felt trapped by her surroundings as well as her circumstance. "You've got some strong feelings about this place, don't you?"

"What gave it away? The aliens or the slime?"

"The whole enchilada. You're shitting all over Cascade Falls."

While Maya was pleased to get such a strong reaction, she suddenly felt embarrassed about having criticized the subdivision that this nice and decent man called home. For all she knew, he loved the place. There were lots of folks who did. "Listen, I think Cascade Falls is great for some people," she explained. "I don't mean to put down anyone's lifestyle."

"Sure, you do," he replied. "Every piece here is saying that this place sucks."

"I'm sorry if I offended you."

"You didn't. I mean, let's be honest. Would anyone throw together a development like this in Siberia? Of course not. It's too freaking cold. People weren't meant to live in thirty below zero, and they weren't meant to live in 120 above in a place with no water. But thanks to a little thing called air conditioning, it's a lot easier to convince the masses that this is okay. Dig some holes, fill 'em up with a hose, and before long, everybody starts to believe they're real lakes. Did you know it takes the average person who moves here two years to adjust to the climate? Two years of bloody noses and giant, dry boogers."

"So, you hate it, too?"

"Not at all. I climatized, both physically and mentally. After a while I realized that even though it's all prefab, the people who live here are like anybody else. They just want a little something to call their own. Nothing wrong with that."

"I know. I just don't...feel alive here."

"Well, you should."

She regarded him curiously. Who was he to tell her how she should feel?

"If it weren't for Cascade Falls, you wouldn't have these." He pointed to what now added up to eighteen canvases.

"I painted them out of desperation."

"And what would you have come up with if everything in your life was perfect?"

"I don't know. That's an interesting question." She took a deep breath, then had to ask: "Do you think they're any good?"

"I do, but what do I know? You ought to show them to some galleries or something."

Maya told him that she had a place in Los Angeles that was interested, based on her previous work. But she'd yet to let them see any of this new series.

Owen couldn't understand her hesitance. "You have a cell phone? Email a couple of photos. You don't have to give away the whole store at once. Start with these two." He picked "Aliens at the Gate" and "Sky Harbor Runway."

JUST AS MAYA BELIEVED that Danny had to feel confident in his coping skills before attempting to come home, she needed to believe in her vision before sending anything off to Judith Aronson. She already had a huge fan in Smoke Shop Bob, and Harley Mason seemed to like the work well enough, despite his scuzzy motives. Owen's reaction felt different though. It wasn't just that he was encouraging her to get the stuff out there. This was a pillar of the Cascade Falls community giving her permission to share her feelings about it with the world.

"I think I will send them," she told him.

"You've got nothing to send until you take the pictures. May I?" He held up his smart phone.

THE HANDYMAN MADE SWIFT work of it, persuading her to let him shoot the whole lot as long as he had the camera out. "I'll text them to you, then delete them all, so you can't sue me for theft or plagiarism."

"You can keep them if you like," she smiled.

"I'd like. Now, don't we have one more room to look at?"

"Right. The family room." Just as Owen had had trouble concentrating on drywalling the other day, Maya's thoughts now had little to do with home repair. She started to lead him out of the studio, then stopped and looked at him. "Thank you, Owen."

"For what?"

She was about to answer, but found no words. Suddenly, she reached up and kissed him on the lips.

Somehow, he seemed less surprised than she was.

"I'm sorry," she blurted out.

"Really?" *He* wasn't. He decided to try kissing her back.

She didn't seem sorry at all.

Rubber Meets the Road

There were a couple of meetings scheduled for the afternoon, and another two the next morning, after which they'd head back to Phoenix, ideally with at least one yea vote in hand. Thanks to Ted's pathological speeding, subject and author arrived in Tucson well ahead of their first appointment, leaving them with hours of time to kill. If Harley Mason thought his boss had been joking about being booked into separate hotels, he became a believer when he saw Ted screech up to the lobby of the Motel 6 and pop the trunk.

"I need to go collect my thoughts. Be outside at 2:15." And with that, the Sultan of Sprawl was Ritz-Carlton bound, primed for some five-star introspection.

THE BREADTH OF TED's soul-searching amounted to little more than an unanswered call to Danny, followed by a nap. Even though his son's abrupt exile had angered the shit out of him, he hadn't stopped trying to reach out. This made the boy's refusal to take his calls doubly frustrating, especially in the current scheme of things. Whether the family business was to survive or go down in flames, Danny Johnson needed to know the score. Tucson was the barometer that would determine the future for everybody.

Had the Johnson paterfamilias possessed the slightest bit of self-awareness, he would have realized that making the call had little to do with the Tucson deal. He just wanted to hear his son's voice. Most people didn't lose their immediate and extended families at the same time, but this was exactly what Ted saw unfolding if Tucson went south. The foundation of his Johnson Homes spiel had always been that family was everything and he still believed that, no matter how many strange beds he'd visited over the years. If his son was having some sort of mental breakdown, he needed to know about it. He'd heard the vague reports of Danny "sorting things out" and "trying to heal" from Maya, but he had no way of evaluating the situation for himself unless he actually spoke to the boy. Was the kid just not picking up, or had he abandoned his cell phone? Or was it something worse, something horrific? Luckily, Ted had the ability to zone out even in the most dire of circumstances, so once he accepted that he was powerless to reach his son, he fell right to sleep and got lost in dreams.

DURING BOOM TIMES, TED would regale audiences with tales of how, since so many of his nocturnal imaginings were prescient, he would act on them the minute he woke up. One night, he'd dreamt of a Phase II clubhouse with an international food court, and by the next afternoon, a plan had been set in motion to install everything from a Panda Express to a Falafel World. Unfortunately, people in the Phases weren't high on ethnic foods and the project had to be abandoned at a substantial loss. Yet Ted remained convinced that the daring notion from his subconscious was simply an idea ahead of its time.

This afternoon's vision proved similarly dicey. An Ultra-Orthodox Jewish Johnson Homes Community, while surely a cutting edge concept, was riddled with inherent flaws. The dearth of Chasidism in Maricopa

County stuck out as an obvious problem, although Ted held to the belief that if you build it, they will come. The bigger issue was that he didn't have the money to build anything, which was, after all, why he'd driven down here. Putting prescience on hold, Ted decided to take a quick shower so he'd be fresh for the Higgenbotham brothers over at Bank of Tucson. Joe and Kenny were good kids and had always shown great respect for his master planning acumen. He owed it to them to bring his A game. Reminding himself how far the Ted Johnson A game had gotten him in the past would pump him up for closing the deal this afternoon.

HARLEY MASON WAS EIGHT feet away from the Town Car when he started smelling the cologne. The author approached the vehicle slowly, wondering how he'd be able to survive riding shotgun while inhaling the lethal combo of lilac and musk. But what choice did he have? Besides, real journalists put themselves in fucking foxholes to get a story. All he needed to do was breathe drug store perfume for a couple of hours. Opening the passenger side-door, he saw a freshly shaven Ted, silver hair slicked back in an eighties Pat Riley do, and donning a dark pinstripe suit. The threads were a bit funereal for Mason's tastes, but they had famously been worn at every one of Ted's big deal closings, regardless of decade or current lapel style. Mason had been instructed to bring a suit of his own, since he would be introduced as a Johnson Homes associate, but since he no longer owned one, he wore a borrowed poplin of Ted's.

"Well, I'm ready to watch the magic happen," the biographer told the boss.

"I'm not a magician. I just make my money the old-fashioned way."

"You earn it?"

"Hell no, anybody can do that. I show other folks how to make money off people who earn it."

BEING KEPT WAITING IN the reception area for over forty minutes was probably not a good omen. Ted did his best to stay energized, reminiscing about his first part-time job at an escrow office. "I got more docs signed in a twenty-hour week than everyone else got in forty. They started calling me Doc Johnson."

As far as Mason could tell, working in an escrow company pushing paper had to be the most boring job imaginable, but to Ted it was a Seven Seas adventure. One thing Mason had to give the man—he loved to work. What was more, he loved offices. And office buildings. What other people saw as corporate prison, he viewed as a cradle of opportunity, the place men went to beat their heads against the wall and walk out with few million bucks. Harley Mason had never had that kind of drive. Sure, he'd taken pride in his early writing, but he was also of the school where you sold your story, got your check, then spent whatever didn't go to rent on booze, drugs, and women. A lot of times, the next job didn't come till after the rent was due, but the biographer lived for the in-between, the spaces in which you could experience things that were outside your comfort zone. By now, he knew that Ted wasn't a guy who did well with spaces.

A CONSERVATIVE, YET PLEASING-LOOKING, redhead, came out to great them. "They're ready for you," she smiled.

"Maybe we're not ready for them," Ted laughed.

The redhead looked flummoxed. "Oh. Do you need some more time?"

"I think he was joking," Mason chimed in.

Ted nodded that he was. Mason hoped that Ted's brand of gaiety would go over better in the meeting.

HARLEY MASON HAD WATCHED a lot of old movies in his time, preferring screwball comedies and Hitchcock thrillers to the current action films and vampire fare. As he watched Ted deliver his spiel to Joe and Kenny Higgenbotham, all he could think of was *Sunset Boulevard*, with the Gloria Swanson role being played by Ted. It wasn't so much that the man was too old, but the use of terms like "Nexting" and "Johnsonization" made him sound like a rag salesman from the Eisenhower Era. While no one would deny the passion of his pitch, in the current marketplace, making an emotional plea to numbers guys had as much chance of success as trying to get an octogenarian pregnant. The Higgenbothams clearly weren't biting. From their perspective, the current housing market couldn't support a development of the scale Ted had designed, and that, combined with the already tenuous financial state of Johnson Homes, made for a mix too volatile to risk an investment.

TED HAD HEARD THIS tight-fisted song and dance before. He remained undeterred, and proceeded to trot out the definitive reason why they owed it to themselves to put their faith in him. "I need to tell you the story of the Three Wise Men."

Joe and Kenny sat back, puzzled as to how their guest thought an impromptu Bible class would win them over. Even Harley Mason couldn't believe Ted was playing the Jesus card.

Ted explained that the Three Wise Men in his story had nothing to do with frankincense or myrrh. This was the moniker that he had personally given the investors who put up the cash for the first Johnson Homes community. "Now why exactly were they so damn wise? Because these fellas went on to make nine hundred percent on their investment. Dewey Rayburn bought a chain of gas stations with his money. Jack Burley got himself a cattle ranch. Al Scofield lost it all in junk bonds, against my advice."

THE HIGGENBOTHAMS NODDED AND smiled politely, but Mason was sure Ted was dead in the water the minute they walked in. The merciful thing now was to have it end as quickly as possible. As little as he'd initially thought of Ted, it was just too painful to watch him unravel. What could be more heartbreaking than seeing a man who lived for offices and real estate get thrown out of an office and be told he could no longer sell real estate?

"Well, I thank you for taking the time," Ted told his hosts, when he finally realized it was over. "You get a change of heart, you know where to ring me up."

"That we do," Kenny smiled.

"Great to see you again," Joe said. "Let's play some golf the next time you're down here."

"That'd be nice," Ted nodded.

Mason hated these kinds of endings. If the whole thing was going to blow up anyway, why did it have to be so fucking phony? He didn't know much about the housing business, but he was always up for a good fight. "You're making a big mistake," he scolded the Higgenbothams.

Ted turned to Mason, shocked to hear anybody but himself making his case.

Joe Higgenbotham spoke first. "We appreciate your opinion—"

"No, you don't," Mason continued. "This guy's a fucking god in the subdivision business. Nobody can make a cookie cutter money machine like Ted Johnson."

"Thanks for coming in," Kenny interjected, anxious to put an end to the commotion.

"I apologize for my associate's language," Ted assured them.

Mason seethed. "Don't apologize to these fat fucks!" "You're better than they are!"

There was little time to consider this possibility as two security guards stepped in to bodily escort them out of the building.

"You don't have to thank me," the author told Ted.

"Thank you? You just killed my chances with those guys!"

"Oh, Jesus. Tell me you had a prayer of turning them around."

"You never know."

"I don't. But I'm pretty sure you do."

Ted absolutely did. Tucson Bank was DOA. And who knows? Maybe this Harley Mason character was right. If you were going to be shown the door, why go out in a blaze of politeness? He had never offered up that filthy an outburst in all his years dealing with banks, but in retrospect, he wished he had. Ted suddenly found himself slapping the biographer on the back. "Good job in there, son. I appreciate the kind words."

THE NEXT MEETING AT Western Federal was practically a carbon copy of the first, minus the phony deference and farewell profanity. Unlike the Higgenbotham brothers, the Western Fed guys hadn't done business with Ted before, so the lack of a personal relationship made the rejection materialize that much quicker. Mason could tell from Ted's demeanor that he was slowly beginning to accept the notion of an Arizona without a Johnson Homes. As he watched the deflation progress, it occurred to the author that in all his years of writing, he had never become attached to a project the way Ted had devoted himself to his company. Perhaps if he'd spent his career writing a single, all-encompassing book, he might have felt that way, but he couldn't say for sure. What he did know was that bearing witness to the death of a dream had moved him. It was like watching the body of a football star or an Olympian get whittled down to nothing by cancer or old age. That the deterioration was happening inside a businessman's head made it no less powerful.

Without a word, Ted hopped in the driver's seat and started off toward Lindy's. There was no law that said you couldn't have a burger for lunch and dinner. If the whole world was blowing up, why not meet your Maker with a Dirty Sanchez? They sat with their meat and beer till closing time, after which Ted dropped the author off at the motel to call it a night. Mason being Mason, he watched the Town Car speed off, then headed to the nearest bar for a nightcap. As an economy measure, he opted for the well Scotch, which, at around 2:00 a.m., struck him as ill-advised. Still, through all the vomiting and diarrhea, he couldn't stop thinking how fortunate he was not to be Ted Johnson.

WHEN TED PICKED HIM up at eight the next morning, he appeared not only refreshed, but enthusiastic about the upcoming meetings. How he had gotten himself in this frame of mind was a mystery to Mason, who felt like he had a dozen steel balls bouncing around in his skull.

"What the hell's up with you?" Ted asked his obviously hungover hire. "That is not a morning after beer buzz, fella. You been shootin' up or somethin'?"

Mason came clean about sharing the rest of the evening with a malt blend called Daggan's Dew, which had the bouquet and taste of paint thinner. He swore that he would not let his sorry state impair his performance at the meeting. Since his role was basically to observe, as long as he didn't fall asleep or collapse, everything would be fine. As it happened, the author's throbbing skull turned out to be a non-issue, as the folks over at Southwest Financial Partners had not merely forgotten about the meeting, but denied ever having entered it in the books. When Ted offered to stay an extra day in order to accommodate their schedule, they said they'd get back to him.

TED JOHNSON WAS ONE burger away from a shutout. Having little left to lose, he indulged himself in a Donkey Punch, boasting a half pound of beef smothered with green chiles, jalapeños, and habeñeros. If he suddenly had to shit himself in the DesertCorp meeting, what difference did it make at this point? Mason, whose eyes were conveniently unable to fully open, couldn't look at food in his current condition. He was ready for the credits to role on their little escapade, after which he would sober up and knock out the best vanity piece he was capable of writing. In some weird way, this assignment had taught him a valuable lesson. Living in a trailer in Kaufman County, Texas, where DAs got murdered for convicting white supremacists, somehow felt safer than Cascade Falls, where the danger and suffering were more subtle and difficult to identify.

THROUGHOUT HIS ADULT LIFE, Mason had always contended that there was good value in low expectations. Sure enough, while he wasn't about to jump to conclusions, the vibe at DesertCorp seemed 180 degrees from how Ted had been received at their other stops. The minute they entered the reception area, they were escorted to a state-of-the-art conference room, where bartenders, waiters, and a platter of local barbecue awaited them. It seemed like such overkill that Ted felt obliged to remind the service staff who he was, thinking that the receptionist might have escorted them to the wrong room. After being assured that the spread was indeed intended for the Johnson Homes meeting, Ted smiled at Mason, who was at once intrigued and nauseated. The sight of eight inch beef ribs made him want to toss his cookies, but he needed to stay in control so he could digest what was about to be said, if not served.

Despite having consumed three giant hamburgers in less than twenty-four hours, Ted dove into the baby backs, the rationale being that he had yet to fulfill his pork allotment. "A whole different animal," he informed Mason.

"Literally," the biographer nodded.

Just as Ted began analyzing the vinegar content of the barbecue sauce, they were greeted by their host, thirty-something Steve Ramirez, who, according to Ted's googling, hailed from one of the most prominent Mexican families in the area. "I've been waiting to shake that hand for a long time," Steve announced, a glint of reverence in his eyes.

Since there was nothing that floated Ted Johnson's boat more than reverence, having it combined with tender pork and a tangy sauce sent his buoyancy off the charts. Mason couldn't help but think positive thoughts as well. Ramirez had no history with Ted, so what reason could there possibly be to make a fuss unless something substantial was in the offing? The thought raced through Mason's head that Ramirez might be angling to buy out Johnson Homes before Tarkanian or Del Webb swooped in for the kill. Then again, it could be something more palatable. Maybe Ramirez had put out this spread to acknowledge the Johnson good years, and his firm was prepared to high roll with a former world champ.

AFTER RECITING A QUARTER-FOR-QUARTER account of Johnson Homes' huge profits in the early 2000s, Ramirez began to ease into another gear. "You've always been an out-of-the-box-thinker, am I right, Ted?"

"True dat," his guest chuckled. Yet despite his reputation as a man who liked to change things up, Ted felt he needed to represent the

Tucson deal for what it was. "In all honesty, JH Tucson isn't any different from the work we've done in Phoenix."

"I'm aware of that," Ramirez smiled. "Which is why I'd like you to consider going a whole other way with the Johnson brand."

Both Ted and Mason smelled a half-rejection, which, while not optimum, still represented a fifty percent improvement over anything the company had entertained in over a year.

Ramirez elaborated. "The housing market's a disaster, we're flooded with vacancies, so what sense would it make to keep building now?"

Ted, not realizing it was a rhetorical question, launched into his boilerplate riff on market fluctuation, until Steve finally cut him short.

"Imagine a world where, even in the worst of housing markets, you can make the Johnson Homes brand a shining star."

"I'm listening," Ted replied, clueless as to where this might be headed.

Ramirez began to map out a multi-point plan, in which a DesertCorp/Johnson Homes conglomerate would go about snapping up short sales and foreclosures in the Phoenix area, where Ted was already a known quantity. "An aggressive buyout strategy would diminish the available inventory, and this, combined with the banks tightening loans to near unqualifiable standards, would pave the way for a whole new market. A market free of regulation and with unlimited growth potential."

Ted was starting to get an inkling of what Ramirez had in mind. The financier suddenly turned to Mason. "You look confused."

"Actually, I'm hung over. And, I have no idea what you're talking about."

"Two words, my friend. Johnson Rentals."

As the phrase made its way from the air into the essence of everything that was Ted Johnson, Mason saw a man transform into a corpse—his face white, then blue, his mouth attempting to speak without the ability to generate sound.

Steve, aware that he'd pitched a radical idea, tried to assure Ted. "I know this would all be new for you, but hey—Nexting. Am I right?"

Ted silently rose from his chair, signaling Mason that it was time to leave.

"I hope I haven't insulted you," Ramirez pleaded.

As off-kilter as he felt, Ted knew he had to set things straight. "Mr. Ramirez, I would sooner shoot my mother in the face and toss her body in a ditch than lower myself to taking advantage of folks in the godforsaken rental market."

"Profit is profit," Steve argued. "Sales, rentals, what's the difference?"

"The difference, my friend, is what made me Ted Johnson. Good afternoon."

TED DECLINED TO SHAKE Ramirez's hand and marched out of the conference room, grabbing a spicy chicken wing as he went. Mason followed him out of the building, trying to imagine what the ride home to Phoenix would be like. His subject unlocked the car and calmly sat down in the driver's seat. Mason took his place riding shotgun, and searched for some words of solace. "Well, that was fun," he offered, figuring humor was at least a good icebreaker. He figured wrong. Ted started the engine, but kept the transmission in park, looking at his biographer with a combination of incredulity and disgust. "We've come to the end of our road, Mr. Mason."

"You can't be sure," the author replied, trying to say something positive, if false. "What about Israel? They're always building shit there."

"I know that. But I was talking about you and me. You'll be paid for your services through today, but as of now, we're finished. I'll drop you off at the motel and you can find your way back to Texas."

"But there's more to the story," Mason argued.

Ted shook his head. "Haven't you squeezed enough scratch out of this?"

"This isn't about money." While most people would be hard-pressed to believe him, Harley Mason was speaking the truth. He was now emotionally invested in how the future was going to play out, not just for Ted, but for Jeannie, Maya, Danny, and the entire community of Cascade Falls.

"Nice try, but it's over. If you choose to honor our agreement, you can email me the finished pages and I'll decide whether or not I want them published."

"You don't have to pay me another dime," Mason told him. "I just need to follow this story to the end."

"You've already done that."

Ten minutes later, they were shaking hands in front of the Motel 6, Mason wishing his former boss a safe trip home. Ted responded that he wasn't necessarily going there right away.

"What about the office?" the author asked.

"Seems like I already said my goodbyes. I'll put in a call to James and Dusty."

Mason couldn't believe what was coming over him. He was actually going to miss this guy. "Hey, Ted, you know what I said to the Higginbotham brothers? I meant it."

"I appreciate that, I really do. And if you knew a rat's ass about real estate, it might be worth something."

"So much for fond farewells," Mason concluded.

"Listen, don't wind up in the toilet with a needle in your arm, you hear? And for God's sake, don't drink anymore well Scotch."

As TED JOHNSON DROVE off into the sunset, Mason discovered that in addition to his hangover being gone, he had no desire to start working on the next one. He was going to begin writing the biography tonight and make his way back to Cascade Falls in the morning. Even if Ted took his time returning, the company would start feeling the effects of Tucson the minute the news arrived. And if this was indeed the end of the Ted Johnson story, what better place to be than "Stucco Central?" The loyal minions, the subdivision soldiers who had served the cause since Day One, would all have plenty to say about this odd, but extraordinary, career. Perhaps now that the dream was over, the faithful could step back and assess it with candor rather than platitudes. Mason suspected they would still judge Ted kindly, but conceded that hard feelings were understandable coming from people who had been left unemployed and without a pension plan. They'd put their faith in their leader and he'd come up empty. Yet, he had done everything in his power to remain worthy of their faith and would never forgive himself for having failed. Folks would either understand, or be so frightened about how they were going to make ends meet that they'd resent him for the rest of their lives. Harley Mason suddenly felt grateful that he had never been inspiring enough to have anyone put his faith in him.

Aftermath

As Maya drove the kids out the Phase II gate for what had to be the two-thousandth time, she was struck by how quiet the subdivision had grown over the last few months. It was true that even when Cascade Falls had first opened in the mid-nineties, the *Phoenix New Times* dubbed it "The place where the dead might visit in order to feel more alive." But it now seemed substantially worse, as if some sort of suburban rigor mortis had set in. When you did happen to see people on the street, they weren't as animated or cheerful. They still enjoyed tooling around in their golf carts, convening for happy hour, and putting on goofy costumes for theme nights in the Phases, but everybody looked lost: their conversations muted, their interactions spiritless. Even Buzzy the guard's wave had grown flaccid, his ever-reliable smile, a foggy memory.

Employees and residents alike had been assured that the new Tarkanian ownership would only improve upon an already-solid foundation, and all signs pointed to a seamless transition. Yet Maya knew that, spoken or not, there was a crucial question hovering over the HOA. "What is a Johnson community without Ted Johnson?" It was completely normal for subdivisions to thrive after the exit of their developers, but this one was a different ball of wax. Here, the majority of homeowners were first generation Johnson buyers, and her father-in-law's presence had permeated every extra they'd tacked on to their units, right down to the upgraded toilet paper holders. Now that the preacher who'd sold the American Dream was gone, how was his flock supposed to get closure?

Ted had never bothered to return after his trip to Tucson, arranging the sale of the company through financial advisors. The rumor Maya had heard was that he'd felt too ashamed to face his homeowners and was now holed up at a condo complex in Hilton Head, a leisure lifestyle Klaus Barbie. The truth was that most folks felt he'd just run into some bad luck and wished him well. Meanwhile, Jeannie was off traveling through Europe while real estate agents showed their renovated home to potential buyers. Maya got asked all the time about Danny. She would always say that he was doing fine, which she hoped was the case. She hadn't heard from him in a long while.

DROPPING OFF MAX AND Dana at school, Maya tried to picture her husband in his current surroundings, wherever they might be. After she'd lectured him about not coming home until he was ready to face his responsibilities, he called a week later to say he was giving up his cell phone. He was busy doing temp work and taking night classes, he said, but assured her that he had people who would lend him their phones when he needed to touch base. Soon after, he began to check in with less frequency.

She became progressively more angry as the weeks went by, yet she felt guilty in equal measure, wondering if her stern action had triggered a far worse reaction. Perhaps she shouldn't have been so harsh when Danny broached the possibility of coming home. As untenable as their situation had become, the last thing she wanted was to destroy him.

Maya took a deep breath, the smell inside the SUV a putrid combination of musty air conditioning and spilled juice boxes. Maybe Danny really *was* healing and getting himself stronger. As much as she wanted to believe that, she just couldn't get it to stick. She was dealing with her own strain of rigor mortis.

Seeing her expression as she walked into Starbucks, Owen could tell right away that she was having a bad morning. He had learned from personal experience that melancholy didn't need much of a trigger. The good news was that if Maya wanted to talk it out, he was there for her. "I ordered your latte when I saw you pull up," he informed her.

"Thanks." She didn't think it was fair to unload her guilt on someone who'd been through so much himself, especially first thing in the morning. "What time do you have to be at work?" she asked, for no particular reason.

"Whenever you get tired of seeing my face."

Maya managed a smile. She would never get tired of seeing his face, and that was part of the problem. "The art gallery from LA called," she told him. "They're going to give me a show."

"That's fucking fantastic!" Owen leaped across the table to give her a hug and kiss, quickly realizing that such public displays of affection were probably uncool given the size of the community.

"I should be happy, right?" Maya started to weep.

"You should be how you need to be."

"How come things can't ever just work?" she sniffled.

He knew she was talking about more than her inability to fully enjoy her paintings being accepted. While something positive had surely come her way, it did so in the context of everything else. Over time, Owen had developed the theory that each bit of good fortune one received always carried with it an obstacle to prevent one from embracing it. It was happening to him right now. He considered himself fortunate to have met Maya and was fairly certain that he was falling in love. As much as he wanted to tell her this, he dared not, concerned that it might spur Maya to declare her love, which would then cause her pain. Her happiness would be tempered by the shame of having betrayed the husband for whose safety now she feared.

ALLOWING HERSELF TO MAKE love to Owen had been an important step for Maya. Taking the leap had shown her that she was still capable of connecting with a man on a higher level than shared chores or daycare. She adored the way Owen talked, how he kissed, what he smelled like before and after their bodies fused together. Yet at the same time, she hated herself for it. If only she could have been satisfied with a Harley Mason one-night stand. Having crossed paths with a good man whom she could love, whom she *did* love, made it excruciating, knowing her husband was drifting somewhere in time and space. If only she could be sure Danny was okay. That he felt like he had a future. In her fantasy world, the one in which good news could be celebrated unimpeded, a couple that drifted apart would be able to find new love while continuing to be excellent parents, enriching their children with their individual strengths. Unfortunately, it wasn't a world she saw herself inhabiting anytime soon.

THE NIGHT THEY SLEPT together, Owen had whispered to her afterward that no matter what happened with Danny, or Ted, for that matter, he would see to it that she and the kids were provided for. This took her aback, not only because it was bold and jumping the gun, but because she knew he meant what he said, and she could envision herself saying yes to his nurturing and protection.

"I'm sorry. I didn't mean to upset you," he told her, seeing how uncomfortable she looked.

"It's okay. It was a really sweet thought."

He wished he could tell her the rest of his thoughts. The ones that weren't sweet, but intense, illogical even. In a perfect world, he would say that he didn't want to lose her. And what was more, that he didn't deserve to lose her since so much had already been taken from him. As self-centered as Owen recognized this confession to be, it was the most honest thing he could offer. And there would probably never be the right time for it.

"Can I ask you something?" he asked softly.

Whatever question he had in mind was already making her heart flutter. *What if he just wanted to refill her latte?* Not every word had to be significant.

"Would you mind if I came to your show in Los Angeles?"

"Wow. No. Of course I wouldn't mind. I'm not so sure I can get there though. Kids, school—"

"Well, if you can't show up, maybe I can report back on how things are going. And if you can get away, maybe we'll meet for coffee."

"Deal." She felt herself blushing.

"You sick of my face yet? Cause I should probably go do some work."

"As a matter of fact, I'm not sick of it at all. But you should go."

"I don't want to."

"I know. Why don't you come over for dinner tonight? Bring Brianna. We'll hang out with the kids."

"You sure that's okay?"

"No. I'm not sure of anything. But everybody knows everybody. It'll just be a good time, right?"

"I know it'll be a good time, but—"

"You're right. What am I thinking? I mean, Danny might call tonight, right?"

"He might." Owen got up from his chair and smiled, letting her know that despite declining the invitation, he was still in her corner. "I'll call you later."

THERE WERE NO EASY answers, Owen thought, as he made his way to the truck. You do your best to be a good person, work hard not to fuck up your life with drugs and alcohol, and suddenly you get hit with a disaster from which you think you can never recover. Against all odds, you manage to crawl out from the wreckage and get your bearings. Then, just as you've reestablished a working order and gotten into a groove, something new catches your eye. You think to yourself, *I want to try this,* knowing full well that doing so will shake up everything you've worked so hard to restore. It was a strange paradox. You got burned and craved comfort. Then you found comfort and got restless. Finally, it became apparent that what burned you wound up taking you to a place you needed to visit. And that should you ever decide to stop traveling, you might as well be dead.

North South

The Civic died not long after Danny's hasty exit from the Juju-Lucky compound. He had managed to make his way to the coast and start heading north from Monterey. Rather than bring the car in for service, he decided to get as far away from Salinas as possible, figuring that should the vehicle become inoperable, perhaps it was meant to be out of his life. Like Katie Barrett. Like Johnson Homes. Certain things had an expiration date and it was better to let go than cling to what had already served its time.

He'd ignored at least seven phone calls and twelve texts, getting as far as Bodega Bay before the engine began to sputter. A half-hour later, he made the decision to sell his only worldly possession for four hundred dollars cash to some guy named Warren. The burly appliance repairman had pulled over to help when he saw the car on the side of the road with its hood up. Danny told him that he was actually looking for help of a different kind—he needed work, if Warren knew of anything. Warren said he had seen a sign up at the local trout farm, looking for someone to clean and gut the fish caught in their stocked pond. Not the most glamorous of professions, but the repairman knew the family who ran the place and they were good people. Danny replied that he'd done worse jobs. Warren couldn't imagine what those might have been. No matter what the work was going to be like, Danny viewed it as an improvement over how he'd been forced to make a living in Phoenix. Accepting this as truth meant that everything would be uphill from here on out.

WHETHER OR NOT IT was just a mind game, it seemed to work. Although Danny wound up making under minimum wage, sleeping in a cold Sears tool shed, and pretty well stinking to high heaven, he chalked it up to life experience, trusting that it would pay unexpected karmic dividends down the line. After a week or so of reenacting the scene in *Atlantic City* where Susan Sarandon rubs lemons all over her body to combat the smell, he realized that trout stink could not be dislodged from the sinuses or the memory unless he and the fish farm parted ways.

He proceeded to hitchhike further up the coast, snagging various under-the-table gigs as he moved northward. Conveniently, the dark beard that seemed to grow faster than it had in the Southwest made him fit right in with the Mexican busboys in Mendocino. Then, as his hair got longer, he assumed the look of a hippie barista, landing himself a two-week gig at a Fort Bragg coffee house that boasted its own bagpipe player. Continuing up toward Humboldt County, he failed to find his cousin, but nevertheless enlisted as a junior leaf clipper on a pot farm. He also began began sitting in on classes at the state university in the evenings. Since his future was now a blank slate, he started by spending each evening in a different class, the diversity of subjects ranging from Russian literature to entry-level accounting. His strategy was that if anything should strike him as interesting, he'd go back for the next session.

Danny found it strangely amusing that the class that most piqued his interest was Introduction to Graphic Design. Maya was the visual artist of the family and he had never shown an interest in painting, photography, or even drawing. Yet it seemed to him now that computer art was the perfect melding of creativity and technology, the bonus being that it was a growing field and would generate lots of jobs, according to the instructor. His only problem now was the lack of access to the technology. Not having a computer or internet account of his own, and unable to log into the school's equipment because he wasn't a registered student, left him at a bit of a disadvantage.

HE ALWAYS SAT IN on the larger classes, so as not to draw attention to himself, but because he was considerably older than a lot of his classmates and tended to wear the same clothes every day, some of the professors had their hunches. None of them said a word. They welcomed older students who wanted to be there, (as opposed to the kids who were either in college to party or because their parents had forced it upon them). The graphic arts instructor, Jane Lefferts, had taken a particular shine to Danny. She seemed to be only a few years older than Katie Barrett, but wore a wedding ring and carried herself as if she were a long-tenured professor. Danny could tell that she really wanted to ask him what his deal was, but she kept her distance, content with letting him know that he made a fine addition to the class. One night, after a particularly in-depth session on painting with Adobe Illustrator, he asked her out to coffee and shared everything. He thanked her for her inspiration, and told her that it had precipitated a life-changing decision. He was planning to return to his family in Arizona and pursue a graphic arts degree.

"I'm sure they'll be happy to see you," the teacher smiled, gratified to have helped a lost soul find new direction.

FROM DANNY'S PERSPECTIVE, HIS series of adventures had given him the strength to at least make a go of it. He knew there was still a lot to overcome, but felt it would make a big difference to Maya that he now had a goal he was excited about. She'd appreciate the artistic bent, and the kids would love that it was all about the computer.

Jane wished him the best of luck and said to keep in touch. He told her he would, but that she might not hear from him right away because it would take time to reintegrate himself back home. She replied that it wasn't a race. He said he was glad of that, because he had been running for too long.

IT TOOK A FEW days of waiting on freeway ramps, as well as a night sleeping in a Wendy's/truck stop, but when he finally hit the Arizona border, he started to get excited. At Wendy's, he'd met up with a young college kid named Dylan who asked if he'd like to hitchhike down to Phoenix together. Dylan was a computer science geek and familiar with all the Adobe programs, so they could talk software between rides. They were just south of Flagstaff when Danny realized that Dylan would be more than happy to lend him a cell phone so he could call Maya.

It had been a long while since he'd felt this brave, but he made the decision to speak with the kids. It would be a whole different ballgame, now that he could tell them with certainty that their father was coming home. He did have to wonder whether or not Maya would pick up. It had been over a month since he'd called, and he couldn't blame her for being angry. At least he had timed it right—after dinner and before the kids got tucked in. Then again, she might interpret it as the worst time, because you never wanted to get kids upset before they went to sleep.

"HI, DANNY," SHE PICKED up right away, her voice flat and non-committal.

"Hey there," he nearly shouted, wishing she could see how happy he was to hear her voice.

"You sound a little better," she said.

"I'm a lot better." He could hear the kids laughing in the background. "Sounds like they're having a good time."

"Who's on the phone?" he heard Max ask.

"What should I tell them?" Maya whispered.

"That their dad wants to talk to them."

"Seriously? You ready for this?"

"I am."

Maya didn't know if she was ready. On the other hand, she had to let him speak with his own children. "Guys, it's dad. He wants to talk to you."

Danny detected no response.

"Come on," she continued, "he wants to hear your voices."

"No," he could hear Dana snap.

"Come back here." Maya started shouting, quickly muffling the phone so Danny wouldn't feel insulted.

He could hear that she was now arguing with Max, who apparently didn't want to talk to him either.

Finally, Maya got back on. "They said they need to go brush their teeth. I baked them brownies—big mistake. They each had four."

Danny felt the tears starting to make their escape. How could he have worked this hard to straighten himself out, only to arrive at a place where his children wanted no part of him? And where his wife, who had every reason to want no part of him, was shielding him from pain?

"I'm better, Maya. I really am." He was weeping now, which didn't do a lot to support his claim. "I guess I didn't get better fast enough."

"They're kids, Danny. A trust has been broken. They don't know what to think."

His sobbing grew louder. "I want my family back."

Maya tried to respond, but even though she felt terrible for him, she had no words.

"I loved you so much," he told her. "I still love you."

After another pause, she was ready to communicate her own ambivalent feelings. She would say that, while of course she truly empathized with him, she had fallen out of love. Then she would explain that she wanted him to come back anyway, so they could talk face to face, begin to sort out their situation, and make sure he stayed healthy. But it seemed she had paused for too long. Now all she heard was dial tone.

The Word

Owen and Maya sat on the sidelines with the other parents, watching the kids' match and attempting to make soccer-appropriate conversation. No one could have suspected the intensity with which they hungered to be alone with one another. After many late-night phone conversations, they had made the decision to cool things down, their recent get-togethers reduced to a run-in at Jamba Juice and two ten-minute Starbucks outings. Still, Maya was aware that Owen had fallen hard and that she was equally susceptible should she allow herself to let go. But that was impossible as long as her husband's status remained in doubt. She went back and forth between blaming herself and Danny, and continued to monitor Max and Dana's moods. She didn't dare bring up their father since she couldn't be certain when or if he'd call again. They had mentioned Daddy once or twice at bedtime, but the most she would say was that he was doing better. He actually sounded like he was doing better, but that was before his abandoned family had given him the impression that it was going to turn the tables and abandon him.

The crowd jumped to its feet as Max scored a goal, putting his team ahead sixteen-fifteen. Defense was obviously not the strong suit of these intramural matches. Parents were cheering and applauding wildly when she felt the phone start to vibrate. Taking it out of her pocket, she saw that the caller ID listed an area code in northern Arizona, which led her to believe that it might be Danny. Owen watched her step away to take the call, and, in a matter of moments, knew that she had not received good news.

When she got back to the sidelines, and for the final few minutes of the game, Maya said nothing. Later, once she got the kids home, she would call Owen and let him know what was going on. That she needed to go to Kingman, Arizona to identify a body.

SHE SOMEHOW MANAGED TO reach everyone, including Jeannie, who was due to land at Sky Harbor Airport the next morning. As expected, Maya was first on the scene, immediately greeted by the police, as well as assorted townsfolk wanting to express their condolences. Escorted into a stark, windowless room and led to the foot of a gurney, Maya felt like her body had been tossed into a deep freeze. As the coroner pulled up the white sheet, all she could think of was "How in God's name had it come to this? That this man, of all people, would die like a hobo in Timothy McVeigh country?" After she verified the true identity of "Smokey," the police began to talk about making arrangements for the corpse. She had a hard time focusing, their words overlapping into a bureaucratic auditory blur. Suddenly, Maya felt a hand on her shoulder. Upon turning around, she found herself in the strange position of being eye to eye with her husband, who had headed straight to Kingman after hearing of the apparent suicide. Luckily, she'd kept the number of his hitchhiking buddy, Dylan, and he had been able to locate Danny.

The man she married what felt like a lifetime ago looked thin and slightly weathered, but incontestably alive, which was more than could be said for poor Ted Johnson.

"Everybody thought he was living in a retirement community in Hilton Head," she told her husband.

Danny shook his head. "He could never retire. Especially outside of Arizona. Johnson Homes and this state were his life. I guess when they took the company away, even Arizona wasn't enough."

Maya examined Danny for tears, or, at the very least, watery eyes, but found neither.

"It's too bad," was all he could muster. Perhaps grief would come to him later. Maybe it wouldn't come at all. No doubt it would take him the rest of his life to sort out the complicated relationship with his father and make peace with its long list of deficiencies. Part of him wondered how it all might have turned out had he blossomed into the go-getter son Ted had always wanted. He imagined that inheriting the go-getter gene would have made *his* life a hell of a lot easier, too.

Maya informed him that the police wanted to know what to do with the body.

"I'll handle it," Danny assured her. "I know where all the wills and stuff are back home, and I'll get in touch with their estate attorney."

He might not have been crying, but what Maya observed struck her as equally poignant. After a hiatus of five years and change, Danny Johnson was not only present, but taking charge. Seeing him now, in the flesh, where expressions could be read and nuances gauged, she surmised that her husband was on the road to some sort of recovery. The purity of this spoke to her. A tortured soul had dug deep and found the courage to face his family—both the dead and the living. Which begged the question: Was he worthy of a second chance?

If so, it posed other questions. Would she be able to fall in love with him again? There were better than even odds the answer was, "No." Would she resent having to cut off her friendship with Owen Shea, the kind of man she'd marry in a heartbeat if she were starting fresh? Undoubtedly, there would be nights where she'd lie awake, aching for what her other life might have been.

However things progressed from here, Maya took comfort in having had the courage to dip her toe into uncharted waters. Being open had gotten her a taste of transcendence, and in a world as fucked up as this, a taste was more than most people were lucky enough to sample. Not to mention those who pressed their luck until they tired of the flavor. In that context, returning a father to his children seemed like the reasonable choice, even without a guarantee as to the outcome. A marriage wasn't a washer-dryer. There was no way of knowing how long the repairs would hold up, but Maya Johnson was prepared to throw herself in for one more cycle and hope for the best.

SOON HARLEY MASON ARRIVED on the scene, distraught by the news of the home developer's demise. To the townsfolk, it seemed a bit strange to see son and daughter-in-law so reserved while biographer blubbered uncontrollably. Of course, the average person had no way of understanding the price an author pays for getting inside his subject— that a piece of Mason would go to the grave with Ted Johnson. Nor could the Kingmanites appreciate the cruel irony of Mason's book now having an ending that would forever elevate it beyond vanity biography.

The concept they seemed to fully understand was gossip. "How could a famous man have let himself go like that?" and "Why weren't we smart enough to figure out who 'Smokey' really was?" Some folks said he was probably depressed. They'd heard that his company went belly-up when the housing bubble burst. Then somebody else quoted the headline of that morning's Kingman Gazette:

"HOUSING STARTS IN THE VALLEY UP 10%. PHOENIX RISES ONCE AGAIN!"

HEARING MURMURS ABOUT THE suicide being a dumbass move, and how much more money Ted could have made if he'd hung tough, the biographer felt it incumbent upon one of the inner circle to speak in defense of the departed. Seeing Danny and Maya remain passive, he ventured forth to address the assembled group.

"Listen, everybody. Like you, I'm convinced that Ted had a whole lot more in him. Had he remained with us, I have no doubt he would have realized his longstanding dream of a Leisure-based International Food Court. But all of us falter, some, more tragically than others. What we need to remember is that no matter how Arizona's future unfolds, Ted Johnson will stand alongside the Grand Canyon as a key building block in the creation of a great state."

It seemed surreal to Danny, listening to a stranger recite an impromptu eulogy for his father, knowing in his heart that it was a more complimentary one than he could have delivered himself. Part of him wanted to believe in the words, but what he took away from them was the same tired promotional packet he'd heard since childhood. For Danny, the only substantive change was that now there would be no one left for him to blame. From this moment on, whatever the rest of his life turned out to be was on him. He was okay with that, and determined to do everything in his power to make sure it didn't suck.

THE END

Acknowledgements

To all who helped me complete the journey to *Cascade Falls*— First and foremost, thanks to Tyson Cornell and his dedicated colleagues at Rare Bird, Julia Callahan and Alice Marsh-Elmer, who believed from the start. Thank you, Marc Weingarten, for pointing out where the prose needed "thinning." Early readers: Chiwan Choi, Rob Scheidlinger, Don Charles, Elliot Shoenman, Marley Sims, David Held, Beth Broderick, and Roy Teicher—your notes helped get me to the finish line and make the work sharper in the process. Additional thanks to Kim Dower, Jennifer Romanello, Larry Kirshbaum, Debbie Stier, Nancy Berk, Maria Berry, Dylan Berry, the Ferber, Rogers, and Lai families.

And forever to Jenise—who watches over us all with a literate and subversive eye.

BRUCE FERBER, before publishing his debut novel *Elevating Overman*, built a long and successful career as a television comedy writer and producer. A multiple Emmy and Golden Globe nominee, his credits include *Bosom Buddies*; *Growing Pains*; *Sabrina, The Teenage Witch*; *Coach*; and *Home Improvement*, where he served as Executive Producer and showrunner. In addition to being recognized by the Television Academy, Ferber's work has received the People's Choice, Kid's Choice, and Environmental Media Awards.

After the publication of *Elevating Overman*, Ferber toured extensively, delivering the closing keynote speech at the Erma Bombeck Writers Workshop. *Elevating Overman* was recently released on audiobook, recorded by Jason Alexander, and is currently being developed for the big screen.

He lives in Southern California with his wife, large dog, and assorted musical instruments.